Praise

What Not to Do on Vacation

"*What Not to Do On Vacation* by Rachel Magee is exactly what we all need on vacation this year! This story has all the things! Those Prestly sisters stole my heart right from the word go. A fast-paced, fun read. Trivia nights, matchmaking, sibling rivalry, and hunky guys. Toss this one in your favorite beach bag and prepare to set the alarm on your phone so you don't forget to reapply sunscreen. I give it five umbrella drinks!"

—Nancy Naigle, *USA TODAY* bestselling author

"This charming, binge-worthy read had me flipping pages long past bedtime, completely caught up in the Prestly family drama, loving every minute of Jax and Cora's slow burn romance! Magee is my go-to for romantic comedies that make me laugh, feel and think. *What Not to Do on Vacation* is the perfect, sweep-me-away summer beach read!"

—Anna Grace, award winning author of the
Harlequin Heartwarming series, The Teacher Project

"Rachel Magee delivers a perfect mix of summer vibes, fake dating, and sibling antics. If you love fun, feel-good romances, don't leave this book behind."

— Jennifer Shirk, *USA TODAY* bestselling
author of *Resorting to Romance*

"*What Not to Do on Vacation* is a tender, banter-filled novel that reads like a lighter, funnier, beachy version of a family saga. I was invested from the start not only in the double dose of romance but in all three sisters' lives and stories. Magee handles big, heavy family topics deftly and with both care and humor. A hope-infused joy of a book!"

—Emma St. Clair, *USA TODAY* bestselling author

It's All Relative

"A delightful story with memorable and heartwarming characters you won't soon forget. Magee does a fabulous job weaving together the complexities of friendship and family, with her trademark light, fun touch. Reminiscent of *My Best Friend's Wedding*, her book is the perfect weekend read!"

—Shirley Jump, *New York Times*, *USA TODAY*,
and Amazon bestselling author

"What a wonderful, whimsical, and witty story of second chances and new beginnings, set against the backdrop of an action-packed island wedding with enough twists and turns to satisfy the most committed Sunday driver. If you want a story that you can get utterly lost in, I highly recommend you add *It's All Relative* to your TBR."

—Kate O'Keeffe, *USA TODAY* bestselling author

"Like being whisked away to a fabulous beach destination wedding! This lighthearted beach read had all the feels, family drama, and plenty of laughs. I loved every page."

—Teri Wilson, *USA TODAY* bestselling author

"*It's All Relative* is a second-chance novel full of complex family relationships and a cast of characters you'll love rooting for as they grow in love and in life. Heartwarming, funny, delightful from the very first page. Fans of Rachel Magee will love adding this book to their shelves!"

—Jenny Proctor, bestselling author of
How to Kiss Your Best Friend

"Though *It's All Relative* proves the route to happy endings is not always smooth sailing, Magee masterfully assures us that (sometimes) rocky seas are worth the ride."

—Ginny Baird, *New York Times* and
USA TODAY bestselling author

What Not to do on Vacation

Also by Rachel Magee

It's All Relative

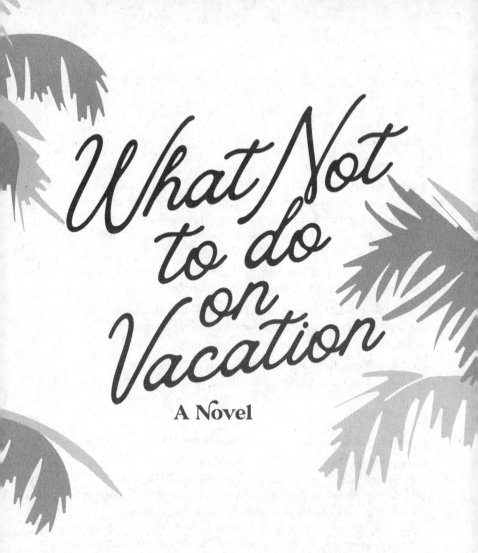

What Not to do on Vacation

A Novel

Rachel Magee

THOMAS NELSON
Since 1798

Published in Nashville, Tennessee, by Thomas Nelson. Thomas Nelson is a registered trademark of HarperCollins Christian Publishing, Inc.

Thomas Nelson titles may be purchased in bulk for educational, business, fundraising, or sales promotional use. For information, please email SpecialMarkets@ThomasNelson.com.

Library of Congress Cataloging-in-Publication Data

Names: Magee, Rachel (Rachel Anne), author.
Title: What not to do on vacation : a novel / Rachel Magee.
Description: Nashville, Tennessee : Thomas Nelson, 2025. | Summary:
   "Ten Things I Hate About You meets the charm (and sisterly
   shenanigans!) of Netflix's Nobody Wants This in this slow-burn, fake
   dating rom-com from the author Kate O'Keeffe says "you can get utterly
   lost in.""—Provided by publisher.
Identifiers: LCCN 2024052291 (print) | LCCN 2024052292 (ebook) |
   ISBN 9780840716972 (paperback) | ISBN 9780840716996 |
   ISBN 9780840716989 (epub)
Subjects: LCGFT: Christian fiction. | Romance fiction. | Novels.
Classification: LCC PS3613.A3434 W53 2025 (print) |
   LCC PS3613.A3434 (ebook) | DDC 813/.6—dc23/eng/20241115
LC record available at https://lccn.loc.gov/2024052291
LC ebook record available at https://lccn.loc.gov/2024052292

Printed in the United States of America

25 26 27 28 29 LBC 5 4 3 2 1

For Mike, my soulmate
There's no one else I'd rather tackle this crazy life with.

1

Cora

*I*f any part of her day had gone according to plan, Cora Prestly wouldn't need a toothbrush right now. But it hadn't, so here she was.

She sat in her rental car and stared at the CVS entrance as rain came down with an intensity that matched Niagara Falls, because of course it did. That was the kind of day she was having.

She knew this trip would be a mistake.

In fact, if she recalled correctly—and she did—that was her exact response when her older sister Savannah pitched the absurd idea that the three Prestly sisters spend a month in Sunnyside, Florida, a small beach town in the Panhandle, to relive their childhood summers. Then Cora followed the statement with her answer: an emphatic *"Absolutely not."*

She didn't care what sort of optimistic spin Savannah put on it, the trip was a recipe for disaster. They were adults with jobs and responsibilities. Well, maybe not Bianca, the baby of the family, but that was a different problem. The point was, they couldn't just pause their lives and spend the summer at the beach like they did when they were kids.

And even if they could, Cora didn't want to.

The Prestly sisters didn't exactly have that kind of relationship anymore. Don't get her wrong, she (mostly) loved her sisters. But in light of everything that had gone down, they now had more of a get-together-for-a-long-weekend kind of relationship. There was a four-day max before things started to get ugly. And last time Cora checked, a month was a lot longer than four days.

"Next time I stick with *no*," she said to the steering wheel.

Although to be fair, *no* wasn't exactly an option.

Savannah had pulled out an unbeatable trump card that forced Cora into coming. This trip wasn't about them. It was about fulfilling their mother's last wish.

Before she passed, Julie Prestly made her three daughters promise her that they would spend one more happy summer on the white sandy beaches of Sunnyside, the way they did every year when they were growing up. And since their mother had lost her battle with breast cancer almost a decade ago, granting her wish was long overdue.

Did Cora think the whole idea was ridiculous, even at the time her mother had requested it? Absolutely. There was no way they could recreate one of those fairy-tale summers because way too much life—and not the good kind—had passed since those blissful days. But what choice did she have? Cora loved and respected her mother too much to just ignore her final wish.

So, when Savannah had put the wheels in motion for the overdue summer trip, Cora had begrudgingly cleared her calendar for the month of July and booked a flight to meet her two sisters in the sleepy little beach town of Sunnyside, Florida.

And so far, her prediction of a disastrous summer had been spot-on. She was only twelve hours into the trip and everything that could've gone wrong *had*. Which was how she wound up here, in the CVS parking lot, trying to judge how wet she would get in the fifty-foot sprint from her car to the store just to get a dumb toothbrush at 9:30 p.m.

"I think we've hit a new low," she told the steering wheel, as if somehow it was involved in this situation. Then she counted down from three before she threw open the car door and made a mad dash to the entrance.

The answer to how soaked she would get during a fifty-foot run through a monsoon? Down to her underwear.

This was officially the worst vacation of all time.

She stopped just inside the door to wipe the rain off her face. The clerk, who was filing her nails behind the checkout counter, temporarily paused her task. With a judgmental eyebrow raised, she gave Cora a once-over.

"Toothbrushes?" Cora asked.

The clerk popped her gum and tilted her head toward the back of the store before returning to her nails.

"Thanks." Cora sloshed in the general direction the clerk had indicated.

The only reason she needed a toothbrush at all was because her journey to get here had been a complete disaster. What was supposed to be an easy two-hour flight from Houston had turned into a twelve-hour ordeal. Cora and her fellow passengers had to deplane and switch aircrafts because of mechanical issues. Twice. Then they were rerouted because of air traffic control, and had to land and refuel at a nearby airport while they waited out a storm. The fact that they'd arrived at their final destination, even if it was ten hours late, felt like a miracle.

Her luggage, however, hadn't shared the same good fortune.

In fact, at the moment the airline wasn't exactly sure where it was. But *of course* they would locate it (they wouldn't use the word *find* because they insisted it wasn't lost, simply unaccounted for), and as soon as they did, it would be delivered to her. She should expect to have it in a couple of days. Three at the most.

So here she was. Replacing things that the airline couldn't locate.

She trudged through the aisles of the deserted store in the direction of the dental care section, leaving a sort of Hansel-and-Gretel trail of water behind her.

Did she need more than a toothbrush? Probably. All she had was what she was wearing and a camera case full of her professional camera equipment. Knowing what she knew now, she'd made the right call to carry on the heavy camera case and check her clothes. Photography wasn't just her profession (which she'd be doing during her stay because the commercial photography industry didn't pause for ridiculous family obligations). It was her passion. But her luggage choice did leave her in a bit of a predicament. She was on a four-week beach vacation without anything to wear to the actual beach.

She paused in front of a rack of cover-ups. "I probably need one of these," she said out loud.

Squinting slightly with serious consideration, she studied the options. Neon palm tree or the bedazzled option emblazoned with *Sun, Sand & Surf*?

"Palm tree," she decided and draped the find over her arm. The endcap next to it had flip-flops in bright coordinating colors, so she grabbed a pair of those, too. After all, one couldn't exactly go to the beach without flip-flops, could they?

With her beach outfit taken care of, she cruised back to the wall of toothbrushes. Wiping some of the dripping rainwater off her face, she scanned the options. She was reaching for one when a deep voice interrupted her.

"I wouldn't go with that one, if I were you."

The voice made her jump, mostly because she hadn't realized there was anyone else in the store besides the gum-popping clerk. With her hand still reaching for the toothbrush, she did a quick sweep of the store to see if there was anyone else she'd missed before settling her gaze on the man standing next to her. Where had he come from?

He was tall and had an athletic build that, although she hated to admit it, looked good in jeans. His dark wavy hair had the unmistakable mix of good genes and an expensive haircut, and his deep blue eyes twinkled. He reminded her of Gatsby, all charm and confidence with a healthy dose of swagger. It was the kind of thing most people probably found attractive.

Cora did not.

"I'm sorry?" Her tone was less asking him to repeat himself and more encouraging him to check himself, although he appeared to hear the former.

"Toothbrushes," he clarified, gesturing to the product her hand was now touching. "You really should go with the two pack. Extra soft. It's the better choice."

Cora was a thirty-one-year-old successful business owner. She might look like a wet mess at the moment, and maybe she had arrived at the point in a particularly bad day where she was narrating her life to stay sane, but that didn't mean she needed some random dude to mansplain a *toothbrush selection* to her. Who did he think he was?

"And what? You're, like, a toothbrush expert?"

Was the comment uncalled for? Probably. But keeping her opinions to herself had never really been Cora's thing. It was something she probably should work on, but she didn't want to. Not if there were guys like this still floating around.

Gatsby flashed a half-hitched grin, which he probably used to make people swoon. "More of a connoisseur, really."

She didn't mean to roll her eyes, they just sort of did it on their own. "I, along with everyone else with an olfactory sense, thank you for that choice."

His grin widened with amusement. "You're not even going to ask me why?"

"Why you made the bold decision to brush your teeth regularly?"

He gave a slight shrug. "A combination of respect for the people around me and a healthy fear of prolonged exposure to the dentist chair."

"Good to know." If the heavy dose of sarcasm wasn't enough of a signal that she was finished with the conversation, she turned her back to him and refocused on the wall of toothbrushes.

"I *meant* why you should go with the two pack."

Cora let out a heavy, annoyed sigh. "The only question I'm asking is, 'Why am I still standing here?'"

Once again, her snark didn't faze him. "Because I've found that it's nice to have a spare. You know, in a backpack or a purse or something." He grabbed the product in question and held it up as an example. "For the times when life throws you a curveball. Which happens a lot more than you'd expect."

"And yet, even with all that knowledge, here you are. In the middle of a rainstorm. Having to buy another one."

Again with the amused, half-hitched grin. "Touché."

"Thanks for your opinion, but I think I'm good." This time she made sure to add an extra dose of annoyance to her voice so he wouldn't mistake her choice of words for actual appreciation. "Besides, the situation that landed me here will *never* happen again." Because if she were traveling for any reason other than to fulfill her mother's final wish, she would've bailed out of this travel day long before now.

"Never say never." He tossed her the two-pack, which she had to struggle to catch with her arms full of beachwear. Then with a wink, he turned and walked away.

Cora glared in his direction. He might have lived his whole life believing the world would bend to his notion, but Cora did not. She returned the package to the rack before grabbing the single brush in the brand her dentist—an actual toothbrush expert—had given her during her last cleaning. And yes, it was a single because she only needed the one. Besides, she *did* have a spare toothbrush. She kept it in her medicine cabinet like a normal person.

Luckily, Gatsby had already disappeared by the time Cora got to the checkout, which she was glad for. She didn't know if she could handle listening to his helpful tips on how to pay for her items.

Still shaking her head with disbelief, she dashed through the rain for a second time and tossed her new finds in the back seat. "Well, that was something," she said to the steering wheel, then pointed her rental car in the direction of their vacation cottage.

Savannah had rented the same beachside cottage they'd always stayed in when they were growing up. Every year, from June 1 until August 15, it was the place they called home. Back then, the blue clapboard house with the navy-and-white-striped awning was one of Cora's favorite sights, and even the thought of it could fill her with buzzing excitement. There was no place in the world she'd rather be.

Some of her favorite memories took place on the back deck that led straight out to the sand. Sparklers on the Fourth of July. Watching movies outside on a white sheet their dad had hung between two beach umbrellas. Their mom making the most mundane day feel special because they were at the beach house with her games and *everything's-*

an-adventure attitude. Just thinking about it filled Cora with a warm nostalgic glow.

Of course, that feeling was followed by an ache deep behind her rib cage, because what used to be hadn't been around for a long time. In fact, there were some days when she wondered if it had been real to begin with.

But that thought was the opposite of improving her mood. She pushed it deep down and switched her playlist to the one she'd named "Beach Tunes." If there were ever a time for Bob Marley to preach about not worrying and being happy, now was it.

The rain slowed from a downpour to a drizzle as she wound through the charming town. The GPS called out her turns, but she didn't need the help. Despite being gone for fifteen years, she remembered the way.

Of course there were several notable changes over the last decade and a half. There was a whole new shopping complex with a big, fancy Publix. The new traffic light at the corner of Emerald Lane and the highway was a welcome and long overdue addition. The heavier traffic, not so much.

Yet, the vast majority of Sunnyside was just the way she remembered it. Main Street was still lined with palm trees. The aptly named T-Shirt Shop next to the beach still had its signature giant conch shell on top of it. Miss Mary's Ice Cream Shop was still on the corner next to the park.

She made two more quick turns, and then there it was. The blue clapboard house.

She turned off her engine and stared at the house for a moment as thoughts whirred around her mind. They were mostly nostalgic ones that hit her more in the feels than she was ready to deal with on a day that had been nothing but one disaster after another, so she did what any normal chronic avoider would do. She buried those feelings deep down with the other topics she didn't care to dive into at the moment. Or ever.

Plus, she really needed to go inside so she could get out of these wet clothes. She was starting to chafe.

Cora grabbed her suitcase-sized camera bag and her drugstore goodies from the back seat and headed through the drizzle to the front door. Then she knocked.

Yes, she was aware that technically speaking she didn't have to knock. For starters, her name was on the rental agreement. She had the code that unlocked the front door.

But the bigger reason she didn't need to knock was that her family stood on the other side of the door.

There was a day when no Prestly sister knocked on a door, ever. Cora couldn't count the number of times Savannah or Bianca had barged into their shared bathroom while she'd been in there. There was a very loose definition of *privacy* among them.

Of course, that had been *before*, when life looked different.

It was only a matter of seconds before the door flung open to reveal both of her sisters standing in the doorway.

"You're here!" Savannah and Bianca squealed in unison and threw their hands up in the air in celebration. The bright lights of the interior shone like a spotlight as they posed, smiles beaming, energy level off the Richter scale.

Yeah. It was going to be a long month.

To any onlooker, it was impossible to deny that the three women were sisters. The Prestly girls had the exact same shade of chestnut-brown hair and rich walnut eyes they'd gotten from their mom and the same button nose they'd gotten from their dad. But there were differences, too. Savannah was the shortest, with always-perfect curls that fell to her shoulders. Bianca, whose hairstyle changed with her mood, was currently sporting new curtain bangs and chunky, wavy layers. Long, lean Cora had always preferred her straight hair to be long with as little fuss as possible.

But if their matching features didn't tip off their relation, the matching pajama sets Cora's sisters were wearing—bubblegum-pink pants with white polka-dots, and a white T-shirt with *Sister Squad* printed on the chest—were a dead giveaway.

Before Cora had a chance to change her mind and turn around, her younger sister Bianca grabbed her wrist and pulled her inside. "Oh my gosh! That took you *forrrrrevvvverrrr*." Bianca threw her arms around her sister in a dramatic hug.

"Yeah, I know," Cora mumbled. "I lived it."

"We're just glad you made it," Savannah said. "But you're soaking wet."

"Rainstorm." Cora gave a *What-do-you-do?* shrug.

"No worries." Savannah ushered her into the entryway with a protective arm. "We've got you covered. Bianca, get her bag."

Except, could this even be called an entryway? They were only two steps away from the front door, but they were already in the middle of the living room / dining room. Cora glanced around, trying to take it all in. Had the cottage always been this small?

Savannah thrust a bubblegum-pink bundle into her hands. "Looks like once again it's matching jammies to the rescue!"

"No one has said that ever. Not even this time."

Savannah gave her a warning look.

So maybe their hairstyles weren't the only differences among them.

Savannah propped her hands on her hips. "Are you going to put them on? Or make fun of them while your wet clothes turn your entire body into a prune?"

Bianca giggled.

"Fine." Cora huffed as she carried her bubblegum bundle to the hall bathroom, although *hall* seemed like a bold title for the alcove between the two bedrooms. She could've sworn this was all larger last time she was here.

"We used to have matching jammies every time we came," Savannah called after her.

"We used to be eight." Cora's voice echoed inside the tiny bathroom.

She peeled off the wet clothes, dropped them on the floor and stepped into the dry set. While Cora maintained the pajama pants were the most obnoxious color of pink, she had to admit they were really soft. If she was going to be stuck wearing something for three days, at least it was comfortable.

"When do they think you'll get your luggage?" Savannah asked through the closed door, as if she were listening to Cora's thoughts.

"I don't know." Cora shrugged on the "Sister Squad" shirt. "Two or three days is what they told me." Although the tracking information online still listed her status as "locating" last time she checked. She gathered up her wet clothing and walked out of the bathroom in her matching pj's. "In the meantime, I guess I should throw these in the dryer."

"Here, let me." Savannah didn't even wait for an answer. She just took the clothes and disappeared into the primary bedroom and en-suite bathroom, which, Cora happened to know from previous visits, was where the stackable washer and dryer were located.

Bianca tucked her arm through Cora's and steered her toward the couch in the living room. "You should've reminded me that you don't do long road trips by yourself. I would've flown out to Houston and driven with you. You probably would've let me control the music."

"You had full control of the music until you proved you had questionable taste. That one's on you," Savannah said as she rejoined them in the living room. "Cora, are you hungry?"

"Starving," Cora said. "Sounds like road trips also haven't changed much."

"Have you heard the stuff she listens to? It's like a bad satire on indie garage bands." Savannah pulled a glass dish out of the fridge and held it up. "Leftover spaghetti?"

Cora nodded and Savannah popped the dish into the microwave.

"It has soul," Bianca retorted. "And passion. Which is a lot more than you can say about the boring formulaic stuff you listen to."

Cora flopped down on the couch. "That's okay. I still wouldn't have let you plug in. My car, my music."

Bianca gasped in mock offense. "Seriously? My own sister."

"Also, I'm not sleeping on the top bunk in that room." Cora nodded in the direction of the room she'd be sharing with Bianca. "Or the extra mattress they keep under the bed as a trundle."

Bianca crossed her arms over her chest and narrowed her eyes. "On what grounds?"

"Seniority." Cora didn't miss a beat.

"What? Are we, like, twelve?" Bianca threw a pillow at her sister, as if she were answering her own question.

"Ah, fighting over beds. Feels like old times." Savannah handed Cora the steaming dish of spaghetti fresh from the microwave. "Either of you is welcome to sleep with me in the primary until Chris and the girls get here in a few weeks."

"In that tiny double?" Bianca wrinkled her nose. "Pass."

"I think it's a queen," Savannah offered.

"Still pass."

Cora tried to imagine Savannah, her husband, and their two little girls crammed into the tiny bedroom that barely seemed big enough to hold the bed. "I'll let you enjoy the space while you have it."

Savannah shrugged. "Suit yourselves. But while we're on the subject of housekeeping, I have another beach house tradition." She swiped a circle of posterboard off the kitchen table and held it up. "Ta-da!"

"Is that the chore wheel?" Cora asked, not bothering to edit the horrified tone from her voice.

"Yes!" Savannah beamed as if the tone didn't bother her. "Just like Mom used to make. With a few updates, of course."

The circle was divided into three sections, each containing cheerful script and hand-drawn illustrations. "Each section has the list of daily and weekly chores you'll be responsible for." Savannah gestured to the chart, clearly proud of what she'd done.

Bianca smirked. "You're kidding, right?"

Savannah shot her the most mom-look Cora had ever seen. "We always had a chore wheel at the beach house."

"For the record, Bianca is old enough to do the regular chores now. She doesn't get to do half the list because she's a baby." Cora blew on her steaming dinner.

"You'd better get ready to rethink your stance on the top bunk, big sis, because you can't have it both ways."

Savannah sighed as if this whole conversation had exhausted her.

"Relax. If either of you had bothered to look in the room, you'd see there are two sets of bunk beds now. No one has to sleep on the top."

Bianca looked at Cora. "Do you think we still fit on a bunk bed?"

Cora shrugged. "I can't even remember the last time I tried."

"You'll fit. It'll be fine. But back to the wheel." Savannah held the wheel out in front of her. "We each have a color, see? You're responsible for everything inside your color. Then we'll rotate each week."

Cora twirled spaghetti onto her fork. "Yeah, I'm not doing that."

Savannah glanced at the wheel, then back at her sister. "What? You're too good for unloading the dishwasher?"

"No. I'll absolutely unload the dishwasher like the adult that I am. But I don't need some chart to tell me when I have to do it."

"I agree with Cora." Bianca gave a decisive nod, then shot Cora a look of solidarity.

"Of course you do," Savannah said. "You've never done your chores. I've been to your apartment. It's a mess."

"She has a point," Cora said.

"Maybe. But that was in the past. I'm different now. I'm turning over a whole new leaf." Bianca straightened her posture, as if it were a sign of her maturity. "In fact, now that we're all here, I have an announcement to make. Something y'all are going to love." Bianca scooted to the edge of the couch and beamed with so much excitement that Cora thought she might spring off at any moment.

"Oh, this must be good!" Savannah clapped her hands together, matching Bianca's excitement. "Let me guess. You got a new job?"

Bianca bobbed her head back and forth, as if she were weighing the guess. "Kind of, but no."

"You finally realized you're about to turn twenty-six and you should probably stop letting Dad pay your cell phone bill," Cora offered.

Bianca glared at her. "I hate you. And no."

"You're dating someone new?" Savannah's eyes sparkled at that suggestion.

"It's even better." Bianca paused dramatically while the air around her crackled with excitement. Even Cora couldn't help leaning in.

"As soon as we get home . . ." Bianca's smile stretched across her face, and she covered her mouth with her hands, as if she were so excited she couldn't contain it. "I'm moving to Idaho!" She let out an excited squeal.

For the first few seconds after the announcement, the room was completely silent. Cora ran the words through her mind again to make sure she'd heard them correctly. Moving? From Atlanta—where Bianca had lived her entire life—to Idaho?

Judging by the horrified look on Savannah's face, Cora assumed she was thinking the same thing.

Then they both fired off questions at the exact same time.

"What?"

"Why?"

Neither the questions nor the obvious hesitation in their voices seemed to give Bianca any pause. In fact, Cora wasn't even sure she'd heard them.

Instead, Bianca launched herself off the couch and threw her hands up in celebration. "Because I'm getting married!"

2

Savannah

Savannah felt like a bomb had just exploded. She was in shock, and there was still a little ringing in her ears. She stared at her sister, trying to make sense of what just happened. "You're what?"

"I'm getting married!" Bianca seemed to sparkle, completely oblivious to the reaction around her. "We're still working out all the details. You know, it's a little hard to plan a wedding there when I'm here." She waved her arms around in a cheerful, animated gesture, as if this were some delightful conversation that made total sense.

It wasn't.

"It's a little hard to plan a wedding when you don't have a groom," Cora said.

Exactly. Savannah would've said the same thing if the explosion hadn't blocked her brain from thinking.

Bianca rolled her eyes. "Ha-ha."

Savannah could feel panic setting in, like danger was prowling around the corner. "No, but seriously. Who are you marrying?" Her pulse quickened, and she took a deep breath to try to slow it down. "I didn't even know you were dating anyone."

Yes, she was aware that she wasn't her sister's keeper, but ever since the day Bianca had been born, it was Savannah's job to keep an eye on her. *"Savannah, watch the baby. Savannah, you're in charge. Savannah, yes, you and Cora can go, but you have to let Bianca tag along."*

She couldn't help it. Since the day baby Bianca came home from the hospital when Savannah was eight years old, it had been her job to make sure her baby sister didn't get into trouble. And when their mom died, that responsibility seemed to double.

"Oh my gosh. Seriously, you never listen to me, do you?" Bianca flopped back on the couch, looking defeated. "I've literally talked about him nonstop since we met."

A slow, creeping awareness started to come back to Savannah. "Wait? Are you talking about that guy from the dating app? Not-a-gym-rat gym rat?" At the moment that was all she could remember about the guy her sister mentioned she'd met online.

Cora chuckled from her side of the couch and twirled spaghetti around her fork. "Oh, this is going to be good."

Bianca shot her an annoyed glance before returning her argument to Savannah. "It's not a dating app. It's a matchmaking site. And he's not a gym rat. He's just really into fitness."

"Which is exactly what Savannah said," Cora said, which earned her another glare from Bianca.

"How long have you known him?" Even as she uttered the question, Savannah searched her memory for every mention of this guy.

Bianca lived fifteen minutes away from her in Atlanta. Although life was busy, they saw each other frequently enough that Savannah kept up with what was happening in Bianca's life. Normally.

And yes, Savannah knew she'd been distracted lately. With all the *developments* she'd been dealing with, her mind had been on other things. But she hadn't been so preoccupied with her own stuff that she'd missed her baby sister being in the middle of a love affair.

Had she?

"Time is irrelevant." Bianca gave an airy wave of her hand to dismiss the thought. "Zander and I connect at a deeper level, so it feels like I've known him forever."

"What does that even mean?" Savannah didn't even try to hide the judgment in her voice.

Also, had the temperature just jumped ten degrees?

Bianca settled into the cushions with a love-swept look. "I think Jane Austen summed it up when she said, 'Seven years would be insufficient to make some people acquainted with each other, and seven days are more than enough for others.'"

Savannah's mouth fell open. Was Bianca even serious right now?

"Yeah, but just for funsies, if you had to circle a date on the calendar when you met, how many of those little boxes are between that day and today?" Cora flicked her fork in the air as if she were using it to count the imaginary calendar boxes.

Bianca huffed, the absurdity of the questions clearly too much for her. "If you must put a number on it, five weeks. We were introduced five weeks ago."

Savannah was starting to feel sick. "Five weeks?" She didn't care what Jane Austen had said. Five weeks was not long enough for someone to meet another person and to move across the country for them. Especially when that someone was her baby sister. "Have you ever met him in real life?" There was a crease between her eyes now. She could feel it. It was probably the kind that would leave a permanent line.

"We FaceTime literally all day every day, which is better than real life. I've been everywhere with him." She settled back into the couch cushions and let out a contented sigh, as if she could picture the conversations. "I'm there when he makes dinner, I ride along with him on his way to work. He's the last person I talk to before I fall asleep. I know everything about him."

"Except what he looks like in 3-D," Cora said.

Bianca shot her a look. "Are you still talking?"

Cora waggled her eyebrows and shoveled a forkful of spaghetti into her mouth.

Savannah let out a heavy sigh and sank into the chair. She was well aware she sounded like a mom, but she couldn't help it. Her sister was behaving like a child. "I have to agree with Cora on this one. How much can you really know about a man you've only known for a month and have never met in person?"

"You're so caught up on this construct of time that it's blocking you from seeing the bigger picture," Bianca said.

"Which is?"

"He's my soulmate." Bianca's eyes fluttered in a look of love. "It was like magic from the very first time we talked."

Cora let out a burst of laughter, and Savannah might have too if she weren't panicking about her baby sister marrying someone she met a month ago. On the internet.

It was like the start of some *Dateline* special.

"Honestly?" Savannah crossed her arms in front of her chest and gave Bianca her best mom-look. "That's the biggest load of bologna I've ever heard."

Bianca looked hurt. "I thought you of all people would understand. Don't you believe in love at first sight?"

"No," Cora said from her side of the couch with zero hesitation in her voice.

Bianca's look of disappointment caused Savannah to soften, and she dropped her hands to her sides. "Look, I'm not saying it can't happen. But with someone you happened to swipe right on? Who you've never actually met in person?"

"First of all, we didn't *swipe right*. We were matched through Soul-Match. It's a new matchmaking app that uses AI to bring soulmates together. It's so effective that almost seventy percent of their matches lead to marriage or lifelong commitments."

Savannah still wasn't buying it. "Aren't there at least ten different dating sites that claim to find your perfect match based on their proprietary method?"

Bianca shook her head. "Not like this. Not to the same level Soul-Match does. It uses the same philosophy as a matchmaker who is only interested in deep, lasting connections. There's no list to *swipe right* on. You only get one match. You chat and go on dates for as long as you need to see if that's your person. If the match doesn't work, you go back into the system to be matched again. This time with new questions about what didn't work to help find a better connection."

"So, you better hope your soulmate decides to try out the dating app the same time you do," Cora said.

"Isn't love always a game of serendipity?" Bianca argued. "You wouldn't question a couple who met because they happened to be at the coffee shop at the same time or went to a mutual friend's birthday party." She turned to Savannah. "You'd probably eat it up if we had accidentally gotten each other's dry cleaning. This is the same thing, with the added benefit of a background check first."

"All those other scenarios have something in common. You live in the same area or like the same kinds of people or are interested in the same things," Savannah countered. Could you feel your blood pressure rise? Because she was pretty sure that's what she was feeling.

"What's your problem with modern technology? Everything else has evolved, so why can't how we meet our soulmates?"

"Because even though the entire world is digitized, human interaction isn't. A computer program can't tell you who to fall in love with."

"This one can!" Bianca stood up, her face turning red and the anger rising in her voice. "It's so good, it could even match Cora with someone she'd fall head over heels for!" She jabbed her finger in the direction of where Cora was sitting.

"Hey! What's that supposed to mean?"

Bianca glared at her. "If the shoe fits."

"Don't drag me into your little fight," Cora said, unconcerned. "If you want to run off and marry some man you've never met because a computer told you to, that's your business. I'm just here for the spaghetti."

Bianca crossed her arms and huffed. "Zander isn't *some man*. We belong together. Everything about him makes me better, and I want to spend all of time—my forever—with him." She turned to face Cora directly. "It's something you know nothing about, because you're allergic to relationships of any kind. Do you want to die alone?"

It was harsh and uncalled for, but it wasn't untrue. And for the first time since Bianca dropped the news, Savannah's panic shifted to another stress-inducing subject: Cora.

"You're being ridiculous." Cora shook her head and went back to her spaghetti.

Savannah agreed, but Bianca's comment sparked an idea, and the wheels in Savannah's mind started to turn.

What if . . .

Bianca kept Savannah up at night because she was reckless. Her baby sister was impulsive, going all in on whatever idea sounded fun at the time, no matter how half-baked the idea was. But Cora was the opposite.

She'd always been the one to do her own thing. She was independent and determined, but she was also skeptical, especially of trusting people. More recently, it seemed that skepticism had grown. Instead of facing her past hurts and dealing with them, Cora had walled herself off. She kept the entire world—even her sisters—at arm's length, hiding away in her Houston apartment. It was making her more and more cranky.

What she needed, in Savannah's humble opinion, was to get back in the real world and let people love her, and the sooner the better. After all, life was never meant to be lived alone. What better way for that to happen than for Cora to fall in love?

Cora finding someone was the reason Savannah interviewed every single guy she ever came in contact with. New hire at Chris's office? She'd corner him at the company Christmas party. Guy in the grocery store without a ring? She'd worm her way to the checkout line in front of him. She could be quite crafty when she wanted to be.

But so far her scheming hadn't done any good. The dates Savannah had managed to set up for Cora had turned into disasters. After the last one, which was over a year ago, Cora had threatened to never come to Atlanta again if Savannah set her up one more time. That hadn't stopped Savannah from being on the lookout for Cora's perfect partner, but it *had* stopped the dates since Savannah hadn't figured out a way to get Cora to go on them.

Until now.

"You might be right," Savannah said as the plan started to form in her mind.

Cora gave a confident nod from her corner of the couch. "Of course I'm right."

"No, not you." Savannah deliberately focused her gaze on Bianca. "You."

"Me?" Bianca looked surprised, pointing a finger at herself.

Savannah nodded.

She still didn't believe AI was capable of cracking the code to true love any more than meteorology had cracked the code to accurately predicting the weather. But maybe it could get close. Maybe it could see something the rest of them were missing. Plus, there was the added benefit that the setup wouldn't come from Savannah.

This could work.

"Maybe your little computer program is on to something," Savannah said.

"Scientifically backed AI," Bianca corrected.

"Sure, we'll call it that." Savannah waved a dismissive hand as she sorted the plan in her mind.

"Maybe we should call it a crock of—"

Savannah held up her hand to stop Cora before she went any further but kept her focus on Bianca. "You really think SoulMatch could find Cora's soulmate?"

"I mean, it can't create a man who doesn't exist. But if he's out there and willing to be found, SoulMatch will find him."

"Interesting." Savannah nibbled on her lip.

"Did it ever occur to you two that maybe I don't want to find my soulmate?" Cora said. "That maybe I'm alone because I prefer it that way?"

Savannah ignored her. Maybe that was the story she was telling everyone else. Maybe that was even what she was telling herself, but it wasn't the whole story.

Savannah *knew* Cora. She was one of the most caring, kind, and selfless people she'd ever met. She loved big.

But she wasn't as tough as she came across. Cora had been hurt before. And each time, she seemed to back away from love, from people, a little more. It was starting to get to the point that if she backed away any further, Savannah was afraid she'd disconnect completely.

The same way Savannah wasn't willing to let Bianca run off with every single person who sparked the slightest interest, she wasn't willing to let Cora give up on love because her heart had been broken. If Cora wasn't going to put herself out there, Savannah would have to do it for her.

The plan brewing in her mind might be crazy, but maybe there was merit to it. Maybe, just maybe, it could work.

"Okay," Savannah said finally.

Bianca narrowed her eyes, looking suspicious. "Okay, what?"

Savannah propped her hands on her hips and squared off with Bianca. "If you can prove your new dating site is so good that it can make Cora fall in love, then we'll have no choice but to admit you were right."

"Who's the *we* in this scenario?" Cora said from behind her. "Because I'm certainly not part of it."

"Let me get this straight." Bianca locked her steely gaze with Savannah's. "If I can prove this dating app is legit, then you'll be okay with me moving to Idaho to be with Zander?"

"I mean, it's far away, but—"

Bianca cut her off. "And get married?"

"If he's really your soulmate, I would never want to stand in your way." That was a big *if*. But Savannah would be the first to admit she'd been wrong before. Maybe she was wrong about this. It seemed highly unlikely, but . . .

"At the end of the summer?"

The anxiety Savannah had been trying to keep at bay bubbled up, but she pushed it back down and kept going. "Seems a little quick. But, sure. I'll even help you plan it. We could do it here."

Bianca cocked a suspicious eyebrow. "And all I have to do is find Cora a date?"

Savannah held up a finger. "Not a date. I could find Cora a date."

"Perfectly capable of finding my own dates, thank you. That has never been the problem," Cora said.

Savannah ignored her and kept going. "You have to find someone she'll fall in love with. Correction: your *dating app* has to find someone."

Baby sister and eldest sister stared each other down like they were a couple of gunslingers at a showdown, the words settling around them like dust on a Wild West road.

Bianca's gaze was steely, as if she were weighing some kind of challenge or a dare. "Done."

Honestly, it felt kind of like a dare, which wasn't exactly Savannah's purpose.

Her goal was to keep her sisters from self-destructing. She'd assumed wise words and encouragement would've been enough for that. But since neither of them was listening, she was forced to take drastic measures.

Cora stepped between them, breaking up the stare-down. "There's only one problem."

"Which is?" Bianca asked.

"I never agreed to any of this."

The realization knocked some of the wind out of Savannah's sails. "But . . ." she started without any idea of where to go with it. Because she knew one thing for sure: it was easier to catch a cloud than to try to get Cora to do what Cora didn't want to do.

"But nothing," Cora said. "I'm not going on a date with some rando. And I sure as heck am not putting my profile on some dating app for a bunch of creepers."

Bianca looked offended. "Not even for me?"

"Especially not for you. I agree with Savannah. You can't marry someone you've only talked to *on the internet*." The extra emphasis Cora put on the last three words made it sound like Bianca was hanging out in some crime-ridden, lawless back alley instead of a site many people spent a large part of their day using.

Bianca, however, looked unfazed. "You know what? Since you have zero experience with falling in love and a phobia to commitment, you don't get to weigh in. Because you have no idea what you're talking about." She held her hand up in the shape of a zero for added emphasis.

It was another low blow, especially since the comment touched on moments from the past Bianca clearly didn't remember. Or maybe, which was equally as likely, no one had ever told her. Since the sisters all felt the same age now, sometimes it was hard to remember that Bianca was still a kid when she and Cora were in college and testing their legs in the adult world.

Savannah sucked in a breath as if she were the one taking the punch and looked over at Cora. Hurt flickered across her face, but it faded quickly as her calm, stoic, nothing-gets-to-me exterior reappeared.

"Careful, sis. That's where you're wrong. I actually know exactly how this is going to turn out. And I don't even need a crystal ball."

Bianca huffed and rolled her eyes, which only seemed to heighten Cora's determination.

"You can match me with anyone you want on your cute little dating site," Cora continued. "But it doesn't matter how compatible we are, he's going to leave. They always leave."

Bianca studied her for a second. "You have to be the most cynical person in the world."

"Realistic. There's a difference."

Bianca rolled her eyes again.

"Fine." Cora crossed her arms in front of her chest, not bothering to hide her judgment. "If you need me to prove it, I'll prove it. Set me up. But if my guy walks away, you don't move to Idaho."

"You know what? Maybe this was a bad idea," Savannah said. Yes, she might have started this, but now that she heard it from the other side, she didn't like where it was going. Someone was going to get hurt.

"And how do I know you're not going to sabotage the relationship?" Bianca glared at Cora, who was looking more and more self-righteous as the conversation went on.

"Because I won't have to. Real life will do it for me. We can have the most perfect first date of all time. Shoot, we can even start dreaming about forever. But as soon as all the drama of reality sets in—which won't take long because I'm sharing a house with my sisters—my *soulmate* will be out the door so quick, he'll set a new record for fastest man alive."

"Seriously? That's what you think?" Bianca matched Cora's posture. "Who hurt you?"

Her answer was meant to be sarcastic, but it hit below the belt. This was starting to get out of hand.

"It's called life experience. Get ya some."

Bianca shook her head like Cora was the most ridiculous person she'd ever met. "You're telling me there's no way even your soulmate would stick around until the end of the summer?"

"That's what I'm saying, assuming your AI bot can find my 'soulmate.'" She gestured air quotes around the last word.

"But if he does stick around, you'll admit you're overly pessimistic and will agree to read whatever self-help book I deem most appropriate?"

"I feel so confident about my stance that if I'm wrong, I'll sing at your wedding."

"Interesting." Bianca considered this for a second. "In front of everyone?"

"The cheesiest love song you can find." Cora held out her hand to shake on it.

"Wait." Savannah stepped in between them. "I don't like this."

Bianca glared at her. "Wasn't it your idea?"

"Yes, but that was before it turned into this." She waved her hand around like she could visibly see the conflict between them. "Someone is going to end up getting hurt."

"Not if I do my job right," Cora said. "The idea is to keep Bianca from getting hurt."

"Or maybe we'll be planning a double wedding." Bianca winked.

"You really are that naive, aren't you?"

"Optimistic. You should try it. It's more fun."

Savannah held up her hands to stop her sisters.

She looked at Cora. "I have to admit, Bianca's not wrong. You tend to err on the negative side. Especially when it comes to relationships."

"Realistic side," Cora corrected.

Savannah gave a *maybe-maybe-not* bobble of her head. "The point is, getting out there and meeting people might not be a bad thing."

"I know plenty of people, thank you very much. But you don't have to convince me. I already said I'll be Bianca's cautionary tale, since apparently she hasn't lived long enough to have her own."

"See? Negative," Bianca said.

Savannah turned to Bianca. "But I'm with Cora on this. I love a good love story more than anyone, but there are some red flags here, Bee. You cannot trust everything you see online. Or on video chats."

"You're making a lot of assumptions about something you know nothing about." Bianca was clearly offended and maybe even a little hurt.

Savannah hurt for her. Part of her wanted to believe her sister's romance was real. Happily-ever-afters were Savannah's thing. She married her high school sweetheart, after all. But this?

Maybe it was because her little sister's heart was on the line. Or maybe it was the threat of Bianca moving away. Or maybe it was something else entirely. But something about this situation didn't sit right. It felt like there was a giant Do Not Enter sign flashing over it.

"I hope for your sake that Zander is everything you say. But if time and experience and Mom taught me anything, it's that not all that glitters is gold."

"Mom? You're actually going to bring Mom into this? Oh, you—"

Before Bianca could finish her sentence, the doorbell rang.

It was like the sound flash-froze the previous conversation along with all of the emotions—which were starting to slide out of control. The room fell completely still and silent except for three sets of questioning eyeballs that laser-beamed at one another.

Maybe Savannah needed to insert a random doorbell into all arguments.

"Are we expecting someone?" Cora whispered.

Savannah stared at the door. "It's the middle of the night. Who would we be expecting in the middle of the night?"

Bianca wrinkled her forehead. "Y'all realize it's not even ten o'clock, right?"

"Do *you* get unexpected visitors at ten o'clock?" Somehow, even when she was whispering, Cora's sass rang through her words.

Bianca seemed to consider the question for a moment before she shrugged. "Should we answer it?"

"No." Savannah didn't even hesitate. In fact, Bianca had barely gotten the whole sentence out before she gave her answer.

"But what if it's important?" Bianca countered.

"It's 9:56 p.m. Either it's important, or it's an ax murderer. And if it was important, someone would've texted." Seriously, did her sisters never watch true crime shows?

Cora cocked an eyebrow. "Do ax murderers ring the doorbell?"

"It's Luke from the property management company." The muffled voice came from the other side of the door. "I, uh, texted that I'd be dropping by to fix the toilet you said wasn't working." After a short pause he added, "I promise I don't have an ax."

"See? Important," Cora said and walked over to open the door.

Standing on the other side of the door was a tall, slender man with bright, friendly eyes and a warm smile. He had a toolbelt slung over one shoulder, giving merit to the claim that he was there to do a repair. Although the rest of him—the open rain jacket, khaki shorts, and HEYDUDE shoes—looked like the definition of a local.

And there was something about him that looked vaguely familiar.

"Oh my gosh, Little Luke Tudor?" Cora asked.

And that's when it clicked. This was the grandson of the woman who owned this house.

For many years, their parents had a longstanding rental agreement directly with Betty, who had always felt like a grandparent to them. And Betty had a few actual grandkids of her own. Savannah hadn't been here in so long that she'd almost forgotten about Lilly and Lacy, who were a couple years older than she was. But the grandchild who spent the most time with them was Lilly and Lacy's little brother Luke, who was Bianca's age and her main playmate while they were at the beach.

He gave a good-humored chuckle as Cora waved him into the house. "No one has called me that in years."

"Luke?" Bianca questioned. "My best friend for all of eternity or . . ." She let the words fall off expectantly.

Luke flashed a smile, revealing a set of charming dimples. "Or until your freezer runs out of Popsicles." He chuckled. "I'd almost forgotten about that."

Bianca looked at her sisters and gave a nonchalant shrug. "He swore an oath when we were eight. So, you know, it's probably still binding." She turned back to Luke. "Although don't hold us to the freezer thing quite yet. We did just get back into town."

He ran a hand through his floppy dark hair. "It's good to see y'all back in Sunnyside. It's been a while."

"Thanks," Savannah said and waved him into the house. "When we were texting about the rental, I didn't realize you were the same Luke. I should have made that connection before now. How's your grandmother?"

"She passed away about five years ago," Luke said. Immediately the air in the room shifted as there was yet another reminder of how much had changed since their last visit.

"Oh, I'm so sorry," Savannah said softly.

Cora nodded in solidarity. "She was a lovely woman."

"Thanks," Luke said. "We've turned all her properties into vacation rentals, so her legacy lives on. I manage them now along with some other vacation rentals in the area." He held up the hardware store bag in his hand. "Which brings me to the reason for my visit."

"Oh right!" Savannah suddenly felt guilty for the earlier text. If she'd known it was Luke, she would've held off sending the text about the toilet that wouldn't flush until normal business hours. It wasn't like it was an emergency. "We would've been fine until tomorrow. We can all share one bathroom for one night."

"It's not a problem. I was out anyway. I'm on my way over to trivia night at Gus's Tavern." He glanced around, probably noting their choice of attire. "But I hope I didn't keep you up."

Bianca waved off the thought. "Us? Not at all. Matching pajamas is kind of a beach house tradition. It doesn't mean we're going to bed."

Although, to be honest, Savannah was hoping to go to bed. She was actually proud that she'd stayed up this late. Late nights weren't really in the cards for her anymore. At least not in her current condition.

Not that she wanted to get into that at the moment.

"Some of us are just finishing dinner." Cora scooped the almost-empty bowl off the couch and held it up as evidence on her way to the kitchen. "Tell us about this trivia night thing."

"It's a summer tradition. Every Monday night at ten. People can get a little competitive over it."

"Sounds like fun," Cora said.

Luke nodded. "It is. Y'all should go."

"Okay," Bianca said cheerfully. "I'm in."

"Now?" Savannah didn't bother to hide her surprise.

Bianca shrugged. "Sure. It's our first night in town. Why not?"

Savannah had a whole list of reasons, starting with it was late. Plus, she already had on her pajamas, and as previously mentioned, it was past her bedtime. And possibly the biggest reason of all, she didn't want to.

She was trying to think of a delicate way to sum it all up when Cora beat her to it. "Yeah, I'm not doing that."

"Why not?" Bianca demanded. "Another pessimistic view of a positive situation?"

"After the travel day I had? I don't think I need another excuse." Cora rinsed out her bowl and stuck it in the dishwasher.

"Maybe we can go next week," Savannah offered, feeling more than a little relieved that she had a decent excuse for bailing. "We can add it to the Summer Bucket List."

Bianca shook her head, looking disappointed. "I can't believe my sisters are so lame."

"Believe it, baby." Cora blew her a kiss.

Bianca shifted her gaze to their guest. "What about you, Luke? Looking for a teammate tonight?"

He seemed surprised. "You want to go with me?"

It was more of a clarifying question, but Bianca jumped on the invitation anyway. "I'd love to, thanks." She gave Savannah a pointed look. "At least one person still knows how to have fun around here. I bet he doesn't even have a problem with dating apps."

"Um . . ." He drew the word out and gave a quick glance around the room as if he wasn't sure how to respond to any of what just happened.

"Just give me a minute to change." Bianca flashed him a smile.

"Great," Luke said. Although his tone didn't sound as enthusiastic as his answer. "And while I'm waiting, I'll fix the toilet."

He looked at Savannah and pointed toward the primary bedroom. She gave him a nod and a sorry-about-all-this shrug, and he disappeared in that direction.

"So, this is off to a fun start," Cora said.

Savannah tried to give her best optimist smile, but she couldn't help the disappointed sigh that escaped.

No, things weren't going according to plan, but it was okay. It was only day one. There were still twenty-seven more. Things would get better.

They had to.

Right?

3

Bianca

Gus's Tavern was located on a stretch of oceanfront property between two condo buildings. It was an octagonal wooden building set up on stilts with a huge, three-level deck on the ocean side. During the day, it was a burger shack, serving up casual fare in paper food trays to beachgoers. At night, it was known for hosting live music out on the sand. And now, apparently, they had added a trivia night to the mix.

Bianca wanted to say that she remembered this place or knew from her own personal experience what it was. Her sisters certainly remembered it. They had mentioned it multiple times in the text thread when they were talking about places they couldn't wait to revisit. Apparently, Cora had big plans for taking down a double order of their fries. Possibly every day.

But Bianca didn't remember it. In fact, there was a lot about Sunnyside she didn't remember, which was hard for her to admit to her sisters.

Sure, she had memories of their summers here, but hers were different. She remembered building sandcastles on the beach with her mom. She remembered playing in the waves with her sisters. She remembered that when she was here, life seemed almost perfect.

But she'd been a kid then. The last time she was here, she'd been gearing up for her eleventh birthday, the summer before she started middle school. She hadn't been old enough to do the things her teenage sisters had done, so her memories were different. Sometimes it felt like a different trip altogether.

But she was here now, ready to make some memories of her own.

Luke pulled his old pickup truck—which would have probably been classified as *old* the last time she was in Sunnyside—into the already-packed parking lot of Gus's Tavern.

"Wow," Bianca said. "You weren't kidding when you said the whole town would be here."

From what she could see, Gus's was packed. An overflow of people hung out on the front deck and the stairs, chatting in small groups. One group waved to a couple as they walked up to meet them, and for the first time since she'd invited herself on this little excursion, Bianca realized trivia was more of a group activity. Luke probably wasn't coming on his own.

Suddenly, she was aware that she had no idea what kind of situation she'd invited herself into. While she remembered Luke and some of their childhood beachy adventures, she knew nothing about him as an adult. For all she knew, he had a long-standing guys' night tradition. Or he could be meeting his girlfriend. Or his wife.

She quickly glanced at his hand. No ring, which meant at least she wasn't interrupting some coveted date night. Probably.

"It's okay that I came, right? I mean, I'm not ruining your plans for tonight or anything, am I?"

Luke shook his head and pulled into what she assumed was a legal-enough spot on the sand. "Naw. I was just meeting up with some buddies. Nothing formal." He shifted his truck into Park. "Besides, it's not every day I get to catch up with my super summer friend."

His old title for her made her smile because: One, it eased some of her embarrassment about crashing his plans. And two: Luke was exactly how she remembered him—kind and inclusive. It was good to know that some things never changed. "Well, I promise I'll be a good teammate. I'm pretty good at trivia. My wealth of random facts runs deep."

"Good to know because it can get a little competitive around here. How are you at buzzing in?"

She held up her hands and wiggled her fingers. "I hate to brag, but thanks to these beauties, I haven't missed getting into a concert queue yet."

Luke chuckled. "Then it looks like I brought the right person with me." He climbed out of the truck.

Bianca followed, stepping out into the warm tropical night.

"Anyway, thanks for letting me come. Things were . . ." She paused, trying to think of the best word to describe the conversation. *Frustrating? Difficult? Ridiculous?*

He shot her a knowing side glance. "In my family, we call it passionate."

That made her lips twitch. "It was definitely that."

"Family. We couldn't do life without them, but sometimes they make it so dang hard to do life with them."

Bianca laughed out loud. "So true. And to think, this is only the first of twenty-eight nights. It could be a long month."

"The beach has a way of healing things. They say it's the salt water."

"Maybe." Although she wasn't feeling optimistic. Even her happy, celebratory news had turned into a lecture. Apparently, she couldn't even fall in love correctly.

According to her sisters, anyway.

She didn't get it. She thought for sure they would be happy for her. She'd fallen in love and figured out what she wanted to do with her life—two things her sisters had been telling her to do for years. Cora and Savannah should've been popping a bottle of champagne and toasting her. Instead, they were trying to talk her out of it.

"What are your thoughts on dating apps?" she asked as they jogged up the front steps to Gus's entrance. The sound of laughter and happy conversations drifted through the open doors.

Luke shrugged. "I've never tried it myself. But I have a buddy who met his wife on one."

"See! Would you please tell my sisters that?"

He waved to a group of guys at a table near the front, then led them over to one of the few open tables, a high-top off to the side. "I'm guessing that's what the fight was about."

"Passionate discussion," she corrected, sliding onto a stool.

He shot her a knowing grin. "Right."

From the stage the emcee called out the two-minute warning and a timer appeared on the main screen. Luke pulled out his iPad and started the process of registering their team. "You, uh, want to pick our team name?"

"How about 'Not Wrong,'" Bianca said without any hesitation. "It's been my stance tonight, even if everyone else wants to debate me."

"I like it." Luke kept tapping away at the screen.

"But this isn't a crazy idea, right? People meet each other all kinds of ways. Why shouldn't online be one of them?"

"Makes sense."

"And if Covid taught us anything, it's that virtual meetings and in-person meetings are practically the same."

"Maybe not quite the same, but they can be effective." He propped up the screen just as the emcee stepped up to the mic.

"Welcome to Trivia Night. The night where it's not just what you know, but how fast you know it." The emcee's voice boomed and the crowd erupted into cheers. "Let's get started."

The first question flashed on the main screen above his head as he started reading it out loud. Before he finished reading the first two words, Bianca reached over and tapped the answer on their iPad screen. "If anything, a connection made over a virtual meeting would be even stronger in person."

"I mean, sure," Luke agreed. He pointed at the now-blank screen. "Was that a guess? Or did you actually have time to process the question?"

Bianca scoffed. "Guess? Please."

As the allowed time to buzz in ran out, the leaderboard popped up on the main screen.

"And it looks like team Not Wrong has taken an early lead."

Luke nodded, looking impressed. "All right."

"The thing is, I don't understand why my sisters would think it was ridiculous to build a relationship that way." The second question flashed up. Once again, while the emcee was still reading it, Bianca pointed at the iPad. "C."

"There's no way you had time to read that. You've gotta be guessing," Luke said as he tapped the answer.

She shot him a sassy little smile and kept going. "Cora lives out of state, and we're not any less close to her because our primary contact with her is FaceTime." She paused and thought through that sentence. "Okay, bad example. The reason we don't feel connected to Cora has nothing to do with FaceTime and everything to do with her being Cora."

"And Not Wrong is living up to their name. But Fact Checkers and The A-Team are holding on to a close second. Looks like we're going to have some real competition tonight."

"I mean, tons of people meet their person online," Bianca continued. "It's not like this is a new thing. It's been around for like thirty years." She flashed her eyes to the big screen and read the new question. "D."

Luke hesitated for a fraction of a second before he hit the correct button. She shot him a judgmental side-eye. "If those were Taylor Swift tickets, you'd be watching the concert two months later at your local movie theater."

Luke chuckled. "I'll work on that. Also, you're going to fit in just fine here."

She gave him a confident grin as the leaderboard showed they were still in the lead.

"Okay, let me make sure we're having the same conversation here," Luke said. "Your sisters think dating apps can't be successful, but you want to give it a try."

Bianca shook her head. "No, I *know* it's successful because I met my fiancé that way." She pointed at the screen. "A."

He hit the answer faster this time. "How do you do that?" He gestured to the screen.

She shrugged. "It's my useless talent."

"Not useless if you want the coveted Trivia Night trophy."

She brightened. "You didn't tell me there was a trophy."

He nodded. "Congratulations, by the way."

Bianca held up a hand in a *stop* gesture. "Slow your roll. We haven't won yet. They might get to a category I don't know. My wealth of random facts might run deep, but it dries up quick as soon as we start talking about geography."

"No, I meant about getting married."

"Oh." For some reason the switch seemed to steal the wind from her sails, which was weird.

She was excited about getting married. Of course she was. It was the whole dumb argument with her sisters that was throwing her off. "Thanks." She reached across and hit the answer because she didn't have the energy to call it out this time.

"If you've already met someone online, why are your sisters anti–dating apps?"

"Because they're lame. They think I can't possibly be in love with someone I've only known for a month and haven't met in person. D."

His eyes widened and his attention focused on her instead of the screen where he was supposed to be entering their answer. "You're engaged to a man you've never met?"

She had to lean over him and hit the iPad for them. No way were they going to be among the fastest on this question. Hopefully The A-Team didn't pull ahead of them. "You sound like my sisters."

He studied her with an expression that fell somewhere between quizzical and amused. "Do you do everything fast? Or just trivia and falling in love?"

"You're making fun of me." She slumped against her chair.

"No. I'm honestly impressed. It must be nice to know what you want as soon as you see it."

To be fair, most of her life wasn't like that. She felt like she'd spent the better part of her "adult" life floundering.

She always put air quotes around *adult* because even though she would turn twenty-six at the end of the summer, she didn't feel like an adult. That seemed reserved for someone . . . older, maybe? Definitely more together.

For example, after three years and four different majors, she'd hit the pause button on college until she could figure out the direction she wanted to go. Four years and five jobs later, she still wasn't any closer to knowing.

Until she met Zander.

Suddenly she felt like she had a starting point. Move to Boise. Marry her soulmate. Start a new career that would build a business they could do together. Maybe this was what she'd been waiting for.

"It is." She breathed in a happy breath. "How about you? Is there a significant someone in your life?"

"Nope." He answered the next trivia question on his own.

She propped her chin on her hand and studied him. "Have you ever been in love?" Was it a personal question? Maybe. But they had once promised to be BFFs for life, so she probably had the right to ask it.

Sure, they were eight at the time, but still.

"Not the kind that ever led to a ring," he answered.

"Maybe you need to try a dating app."

He chuckled. "I'm good, thanks."

Bianca shrugged. "You never know. It could change your life."

Luke gave her a look like he didn't believe her, but that was fine. Like he'd already admitted, he'd never been in love. Not the kind that made the impossible seem possible, anyway. The kind that made her want to get married now because she didn't want to wait a single day longer than necessary to get started on the life she'd been waiting for.

He didn't get it because he hadn't been there. Just like Cora had never been there. And she didn't know what Savannah's problem was, except that she could be judgy about a lot of things Bianca did. She had impossibly high standards. She always had.

But they would change their tune when they saw how great she and Zander were together. Seeing was believing, after all.

Plus, it wouldn't hurt when she won her bet with Cora.

"And with that, the first round is over," the emcee called from the stage. "Let's take a look at our leaderboard. Know-It-Ales snuck into third position right there at the end." A team of college-aged guys cheered from a four-top out on the deck. "Second place is The A-Team." The table next to them with an older man and a guy probably in his mid-thirties waved. "And blowing everyone else away is Not Wrong. Come on up and claim your prize for round one, a free appetizer. Which you might need because we have four more rounds before we crown tonight's trivia champ."

"We go up there?" Bianca asked, pointing at the stage.

"If you want your prize, you do." Luke stood up and made his way through the tables to the front. Bianca followed him.

At the request of the emcee, they hopped onstage and took a bow. Bianca accepted the certificate for a free appetizer and held it over her head like a trophy. The crowd cheered and her optimism shot up.

So what if her sisters didn't think she knew what she was doing? Clearly she did.

"Should we cash it in now?" Bianca asked as they hopped off the stage.

"Sure. What do you want?"

"I honestly have no idea what's on the menu. What do you suggest?"

"Do you like fried calamari?"

She nodded.

"Great. I'll put in the order at the counter. It'll come out faster that way."

He headed with the certificate over to the counter while Bianca made her way to the table. Back on her stool, she did a little people watching. Naturally, her attention went to the table next to them, where The A-Team was sitting. The two men seemed to be in the middle of a serious discussion.

"You and I both know you're making a mistake. Neither Brody nor Trina has what it takes to do the job. There's no debate that I'd make the better Senior Vice President of Operations," the younger of the two men was saying.

He was undeniably handsome in a rugged sort of way. His dark wavy hair was fixed without being overly styled, and his bright blue eyes sparkled with passion. Even though it appeared to be a serious conversation, he was relaxed. Comfortable. In charge.

But he also carried a hint of danger.

Bianca didn't know how to explain it. Maybe it was his muscular build or his undeniable confidence. Or the scar he had on his arm that looked a lot like a bullet wound. Whatever the reason, he looked like the kind of guy who had stories, but he couldn't tell them to you. The kind of guy you might want if you ever needed help getting out of a sticky situation. Basically, he reminded her of a real-life Jack Ryan or James Bond.

He was intriguing. And more than that, his conversation was intriguing. So, while she probably should've minded her own business, she leaned in to hear more.

"What Trina and Brody have is predictability. I know where their priorities lie."

The older man shot 007 a pointed look. "They're not going to disappear when we need them most."

"That's not fair, and you know it," 007 argued. He leaned back against the stool. "Besides, I've changed."

"Leopards can't change their spots."

"Then it's a good thing I'm not a leopard."

The older man heaved out a sigh. "Look, do I think you'd make a better SVP than Brody or Trina?" The pained expression that passed over his face was so obvious that it made Bianca want to pull her stool over to their table and demand they spill the tea on poor Brody and Trina. But before she could embarrass all of them, the older man kept going. "But competence is not the only factor at play here."

"Their fashion sense is a concern, too, isn't it?" 007 said, pulling a face.

Older man shot him a reprimanding look. "This is your sister and cousin we're talking about."

Oh, now this was getting good! Bianca glanced around to see if anyone else was following this drama, but everyone else seemed to be happily engrossed in their own conversations.

"And there's nobody I'd rather spend Thanksgiving with," 007 was saying. "But they can't run a company."

"You know what they can do? Show up. I know if I schedule a meeting with them next week, they'll be there. If I have a question at any point during any day, I don't have to wonder what time zone they're currently in."

"And that's the kind of person you want running your company? Someone who's afraid to venture out of their office?"

"Someone who's not afraid to stay," the man said in a firm voice. "Of course I'd rather pick you, but you have nothing keeping you here and a history of not sticking around. I can't leave our family's legacy to someone who could decide to cash out tomorrow and move to Tahiti."

"First of all, I'd never move to Tahiti," 007 said. "New Zealand, maybe. But not Tahiti."

The older man didn't seem amused.

"And secondly, I'd have the company keeping me here."

"Which you've left before."

"That couldn't be helped, and you know it."

This was better than a movie! Bianca leaned in even farther.

The older man sighed like he'd lost all his fight. "Listen, this isn't a personal attack. You had to do what you had to do. I get that. But I have to do what is best for the company. And the family. You haven't been able to commit to a dry cleaner. Why would I think you'd be able to commit to this?"

"Because I said I would. And I keep my word."

"I'm not saying your lifestyle is bad," the man continued, as if he hadn't heard 007's comment. "If anyone can relate with wanting freedom, it's me. But you have nothing tying you here. You have no spouse, no kids. And while you always seem to have a date, it's never the same one. Have you ever had a long-term relationship?"

"Like I said, that's not who I am anymore."

"No one wants to believe that more than I do."

"Then what's it going to take?"

"The proof is in the pudding," the older man said. "If you want to prove you're a family man, be a family man. Settle down. Buy a house with a two-car garage. Coach Little League on the weekends."

At that, 007 crossed his arms and leaned back on his stool, looking obstinate. "The board meeting is next month, Uncle Anders. I can't exactly conjure up a family by then."

"No, that kind of life takes time. But it starts with a commitment. To a relationship." The older man raised an eyebrow as he tossed the challenge out there.

The challenge hung between them for a second, and Bianca could've sworn 007 was visibly trying to work out how they could circle back to the Little League thing.

"So, a girlfriend," he said eventually, his confidence returning. "You want me to get a girlfriend."

"No. I want you to be in a relationship. A serious, committed relationship. One that's built on trust and mutual respect. One where neither of you is going to run when things get hard." He gave the younger man a knowing look. "One where plans for the future mean years, not next weekend."

"And you think I can find that in a month?" There was a heavy note of *this is ridiculous* in his voice.

"If you're lucky, you'll find it once in your lifetime. But I'm announcing the position in a month. Where you are on that journey is up to you."

The wheels in Bianca's mind started to spin.

This guy needed a serious relationship that lasted until the end of the month.

For her to win her own bet, Cora's SoulMatch date needed to stick around for a month.

What if . . . ?

"Two-minute warning," the emcee called out, and again the time appeared on the big screen.

Luke slid onto the stool next to her and put two drinks and a paper tray full of steaming calamari on the table. "Looks like our order came out just in time."

"Who's that?" Bianca gave a discreet nod of her head in the direction of where 007 now sat alone.

"Who? Him?" Luke, on the other hand, was not as discreet. He popped a couple of steaming calamari rings into his mouth. "That's Jax Verona."

"Is he from around here?"

"Yes and no."

"That's a cryptic answer."

"He's a cryptic guy." Luke grabbed another couple of calamari and dunked them in the rémoulade sauce. "He's part of a longtime Sunnyside family. They own Padua Resorts, a chain of coastal boutique hotels. But Jax is somewhat of the black sheep. He's the only family member who doesn't work for Padua Resorts and sometimes he disappears for months at a time."

"What does he do?" she asked.

Luke shrugged. "No one knows for sure, but there's a lot of speculation. My favorite, and frankly the most believable, is that he's a hit man. But a lot of people make the case for international art thief."

Bianca gave him a warning look.

Luke held up his hands in a *don't kill the messenger* gesture. "I didn't make it up. I'm just giving you the facts."

Bianca studied 007. The last thing she wanted was to put her sister in danger. But this man looked kind. Yes, it was kind in a tough sort of way, but maybe that was a good thing.

Besides, the beauty of SoulMatch was that they would do a background check. If there was something sketchy about him, they'd never get matched in the first place.

"I want to meet him."

Luke looked surprised. "The hit man?"

"First of all, he's dressed way too nice to be a hit man. I'm leaning toward art thief."

"Hit men have a dress code?"

Bianca rolled her eyes.

"Okay, but don't say I didn't warn you."

Luke started to move off his stool in the direction of the table next to him, but Bianca caught his arm. "Wait. Let me beat him first. I think the conversation will go better that way."

Luke chuckled. "I love your confidence." He settled back on his stool as the first question popped up on the screen.

Twenty questions later, Not Wrong had another winning round under their belt.

As soon as the emcee announced them as the winners, Jax Verona shifted to look behind him. He shot her a half-congrats, half-impressed look.

"Now," she whispered to Luke.

Luke stood up. "Hey, Jax. Good to see you. How've you been?"

Instead of answering, Jax studied him as if he were trying to assess the threat level of the question. Or maybe he was assessing the threat level of the *questioner*.

Either way, the stare caused Luke to back down. "Great." He cleared his throat. "Anyway, I'd like to introduce my old friend and one of my tenants, Bianca Prestly."

Bianca gave him her friendliest grin. "Nice to meet you."

Jax maintained his same serious look. "Bianca Prestly, are you cheating?"

"Are you saying that just because I'm a woman, I couldn't possibly win?"

"I'm saying you haven't gotten one wrong yet. Not even the one about the stolen van Gogh being in an IKEA bag. No one got that right."

"Except you," she said. And to be fair, he'd buzzed in before she did because it took her a second to remember the whole story she'd read.

"I had an advantage." He paused, letting those words sink in. "I was there."

The confession caught her off guard. Luke wasn't wrong. There was merit to the occupation theories.

But maybe that was just what Cora needed. He was independent. She was independent. He was interesting. She . . . liked interesting people? Regardless, they were a match made in heaven.

Plus, and possibly most importantly, he was committed to sticking around for a month, which meant Bianca would win her bet. She had to admit, the idea of Jax being Cora's SoulMatch was becoming more and more interesting. Now all she had to do was convince him to do it.

And figure out a way to guarantee they would match. But first things first.

She got up and slid into the seat his uncle had just vacated. "And even that experience wasn't enough to qualify you for the job you want?"

He narrowed his eyes on her with a questioning look.

She shrugged. "I couldn't help but overhear your conversation earlier." Maybe it would've been more accurate to say *didn't want to avoid* overhearing his conversation, but why get tangled up in semantics? "But I might be able to help you with your little problem."

"Convincing my uncle to let me run the family company because I'm the most competent choice?"

"Helping you find the committed relationship to prove you're serious."

He studied her with a look that could only be classified as amused. "Are you offering to date me?"

"I'm engaged, thank you." She held up her left hand to put the ring on display. "Besides, if you're going to meet someone who seems serious enough to marry, I'm pretty sure it's not going to be in a bar."

"Technically, this is a tavern, which is closer to a restaurant."

Yeah, he was going to be perfect for Cora. They were cut from the same cloth.

"What I'm proposing is a matchmaker app," Bianca said.

The amusement vanished and he turned away. "Like Tinder? No, thanks. Not really my thing."

She raised an eyebrow. "How about winning bets with your uncle? Is that your thing?"

He studied her for several long seconds before answering. "And what's in it for you? Is this your app?"

"Nope. I'm just a satisfied customer in a happy relationship who can't help but pass on the recommendation to everyone I meet." She tried to glow. She wasn't entirely sure one was capable of forcing that kind of thing, but it wasn't going to be for lack of effort on her part.

Apparently her effort didn't work, because he didn't seem convinced. If this plan was going to work, she was going to have to up her sales pitch.

"Hear me out," she continued. "This isn't just another dating app. It's a virtual matchmaker whose job is to help you find a long-term, committed relationship."

"And you think I can't find that on my own?"

"In . . . How long did you have, again?" She could tell her argument had struck a chord with him when he glanced down, ever so briefly, at his hands. So, she continued. "The main benefit here is that everyone on the app is also looking for something long-term. You automatically weed out anyone who's looking for something more . . . fun."

When he still didn't look convinced, she tried again. "Or, your other option is to pull up your contact list and see if there's anyone who would be willing to give you a second chance."

She could tell he was starting to come over to her side, but he was still suspicious. Being an international criminal probably did that to you.

"What's in it for you?" he asked.

She gave him her most innocent grin. "What can I say? I'm a hopeless romantic."

It wasn't entirely true, but it wasn't a flat-out lie. Besides, she still stood by her claim that SoulMatch was a great way to find your forever-person. Plus, it was possible he wouldn't get matched with her sister, which meant Bianca was really doing this out of the goodness of her heart.

Of course, she could narrow the search radius to as small as she wanted. And really, how many people were joining tonight in a twenty-mile radius of this tiny town? Plus, she wasn't above helping him *structure* his answers so the computer could see the same potential she did.

Not that she didn't believe in the system. She did. The success rate didn't lie. But even fate needed a gentle nudge every now and again.

In fact, maybe she should recommend he put in a fifteen-mile radius, just to be on the safe side.

Who knew? Maybe she and Cora would be planning a double wedding.

"So, what do you say?"

Jax studied her with an expression she couldn't read. After what felt like an eternity, he shrugged. "Okay. I'm in."

4

Jax

The fact that Jax was setting up an account on some dating app was a testament to how ludicrous his uncle was being.

Had he left the company once? Yes. But he had a good reason. It was the right thing to do.

As far as he was concerned, that decision had zero to do with the Senior Vice President of Operations job. It was a different time under a completely different set of circumstances. One had nothing to do with the other, and his uncle knew that.

But Jax was made for this job. He was born to run this company. And as far as the competition? Well, there *wasn't* any competition.

Trina, his sister, had made it clear that she didn't want to run the whole show. She liked running one hotel. The person who wanted to run the company was Trina's jerk of a husband. Jax didn't trust him as far as he could throw him. No way was he letting that money-grabbing jerk anywhere near their family legacy.

And Brody? Sure, he was good with numbers. He would make a fantastic CFO. But he was about as assertive as a bunny rabbit. He'd cave under the threat of opposition, whether it came from the inside or the outside. Five years with Brody at the helm, and if the company didn't go under, they'd be selling to a big corporate shark who only cared about the bottom line.

Padua Resorts had been in his mother's family for fifty years. It was one of the few independent hotel chains left. Jax wasn't going to sit by and watch Brody or Trina's husband destroy it. If finding a girlfriend was what it was going to take to convince his uncle to do the right thing, so be it. He'd stared danger in the face more than a few times in his life. Surely, he could figure out how to be in a relationship for a few weeks.

Okay, fine. He'd be the first to admit the prospect made him uneasy. He'd even go so far as to say that pushing his two-date rule aside for something longer made him nervous. But high-speed car chases made him feel uneasy and he did those, so . . .

While they were between trivia sets, Jax entered his personal information and created a password just to prove how much he was willing to defy his nerves.

Are you ready to meet your forever?

The words flashed across the screen.

A corner of Jax's mouth pulled up. *Absolutely.*

Although he felt fairly certain he and the site weren't thinking the same thing. His forever included a nameplate on the door and a big corner office.

But companionship wasn't bad either.

He clicked the Get Started button.

On the next page sat questions on top of free-response dialogue boxes. He scrolled down to the first one.

Describe your ideal forever relationship.

They got straight to the point, didn't they?

Maybe he'd start with something a little lighter and circle back. He went to the second question.

What are the top three qualities you're looking for
in a partner, and why are those important?

Nope. He wasn't starting with that one, either.

He continued scrolling, scanning the questions as he went. His stint in the Army, when he shared a single room with eleven other men, had not been as invasive as this questionnaire.

He shifted around to look at his new friend Bianca, sitting at the table behind him.

"It's a little intense."

"What? Were you hoping it would just let you pick the prettiest face?"

Fair. "But is writing a dissertation necessary?"

"To match you with the right person, they have to have all the information. Just answer from the heart."

Jax stared at the questions again.

How ambitious are you? What level of ambition would
you like your forever partner to possess?

"I'm starting to think scrolling through my contacts might've been the better way to go here," he said.

She breathed out as if he were a child exhausting her patience. "Do you need me to help you?"

"Yes. Because if I'm being honest, I've never once thought about what kind of relationship I expect my future partner to have with my family. I've barely even thought about my future partner."

She rolled her eyes but reclaimed her spot on the stool next to him and held her hand out for his phone. "May I?"

He handed it over.

"Let's see. What qualities are you looking for?" Her thumbs flew across the screen without even waiting for his response. "You want someone who is trustworthy, confident and . . ." She squinted her eyes and studied him for a second. "Has a good sense of humor."

Not a bad lineup. "A drop-down list would've helped."

She gave a slight shrug and moved down to the next question.

"You view ambition as an admirable quality. You like strong, successful, independent women." She spoke the words out loud as he watched her type them on the screen.

"You got all that from eavesdropping on my conversation?"

She gave him a quick side-glance but didn't stop. "Do you want children, and if so, how many?" Instead of answering this one, she turned and looked at him expectantly.

"You're not going to answer that one for me?"

She shrugged. "Didn't come up in your conversation."

"Sure, at some point." He thought about that for a second. "In the *very* far future."

"Absolutely," she said as she typed. "When the time is right. After we've had some adventures on our own."

Yeah, that sounded better.

"Your ideal date." She paused and looked at him with narrowed eyes. "I'm going to say . . ."

"That one I can cover." Before she could go there, he took his phone out of her hand and started typing. "Forever relationships haven't been my thing, but I'm not lacking game."

"Or confidence," she muttered. She read over his shoulder as he typed his favorite first date. "Nice. But add 'stargazing on the beach' at the end. You're looking for a fifty-year anniversary forever, remember? Not a one-night stand."

Fair enough.

They went through the rest of the questions. Fifteen minutes later he was ready to hit Submit.

"How long does it take to match?"

She shrugged. "That depends. It's a longer process since they run background checks. And, of course, it depends on if there's anyone in the system you match with. But I'd say probably a day. Maybe two."

"And what makes you so confident that this is going to work?"

She gave him a knowing smile. "I have faith in the system."

Jax was good at reading people. It was one of the things that made him successful at the poker table and imperative for the job he'd been doing for the past five years. And he could tell there was something this Bianca person wasn't telling him.

He didn't bother calling her out on it. He just refocused his interrogator gaze on her.

He was pretty good at that, too.

After a second, she caved. Her shoulders slumped, and her eyes drifted from him down to her lap. "My sister's on it, and I think y'all would be a good match. You seem like her type."

"And you think she'd be *my* type?"

She nodded at his phone. "Are you really looking for the kind of woman you described there?"

"Technically, you described it." He mentally reviewed what they'd written. "But, yeah."

"Then she's your type." Bianca nodded confidently.

"So why not set us up?"

She seemed to consider the question for a second. "She'd be more open to it if it came from . . . someone else."

"Plus, you wanted the background check."

"You can never be too careful these days." She looked at him, curious. "You're going to pass the background check, right?"

He gave her his best smoldering, mysterious look. It was the same one he used anytime someone asked him about his dangerous reputation. "Would I be any good at my job if I didn't?"

It was hard to keep up with the rumors about his mystery occupation. He'd heard it all. Spy. Black mission operative. International art thief.

That one always made him laugh. People had way too much time on their hands.

"Anyway, I guess we could be seeing a lot more of each other." She paused to think for a second. "And if not, best of luck on winning your bet."

"That's it? You're just going to leave me?"

"I got you set up. It's your job to woo her. And I thought you said you had that part covered."

"Even so, it never hurts to have some inside information."

That seemed to get her attention.

"What's your sister's name?"

"Cora." Bianca paused, seeming to consider his request for insider information. "And don't bring her flowers. She's more of a booklover kind of girl."

He nodded, and she turned to walk away.

So, this is where life had taken him? Signing up on a dating app run by AI?

But if that's what it took to save the company from demise, then that's what he would do.

He'd been in life-threatening situations before. Stared down the wrong end of a gun more than once. He was pretty sure he could handle a relationship for a month.

5

Cora

Cora had a date.

Well, what she really had was a match. But a match would lead to a date. And a date would lead to a breakup, which meant she won the bet.

Okay, yes, that sounded a little off, even to her brain. But a surge of triumph rushed through her anyway. She was about to win the bet with Bianca.

Cora was a competitive person, so winning any bet was enticing. But winning this particular bet came with the added benefit of proving her point to her sister. Bianca was naive, and Cora felt a sense of responsibility to keep her from getting hurt.

More than half of marriages ended in divorce, and those were just the relationships that were committed enough to make it to the altar. Statistically speaking, this internet-based relationship with a person Bianca had never met had zero chance of going the distance. And then what? She'd be stuck in another state all by herself, trying to put the pieces of her life back together?

Unfortunately, Cora knew all too well how that song ended. She'd already lived it once.

But there wasn't going to be a repeat performance because Cora was going to win the bet and prove her point to Bianca. And the poor shmuck who was going to help her do it was . . .

Jax V.

SoulMatch used last initials instead of full last names to protect privacy, believing that each person should be able to share their personal information when they felt most comfortable, which Cora could respect.

Although if she was being honest, being called "Cora P." made her feel like a contestant on *The Bachelor*, which wasn't a selling point for the site.

But she digressed. The main thing was that she had a match.

She skimmed Jax V.'s information. He was a couple years older than she was and had never been married. His hobbies were kite surfing, traveling, and hanging with his family. A fun fact about him was that he had his pilot's license but didn't have his own plane—yet. And his ideal relationship was one where forever didn't seem long enough. All in all, Jax V. sounded like a pretty great guy.

Of course, it could all be a lie.

Okay, yeah. Maybe Bianca had a point about her being cynical.

Although whether Jax V.'s story was a lie or not didn't really matter. It wasn't like she was looking for a future with this guy. All she needed was a perfect first date and maybe a pretty awesome second date. As soon as he seemed interested, she would flip the switch to Real Life and count the minutes until he bolted. Hopefully she got to count in days, but she supposed being dumped in the middle of a meal would make a more impactful point. She scanned the profile a bit more before she opened his message.

Honestly, she was a little disappointed she didn't get to send him the message first. She would've liked having the first word, starting off more in control.

But this app worked like a real matchmaker, someone who would introduce a couple based on whatever criteria she thought would make a connection. In this case, the introduction happened in the form of a message sent to both people simultaneously. Apparently, Jax V. opened his message before Cora did.

She made a mental note to change her notifications so that wouldn't happen again.

> Nice to meet you, Cora P.
> Three things you should know about me, in case they are deal-breakers.
> I love hot dogs. I know I shouldn't. I know they're made of nothing good, held together by chemicals, and will probably kill me. But if death by hot dogs is how I go down, so be it.

He didn't start off with a cheesy pickup line or some comment on how she looked, which was a solid start. Plus, it made her smile.

She kept reading.

> While I agree that Taylor Swift is a talented musician, I don't know if she's the greatest of all time. That designation is reserved for Elvis. I could also be talked into Dolly.

Clearly, he'd read her bio. He was wrong, but she gave him points for trying to connect.

Although, she did like Dolly.

> This is my first time doing anything like this, so I apologize if I'm doing it all wrong. But if I haven't offended you too much so far, I'd love to chat.
> —Jax (My last name is Verona, by the way. In case you want to look me up on social.)

She had to admit, she was intrigued. Before she gave herself too much time to overthink it, she hit Reply and started to type.

Hot dogs, huh? Seems like an unfortunate way to go.
If you're going to have death by something unhealthy,
sugar is a much better option. Think of all the delicious
culprits. Ice cream. Chocolate. Donuts. Pretty much
everything served at brunch.
But as long as we're discussing deal-breakers, I don't
trust people who don't eat dessert. Seems ... wrong.
—Cora

She hit Send and was just about to open the profile page with his
picture when she was interrupted by the sound of the glass door sliding
open.

Savannah stepped out on the deck clutching a coffee mug between
her hands. "I mean, there really isn't a better view in the whole world,
is there?"

"Not as far as I'm concerned." Cora snapped her laptop shut and
set it on the wide arm of the Adirondack chair. She wasn't sure why she
snapped it shut. It wasn't like she was trying to hide anything. Both of
her sisters were aware of her dating plan. But for some reason, this part
felt . . . personal.

Either Savannah didn't notice the laptop or didn't care, because she
settled in the chair next to Cora and let out a contented sigh. "Now,
this feels familiar."

"Right?" She jerked her thumb over her shoulder. "But the house
used to be bigger, didn't it?"

"It's like someone threw it in the dryer. It looks the same, just two
sizes smaller than it used to be."

Cora laughed. "Exactly."

"It's good to be here, though."

"Mmm." It was a noncommittal response, because the verdict was
still out on whether or not it was good to be here. Although, if the first
twenty-four hours were any indication, it wasn't looking good.

"Any word on your lost luggage?" Savannah asked.

"It has been located." Cora gave a dramatic pause and turned to look at her sister. "In Fargo, North Dakota."

"How did that happen?"

"I have no idea." People's incompetence exhausted her.

Of course, sometimes people in general exhausted her, but that was a different topic for a different day.

"I have a swimsuit you can borrow today," Savannah offered.

"Thanks." Cora took a sip of her Diet Dr Pepper. "I thought I'd drive to Panama City and buy a few things to hold me over while I wait."

"Today?"

"Yes. What else do we have to do?"

Savannah motioned out toward the water. "I thought we'd have a beach day. Like we always did. First day of the summer vacation was always a beach day."

"Every day of the summer was a beach day."

"Yeah, but the first day was different. The first day was a designated beach day. Remember?"

Cora sighed. "Fine. I'll drive to town tomorrow." She tossed Savannah a judgmental look. "But you're not going to try to make this trip an exact replica of how it used to be, right?"

"What's so bad about holding on to traditions?"

"Because life isn't the same as it used to be. Maybe it's time to let go of the past and embrace the present."

"But that's the beauty of traditions. Even if everything else changes, some things stay the same."

It was a nice sentiment, maybe. But just because they went to the beach on the first day of vacation didn't make any part of this trip—or this family—the same as it used to be.

The sliding glass door opened again, and Bianca cruised onto the patio holding an energy drink in one hand and a hideous, three-foot-tall trophy in the other. "Let the record show that bunk beds are not as fun for adults as they seemed to be when I was a kid," Bianca said, almost as if she were trying to prove Cora's point from the previous argument.

"What is that?" Cora pointed at what appeared to be an old T-ball trophy covered in stars and doused in gold spray paint.

Bianca hoisted it up proudly. "Only the most coveted souvenir in Sunnyside. Y'all can thank me later."

"Yeah, I'm pretty sure that's not going to happen," Cora said.

Bianca ignored her and propped herself on the deck railing directly across from her sisters.

"Okay, I'll bite," Savannah said. "Why is that thing coveted?"

"It's the Trivia Champions trophy. You should've been there last night. The entire town showed up, locals and tourists. The place was packed."

"And you won the whole thing?" Savannah sounded impressed.

Bianca nodded. "Well, Luke and I did."

"And yet, even with all that knowledge in your head, you still thought it'd be a good idea to move across the country and marry a man you've never met," Cora said.

Bianca rolled her eyes. "You're not going to let that go, are you?"

"The fact that you're moving across the country to marry some man you've never met? Nope. Not letting it go."

"You have to admit, Bee, it seems a little impulsive. Even for you," Savannah said in a diplomatic tone.

"Soulmate. I'm moving to marry my soulmate."

"Who you met online," Savannah countered.

"Who I was matched with using state-of-the-art AI technology." Bianca had an *I'm-running-out-of-patience* tone. "I thought we went over this last night. Cora's going to try it out. Confirm its validity."

"Wait, we're still doing that?" Savannah asked.

"Absolutely. Someone has to save Bianca from herself." Cora settled into her chair, feeling confident. "In fact, I've already gotten a match."

Bianca brightened. "That was fast! Should I pick out my own bridesmaid's dress, or do you want to choose for us?"

"Or, by this time tomorrow night, you'll be canceling your moving truck reservation." Cora shot her a satisfied smile.

Savannah let out a mom-like, tired sigh. "If you two are going to go through with this—"

"Three," Cora jumped in. "In case you forgot, you were the one who came up with this plan."

"Fine. If *we* are going to go through with this, there need to be some ground rules."

"Good idea. Rule number one: Cora can't sabotage the dates," Bianca said. "She has to at least give him a chance."

"I promise to be my normal charming self." Cora cupped her hands around her face, giving her best angelic look.

"That's my fear," Bianca mumbled.

Savannah gave Bianca a warning look. "Cora can't sabotage the relationship, but, Bianca, you can't do anything to unnaturally prolong it."

"What does that even mean?" Bianca asked, clearly offended anyone would suggest she'd do such a thing.

"You know, talking Cora's date into trying again after he's already decided to move on, or being his relationship counselor."

"Or bribing him," Cora added.

Bianca sucked in a breath and pressed her hand against her chest, looking shocked. "I would *never* dream of bribing anyone, because I know whoever SoulMatch matches you with will be perfect for you. Just like Zander's perfect for me. The program will speak for itself."

"We'll see, won't we?" Cora was confident how this would end, and it wasn't going to be a victory for Bianca or her AI matchmaker.

"And the bet runs until Chris and the girls get here," Savannah added. "We're not dragging this out all summer. If Cora's still happily with her guy after three weeks, we all agree there is merit to this Soul-Match thing, and, Bianca, we'll help you pack."

"And Cora sings at my wedding. That's what we said last night." Bianca started singing the opening lines to a classic song. "'Going to the chapel and we're . . .'"

Savannah held up a *but wait* finger. "But if she's not, you agree that you will not move to Idaho at the end of the summer. And you won't revisit the move for at least six months."

"What?" This time Bianca didn't have to feign the shock.

"I just want you to give your relationship with Zander a little time. Make sure this is what you really want. If it's the real deal, a couple months won't hurt anything."

"Six is more than a couple."

"It's for your own good," Cora added, because the only reason she was doing this was to protect Bianca.

Bianca was silent for a moment. "Fine," she said eventually.

Cora thought everything was set and Savannah was going to officially declare the bet, but instead she turned to Cora.

"And you have to try to connect. Actually allow yourself to be open to letting someone in." There was actual concern in her voice. "It's for *your* own good."

"Fine. Of course. Whatever it takes." A flash of nervousness zipped through her, but she washed it down with another sip of Diet Dr Pepper. After all, she didn't believe this AI thing was effective, so really there was no risk. She'd be fine.

Savannah shrugged. "In that case, I guess we need to add 'Cora dating' to the Summer Bucket List."

"What is this bucket list you keep talking about?" Bianca asked.

"Another one of Savannah's traditions," Cora clarified.

"Another one of *all* our traditions. Hang on." Savannah pushed herself out of the chair and disappeared into the house. When she came back, she was holding a large piece of brown butcher paper. "See? Just like we always had."

Bianca stared at the list. "I don't remember anything that looked like that."

"That's because it didn't look like that," Cora said.

"I made a few upgrades."

Cora agreed—if, by "few," Savannah meant "a total overhaul." The bucket list they'd had as kids had been a hodgepodge of handwriting on a white posterboard. Anyone could add to it in the weeks leading up to summer, and it often included everything from ice cream at Miss Mary's to movie night. This version had been done on butcher paper, with fancy writing and colorful sketches to illustrate each activity. It looked like something that walked off a Pinterest page.

Cora scanned the items on the new list. "You really think we need to have a campout on the deck?"

"It's tradition," Savannah said.

"Sleeping on the hard ground two feet from the back door because it was an *adventure* we used to do as kids? A hundred percent, if there's a bed anywhere in the vicinity, I'm sleeping in it. Period." And no one was going to change Cora's mind on that.

"I agree with Cora on this." Bianca nodded in solidarity.

"Okay, maybe sleeping on the deck was a little much. But tradition dictates that we spend the first day here on the beach. That, I'm not backing down from." Savannah pointed to the top item on the list. "And we *will* boogie board." She emphasized the last point with the kind of stare that seemed like a challenge.

What had gotten into Savannah?

"Of course we'll boogie board. Have you seen those waves today?" Cora said in a dismissive tone.

"Boogie boarding. That, I remember," Bianca said.

"Great!" Savannah exhaled, and Cora could've sworn she looked worn out, even though it wasn't even ten yet. "Should we start getting ready?"

Bianca yawned and stretched. "Before breakfast?"

"I have a couple emails I need to send first." Cora motioned to her computer. "I mean, it is a workday for most of the world."

"Sure. After breakfast and emails." Nothing about Savannah's posture changed and her careful smile remained in place, but Cora could've sworn her sister actually deflated. "I'll pack some snacks."

She disappeared inside with her bucket list.

Cora stared at the empty chair for a few seconds before she looked up at Bianca. "Is she okay?"

Bianca gave a dismissive shrug. "You know Savannah. She's high maintenance."

Cora's mouth twisted to the side as she considered it. "Maybe."

Although, she wasn't convinced. Something seemed off, starting with the dark circles under her eyes.

"Anyway, I'm going to get some breakfast." Bianca slid off the railing and grabbed her trophy. "You want anything?"

Cora shook her head. "I'm going to knock out these emails."

Bianca nodded. She followed Savannah into the house, and Cora grabbed her computer.

If there was a problem with Savannah, she'd figure it out later. Right now, there were other things that needed her attention.

Two hours later, Cora was back on the deck. This time she was wearing one of Savannah's swimsuits and her neon palm tree cover-up.

For the record, the cover-up looked a hundred times worse in the light of day than it had in the store. It was so bad, in fact, that she started to wonder if the gum-popper had switched it when she rang it up. No way had she bought this on *purpose*.

She was officially banning herself from impulse purchases at convenience stores. Especially fashion-related ones.

But, since her outfit choices were between the cover-up and the Sister Squad T-shirt, here she was. Desperate times called for desperate measures.

While she was waiting for her sisters to finish getting ready, she took the time to edit some photos. Cora had scaled back her business for the month, but she couldn't completely take the month off. There were far too many projects on her docket.

She was just getting started when her phone buzzed.

You have a new message on SoulMatch.

She stared at the phone for a second. The smart thing to do was to finish her edits first, then check the message. Work first, fake dates second. Sure, she wanted to win her bet, but she still had her priorities in line.

Although she only got halfway through the edit before curiosity won out.

She put her computer aside and grabbed her phone.

> Cake, donuts, ice cream—sure. But the real question is:
> How do you feel about pie?
> —Jax

An almost-grin tugged at the corner of her mouth. She had to admit, this guy was entertaining. She thought about her answer for a second and then hit Reply.

> When it comes to pie, it's all about the crust.
> —Cora

She was about to close the app when his response popped up in the chat section.

> **J:** I couldn't agree more.
> **C:** Also, it's not officially Thanksgiving unless there's at least one pie. Preferably pumpkin, but I can be swayed.

She thought about it a second and then typed a second message.

> **C:** Nvm. Can't sway. Pumpkin has to be on the menu. Just FYI, while we're getting our deal-breakers out there.
> **J:** Got it. Must eat sugar and bring pumpkin pie to Thanksgiving. Any other deal-breakers you forgot to put on your questionnaire?

She thought for a second.

> **C:** You have to like animals.
> **J:** Are there people who don't? I mean, I get some peo-
> ple have a normal fear of sharks or birds, but who's got a
> problem with a hedgehog?
> **C:** You have a fear of birds?
> **J:** People. I said *some* people might have a fear of birds.
> **C:** Speaking in a general sense, is it all birds or only certain
> types that *people* are afraid of?

There was a pause.

> **J:** Anything with a wingspan over six feet. Because
> let's face it, that's like a hang glider with a beak and
> a vendetta.
> **J:** And blue jays.
> **C:** Blue jays, huh? Those sweet little birds that sit outside
> the window and sing pretty songs in springtime?
> **J:** They're not sweet. They just want you to think they're
> sweet with that charming color and tiny size. One of
> those "sweet" little blue jays attacked my dog when I was
> growing up.
> **J:** The dog was fine, by the way. I'm still a little broken up
> about it, though. Thanks for asking.

Her almost-grin tugged a little higher, threatening to break into a
full-fledged smile if she wasn't careful.

> **C:** Your poor dog. And fine, I can take fear of birds off my
> deal-breaker list.
> **J:** I appreciate it.
> **C:** Anything else we need to get out of the way?
> **J:** What are your thoughts on Mexican food?

C: Pro

J: And boy bands?

C: Negative

J: Interesting. What about skiing?

C: Totally dependent on the crowds and the snow. Long lift lines? No. Not much snow? No. Icy? Hard pass.

C: Also, I snowboard.

J: Good to know.

J: And while we're on the topic of pie…

C: But were we? On the topic of pie?

J: Well played. Let me try that again.

J: Circling back to pie, do you want to meet tonight? For pie?

Wait. What?

Of course, she knew she'd have to go on a date in person with whatever man she was matched with. Sticking to the safety of online banter from the comfort of her own home was the very thing she had given Bianca a hard time about.

But knowing about the date in theory and facing it in real life were two very different things. Suddenly her mind was flooded with a million excuses for why she couldn't go.

This was fast, wasn't it?

Before she could overthink it too much, her phone buzzed with his next message.

J: Normally I'd wait until we got to know each other a little better. But there's this pie thing happening that's only tonight. Since you're a fellow crust connoisseur, I thought you might like to join me.

Well, that made her feel a little better. There was a reason for moving fast. Of course, he could be making it up . . .

She shook off the negative thought because who cared if he was making the whole thing up? It was a fake date to begin with—on her end, at least. If he turned out to be a lying jerk who was nothing like his online persona, that worked in her favor.

As long as the whole thing was safe. She wasn't willing to put herself at risk.

> **J:** It's in a very public place with plenty of people around. Technically the event lasts two hours, but you're free to leave whenever you like.

Okay, now this was getting creepy. It was like he was reading her mind.

> **C:** Interesting proposal. But how's their crust? Bad crust is a deal-breaker.
> **J:** I can't speak to the quality of the crust. What I can say is that if it's not good, you have no one to blame but yourself.

So, a cooking class, maybe? That actually wasn't a bad idea for a first date. It sure beat sitting across a table and trying to come up with conversation topics.

> **C:** In that case, how's *your* crust?

Savannah chose *that* moment to join Cora on the deck.

"I could've written a memoir in the time it's taken Bianca to get ready." She flopped into the chair next to Cora. "What's got you smiling over there?"

"TikTok." She wasn't sure why she lied about it. It wasn't like she was trying to hide anything. Both of her sisters were aware of her dating plan. They had clearly outlined the bet, after all. But for some reason, this part felt . . . personal.

"You're focused on TikTok with a view like that?" Savannah waved in the direction of the beach. "The beach should be a no-phone zone."

"You really have become a mom, haven't you?" Although, watching the aqua waves rolling into the white sand shores *was* awe-inspiring.

Savannah shot her a confident look. "Let's see how much you're judging my mom-skills when you're wanting one of my snacks out on the beach."

"Don't worry. I can judge *and* eat your snacks. It's a talent." She grinned at her sister while Savannah just shook her head.

Meanwhile her phone buzzed with Jax's response.

J: Never made one before. But I'm confident it won't disappoint.

Cora tried to keep her face neutral as she responded.

C: Bold claim.
J: What can I say? I'm dedicated to my desserts.
C: Well, I feel like I can't say no now.
J: So is that a yes?

She thought for a second. It still felt rushed to go on a date with a person she knew nothing about, except he had questionable taste in music and the only thing vouching for him was a green stamp on his background check.

Still, it wasn't like she was going to marry the guy. If she was looking for someone to marry—which she wasn't—she absolutely would not find the man through a dating app.

She typed out her response.

Sure. Why not?

Her thumb hovered over Send for a fraction of a second. *Fake. It's just fake*, she reminded herself, and pressed the button.

His reply came back almost instantly.

J: Not usually the response I get when I ask someone out,
but what the heck. Here's to all kinds of firsts.

That made her laugh out loud, which she covered up with a cough
when Savannah glanced in her direction.

C: I'll see you at five.

Cora typed her last response quickly, then slid her phone in her bag
before she had to make up any more excuses for what she was doing on
her phone. Or why she was smiling while she did it.

Maybe this date wouldn't be awful.

Bianca came out dressed in a swimsuit and cover-up with a towel
over her shoulder. "Y'all ready?"

"Finally," Savannah said, standing. "Can we go now?"

Cora held her computer up. "Let me just put this away first."

"Oh, that reminds me. I should grab my book," Bianca said. "And
do we have time for me to make a smoothie real quick?"

"I could go for a smoothie," Cora said. "We have strawberries, right?"

Savannah flopped back into her chair with a huff. "It's like herding
cats."

Family bickering. Yep, it felt just like old times.

6

Savannah

This trip was not off to the start she'd hoped for. Or even the start she'd expected. In fact, she'd go so far as to say that up to this point, this trip had been a disaster.

There was a day when the Prestly sisters had been inseparable. They did everything together. They knew everything about one another. Yes, they had three very different personalities, but somehow that made them even closer. Growing up in the Prestly family had been a dream.

And then the divorce changed everything.

Technically speaking, their parents' divorce had been amicable enough. They didn't fight over assets or have long, drawn-out court hearings. Savannah and Cora were essentially adults at the time, and since Bianca was almost a teenager, their parents let her have a major say in her custody arrangement.

All in all, the whole thing seemed to be pretty seamless—to Savannah, at least. One day her parents were married, and the next they just . . . weren't.

Although the one thing she hadn't been ready for was how their parents' split would split the sisters.

Cora took the news the hardest, siding with their mom and putting all the blame on their dad. It strained Cora's relationship with him so much that eventually she stopped talking to him altogether.

When Savannah didn't take that same stance, she felt a wedge form between her and Cora. Of course, there were things Cora didn't know. Things Savannah had kept from her, for the sake of keeping the peace. And almost overnight, Cora and Savannah went from two sisters who were inseparable to two polite acquaintances who kept in touch on birthdays and major holidays.

Bianca was caught somewhere in the middle. She didn't take sides. Savannah couldn't tell whether her baby sister's stance was a conscious decision to remain neutral or a product of her go-wherever-the-wind-blows personality. Either way, Bianca flitted through life blissfully unattached to anything. She never finished a project. She was the most likely sister to show up late or skip a family event because she forgot or was double-booked.

Admittedly, her childhood had looked very different from hers and Cora's. She was the only one who grew up in a single-parent household. She was the only one who was still a minor and living at home when their mom had died. She had the fewest memories of what life was like before, when the sisters were close and everyone got along.

Which was why this trip was so important. This was their chance to recapture what they once had. Their last happy family moments had been right here, in this cottage, and Savannah had hoped that if they could just revisit the place and do the things they once loved to do together, maybe the sisters could remember how good it had been. Maybe they could find their way back.

Which was the reason Savannah had put so much time and effort into the Summer Bucket List. It was the blueprint of her plan. Were her sisters as inspired by it as she'd hoped? No, but perhaps she should've expected that. At the end of the day, the beautiful aesthetic of the list wasn't going to save their relationships. But the experiences and laughter and fun they would share just might.

Of course, they'd have to actually *experience* those activities first.

Savannah was no stranger to the amount of patience it took to get a group of people out the door. She was a mom of preschoolers, after all.

What she didn't expect was that getting preschoolers, who were distracted by any little thing, out the door was considerably easier than getting her grown-up sisters to do the same.

She was just about to head into the house and find out why it was taking so long to grab a book and make two smoothies when Cora finally walked out the back door. By herself.

"Bianca had to switch her swimsuit. Again. She wasn't vibing with the last one," Cora said with an eye roll. She handed Savannah one of the two smoothies in her hand.

"I said it wasn't comfortable," Bianca yelled from somewhere in the house.

Cora seemed unconcerned as she sipped her smoothie. "We could always leave her."

"That would be rude, Cora." Bianca's voice drifted out the open sliding glass doors.

Savannah sighed and flopped down into the chair she'd just vacated. "We should wait. We'd want her to wait on us."

"Would we, though?"

Savannah didn't even bother responding. She just took a sip of her own smoothie.

Several minutes ticked by before Bianca cruised out of the house dressed in a bikini and cutoff jean shorts, with a towel over her shoulder. "Are we going to sit around here and talk all day, or are we going to the beach?"

"Finally," Savannah said and started to gather everything they needed to take down to the beach.

The first trip of the day was always the worst. There were coolers and umbrellas. Chairs and boogie boards. It was all stuff they would enjoy having once they were by the water. But even though the water was only a couple hundred yards from their back deck, getting there with all this stuff felt like trekking across the Sahara.

By the time they got to the spot where they were going to set up, Savannah was out of breath. Which, she told herself, was normal. Everyone was out of breath after that hike. It had absolutely nothing to do with . . .

Well, anyway, it was totally normal.

She pretended to busy herself with stacking the things she'd carried down in the sand while she tried to catch her breath.

Bianca stepped up next to her, a serene expression on her face as she surveyed the scene in front of them. "I mean, it doesn't get more perfect than this." She let out a contented sigh.

Cora started the process of putting up the umbrella. "After the travel day I had yesterday, I definitely earned the right to relax in the shade, listen to the waves, and eat all the salty snacks."

Bianca grabbed a chair and set it up in the sun. "I'll do the same. Out of support, of course." Then she shimmied out of her shorts and sank down into the chair, stretching her legs out over the sand.

"But first, we break in these little beauties, right?" Savannah picked up one of the brand-new boogie boards she'd bought just for the trip and gave it a little shake. "Boogie boarding. Remember, we always start with boogie boarding."

"Seems like a later kind of thing." Cora opened her own chair and set it in the shade of the umbrella she'd just set up.

"Yeah, maybe we should work up to it." Bianca closed her eyes and tipped her head toward the sun.

"Work up to what? We never had to 'work up' to boogie boarding before."

"We were never in our thirties before," Cora said.

"Some of us still aren't." Bianca shot Cora a look. Then she shifted her gaze to Savannah. "But I'm still not getting in the water yet. Aren't beach days supposed to be relaxing?"

"Yes. Totally. We should relax first." Savannah set up her chair in the shade next to Cora and sat on the edge.

"That's your problem. You don't relax well. You always have to be doing something," Bianca said.

"That's not true," Savannah shot back and slid a little farther back in her seat.

"It's kinda true," Cora agreed.

"I'm great at relaxing. Look, I'm relaxing right now." Savannah leaned back and stretched out her legs, mimicking Bianca's pose. Although even she had to admit she looked a little stiff.

Honestly, it wasn't that she always had to be doing something. She just felt more at peace when everything was scratched off her to-do list. She could argue that a lot of people were that way. Maybe even most people.

The problem was that lately she couldn't seem to get everything scratched off.

She'd always been somewhat of a high achiever. She was a star student, and after she graduated, she went to work as a graphic designer. In the few years she was in the workforce, between getting married and having Genevieve, she'd advanced quickly. Then, when she became a mom, she and Chris had decided she'd stay home with their kids. It was a move she was excited about because she'd been dreaming about it for a while.

She loved being a stay-at-home mom. She did. But sometimes it felt like the kind of task where she couldn't win. There was always something else she could be doing or something she could be doing better. And with Pinterest and Instagram, there was always visual proof of what "better" looked like. Not to mention that as soon as she got a particular age or stage figured out, they'd move on to the next one.

Keeping up with it all was exhausting.

Plus, there was this whole thing with her sisters not getting along. And Cora turning into a recluse. And now Bianca's new life plan. Not to mention trying to do the house upkeep and the never-ending pile of laundry and feeding her always-hungry family.

Then there was the whole health thing she didn't want to think about . . .

The bottom line was that her life seemed to be spinning out of control, and the list of things she needed to do to fix it kept growing. So yeah, she was having a hard time relaxing.

But resting was as much on her to-do list as reconnecting with her sisters. The doctor had ordered it. Chris had rearranged his work schedule so he could solo parent while she took what he called "a well-deserved vacation." She needed to honor her end of the deal.

Since she'd already pledged to make the beach a screen-free zone, she pulled a magazine from her bag and forced herself to settle into the chair. See, she could relax if she wanted to.

She flipped through the pages, trying to focus on the articles that weren't holding her attention and the pictures she didn't care about. When she got to the end, she glanced around, taking in the scene as she tried to decide if she should reread the only magazine she'd brought by starting over at the beginning or flipping through it backward.

Backward. Pages flip easier in that direction.

She was just about to get started on her second backward-this-time pass when she was distracted by a muffled chuckle coming from Cora.

"More TikTok?"

Cora startled as if she'd just been caught. "Just keeping up with the new trends." She quickly slid the phone into her bag and grabbed the board that was at her feet. "Are we going in or what?"

Before anyone had the chance to respond, she headed out to the water.

"That felt more like a demand than a question," Bianca said from her position stretched out in the sun with her eyes closed.

"Yeah, but we're burning daylight." Savannah repeated one of their mother's favorite lines and grabbed her own board.

"You've officially turned into Mom," Bianca said. And while it might have been meant as an insult, Savannah took it as a compliment.

She headed to catch up with Cora, who was already wading out into the crystal-clear water. The water wasn't cold, per se, but after sunning on the shore, Savannah felt there was a chill to it. Wading in, the water seemed to get chillier as the waves got closer to her abdomen. She held her board up, doing her best to keep the top half of her body from the cool water.

"You're doing a great job keeping that board dry," Cora joked as Savannah shuffled closer to her.

"I'm trying to get used to the temperature." Savannah tried to bounce over the next wave, but she couldn't avoid the splash that hit her stomach.

Cora seemed amused. "And keeping the board over your head helps?"

"It helps me not have to put my arms in. And if my arms are dry, at least part of me is warm."

"Dive under. You'll get used to it faster."

"Absolutely not."

"She doesn't like cold water," Bianca said as she paddled on her board behind them.

"And this is cold?" Cora questioned.

"It's not warm." Savannah bobbed around with her arms held high above her head. "Just give me a second. I'll acclimate."

"Suit yourself. But while you bounce around like a jumping bean, I'm going for a ride." Cora positioned the board in front of her, the way she used to do when they spent the summers here.

"Do you remember how? Or should I give you a tutorial?" Bianca teased.

"Please. It might have been a minute since I've been here, but boogie boarding is like second nature." She glanced over at Bianca. "But do you need me to push you into the wave like we used to?"

Bianca slid off her board and stood up in the deeper water. "Just because I couldn't beat you back then, doesn't mean I can't beat you now. Watch and learn."

Bianca looked over her shoulder at the waves. Just before the biggest one reached them, she pushed her board forward, landed on top of it, and started kicking.

Only she hadn't timed it right, and instead of catching the wave, it rolled right over her. She came out on the other side looking like a drowned rat, coughing and wiping the salt water off her face.

Savannah tried not to laugh. "Are you okay?"

Bianca wiped the water off her face. "I let that one get away from me."

"Okay, my turn." Savannah lowered her arms to the water but kept bouncing to keep her body heat up as she turned to check out the waves rolling in. "That's it. The third one."

"Are you calling it? Like shotgun?" Cora asked.

"Just making you aware of when you should watch." She shot a side-eyed glance at Cora. "And yes, stay off." She fixed her eyes on the waves and counted down. "In three, two, one." She jumped forward, slamming her board down on the water.

Nothing happened. She went exactly nowhere.

Waves kept rolling by, and she just bobbed over them like a boat floating at sea.

"Should we count down again?" Bianca teased.

Savannah looked over her shoulder at the waves rolling in. "Did I miss it?"

"You didn't catch it," Cora said.

Savannah slid off the board. "Well, that didn't go as planned."

Cora got her board ready. "Am I going to have to show y'all how it's done?"

"What? You think you're better than us?" Bianca said.

"I certainly can't be worse." Still looking over her shoulder, she launched into the wave.

To be fair, Cora went farther than the rest of them. She caught the back part of the wave, and it carried her about ten feet before she dropped out the back. She floated there for a second and watched her wave roll into shore without her.

She bobbed back to her sisters. "This used to be easier."

Savannah nodded her agreement. It seemed to be the theme of their summer so far. All of this used to be easier.

Meanwhile a group of kids two umbrellas over from them bounded out into the water with their own boogie boards. One after the other, they each caught waves and rode them all the way into the shore, like they were stepping on a moving sidewalk.

Savannah watched the next kid hop on a wave and do a trick. "There's no way I'm letting them out-board us. We've got way more experience than they do."

Bianca squinted at the group. "I don't know that your kind of experience is a benefit here."

"We'll see about that." Savannah stared at the waves, determination pulsing through her. She lined up her board again.

Yes, it was just a wave and only one brief moment of their summer. But at the moment, it felt like her entire to-do list hinged on this one ride.

So far, nothing had gone according to plan. Nothing about this trip had turned out the way she'd thought it would. But she wasn't willing to go through the entire summer watching one thing fail after another. This was her family. Her trip. Her responsibility. And she was going to make it work if it took everything she had, starting with boogie boarding.

"Bring it," she whispered to the waves.

This time she didn't wait for the best wave, she just went with the next one. She kicked with everything she had. Nothing was going to stop her. She was catching this wave. This was her moment!

Except it wasn't.

The wave rolled right past her. Then another followed in its wake. Frustration and disappointment washed over her, but she didn't stop. Savannah kicked with the board tucked under her belly like a kid at swim lessons.

"Are you going to kick all the way to shore?" Cora joked behind her.

"Maybe." Because it was either that or start crying.

"Woo-hoo!"

Savannah turned in time to see Bianca sail right past her, riding on a wave. A huge smile was spread across her face, and she pumped a fist in the air as she passed.

Savannah might not have caught the wave, but watching her sister succeed was almost as gratifying. She slid off her board and watched Bianca ride the wave to shore.

It was the biggest wave they'd seen so far, and it continued to swell as it got closer to the beach. By the time Bianca's wave was almost to the sand, it had grown into a huge, crashing monstrosity, and as it hit the beach, it rolled right over Bianca.

For a second Savannah lost sight of her sister, but by the time the wave retreated, she spotted Bianca again, sitting in the ankle-deep water.

"Go, Bianca!" Cora cheered from behind them.

"Are you okay?" Savannah asked.

"I lost my . . ." She wiped her face at the same moment as saying the last word, which made it impossible to hear over the sound of the waves and other noise at the beach.

"You what?" Savannah called.

"My bottoms! The wave took my *swimsuit bottoms*!" Bianca yelled, just before another wave knocked into her.

Savannah looked back to where Cora was standing, and, without any words exchanged, they both burst into laughter.

"It's not funny!" Bianca whined, continuing to wipe salt water off her face with one hand while she held her board over herself with the other.

"No, you're right. It's not funny." Savannah tried her best to stop laughing, but she looked over at Cora, who had caught up to where she was, and another round of giggles erupted.

"It's freakin' hilarious!" Cora said.

The harder Cora laughed, the harder Savannah laughed until it got to the point that Savannah was having trouble swimming and Cora had to wipe the tears out of her eyes.

Bianca on the other hand seemed less amused. "Well, could you at least laugh and swim at the same time? I have sand going places it doesn't need to be." Another wave washed over her as she tried her hardest to keep herself firmly seated on the sandy bottom.

"Coming, coming," Cora said.

Cora got to the beach first and ran up to the chairs to get a towel. Savannah tossed her board on the sand and waded through the water in hopes of locating the missing swimsuit. When Cora returned to the water's edge, the three sisters worked together to shield Bianca while she wrapped the towel around her.

Was it the boogie board experience Savannah had planned? Not even close. But it was their first bonding moment. And as she and Cora struggled to get their giggles under control, Savannah felt a glimmer of hope that all wasn't lost. That maybe, just maybe, they could find their way back after all.

With the towel firmly wrapped around her waist, Bianca turned and stomped toward the house. "You two are ridiculous."

"Us? What did we do?" Cora asked, still laughing.

"Are you coming back?"

"Not sure!" Bianca yelled without turning in their direction.

"Should we go after her?" Savannah asked Cora.

"Naw, she'll calm down." She walked to their umbrella and flopped into her chair. "But it feels like snack time. Do you have any salt and vinegar chips in that cooler of yours?"

Yep, everyone was always hungry.

"Sure do." She joined Cora and opened the cooler.

It wasn't the start she'd been hoping for, but it was a start.

7

Cora

Cora pulled into the parking lot of the outdoor shopping complex for her date at exactly five o'clock.

She wasn't nervous because there was nothing to be nervous about. Whether this date went perfectly or flopped like an overhyped movie made no difference to her. She could accomplish her goal either way.

The only way she'd lose this bet was if she actually fell in love with Jax Verona, and there was zero chance that would happen. She almost felt bad for Bianca.

But since she was saving Bianca from her own self-destruction, Cora didn't feel *that* bad.

Still, she felt a slight niggle in the pit of her stomach that she couldn't shake. It wasn't butterflies. It was more like butterflies' annoying little cousin, if that were a thing.

Excitement—that was it. She was probably just excited to make a pie.

She'd looked up the cooking class they were taking tonight. Kiss the Cook was a test kitchen attached to one of the local restaurants and specialized in cooking classes of all sorts. The kitchen was set up so that two people shared a cooking space, but every participant made their own dish. After the cooking lesson, participants were invited to stay and enjoy their creations, which in their case was blueberry pie.

Of course, how much time Cora spent chatting over pie would depend on the cooking part of the date. So far Jax had been funny and seemed interesting. But Cora knew that in real life, not everything was as perfect as it appeared online. She was prepared for, well, anything. She'd even brushed up on her self-defense moves. Not that she intended on using them, but one could never be too careful.

The one thing she didn't know was what Jax Verona looked like.

His profile picture on SoulMatch didn't help much. It was an artistic shot of a breathtaking sunset in a setting she couldn't quite identify. A man, presumably Jax, was standing in the distance, back mostly to the camera, watching it. And while it was a beautiful picture, the distance combined with the shadows of the setting sun made it impossible to make out any of his features.

And a quick social media search hadn't helped much, either. The few accounts she found listing a "Jax Verona" didn't have many pictures. Clearly Jax Verona valued his privacy. Or had something to hide.

Okay, yeah. She was definitely cynical.

But again, it didn't matter what he looked like. It wasn't like this was a beauty contest. Cora didn't even have to be attracted to him. All she had to do was charm him enough to get him to stick around for a few more dates. And she could be charming. When she wanted to be.

Pushing the annoying mini butterflies aside, she took a deep breath and stepped out of her car. Showtime.

She smoothed out her shirt and adjusted how it was tucked in as she strode toward the cooking school with confidence. She was dressed in the same black T-shirt and black joggers that she'd worn on the plane.

The outfit, which was half a step above loungewear, wasn't what she normally would've chosen for a first date, but the only other clothing she had was the neon palm tree cover-up. And since she'd already promised not to sabotage the date, that choice was clearly out. At least Bianca's gold necklace Cora had swiped off the bathroom counter helped dress up what she had. Kind of.

Plus, she'd be putting an apron over it as soon as she got into the kitchen anyway.

The state of her missing suitcase was annoying. After the airline "located" her bag in Fargo, its status had now been updated to "waiting to be loaded" in Portland, Maine, with a TBD arrival time. Why was the bag in Maine? None of the airline reps she talked to seemed to know the answer to that question. Or any question, really. It seemed they were reading the same limited information from the website she had access to. The only difference was they ended every conversation with "Trust the process, ma'am" and "As soon as we have additional information, we'll let you know."

Still, she made a mental note to call again in the morning. Because the one thing she knew about the system was that the squeaky wheel tended to get the oil.

Also, she didn't care what was on Savannah's agenda tomorrow; shopping for a few essentials to get her through the next few days was nonnegotiable. And with all the new stores in this shopping complex, maybe she wouldn't have to drive as far as she'd first thought.

She glanced in the window of the store she was passing. Three white wedding gowns hung in the front display.

Okay, maybe not that store, but she'd for sure hit some of the other ones. She loved supporting local businesses, after all. She looked over her shoulder to study the stores farther down the sidewalk and gauge their selection.

"Cora?"

The sound of the deep, smooth voice calling her name sent the mini butterflies back into flight and she turned, ready to meet the man who would help her win her bet.

Only when she caught sight of who it was, her charming smile and witty greeting fell away.

No. Way.

She let out a tired sigh that could most closely be interpreted as *You've got to be kidding me* and took the last few steps to join the man she'd already met before. Kind of.

"Well, well, well. Jax Verona." Or, as she knew him, Gatsby from CVS.

Should she have tried to sound delighted or even entertained by the coincidence? Maybe. But she couldn't help that he was standing there looking as smugly amused as he did in the dental care aisle. She found that look incredibly annoying. Again.

"It's nice to meet you officially." His smolder widened into a grin. "How's the toothbrush?"

"It's perfect." She had a feeling she looked self-righteous, but she didn't care. "I went with a different brand than you suggested. And stuck with a single. Since I, you know, only needed the one."

He tucked his hands into his pockets. "Glad it worked out. After all, you gotta do what's right for you."

What was right for her was *not* going on a date with this doofus. She knew his type. He was overly confident with his macho swagger, walking around as if it were a treat to meet him. He probably spent more time getting his perfectly straight teeth that white than he did keeping up with current affairs.

And, yes, she realized that in order to come to that conclusion, she had to notice his nice smile. But since the majority of their conversations so far had revolved around dental care, it would've been weird if she hadn't.

The more important thing was that she hadn't been dazzled by it.

"But you know what I've been wondering?" she asked.

He raised an eyebrow, looking amused. "You've been wondering about me?"

Okay, she walked right into that one. But since she wasn't going to let him get to her, she ignored it and kept going. "What kind of person can't keep up with their toothbrush? Typically speaking, it's not something that gets misplaced a lot. It generally stays right there, in the bathroom, where it's used."

He chuckled. "It's more of an occupational hazard. I travel a lot for work."

"And you keep forgetting to pack it?" She gave him a look of mock sympathy. "I hear a packing list can help with that."

"Sometimes the trips pop up last minute. No time to pack." He shrugged as if that were a normal problem.

"Right. I hate when that happens." She couldn't tell if he was serious or joking. What kind of job had him leaving so fast, he didn't have time to pack a bag? "What was it you do, again? Your bio was a little vague about it."

To be technical, his bio only listed one word under occupation: *consultant*. There were zero references to what he consulted about. Or with whom.

"I'm actually in a period of transition at the moment."

"So . . . unemployed," she interpreted with a look that might have been considered challenging.

It wasn't that she cared if he was unemployed. Life was known for dealing all sorts of unexpected turns. What bothered her was that he was enhancing the detail to try to come across as more impressive than he was.

But instead of seeming offended by her calling him out, or even sputtering another excuse, he seemed more amused. "Not exactly."

Let the record show he didn't give any more details, Cora thought. Which she also wasn't willing to let go of. "What, are you like a spy or something? You'd tell me what you do, but then you have to kill me?"

"You know, that phrase is widely misrepresented. Telling you something you shouldn't know might result in a relocation or, way more commonly, heightened monitoring. But rarely is there killing over it. Too much red tape."

Once again she rolled her eyes, because who did this guy think he was? She didn't know who he was used to dating, but the dangerous and mysterious act didn't work on her. She wasn't a damsel in distress looking for a hero, or someone who was easily impressed by his muscular forearms. Frankly, she'd be more impressed by someone who had a regular schedule for cleaning his home.

Although, he did have nice forearms.

Before she could be distracted by that thought, he opened the glass door that led to Kiss the Cook and flashed one of his grins. "On that note, shall we?"

Cora stared at the open door. What she wanted to say was *See ya never* and head home to binge Netflix in her pink polka-dot jammies.

But walking away would mean she'd have to start over. There would be more questionnaires to fill out. More online chatting. More meeting someone who turned out to be nothing like he said he was. She didn't want to prolong this bet any more than necessary.

And since SoulMatch's AI failed miserably on their first attempt, she didn't want to see who they'd set her up with on the second try. For the sake of winning the bet in the quickest way possible—and for that sake only—she refreshed her smile.

"Let's." Her answer might've come out a little more fake than she'd intended it to, but to be fair, she'd never been good at faking her emotion. And since she wasn't allowed to sabotage the date, she took another stab at pleasant conversation. "Do you come here often?"

As soon as she heard how it sounded, she wanted to take it back. If she could've face-palmed herself, she would have. What was it about this guy that threw her off her game?

Half of his mouth pulled up into an amused grin, and he propped one elbow on the vacant front desk. "Did you just use a pickup line on me?"

She straightened, owning it. "Where I'm from it's called a conversation starter."

"Huh. 'Cause it sounded like a pickup line." Laughter sparkled in his eyes.

"What I meant was, do you take cooking classes often? I wasn't just trying to get to know you. I'm also trying to figure out if I need to locate the nearest fire extinguisher before we get started." Okay, so maybe she needed to work on the pleasant conversation part.

"I never make guarantees, but I can say that you can trust me." He flashed her a flirty look that didn't need any practice at all. Before she could respond, something behind her caught his attention and he straightened. "Gracie Blakeley. I didn't know you were working here."

Cora turned to see a woman about their age in chef whites walking up to the counter. The name *Gracie* was monogrammed under the words *Head Chef* on the left side of her chef coat.

"I got this role when I took the head chef position at Coastal Kitchen." She shot him an accusatory look. "Which you would've known, if you were around."

"Can't be helped." Jax gave a faux-innocent shrug that was full of his signature swagger.

"Never can be." Gracie's tone said that she didn't believe her answer any more than she believed his. Then she shifted her gaze to Cora. "Where are my manners? Welcome to Kiss the Cook."

"Gracie, I'd like to introduce you to my friend Cora," Jax said.

Gracie extended her hand. "Nice to meet you, Cora. Let me get you checked in." She turned her attention to the computer in front of her and clicked several things before looking up again. "You two will be at station six. Come on in and get settled. We'll get started in a few minutes."

"Thanks." Jax gave Gracie one last smolder, then held his hand out toward the door for Cora.

"Nice to meet you," Cora said to Gracie.

In return, Gracie leaned in and lowered her voice to a stage whisper. "Careful with that one." She gave a slight nod in Jax's direction. "He's a heartbreaker."

She fixed Jax with one last accusatory, side-eyed stare before she disappeared to the left while Cora and Jax made their way through the door and into the kitchen.

For the record, Cora liked this Gracie already.

"Ex-girlfriend?" she asked as they wove their way through the cooking stations to the one with the giant number 6 on the front.

"Old friend."

"Do all your old friends warn your dates?"

"It's a small town. People talk a lot." He picked up one of the aprons that was folded neatly on the counter and handed it to her.

"And let me guess, they have a lot to say about you?"

"You can't believe everything you hear." Again with the smolder. Only this time Cora felt a slight reawakening of the mini butterflies, which was annoying. She wasn't supposed to find this man attractive. He was arrogant and apparently a heartbreaker, and she was immune to his charming smile. She'd already said so.

"How about you?" he asked. "Any old friends with words of wisdom I need to know about?"

"The first date is a little early to dive into past relationships, don't you think?" She kept her gaze locked with his as she slipped the apron over her head and wrapped the strings around her waist.

He pulled on his own apron. "You think we should wait until, what, the fourth date for that kind of thing? It seems more appropriate, doesn't it?"

"You're already planning on us having a fourth date? Bold."

He shrugged. "I like to dream big."

"I hope your piecrust can measure up."

She let the challenge hang in the air between them as Chef Gracie stepped in front of the kitchen. "Welcome, everyone. It's so good to have you here. Tonight, we are making a summer classic: blueberry pie. I'm going to walk you through every step of the process, but our goal is not perfection. This is a judgment-free zone. We're here to have some fun and learn a new skill or two. At any point if you need me to slow down or explain something again, don't hesitate to ask."

Cora leaned in toward Jax. "I don't care what she says. Station six is still a judgment zone."

"Trust me, my pie will be nothing less than impressive." There was just the right amount of confidence in his whisper to make her lean in, which she also found annoying.

"Those are strong words coming from a guy who's never made a crust before."

"Then it's a good thing you don't have to take my word for it. The proof is in the pudding."

"The only problem is we're making pie. Not pudding."

Her wit earned her a grin.

Well, technically speaking, he was grinning at his bowl, and it was different from his other grins. More authentic, like he couldn't help it. And while all his expressions had a certain undeniable charm to them, this grin was in a class of its own. It hit her in a way the others didn't.

She immediately turned her attention to rearranging the supplies on her part of the workstation and did her best to push the grin out of her mind. After all, she didn't need one of his smiles to make her do something stupid, like drop her own defenses.

For the record, if she was looking for someone to date—which she wasn't—Jax would be the anti-example. She knew his type; he was a macho tough guy with a bit of a hero complex. If she wasn't here to prove Bianca's AI matchmaker was bogus, she would've noped this situation already, so she certainly wasn't going to let herself fall victim to his charm act.

Chef Gracie continued with her instructions. "We're going to start with the piecrust. And the secret to a nice flaky crust is the butter. The colder, the better. If your butter gets too warm, there's no way to recover, and you'll be left with a soggy mess. Which means we need a few ground rules."

Ground rules. Cora could solidly get behind those.

"I want everyone to put your hands against your cheeks. Go ahead, do it." Chef Gracie paused, waiting for the class to follow her instructions. Cora lightly placed her fingers on either side of her cheeks and turned to see if Jax was doing it, too.

Jax's gaze met hers at the exact same time as she turned to him. Only instead of just his fingertips, he had his palms pressed against either side of his face. Which was accompanied by Macaulay Culkin's wide-eyed, gaping expression he'd made famous in *Home Alone*.

Cora shook her head at the ridiculous sight and couldn't help it when a chuckle slipped out of her mouth.

Fine, she was willing to admit he could be entertaining.

Gracie continued, "If your response was anything other than, *Wow, that's cold,* your job is to never touch your dough with your hands."

"Warm hands, warm heart." He held her gaze with a sizzling look that threatened to heat up all the butter in the room. "Utensils only for me."

Oh, this guy was good. She had the feeling this wasn't his first cooking class date.

Cora smirked. "Now, if only there were something we could do about your confidence problem."

He waggled his eyebrows and shifted his attention back to the front as Gracie went through the directions for combining the dry ingredients.

By the time Gracie finished her instructions, the entire room was working on cutting the cold butter into the flour. Each cook rocked their chilled pastry cutters along the bottom of their chilled mixing bowls, chopping the butter into pea-sized pieces.

As she and Jax got to work on their piecrusts, there was a slight lull in their conversation. Since she was trying to be nice and attentive and all those other things, she decided to take it upon herself to keep the conversation rolling.

"So, your first time with online dating, huh?" Cora said. "What made you decide to take the plunge?"

Jax seemed to consider the question for a second. "I guess I was ready for a change."

"Is that code for 'I broke too many hearts in my current circle, so I had to widen my search'?" Yes, she knew she was supposed to be flirty, but some habits were hard to kick.

Luckily, he seemed to find her line of questioning amusing. "Something like that."

Then he did something that surprised her. He got quiet while he concentrated on the process of mixing the butter into the flour. She would've dismissed the action, contributing it to him focusing on the task at hand since cold butter had the same consistency as a rock. But there was something about the look in his eyes that made her wonder if his thoughts were actually on piecrusts. She couldn't quite describe that look, and it was only there for a second, but it told her that maybe there was more to the story of how he ended up on this date. It intrigued her, like maybe there was something more to him altogether.

After a couple seconds, the look vanished and his casual charmer persona returned. "The truth is, I've done the casual thing for a long time, but I'm ready for something more. Something deeper. I know enough to know that if I want something different, I'm not going to find it in the same place." He shrugged. "Since I was broadening my horizons, I thought I might as well bring in the experts to streamline the process."

She cocked an eyebrow. "And a computer is the expert in this scenario?"

"Not just any computer. 'A revolutionary new way of connecting soulmates.'" He repeated the company's tagline with the sort of playful, mocking look that made her laugh.

"What about you?" he asked, smiling at her in a way that made her feel almost . . . comfortable. "What inspired you to fill out twenty-five deeply personal questions for the benefit of strangers you've never met?"

Cora gave him her best flirty look. "See, that's where you're wrong. Because we *had* met."

"Sorry. Let me rephrase. Twenty-five deeply personal questions for the devastatingly handsome man you met at the drugstore." He transfixed her with a knowing grin.

She wasn't silent for long. "Devastatingly handsome? Yeah, I don't think I've met him. You were the only person there that night."

"Ouch." He put his hand over his heart and feigned a hurt expression. "Although you're avoiding the question."

He wasn't wrong. She hadn't thought through how to answer this particular question, which was an oversight on her part. She should've anticipated it would come up. And it wasn't like she could say the truth. *I'm trying to prove to my sister that the dating app is a hoax and that you're a jerk who will bolt at the first sign of trouble*, seemed offensive. Plus, it would pretty much guarantee there wouldn't be a second date, which she kind of needed to prove her point.

Still, she didn't want to outright lie to him. It seemed . . . wrong.

"I, uh . . ." She mashed the butter in her stainless-steel bowl as she thought through the entire situation. "I'm at a point in my life where I'm looking for someone who wants a serious relationship." It was pretty much true. She just left out the part where she was at that point because she was trying to prove something to her sisters.

"And you had to come five hundred miles to do that?"

The question caught her off guard. "What?"

"I read your bio, remember? Aren't you from Houston?"

Huh. She hadn't quite thought through how to address that, either. "Like you said, if I wanted something different, I wasn't going to find it in the same place I'd been looking before."

"You ran out of prospects in a city of two million people?" He gave her a skeptical look.

"It was an exhausting search."

He chuckled. "I bet."

They paused their conversation as Gracie went into more details about how to add the right amount of water to the mixture.

"What brings you to Sunnyside?" Jax asked. "Besides widening the search for your soulmate."

Finally, a question she could answer. "I'm spending the month with my sisters. It's a whole 'reliving our childhood' kind of thing."

"That sounds fun."

She shrugged. "The verdict's still out. For starters, I'm spending the month with family, so there's that. Plus, we haven't gotten off to a stellar start. My sister had a surprise not-so-great announcement, and I'm still waiting for the airline to find my luggage."

"Ah, that explains the pit stop for the toothbrush. And why you're wearing the same outfit."

She studied him for a second. "You noticed that? You only saw me for, like, five seconds."

"Time is irrelevant when staring at such beauty." He even delivered the cheesy line with Don Juan–type smoothness.

She wanted to roll her eyes but instead a flattered warmth bloomed in her cheeks. Was she blushing? Since when did cheesy pickup lines make her blush?

She pretended to focus on her dough to divert attention away from her traitorous cheeks. "Does that line ever work?"

"You'd be surprised." He waggled his eyebrows, then switched to a more sincere tone. "But of course I noticed you. Why do you think I talked to you? My toothbrush wisdom isn't for just anyone, you know."

"If your method for finding a serious relationship is picking women up at the drugstore, then you definitely needed the help of an expert computer."

"And yet, both methods yielded the same result." He grinned at her in a way that did nothing to help the cheek situation.

"Unlucky coincidence."

"Or was it serendipity?"

There was that word again.

The thing was, she didn't even believe in serendipity. Was it a coincidence that the only other person she'd met in town was the very same person Bianca's dating site had matched her with? Yes. But that's all it was.

She didn't think they were meant to be together any more than she thought not-a-gym-rat gym rat was meant for Bianca. "It was something." She added another spoonful of ice water to her dough and kept mixing. What had started out as dry flour and a stick of almost-frozen butter was turning into a smooth dough. "I think mine is getting close."

He stared down at his bowl. "I'm not entirely sure what I'm looking for, but this is starting to look less like sand and more like dough."

"The next step is to wrap the dough in plastic wrap and put it in the fridge, right?" She glanced at a couple to her left, who were putting wrapped dough balls into the chilling drawer. The set of friends on their right were already relaxing on their stools while they waited.

A quick glance around the room told the same story. Everyone had finished mixing their dough. Everyone but them. And if there was one thing Cora hated, it was losing.

"I think we're behind. We should probably speed up."

Jax continued mixing his dough slowly and methodically. "You can't rush perfection."

Cora gave her dough one last turn to form it into a big ball, then grabbed the plastic wrap from the supply shelf. "Yeah, but the only two groups who aren't finished are us and that group in the front who had to start over twice because they can't follow directions."

Jax looked up from his dough and glanced in the direction of the group in question. "Yeah, we gotta speed this up."

"Finally, we agree on something." She tore off a piece of plastic wrap and lay it out on the counter in front of Jax, then did the same for herself.

Jax stared down at his bowl. "How am I supposed to get it out?"

"Picking it up seems like the easiest option."

Jax shook his head. "Nope. Warm hands, warm heart, remember? I'm not going to let my warm, sunny personality ruin my piecrust." He narrowed his gaze at her. "Unless you're trying to sabotage me."

She picked up her own ball and plopped it down on the plastic wrap. The whole move took less than a second. "I'm willing to risk it. Live dangerously." This time, she winked.

Jax picked up his bowl and dumped it over the plastic wrap. He had to shake the bowl until the sticky ball rolled out and landed on the counter with a soft thud. "*Voilà.*"

He pulled the four corners of the plastic together over the top of his ball and twisted them until they were tight. Then he picked up the bundle by the remaining plastic wrap and carried it to the chilling drawer on the opposite side of their workstation. "Be prepared for the best."

She picked hers up and set it in the drawer next to his. "I'm on pins and needles."

An hour and a half later, they kneeled in front of the oven door and stared through the glass as if they could make out the status of the pies. They couldn't. At least she couldn't.

The best she could report was that there were, indeed, still two pies inside. As to the condition of said-pies, there would be no way of knowing until they opened the door.

"Do you think they're done?" Jax asked, his oven mitt–clad hands held up like a surgeon waiting for surgery.

Cora twisted her mouth to the side as she studied the glass. "Sure. I mean, the timer went off. The recipe says they're done."

He shot her a challenging look. "Do you always live your life following the recipe exactly?"

"If we're keeping score on taking risks, I was the one who wasn't afraid to touch the dough with my fingers."

"A decision we're all still questioning a bit."

She met his gaze with a confident one of her own. "I feel good about my choices. You worry about you."

"I'm really more of a *hakuna matata* kind of guy myself."

Geez, what was she getting herself into?

"I say they're done." And without bothering to wait for him to agree with her assessment, she pulled the oven open and reached in to grab her pie. He did the same, and they stood to face each other, pies held with mitted hands between them.

She had to admit, both pies looked amazing. The latticework tops were golden brown with a perfect sheen, and the curls of steam wafting up from the middle were so ideal they almost looked fake.

"Perfection." Cora lifted her pie up to her face and breathed in the sugary, blueberry scent before she spun around and set it on the counter next to his.

Jax had taken off his oven mitts and was leaning against the counter with his signature swagger. "Not bad, if I do say so myself." His gaze flickered to the pie in question.

"Just because it's pretty doesn't mean it's a keeper. You promised the perfect crust, after all."

"I think the exact promise was that it wouldn't disappoint. Which it won't." He grabbed the pie cutter and the two plates stacked on the counter. "But if it's not perfect, it's pretty darn close. Yours, on the other hand?" He gave her a pained look. "You did touch the dough."

She shook her head at his ridiculousness. "Lucky for us, we don't have to keep speculating on whose is better. It's time to put your money where your mouth is." She gestured to the pies on the counter. "Or, in this case, pie."

"Should we get an unbiased judge? We can call Chef Gracie over here for a blind taste test."

"I'd hardly call your ex-girlfriend an unbiased judge."

"Old friend."

"Sure," she said in a tone that said she didn't believe him for a second. "But I don't need a judge. I'm a big enough person that I can admit when I've been beat." She fixed him with a challenging look. "Are you?"

"Absolutely," he said without any hesitation. "Although it's never happened before, so I don't know exactly what it would feel like."

She shook her head. "Just cut your pie."

She picked up a second pie cutter and sliced into her own pie, but she wasn't ready for what it revealed.

As she lifted a perfect-looking piece out of the pan, an explosion of mouthwatering scents filled the air, causing a wave of nostalgia to slam into her.

Blueberry pie had been her mom's specialty, and not a Fourth of July went by without Julie Prestly making her famous dish. Of course, she also made it for special occasions or a fun summer treat, but blueberry pie was a staple at the beach house on Fourth of July. Which meant it was the official food of the time when life was perfect.

The memories hit her right in the feels, the good ones and the painful ones and the still-tender ones. And the thing was, Cora didn't do feels. Messy and emotional weren't really her things. She preferred things neat and tidy and controlled. Safe. And that went double for when she was on a first date.

So naturally, when the ache started to grow under her rib cage and the lump formed in her throat, she pushed them away and tried to focus on something else. Anything else. The design on the plates. The happy chatter that filled the room. The hypnotic nature of Jax's gorgeous smile.

Okay, definitely not that last one, because falling under his spell was the opposite of tidy and controlled. Perhaps it was best to avoid looking at it directly. Kind of like Kaa in *The Jungle Book*.

She drew in a deep breath and focused on plating two perfect pieces of her pie. Jax did the same until each plate held two almost identical slices.

"The moment of truth." Jax picked up his plate and fork.

She stared at the two pieces on her plate, trying to decide if they should start with his or hers when another annoying emotion zipped through her.

Nervousness.

She wasn't feeling the fluttery kind of nerves that went with excitement. She was feeling the cold kind, the kind more closely related to anxiety or the fear of not measuring up.

It was dumb, of course, because who cared if her pie wasn't better than Jax's? It wasn't like this was her recipe or she had used her special methods. They had followed the directions of the cooking class. If anyone were to blame for the pies not turning out well, it would be Chef Gracie.

Besides, what did it even matter? The prize was getting to go on another date with the most arrogant, ridiculous man she'd ever met—even if he did have a good smile and great eyes. And, fine, she could also admit that he was slightly entertaining, in an annoying, self-righteous way.

Anyway, the point was she didn't even want to go out with him. The whole reason she wanted a second date with him was to prove to her sister that he was a jerk who would promise the moon, then hit the road as soon as things got tough. She had absolutely nothing to lose here, even if her pie happened to be inedible.

Although if the mouthwatering scents drifting up from her plate were any indication, both pies were far from inedible.

"Ladies first," Jax said. His fork hovered over the slice of her pie.

"Prepare to be wowed." She pushed the nerves deep down inside next to all the other unwanted emotions and plunged her fork into the pie. Keeping her gaze locked with Jax's, she took a bite.

If the scent of the pie made her nostalgic, the flavor bomb that went off when the pie hit her tongue doubled as a time machine. The pie was sweet and bright and tasted like the goodness of summer. She closed her eyes as she was instantly transported back to her childhood. Suddenly she was a kid again, on the back deck on a warm summer night, laughing and lighting sparklers. They were sweet memories of a time when life was happy and less complicated.

But this time, before she could let the happy memories of the past conjure up any other feelings, she forced her eyes open and focused on the bet that was standing in front of her.

Jax was smiling at her. "I'm no expert," he said through a mouthful. "But that crust sets the bar pretty high."

"Buttery, flaky, not at all soggy." She listed off the attributes with a smug grin.

His eyes met hers in a way that stirred up other familiar unwanted feelings. "Perfection."

He held her gaze, and she couldn't help but feel adored. She blamed the annoying phenomenon on all the other rogue emotions floating through her.

She quickly looked down to retake control of her thoughts. Of course he would try to flatter her. He didn't get the reputation for being a heartbreaker on accident.

She moved to his slice of pie. This time, she cut off a bite that had more crust than blueberries, so she could judge his "perfection" promise more easily.

Also, she didn't have any childhood memories connected with the piecrust on its own. It seemed like a safer zone to stay in while she was trying to get her feels back in check.

With the ideal bite on her fork, she held it up. "Any last words before we dive in?"

He held up his own forkful of pie. "Cheers."

As expected, his pie tasted almost identical to hers. Chef Gracie's recipe was divine. But this time instead of being caught off guard by a flood of feelings, she was able to focus on his crust.

She had to admit it was good. Maybe even better than good, although she would never say that to him. He didn't need any more compliments puffing up that pretty little head of his.

"Not bad for a first-timer," she said.

"As promised, I do not disappoint." He had a sort of boyish excitement to him that made him seem authentic and playful, though she got the feeling he was talking less about his crust and more about their time together.

She was surprised to admit it, but she agreed. The date had been . . . fun.

"You know what this pie really needs?" Jax continued. "Ice cream." He grabbed a pint of ice cream from the freezer and popped off the lid. "For you?" He offered, holding up the ice cream scoop.

"I'll pass, thank you." She took another bite of her perfectly plain pie.

He scooped out one perfectly round scoop and plopped it in the center of the two slices on his plate. "Not an ice cream fan?"

"On the contrary. I love ice cream. Actually, it's my favorite dessert. I just don't like it on blueberry pie."

"Well, then, that settles it." He shoved a giant bite of pie and ice cream into his mouth.

"Settles what?"

It took him a second to swallow his bite before he could answer. "Our next date." He wiped his mouth with a napkin. "We'll have to get ice cream. Or, maybe another contest to see who makes it best?"

A slight victory grin tugged at the corner of her mouth because she'd done it. She'd gotten a second date, which meant she had practically already won the bet with her sisters. No way was this Casanova sticking around longer than a week. She pretty much had Chef Gracie's guarantee on that.

"Two things. First," she said, as she held up one finger, "no one in this town makes better ice cream than Miss Mary. It's a proven fact. We don't even have to debate it."

He bobbed his head back and forth as if weighing the merit of her statement before giving a slight shrug of agreement.

"And two." She held up a second finger. "Don't assume. If you want a second date with me, you're going to have to ask."

He took another bite of pie. Her pie. Which she knew he did to flatter her, but still, she couldn't help but feel flattered. Dumb rogue emotions.

Then he did something that caught her off guard. He looked at her with more sincerity than she'd seen all night.

"I really enjoyed tonight. I'd like to see you again."

"Me, too." The authentic answer popped out of her mouth before she'd given it permission to. What was happening to her?

Sure, going on a second date was part of her plan, so technically it was a no-brainer. But she at least should've considered it first. It was a date with *him*, after all.

She blamed it on the pie.

"How about Friday? Are you free?"

She at least managed to stop herself before an automatic agreement came flying out of her mouth.

"I'll check my schedule." She even finished it off with a nonchalant little shrug.

Only this time, she'd make sure they didn't go anywhere near blueberry pie. She didn't need any more rogue emotions as she entered into Phase Two of her plan.

8

Jax

After they finished eating their pie—both pieces along with the full scoop of ice cream, in his case at least—they hung up their aprons and walked to the front of the store.

Gracie was sitting at the reception counter, thanking customers as they left, and Cora stopped to talk to her.

"Thanks for a fun evening. I really enjoyed the class."

"My pleasure," Gracie said. "I hope we see you again."

"Thanks, Gracie." He held a hand up in a wave as he used his other arm to open the front door.

She gave him a nod of acknowledgment along with a look of unbridled judgment. With a slight *What-do-you-do?* shrug, he joined Cora on the sidewalk outside.

"I guess you were right after all," he said.

"Naturally." She dug through her purse and pulled out her keys. "But to which specific occasion were you referring?"

"You can't trust a person who doesn't eat dessert." He couldn't help the hint of a grin. "I don't know if food can make you happy, but after eating that, I'm not unhappy."

She chuckled, causing the cutest little crinkle lines to form around her eyes. "Right? Dessert is seriously the best part of the meal."

"Agreed." For a brief moment he was distracted by how attractive she was. And not just externally. She was funny and witty and sometimes infuriating but mostly . . . "It's been a long time since I've been on a date with someone where I had this much fun."

He didn't actually mean to say that last part out loud, but now that it was out there, he might as well own it. It was true after all.

His statement seemed to catch her off guard too, and there was a flash of vulnerability in her normally controlled exterior. It was the same look she had when she tasted the pie for the first time. There was something about it that intrigued him.

Although, if he were being totally honest, there was a lot about her that intrigued him.

"Agreed. It was . . ." She paused as if searching for the right word. "Unexpected."

Not the normal response he got after a date. He arched an eyebrow. "In a good way?"

She seemed to consider that for a second. "Hard to say. I'll let you know after Friday." She shot him a look that sent an electric bolt zinging through him, which was absolutely unexpected.

"I'm looking forward to it." And he meant it.

"Until then." She held his gaze for a second, then turned to walk toward the parking garage.

He watched her go, hands still tucked into his pockets.

"Who is she?"

The singsong words broke his reverie, and he turned to see Chef Gracie standing next to him.

"Cora. You met her." Although he knew that wasn't what she was asking.

"Yeah, I did." She looked over at him with an accusatory stare. "But who *is* she?"

"Don't you have people inside you need to attend to?" Was he avoiding answering the question? Maybe. But did that mean he was totally enthralled with his slightly-infuriating-but-mostly-intriguing-witty-and-beautiful AI match?

Okay, yes it did. But he still wasn't ready to talk through it with Gracie.

"The only two left inside are the young parents on a date night who will likely sit in there until I kick them out. So from now until I need to lock up, I have nothing to do but stand out here and find out about the mystery girl who captivated Jax Verona."

"I'm not captivated." Interested? Maybe. Entertained? Sure. But definitely not captivated. He didn't get captivated.

"Hmm." She crossed her arms and studied him. Her furrowed brow said she wasn't buying it.

He matched her cross-armed stance, except he switched out her skeptical expression for his own confident one. "Maybe I was really excited about the pie."

"Maybe."

He could've kept denying her claim—which *was* bogus, by the way—except another thought occurred to him. If he was going to pull off this charade and prove to his uncle that he could be in a committed relationship, he needed to convince the world that this was a committed relationship. Which meant he needed to appear smitten, right? Because people in that kind of relationship were smitten.

And in a town where the official language was gossip, here was his chance to start building the story in the rumor mill.

"She was pretty great, though, huh?" He relaxed his stance and even allowed what he hoped was a dreamy look.

"She seemed to keep your attention."

"I'm seeing her again on Friday."

"Two dates?" Gracie let out a low whistle. "She *is* special."

Instead of answering, he just smiled.

Gracie raised a skeptical brow. "Is she aware of your two-date rule?"

"Maybe I'm not going to put a limit on it this time. Maybe we'll see where it goes."

She sucked in a fake gasp. "Jax Verona? In a real relationship?"

It was a fair comment. Up until one day ago it would've been his response, too. But here they were.

"I don't know." He gave a little shrug. "This one feels different."

There was a little more truth in that statement than he'd like to admit. Being with Cora *did* feel different and he was looking forward to Friday. He'd hit the jackpot with this match. If he had to spend his summer dating someone, at least he knew they'd have fun together.

But that didn't mean tonight had changed his thoughts on forever. He had the same stance he'd always had. Maybe it worked for some people, but not for him. Too many unknown factors. Too many things outside his control. Too many ways to get hurt. In his opinion, as a man who'd spent the majority of his adult career evaluating risk for a living, falling in love wasn't worth the risk.

That's why he'd instituted the two-date rule to begin with. The max number of dates he went on with any woman would be two. No more. He'd wanted to be up front about his intentions so everyone was on the same page. Falling in love would never be part of the deal. For anyone involved. He preferred to keep things fun. Light. Unattached.

But he'd said it before, and he'd say it again. If he needed to make the entire world think he'd changed his views on love and commitment to get the job that should've been his anyway—the job he was made for—he'd do it. And apparently that task started with convincing Gracie Blakely.

"Well, this one I'm going to have to see to believe," Gracie said.

Jax didn't say anything. He just gave the same slight shrug with the same dreamy look.

Challenge accepted.

And he liked the prospect of facing this challenge with Cora. She wasn't like the women he usually dated. He didn't know how to describe her other than she was . . .

Unexpected.

9

Bianca

Thursday afternoon Bianca decided to go for a run.

There were a few reasons for this. For one, she kept saying how she needed to start some healthier habits, including getting into a regular workout routine. Generally speaking, she considered herself a healthy-enough person and didn't mind a good workout. But who had the time or energy to work out every day when they were working full time? By the time she left her nine-to-five, what she really wanted was to chill on the couch, eat dinner, and sleep—and not necessarily in that order.

Yes, she was aware there was a group of people who got in their workouts before work. They got up at four in the morning because they didn't want to wait until after work when they were too tired. Bianca, however, felt more inspired to sit through a root canal than get out of bed at four to hit the treadmill.

Still, she knew she needed to get into the habit, because Zander was into having a healthy lifestyle. Not a day went by that he didn't make it to the gym—sometimes twice. She had no intention of working out the same way he did, but she would have to stop fudging the details of how regularly she did it when she moved to Idaho. Since she had plenty of spare time at the moment, now seemed as good a time as any to start.

Her second reason for choosing to go for a run was that she was bored.

It wasn't that she didn't like relaxing at the beach. She did. And of course there were all of Savannah's Summer Bucket List activities. But after four days of lazy summer vacationing, she was starting to feel restless.

She crossed the small front yard that was covered with pea gravel and tropical plants and stopped on the street. With her hands on her hips, she looked both ways. Honestly, it didn't matter which way she chose to run. She had zero idea what was in either direction.

Maybe it would've been smarter to look at a map and plan out a route. That's what Cora would've done. Or she could've gone to a pretty running trail in some idyllic place. That's what Savannah would've done.

But Bianca didn't want to waste time stressing over the details. She just wanted to go. There would be plenty of time to figure out the plan while she was on the way. If she got lost, she always had direction apps on her phone to help her find her way home. If she got *really* lost, she could call one of her sisters to pick her up.

She'd call Cora, of course, because while Cora always had something to say about everything, Savannah would give her the disappointed-mom look. And she wasn't in the mood to be a disappointment.

She turned to the left, mostly because that would put her facing oncoming traffic without having to cross the street, and started running.

See, she put plenty of thought into where she was going.

She jogged through the little neighborhood, taking in the cute, cottagey houses that lined the street. Sunnyside was the kind of small, charming beach town that looked like it walked right out of a picture book. Other than a few designer brands in the shopping complex, she hadn't seen one chain store or restaurant yet. Not even a Starbucks. It provided the perfect backdrop to escape from the normal hustle and bustle of life. She could see why their family would choose to come back here year after year. Sunnyside almost seemed too good to be true.

Kind of like her childhood.

The last time she was here was the summer she was ten, which seemed like a turning point in her life. Before her eleventh birthday she was a kid. Life was carefree, and she did things that normal kids did. She went on family vacations where she ate saltwater taffy that was made right there in the magical taffy shop. She built sandcastles on the beach and wondered exactly how high she'd have to go on the swings at Founders Park to be able to go all the way around. Her biggest worry was who she should invite to her birthday party and what kind of cake they should have.

Then she turned eleven, and everything changed.

The day after her eleventh birthday party, which was one week after they'd arrived home from their last trip to Sunnyside, her parents sat the three sisters down and informed them they were separating.

To Bianca, this development had come out of the blue. She'd had no idea there was a problem that would have led to something like this. Her parents were unhappy? There was something wrong with her family? When had this happened? They'd just gotten back from the beach where there had been fun and laughter and giant bags of taffy.

Her dad moved out the same day.

Less than three weeks later, the four now-independent ladies loaded up their mom's SUV and drove Savannah to college. They'd sweated all day, moving her into her freshman dorm; gone to dinner; and then left her oldest sister there.

The drive home had seemed odd. She had the entire back seat to herself, which had never happened on a road trip before. And as soon as they got home, Cora moved out of the room they'd always shared and into Savannah's now-vacant room. Their house—and Bianca's life—had never felt so empty.

The only constant after that summer was that nothing stayed the same. A year later, her parents were officially divorced. A year after that, Cora left for college in Texas. A year after that, her mom got her first cancer diagnosis.

Before Bianca had even graduated from high school, she was standing at her mother's funeral, and her entire world looked different.

Starting from the moment she blew out the candles on her eleventh birthday cake, life had been a series of major changes. It was all Bianca could do to try to keep up.

The road she was running on had come to a dead end at a T-intersection, forcing her to choose between going right or left. She stopped and wiped the sweat from her forehead as she surveyed each direction.

Right. Right was always right.

Confident in her decision, she started jogging again.

But the truth was, the lazy vacation days weren't the only reason she was feeling restless. She'd been restless for a while. She felt like her life was in a holding pattern while she tried to figure out what came next. The only problem was that she'd been in that holding pattern for as long as she could remember. Maybe even as far back as her eleventh birthday.

She had dropped out of college because after three years and four different majors, she was no closer to figuring out what she wanted to do with her life than when she'd started. And since funds were running out, she decided to put college on hold until she had a better idea.

That was almost four years ago, and she was no closer to having it figured out than the day she'd hit the Pause button. Sure, she'd had plenty of jobs in that time, but there wasn't a single one she wanted to do for the rest of her life. Most of them she hadn't even wanted to do for the rest of the year.

She was aware of what people thought of her, especially her sisters. They thought she lacked work ethic or was flighty. They thought she was undisciplined or a screwup.

But what she really was . . . was lost.

Her road came to another dead end that forced her to choose a new direction. She started to turn right but changed her mind. Right would put her heading back toward the house, and she wasn't ready to head home quite yet. Maybe she didn't know where she wanted to be, but she knew where she *didn't* want to be.

And this was the reason why meeting Zander was so amazing. Here was this great guy who was funny and attentive and romantic. But even more than that, for the first time she could finally see what her future was supposed to look like.

He already had a job lined up for her as a receptionist at his law firm. It was a starting position that would give her the training she needed to run the office side of a law practice. Eventually, when she got familiar with the legal world and he had enough experience under his belt, they would open a practice of their own. They'd be the ultimate team.

They'd also talked about having a family, but not right away. They needed to buy the right house first. He'd even sent her listings of places that were zoned for highly ranked elementary schools. They were already talking about elementary schools!

Finally, her future was figured out. All she had to do was get to Boise and get started.

Of course, she still had to convince her sisters this was all a good idea. That Zander was a good idea.

All she had to do was win the bet with Cora and Savannah. By the end of the summer, she'd be well on her way to getting her life on track. She was sure of it.

Mostly sure of it, anyway. Yes, she had a slight hesitation, which was totally normal. Everyone felt a little apprehensive when starting out on a new adventure. It would be weird if she wasn't a little anxious.

She came to another intersection, but this time she didn't guess which way to turn. A smile crept onto her lips as she saw exactly where she wanted to go. The cutest little pink and white coffee truck, the one where she and Savannah had stopped the day they'd arrived, was parked on the corner. One of their shaken berry green teas sounded like the perfect way to reward herself for a long run.

See. Sometimes aimless wandering led to exactly the right place.

She slowed to a walk as she headed toward the coffee cart. There was already someone ordering at the window, and as she got closer she noticed they happened to be the only other person she knew in town: Luke. This jogging trip had brought up all kinds of great surprises.

"Look who it is!" she called as soon as he was within earshot.

He turned to her, and an authentic smile lit his face. "Hey! What are you up to today?"

"Just out for a little run and thought I'd get something delicious to reward myself. You?"

"Headed to a jobsite but had to stop for a little incentive first." As he finished his sentence, he accepted two frozen drinks piled high with whipped cream.

"Those look yummy."

"According to Sylvie, they are the only acceptable payment for helping me with a job. So . . ." He gave a little shrug.

"So naturally you had to get one for yourself, too?" Bianca didn't know Luke had a girlfriend. When they had talked about relationships the other night, she just assumed . . .

Anyway, it didn't matter. Luke was great. Of course he had a girlfriend. How sweet that she helped him out. Pretty soon that would be the same kind of couple she and Zander would be.

Although she didn't know if Zander drank drinks like that. He was more of a protein shake kind of guy.

"Well, Sylvie seems to be onto something," Bianca continued. "Maybe if I had one of those every morning, I would feel differently about my job."

As soon as she finished saying it, a little girl about eight or nine walked around the other side of the coffee truck and held her hands out for the drink. "Thanks, Uncle Luke." She licked the top of the whipped cream before she took a long slurp of the drink.

Suddenly Bianca's mood brightened. "And this must be Sylvie."

Luke nodded. "This is my niece. Sylvie, meet my friend Bianca."

"It's nice to meet you, Bianca." Sylvie had the formal tone of someone who was wiser than her years. She stuck her arm out, elbow locked, for a handshake.

Bianca liked this kid already.

"Likewise." She shook the little girl's hand. "And what is this fabulous drink you conned your uncle into ordering for you?"

"It's a frozen raspberry butterscotch latte. It's really good." She took another long sip to illustrate its deliciousness.

"Well, with that kind of recommendation, I can't really leave without trying it." She looked at the barista. "I'll have one of those, please."

"Good choice," the barista said. "Would you like it like his or hers?"

Bianca's brow furrowed as she looked back and forth at the two drinks. "What's the difference?"

The barista leaned forward and lowered her voice. "With the caffeine or without?"

"Oh, caffeine. All the caffeine."

"I got ya."

The barista got to work, and Bianca turned around to focus on Luke and Sylvie.

"What fun job has your uncle roped you into today?" She glanced up at Luke. "Another toilet repair?"

"Ew! Fixing a toilet." Sylvie squeezed her eyes shut and stuck her tongue out, disgusted.

Luke chuckled. "Luckily, all toilets seem to be running just fine. Today's task is part of a new service L & C Property Management is offering."

"And what is this new venture?"

"It's called the Custom Concierge Service. I got the idea when a few of my renters over the holidays asked if I knew anyone who could decorate their house for Christmas."

Sylvie raised her hand. "Me. It was me. I decorated their house."

Luke chuckled. "It's true. She helped me finish one of the houses because I didn't realize it was an early release day at her school."

"And here we are. Still decorating things," Sylvie reported.

"Sounds like a pretty cool service," Bianca said.

"The renters have thought so," Luke agreed. "We've expanded from decorating to setting up custom experiences that make their trip extra memorable. You know, family photo shoots on the beach, special birthday parties, custom tours they want to do. All for a small fee, of course."

"Naturally. What custom experience are you setting up today?"

"A romantic dinner on the beach."

"Wow, that sounds fun." She glanced at her watch. It was only three o'clock. "But isn't it a little early to be setting up for dinner?"

"Typically, I'd say yes, but I'm giving myself some extra time. Arranging for a bounce house is one thing. But setting up a romantic dinner that will be the backdrop of a proposal?" He gave her the wide-eyed look of being overwhelmed.

"Uncle Luke doesn't know what he's doing," Sylvie filled in.

Luke held up his hands in surrender. "She is right. I have no idea what I'm doing. What I do have is an inspiration picture and a truck full of supplies, so we're going to figure it out."

"Sounds like a fun problem to figure out," Bianca said, accepting her frozen raspberry butterscotch latte from the barista. "I love that kind of stuff."

"Really?" Luke seemed shocked by her statement, as if they were still on the subject of toilet repair.

"Sure. Decorating with someone else's money? What's not to love?"

"Um, everything. I have some guy's proposal dreams hanging on the hope that I can set up something that will wow his girlfriend."

"The proposal does step it up a notch." She took a sip of her drink—which was divine, by the way—and considered Luke's dilemma. "Just make sure it photographs really well from one side and tell him to walk in from that direction. And maybe give the photographer a heads-up on where to stand."

Instead of giving him confidence, the helpful advice appeared to make Luke even more stressed. "You think there's a photographer?"

"Of course there will be a photographer. Who proposes on the beach with that kind of setup without a photographer?"

"Huh." Luke stared at the ground, his brow furrowed in thought.

Bianca probably should've stopped there, but she was too excited. Maybe it was the thought of the project that inspired her or thinking about the romantic moment of someone saying yes. Whatever the case, she kept on rattling. "And if he didn't think to get a photographer, you should probably offer to hang around to take some pictures. She will want them. Also, make sure you have champagne." She stopped to think for a second. "Unless it doesn't go as expected. Then they won't want the pictures or the champagne, or really for you to be around at all. So, be ready to disappear if that's the case. With the champagne. And delete the photos."

It wasn't until she saw fear flash across his face that she realized she'd gone too far.

She quickly waved her hand in the air to erase the thought. "Don't worry. That's not going to happen. And even if it did, that would have nothing to do with your setup. She would've said no even if it was the most breathtaking scene. Although, yours *will* be breathtaking. It'll be great. They're going to love it."

Seriously. Why did words keep coming out of her mouth?

"Yeah. I'm in way over my head." Luke let out a long sigh and twisted his mouth to the side as he thought. After a couple seconds, he looked up at Bianca with a hopeful expression. "Any chance you have some free time and want to look at the plans? I have them in the truck."

Yes. Yes, she did. But she tried to play it cool anyway.

She looked over at Sylvie. "Is this how he roped you in, too?"

"Pretty much." Sylvie gave a serious nod as if she, too, knew she'd been duped. Then she took a sip of her raspberry butterscotch deliciousness to prove it was worth it.

Bianca looked back at Luke. "I'd love to help. I happen to have a couple hours, so maybe I can do more than just look at the plans. Let's see what you got."

Relief washed over Luke's face. "Thanks. I really appreciate it."

She followed him to his truck, and he pulled a binder from a rubber bin in the bed. Inside there was a data sheet that had a picture paper-clipped to the top of it.

The setup was simple enough. There were three long bamboo poles arranged kind of like a teepee, with a small two-person table underneath. The poles were wrapped in white gauzy fabric, and where the poles met there were twinkle lights with a candle lantern hung like a chandelier. The scene was surrounded by tiki torches.

It was a beautiful setup, and it would make a great backdrop for a romantic evening. But with a few minor touches, it could be stunning. And with something as big as popping the question, "stunning" needed to be the target. "Magical" would be preferable.

Luke studied her intently. "You don't like it." He seemed to deflate.

"No, I do," she said in her most optimistic voice. "I'm just thinking through the whole setup. Where is this happening?"

"On the beach, right outside of their town house."

Bianca nodded, envisioning the space. "They're not there, are they? While you're setting up?"

"No. They're out on a kayaking excursion. They won't be back until after five. Which is why we're setting it up now, so we can be out of the way before they get back."

"And he's going to propose right when they get back? When they're all sweaty and gross from kayaking in the sun?" Technically she'd been proposed to over a FaceTime call when she was wearing bunny slippers and eating Kraft Easy Mac, but just because her proposal wasn't Instagram-worthy didn't mean Bianca didn't have high expectations here. This soon-to-be groom was paying for something of that caliber, after all.

Plus, Zander promised a more romantic proposal that would make a better story when they were finally together, so her moment would come. Maybe she should even point him in Luke's direction.

But she was getting off track. What was important today was this proposal.

"I think he was planning on doing it during dinner. Catering is scheduled to arrive at six thirty. My guess is they'll shower first and get ready. He ordered a pretty fancy meal."

Bianca thought for a second. "Are you open to making a few changes?"

"As long as it's in the realm of doable, change away."

Bianca's grin started from the inside, and she felt more excited for this project than she had for anything else she'd done while she was in Sunnyside. Which was normal, right? Because who didn't love a good proposal?

"Okay, here's what I'm thinking. We need to add rose petals to form a little barrier. All it will take is a couple dozen roses, and we can grab them from the grocery store. Then we can add some big seashells on top. Our house has a few being used as decorations that we could bring over. And I think it would be cool to have a path outlined by candles. That many candles might be a little trickier to find, but let me see what I can come up with. And maybe a few flowers here and here." She pointed at spots on the pictures.

Sylvie slurped her drink. "Her idea is better."

Luke nodded in agreement. "I think we can do that. I even have some candles left over from some of the Christmas setups. We can use those."

"Perfect!" Bianca beamed. "But here's the kicker." She clenched her teeth together in the nervous-emoji look. "We need to set it up while she's in the shower. *After* they get back from kayaking."

Luke looked at the truck bed full of supplies and then back at her. "I don't know if I can do that."

"Sure, you can. We can practice setting everything up now in a different location, like Founders Park or something. Then we'll just fold it up and have it standing by. As soon as she's inside and away from the windows, we pop it all back up."

"And you think we can *pop it up* in less than an hour?"

Bianca gave his hand a squeeze. "Of course we can. I'll even stick around the whole time to help."

Sylvie kept her no-nonsense gaze on her uncle while she nodded at Bianca. "You heard the lady."

"I guess I've been outvoted."

"Yes!" Bianca turned and high-fived Sylvie.

"But you're sure you want to spend your day doing this?" Luke asked again.

Bianca grinned. "Like I said before, I love this kind of stuff. This isn't work. This is like playing."

Luke shrugged like he still didn't get it but returned the binder to the bin. "It's your vacation."

✄

Forty-five minutes later, after Bianca had a quick shower and Luke picked up the other supplies they needed, she met him and Sylvie at Founders Park to practice the setup.

"Are you ready for this?" She waggled her eyebrows as Luke and Sylvie walked up, each carrying an armful of supplies.

They hadn't quite made their way to Bianca when kids playing at the splash pad at the other side of the park called out to Sylvie. "Come play with us!"

Sylvie looked up at her uncle with a hopeful expression. "Can I?"

"Yeah, go ahead. Just make sure you stay where you can see us."

"Thank you, Uncle Luke!" She handed her armful of supplies to Bianca, then skipped off toward her friends.

"She's a great kid," Bianca said, watching her run up to her friends. "Does she hang out with you often?"

"Every day."

Bianca couldn't help the surprise. "Like full-time?"

Luke chuckled. "No, not like that. My sister is a single mom and full-time nurse practitioner, and I help out during the summer breaks and holidays. I drive Sylvie to her summer camps and let her hang out with me on days when she doesn't have anything."

"And buy her sugary drinks?"

"I didn't say my services were free."

"Well, she's lucky to have you," Bianca said.

"Family is important. We have to stick together."

"Mmm." Bianca agreed.

"Speaking of family, I heard your little ploy to set up Jax Verona with your sister worked."

It was exactly the segue Bianca wanted before she got distracted by the proposal project. "How'd you hear that? They just went out, like, two nights ago."

He shrugged. "It's a small town. People talk."

"And what else are they saying?"

"That there's a second date."

"So, not a lot." She didn't know what she was expecting from Luke's town gossip, but she was hoping for something more . . . substantial.

"Not a lot of people get a second date with Jax Verona. Trust me, it's newsworthy."

"I have a feeling he's going to stick around awhile this time."

Luke studied her. "Do I even want to know why?"

Did she feel bad about stacking the deck so she'd win her bet? Maybe a little, but she also felt justified. For her entire life she'd been trying to prove to her sisters, especially Savannah, that she was enough: old enough, mature enough, responsible enough. And, okay fine, there were times when she had proven she wasn't, but just because it had happened didn't mean it was the norm. She was tired of her sisters second-guessing her, tired of them thinking they knew best.

She was tired of failing.

For so long she'd felt like she was trying to find her way, and now she'd finally found it. She'd been introduced to someone she'd fallen in love with. They had a plan for the future that made sense. Moving to Idaho and marrying Zander was a good thing. She knew what she was doing, and if winning this bet was how she had to prove it to her sisters, then so be it. She was not a disappointment.

But her reasons weren't entirely self-motivated. She believed what she'd said about Cora. Getting out and having fun and connecting with people would do her some good. She'd gotten so grumpy. So distant. So . . . boring. She needed a little spice in her life. Cora needed this. Someday she would thank her.

Probably.

"Any chance your rumor mill had any details about their second date?"

"If it did, I didn't care enough to pay attention." Luke seemed unconcerned, busying himself with unloading supplies in an open patch of sand. "Although, don't you live in a house with someone who could give you that information?"

"She's not exactly one for sharing details." Bianca twisted her mouth to the side and thought. "You don't happen to have his number, do you?"

"No. We're not exactly friends. But trust me, Jax has never had a problem impressing the ladies."

"Yeah, but he's never tried to impress my sister before."

This would be the date when her sister would drop whatever charm she used in the first date and bring out the true Cora, who was an expert at pushing people away. And Bianca didn't exactly want to warn Jax about what was coming. There was too much of a risk that he'd take off, not that she would blame him. It would be easier to convince a lion to become vegan than to get Cora to fall in love. There were easier routes for him to win his bet.

But for her to win hers, she needed him to stick around. She had a few tips for him that might help that happen.

For the record, sharing tips about her sister's likes and preferences wasn't artificially prolonging the relationship; it was helping to make the experience better for both of them.

"Are you sure this is the guy you want for your sister?" Luke asked.

"Trust me, he's perfect."

"And you're not worried about his mysterious past?"

She shrugged. "His background checked out, so I find 'hit man' hard to believe."

"International art thief?" He raised a questioning eyebrow.

Okay, even she had to admit that one was starting to seem plausible, especially after the van Gogh answer. "But is an art thief really dangerous? One could make the argument that they're cultured."

"You're hopeless."

"A hopeless romantic." She grinned up at him innocently.

"But not hopeless enough to let it play out on its own."

Bianca had said it once, and she'd say it again. "Even fate needs a little nudge sometimes."

10

Savannah

*F*riday afternoon Savannah's phone buzzed as she sat on the back deck reading. She smiled when she saw who the call was from and picked it up.

"Hi, Mommy!" The two sweetest voices she knew rang out as soon as their faces appeared on the screen, followed by their signature giggling. Three-year-old Juliette and five-year-old Genevieve danced on the other side of the screen.

"Hello, my sweet peas! How are you today?"

"We're getting pancakes! For lunch!" Genevieve announced, as if no further explanation of the status of her day was needed.

"Wow! That sounds exciting," Savannah said.

"It's possible that pancakes were promised yesterday, and I forgot to make them for breakfast," said her husband's voice from somewhere behind the phone.

Savannah chuckled. Her girls were nothing if not persistent. Genevieve would make a great lawyer someday.

"And then Nana's coming!" Juliette added. Her lopsided pigtails bounced as she jumped around.

"So fun!" Savannah agreed.

"And we got to tear a loop off the paper chain today. Only seventeen more loops until we come to see you and Aunt Bee and Auntie Cora!" Genevieve threw her hands up in the air and spun around in celebration. Since she was holding the phone, the sudden view of the swirling gave Savannah slight motion sickness vibes.

Although Savannah didn't mind. She missed her girls. Even a look at the spinning ceiling made her heart sing.

"I can't wait. You two are going to love it here."

"All right, you two, my turn." There was more bobbling, and then the familiar comfort of seeing her favorite human on the planet warmed her whole body as Chris's face filled the screen.

"How's life on the beach?"

"Perfect. As usual." This was her happy place and being here now, even with all its struggles, fed her soul. "Although I miss y'all."

"We miss you, too," Chris said. "And how are things with your sisters? Going any better?"

"Oh, you know." There was a hint of disappointment in her voice that she couldn't help. She'd thought her plan would be further along by now, that there would've been more bonding. She thought more boxes on the Summer Bucket List would've been checked off.

But the huge gaps that stood between the sisters were still as big as ever. Once again Savannah found herself asking how they'd ended up here. How she'd *let* them get here.

"You're letting them help out, right? Your chore chart is working?" There was obvious concern in Chris's voice.

"Of course they're helping. They're my sisters."

It wasn't exactly the truth. They hadn't done one chore that was assigned on the chore chart—she was pretty sure Cora was avoiding them to prove something—but her sisters were picking up after themselves. Kind of.

Of course, she still had to wipe down the kitchen every night regardless of who had done the dishes and cleaned. It just felt cleaner if she did it herself. It was probably one of those perfectionist habits she needed to work on, but how much time did it take from Savannah's day to wipe down counters?

The concern from his voice pooled in his eyes. "You should tell them. They'll want to know. No more secrets, right?"

A wave of guilt washed over her, which she did her best to push away. "I will. Just not yet. I want to get in a few more fun days first."

There was enough big news already. She didn't need to add any fuel to the flame. Not yet, anyway.

"But you're going to tell them before we get there, right?"

"Right. Of course." Or maybe when they got there.

But definitely before the month was over.

Probably.

As if he could read her mind, Chris gave her an accusatory look.

She let out a sigh. "I know. I promise I will. I'm just waiting for the right time."

"Make sure you get some rest. That's the whole reason you're there, remember?"

"I thought the whole reason I was here was to reconnect with my sisters and fulfill my mom's last wish," she tossed back in a lighthearted tone.

"It's an agenda-packed month." He looked over the camera at something in the background, and the source of his concern shifted. "Juliette, get down." He glanced back at the camera. "Hang on a second."

The ceiling filled her screen again while she could hear his muffled voice in the background. She wondered what sort of trouble her second-born was getting into. Fiercely independent, adventurous, and untethered by rules. She would do great things, that was for sure. But it wouldn't be without giving everyone who cared for her a headful of gray hair.

It reminded her of a certain other second-born. Maybe it was their anthem.

As if on cue, the sliding glass door opened behind her, and Cora stuck her head out. "There you are. We've been looking for you. You ready to go?"

Savannah held up her phone. "Yes. Let me say goodbye to Chris and the girls first."

"Oh, I want to say hi to those cuties." She stepped all the way onto the deck and propped herself on the arm of Savannah's chair. "Hey, girls!" She waved at the camera.

"Auntie Cora!" At the sound of her voice, the two giggling faces filled the screen again.

Or perhaps it would be more accurate to say parts of their faces filled the screen. It was mostly just Genevieve's eyes and a shot up Juliette's nose.

"How are my favorite minions?"

For as much as Savannah gave Cora a hard time for not being involved with the family, her sister loved the girls well in her own way, which was with gifts. She gave big, elaborate gifts and on the rare occasion when she was in town, she took them on big, elaborate outings. She took Fun Aunt to a whole new level. She was so fun, in fact, that this past Christmas, Juliette didn't want to put the biggest wish on her list to Santa because *"Auntie Cora gives better presents, and I don't even have to be good to get them."*

"We get pancakes! For lunch!" Juliette sang out.

"There are only seventeen more paper chains until we get to see you," Genevieve said.

"Did you get us presents?" Juliette asked.

"Juliette, baby, you can't ask that. It's not polite," Chris said from somewhere behind them.

"Pancakes sound delicious, and I guess you'll have to wait seventeen days to see if I have a gift for you or not." Cora shrugged like it was a big secret, then she leaned into the phone and whispered, "But of course I do!"

"Yay!" The video feed bounced around as Savannah could only assume the girls were jumping with excitement.

Chris reclaimed the phone. "And with that exciting news, I'm going to go so I can give them more sugar to add fuel to this frenzy. It's good to see you, Cora."

"Hey, Chris. Can't wait for y'all to get here." She gave him a little wave, then slid into the chair next to her sister, and Savannah centered the phone on her own face.

"Y'all have a good weekend, and I'll see you soon." She blew him a kiss.

"You, too." Her husband gave her a sympathetic look. "And Savannah, remember what I said. You should tell them."

She nodded and blew him one last kiss before she clicked off.

Cora gave her a quizzical look. "Tell us what?"

Savannah had kind of hoped Cora hadn't heard that. But since nothing escaped her sister, she put on her best carefree expression. "That Chris is thinking about coming a day or two early. Y'all wouldn't mind, would you?" It wasn't exactly the truth, but she needed to work up to the other conversation.

"Not at all," Cora said, although Savannah could tell by the way she was looking at her that her sister wasn't convinced it was the truth. Luckily, Cora didn't press the issue.

"Are we ready to go to the pier for lunch?" Not only did Savannah not want to talk about her little problem, but she was still trying to actively avoid thinking about it when she could.

"Let's do it."

She stood and followed Cora into the house, locking the sliding glass door behind them. She grabbed her crossbody bag from the kitchen table and headed to the front door where Bianca was waiting.

"Who's driving?" Bianca asked.

"No one's driving." Savannah pulled open the front door and waited for everyone to file out. "We're riding bikes. Like we always did. It's tradition."

Cora turned to Bianca. "Let me guess. You don't remember riding bikes."

"I totally remember riding bikes. Just not with you guys." She looked around the living room as if the bikes would be there. "Do we have bikes?"

"Sure. In the shed." Savannah waved everyone out the door.

"We have a shed?" Bianca asked as she stepped out onto the small front porch.

Cora just shook her head and walked over to the left side of the house where the shed was located. "And you wonder why we question if your move across the country is a good idea."

Maybe that was a little harsh, but Savannah had to admit Cora was right.

The shed was clearly visible from the street. And it was mentioned in the welcome letter with the instructions for the house. Twice.

Cora was already unlocking and opening the shed when Savannah rounded the corner.

"Huh. Look at that. Bikes." Bianca was the first one in to sort through the tangle of bikes mixed in among the other beach items.

Clearly, the house catered to families, because there was a wide selection of different-sized bikes. There were three adult bikes, two midsize bikes that looked to be for older kids, and two smaller bikes that would be an ideal size for someone around Genevieve's age. And, of course, there was a cart that could go on the back of an adult bike to pull toddlers.

"Perfect." Savannah clapped her hands together after scanning the inventory. "One for each of us."

"Let's do it." Cora grabbed her bike and pushed it out toward the street. They all followed.

When they were at the end of the driveway, Savannah climbed on her bike and followed her sisters toward the pier.

She had a passing thought that perhaps riding a bike wasn't *taking it easy*, but since the pier was just over a mile and on completely flat terrain, she wouldn't consider the ride vigorous, which was what the doctor had told her to avoid. She'd be fine biking this once.

Yes, she was aware she was not a great patient, which was largely because she didn't want to be a patient. She didn't want this problem that had popped up at the most inopportune time.

But was there ever an opportune time to find out you had a hole in your heart?

Technically speaking, it had been there her entire life. The official diagnosis was a congenital heart defect called atrial septal defect. It was something she was born with, although in her case, it was such a minor defect it went unnoticed for years. Her heart had found a way to compensate, and she got through life with hardly any signs. Was she always a little more winded during exercise than most? Sure. But she'd blamed it on not being athletic. It was a good excuse to focus on crafting instead of running.

But at some point, either the hole got bigger or her heart got tired, because the symptoms became unavoidable.

It happened around the time she was pregnant with Juliette, so naturally she'd blamed the unusual tiredness and shortness of breath on the pregnancy. It wasn't until after Juliette was born and she still couldn't carry groceries from the car to the house without getting winded that Savannah started thinking there might be a different problem.

The good news was that her condition was treatable. The bad news was it would require open heart surgery, a detail she was still wrapping her head around. Which was why she hadn't told her sisters.

The prognosis was good, but it was still scary. There were risks. Normally, that made anything medical seem scary. But since they had experienced the trauma of losing their mom, anything medical brought up an extra truckload of anxiety. For all of them. She didn't want to make her sisters' worry about her own medical issues.

Did she need to tell them? Yes, especially now that the surgery had gone from *someday* to *soon*. But she needed to wait for the right time, when they were ready to handle that kind of news. She didn't want to do anything to damage their mental health. Or their already-delicate relationships.

In the meantime, she'd take it easy. Look at the tortoise and the hare. The tortoise kept up with the hare, no problem. She just needed to stay on the slow and steady track. She could do this.

Halfway into their ride, though, her energy level dropped from *probably enough* to *nothing left in the tank* almost instantly. She felt like she couldn't pedal one more rotation, which frustrated her. In fact, every single thing about her condition frustrated her. It was stupid and unfair. She wanted it to go away so she could at least control her own body instead of the other way around.

But since her heart didn't seem to care about her ever-growing to-do list, she gave in and did what any normal person would do. She pretended to drop her phone so she had to stop and pick it up.

"Oops," she called as soon as her phone hit the ground, hoping her new screen protector did its job. "Y'all go ahead. I'll catch up." She climbed off her bike, grabbed her phone, and then rested there for a second. When she had caught her breath, she decided to walk her bike for a few minutes. Just until she felt her energy meter rise again.

When she finally reached the bike rack where her sisters were, quite a bit after they had gotten there, she gave them her cheeriest smile to distract them from how out of breath she was. Or how late she was. "Hot dogs on the pier might be my favorite item on the bucket list."

"So far every item has been your favorite," Cora said as she studied her. "Are you okay, Van? You look pale."

Bianca waved off the question before Savannah could answer it. "She always looks pale now. It's her new we-have-to-stay-out-of-the-sun-to-protect-our-skin routine, along with the SPF 1,000 she wears. I'm surprised she hasn't made you start wearing it."

It wasn't exactly true, but since Savannah wasn't ready to tackle the other topic, she played along. "Can you blame me for wanting to protect my sisters from wrinkles?"

Although neither of her sisters heard her because they were both distracted by the scene in front of them.

"I know my memory is fuzzy, but the pier didn't look like this, did it?" Bianca asked, walking from the bike racks to the activity around the pier.

"No, this is different," Cora agreed.

Savannah sat back against the bike rack and surveyed the scene.

Back in the day, the long fishing pier that stretched out over the water was a fun place to hang out, but it was never very crowded. There were always a few street performers who seemed to rotate regularly and small vendors selling things like balloon animals or cotton candy. The only food stand was The Original Hotdog Guy, who made fresh kettle chips that, to this day, were one of the best things Savannah had ever eaten.

But the scene in front of them was totally different, starting with the giant "Weekend at the Pier" banner that flew over the entrance. It was packed, both with people and pop-up shops under canopy tents selling everything from local art to fancy lemonades.

The food selection had expanded, too. Savannah could see several permanent food stands that lined the pier, along with some food trucks on the highway that seemed to show up just for the occasion.

"Wow. I knew it had gotten bigger, but I had no idea it looked like this."

"Good thing we brought the bikes. No way would we have found a parking spot," Cora added.

The comment made Savannah feel a little more justified about the call, even if her heart was pumping faster than her doctor would've said was allowable. With cars stretching down both shoulders of the highway for as long as she could see, they would've had to walk almost as far as they had ridden.

See, she wasn't being vain. She was being responsible.

Bianca headed for the stand not far from where they were standing. "I don't know about y'all, but I'm starting with one of those sparkling unicorn lemonades."

Savannah followed, squinting at the poster of the turquoise and pink drink that had multicolored ice cubes. "What's in it? That cannot be natural."

"Don't know, don't care. It looks delicious," Bianca said.

There was glitter floating in the drink. Actual silver sparkles. "That's a no for me," Savannah said. "I don't like glitter in my house. I am definitely not about to put it in my drink." Not to mention that it couldn't be good for you, no matter what kind of "edible" material it was made from. "I gotta go with something else. Like maybe the peach basil lemonade. What about you, Cora?"

When Cora didn't answer, Savannah twisted around to ask her again. Only, Cora wasn't standing where she thought she'd be. In fact, Savannah didn't see her anywhere in the area.

"Where'd Cora go?" she asked Bianca.

Bianca seemed unconcerned. "There's no telling. Keeping up with Cora is a lost cause."

"But you don't think she got lost, do you? She knew where we were going, right?" Savannah kept scanning the area.

"Cora lost? No way." Bianca laughed. "She does her own thing. She'll be here when she wants to be."

"But we were doing this together."

"I don't think that's how Cora operates. But she'll turn up. She always does."

It was more of a statement than a critique, which gave Savannah pause. Perhaps there was something to Bianca's wisdom she needed to consider.

Although now wasn't exactly the time. With the exercise and trying to find Cora, Savannah's brain didn't have extra capacity at the moment.

Later. She'd think through that later.

After they'd ordered and gotten their drinks, Cora still hadn't reappeared. Savannah tried to appear chill as she and Bianca browsed the booths, but she couldn't stop searching for her sister.

They had browsed a few booths and Savannah had shifted her search to the end of the pier when she heard the familiar voice.

"What are we looking at?" Cora's relaxed tone sounded as if she'd been standing next to them the whole time.

"Macramé for my new condo as a married woman." Bianca picked up the wall hanging to display it.

"Where did you go?" Savannah asked. She knew it sounded a little like a reprimanding mother, but she couldn't help it. It was her nature. She'd been a mini mom ever since she'd been given a sister only twenty-two months into life on this planet.

"What do you mean? I've been here the whole time." She took a bite of the snow cone that proved she had not, in fact, been with them the whole time. Where was there even a snow cone stand?

But if Cora heard the annoyance in Savannah's question, she didn't comment on it. "Does Zander like stuff like that?" She motioned with her snow cone to the item in question.

Bianca stared at the macramé wall hanging and then at Cora. "Doesn't everyone?"

Cora shifted her gaze to Savannah. "Do you have anything like that in your house?"

Savannah wanted to circle back to the conversation about where Cora had just been. Ditching them was a big deal. They were supposed to be spending time together. Plus, she'd been worried.

Okay, she really was turning into their mother.

"Not in my house, no. It doesn't really match my style."

"See. Savannah doesn't like macramé."

"That's not what I said," Savannah tried to argue, but even as she said it, she could tell she wasn't really involved in this conversation.

"So? Savannah isn't everyone."

"Is Zander?"

Bianca huffed and returned the wall hanging to the rack. "You are exhausting."

"Because I'm right."

Honestly, Savannah thought they were both exhausting. But before she got the chance to weigh in on the macramé discussion, they were interrupted.

"Hey! I wondered if we'd see you here," Luke the landlord said.

Bianca picked up the wall hanging again. "Would you hang this in your house?"

He looked like he realized he'd just walked into a trap, but he wasn't sure what the trap was. "Maybe?"

"I like it!" the little girl next to him said with all the enthusiasm. "I like the ones with the plants in them, too." She pointed at a similar wall hanging that housed a plant.

Bianca beamed at the little girl. "Me, too." Then she turned to Cora with a smug look.

"One out of the four people here back you. Odds aren't really in your favor, babe." Cora took a self-righteous bite of her snow cone.

Savannah couldn't help the hint of a chuckle. Cora had always been impossible to argue with. And since Savannah didn't have any skin in this fight, she didn't mind watching.

Bianca, on the other hand, just huffed and glared.

Savannah shifted her attention to their landlord. "It's nice to see you again, Luke."

"You, too. The toilet's working fine, I assume?"

"No issues. Thanks."

Bianca turned to Luke with rapt attention. "So, I'm dying to know. How did it turn out?"

From the way Bianca was lit up, they weren't talking about toilet repair. Since the only other thing Savannah knew Luke had been involved in was trivia night—and they already knew the outcome of that—Savannah had no idea what was going on here.

"She said yes!" The little girl pumped both fists in the air in celebration. If there had been confetti cannons, they would've gone off.

Luke nodded in agreement, looking very proud. "And even better than that, they were both more than impressed with the setup."

"Really?" Both of Bianca's hands covered her mouth, and she let out an excited squeal.

What was happening here?

Luke nodded. "He said it was even better than he'd imagined, and she can't stop sharing the pictures with everyone they know. Which is all because of you."

Bianca gave a humble shrug. "It was a team effort."

"What did you do?" Cora asked.

"Remember yesterday when I said I had to help Luke? We were setting up a proposal for one of his renters."

"It was the most amazing thing ever. You should've seen it," the little girl said.

Luke nodded. "So amazing, in fact, that I just got two more requests this morning from people who saw it and want a romantic dinner like that for themselves. One is for tonight. An anniversary dinner." He turned to Bianca. "Any chance you're available to help me set it up? I'll pay you for your time." He pulled up something on his phone and spun it around so she could see it.

Bianca studied it for a minute, her expressive face filtering through a wide array of emotions. "Wow . . . Huh . . . Okay . . . Yeah, I think we can do that." She glanced at her watch and looked surprised. "Yikes, but we should probably get started."

"Sylvie and I were about to head that direction. Do you want to ride with us?"

"Sure. I mean, I have my bike here, but I can come back for it later."

Luke waved the thought away. "No problem. We can throw it in the back of the truck."

"Yay!" cheered the little girl. "More frozen lattes!"

Bianca swung her gaze over to Savannah. "I guess I'll see y'all back at the house, then."

Before Savannah even knew what was happening, the trio swept out of the tent and disappeared into the crowd on the pier.

Savannah stared in their general direction, stunned. "What just happened?"

"I know. She didn't even stay for a hot dog." Cora shook her head as if that were the biggest shock of the whole ordeal. She meandered over to the next booth to check out the jewelry made of local seashells.

Savannah followed, still trying to make sense of Bianca's absence. "Is she working for Luke?"

Cora shrugged. "That's what it sounded like."

"Does that seem weird to you?"

"The girl just quit her job, which was at least her second one this year, because she wants to move across the country and marry a man she's never met. A man, I might add, who has a striking resemblance to Captain Underpants if Captain Underpants grew up and did semi-legal steroids." She took a bite of her snow cone. "At the moment, most of her decisions seem odd to me."

"Fair."

"So, are we getting hot dogs or what?" Cora asked.

"Please," Savannah responded.

After weaving through the crowds and finding the original hot dog stand—still called The Original—they put in their order for hot dogs and chips and found a spot at a picnic table under a tent.

"Is it possible to taste memories?" Cora asked after her first bite.

"I was just thinking the very same thing." To Savannah even the smells were familiar. It all took her back to being a kid. Back to when things were . . . less complicated.

"Remember that time we saw the dolphins jumping off the pier?" Cora asked.

"Of course. Before we saw that I had no idea dolphins flipped like that in the wild."

"Me, either." A grin tugged at Cora's lips, and she glanced around looking the most nostalgic Savannah had ever seen her. "I used to love it here."

"Me, too." Savannah closed her eyes and drew in a deep, cleansing breath and savored the moment. This was why they were here, so that they could remember. And if they could remember, maybe they could find their way back.

"Oh, wow, look at the time. I didn't realize it was that late."

Her sister's hurried tone made Savannah's eyes pop open. Cora shoved the last bite of hot dog into her mouth, then pushed what was left of her salt and vinegar kettle chips toward Savannah. "Do you want the rest of these? I have to run."

"Run?" Savannah glanced around as if she was reorienting after a long nap. Weren't they in the middle of sharing a moment? "I thought we were eating hot dogs on the pier."

"We did." Cora pointed to her empty basket as proof. "And now I have to go."

"Where?" They were on vacation, weren't they? Why was everyone rushing off?

"To stop Bianca from marrying the gym rat." Without any more of an explanation, she stood and started down the pier toward the sidewalk.

"Huh," Savannah said out loud to no one in particular, since she was now sitting at a table by herself. She munched on chips while she watched vacationers wander from booth to booth with their friends and family. Once again here she sat, finishing a bucket list item all on her own. She wasn't quite sure how this kept happening.

On the bright side, at least she could ride home as slowly as she needed without anyone questioning her about it.

But she would tell them. Of course she would.

As soon as the time felt right.

11

Cora

*D*ate number two.

The most authentic part of this date was how excited Cora was for it. She genuinely felt giddy, which was not something she usually felt. Generally, that kind of feeling was reserved for when she captured the most incredible photos or won a tournament.

But to be fair, tonight kind of was like winning, because she had the most perfect plan to tank her date.

Wait, no, that wasn't right. She wasn't *tanking* the date. That sounded a whole lot like sabotaging, which was against the rules. She was simply planning to use real-life situations to prove that when the going got tough, Prince Charming was going to take off.

Were the situations she was planning slightly exaggerated? Maybe. But since they were in a little bit of a time crunch, concessions had to be made. It was only reasonable.

Did she feel bad using Jax as a pawn? Absolutely not. Word on the street confirmed he had the reputation of being quite the heartbreaker, so he clearly deserved whatever he had coming his way.

Her biggest regret was that she wouldn't be the one doing the dumping. She thought the man could stand being on the receiving end of a breakup. It might knock him down a peg. But since she was about to spend her day knocking him down a peg, having him doing the dumping wouldn't be a total loss.

Her plan was simple, really. She'd start off being totally self-consumed. She'd be late, make him wait, and put work ahead of him.

Then, she'd flex on the pickleball court.

She'd been playing in a league for months to get a little exercise, a detail she hadn't bothered to tell him when he invited her on the date. And she was good, something she rarely apologized for. She felt fairly confident she could beat him, and serving up a loss would no doubt bruise his ego.

Then, if all of that didn't rattle him, she'd serve up a little family drama, too.

Let the games begin.

She pulled up to the pickleball courts fifteen minutes late, which was a lot harder to do than she'd thought it would be. She'd had to drive around the block twice to kill some extra time. Where was all the traffic when she needed it?

Still, she could see him waiting on the court when she pulled up, so the first part of her goal was accomplished. For part two, she needed her assistant.

Janna, who was not only her assistant but also a friend, picked up on the first ring.

"Why are you calling me? I thought we agreed that I'd handle things here, and you would take a much-needed break to spend time with your sisters."

"This isn't about work. It's actually a vacation thing . . ." Kind of, anyway. "But while I have you on the phone, how's that problem with the Lolly and Vine account?"

"Not that we're talking about it because you're on vacation and this isn't your prearranged weekly check-in meeting, but you were right. I made that one little change you suggested, and they were back to singing your praises." Janna's sparkly voice sang out. "Now, what's your vacation thing?"

"It's a long story. Just act like we have a major problem and go with whatever I say." She stepped out of her car and made her way over to the courts where Jax was waiting.

"For the record, I like long stories," Janna said.

Cora ignored her. There would be plenty of time to explain later, when her goal had already been accomplished.

As she neared the courts, Cora started her plan. "Seriously? Right now? He needs it right now?" She let out her best annoyed huff and checked her watch.

"Oh, is this the part where I tap into my junior high acting classes?" Janna cleared her throat and continued in a deadpan voice. "Oh no. It's a crisis. Please help."

Cora kept most of her focus on Jax. She met his gaze from across the court and held up her brand-new pickleball paddle in a wave.

He returned the gesture, and his charming smolder-grin spread across his face. He really was very attractive, which she found equally delightful and annoying.

She motioned at her phone to show him she was in the middle of a very important—even if it was very fake—conversation. "Do you have the original files from the last shoot? I can probably use one of those and edit it to make it work."

"The files. Oh no. Where are the files?" Cora could almost see Janna rolling her eyes as she spoke in her robotic voice.

"You know what, I have my laptop here. I can pull it up and make the change." She held up a finger to signal to Jax that she needed a moment to deal with this very important crisis.

"You saved the day. Woo-hoo. I am so happy."

"Not yet. But I will. Give me five minutes, and I'll give you an update."

"I'll be on pins and needles until you do," Janna said. "Oh, and Cora? Go enjoy a margarita on the beach like a normal person on vacation."

"I'll take that into consideration." She kept her gaze focused on Jax as she said it. Then she hung up and tucked her phone into the pocket of her brand-new tennis skirt. "Sorry about that."

"Let me guess. Work crisis?"

"It's always something." She gave a *What-do-you-do?* shrug just to sell it. "Anyway, I hate to do this, but I need a few minutes to handle something. You don't mind, do you?"

"Not at all. Take your time. I'll just be over here working on my dink shot." He shot her a flirtatious grin that, she had to admit, was pretty alluring. He certainly had the charming act down.

She walked back to her car and pulled out her laptop bag. After powering up her computer, she checked her email, added a couple things to her calendar, and looked up the status on the suitcase. For the record, the suitcase was now reportedly in Tulsa, Oklahoma, which she supposed was closer than Maine. But since it wasn't here and the estimated delivery date had been pushed back again, she pulled up Amazon and ordered a few more things to hold her over. She probably could use her own moisturizer instead of using up all of her sisters'.

After she checked out, she called Janna back. "Okay, thanks for your help," she said as soon as Janna picked up.

"Anytime. It's what I'm here for. But this better have a great story."

"Don't worry, it will. Now if you'll excuse me, I have to go beat the pants off my date on the pickleball court."

"There's so much in that sentence we need to unpack."

After Cora hung up, she tucked her laptop back into her bag and rejoined Jax on the court. "Sorry about that. Couldn't be helped."

Jax walked toward her, his eyes sparkling. "It never can be." He held up a pickleball. "You ready to take out some of that work aggression?"

"I think the better question is: Are *you* ready for that?" She met his gaze with a playful challenging one of her own.

"Competitive. I like that."

Yeah, she'd see about that. In her experience men—even ones who claimed they weren't competitive—rarely liked to be beat by a woman. Which was exactly what she planned on doing.

He headed to the other side of the court, and she took up her position.

"Do you want to warm up first?" he asked.

She shook her head. "I've kept you waiting long enough. We can just jump right in."

"You sure?"

She gave a decisive nod. Plus, she'd warmed up on her own before she got here, a little detail she kept to herself.

"In that case, ladies first." He tossed her the ball.

She caught it and waited for him to get in position before she served. As she waited, a couple of ladies who were walking in the park paused where the path passed by the fence and waved. Jax did his whole charmer thing with a nod and a mini wave.

Then the ladies turned to Cora with more serious, wide-eyed expressions. *"Run. Run now,"* one of the ladies mouthed. The other nodded her head in agreement, giving a discreet point toward the exit before the path curved and led them away from the courts.

Cora nodded her head in their direction. "More friends of yours?"

"I might've been the one in green's date to the one in blue's wedding." He shrugged as if it were a minor detail.

She gave a *you're-ridiculous* shake of her head. Then, she held up the ball, signaling that she was going to serve. "Zero-zero."

When she served, he hit the ball back and she returned it, setting him up for an easy dink. Giving him an easy first win as a mini ego stroke was all part of her plan.

He ran to the net and tried to tap the ball over, but his angle was off and the ball didn't have enough height to make it over the net. It rolled down the net and landed at his feet.

"Guess I didn't give you enough time to work on that shot after all." Maybe this win was going to be easier than she'd thought.

"Just wanted to make sure you got on the scoreboard." He scooped up the ball and tossed it back to her.

"How sweet." She held his gaze. "One-zero."

She served again, putting a little more spin on it this time, just to give him a taste of what she was capable of. And after she won that point, she served again. In fact, she picked up the next four points before he hit a shot into the far corner with so much heat, there was no way she could get to it without superhero powers.

He flashed a playful smile. "Oops. Did that one get away from you?"

She shrugged and pulled another ball from her pocket and tossed it to him. "Can't win 'em all."

"My opponents tend to say that a lot." His gaze met hers with the kind of look that gave her a fluttery feeling, which was annoying. So he had nice eyes. Big deal. It didn't mean she was going to fall for him.

She returned her focus to the game, getting in her ready position. "Do you play a lot of pickleball in that dangerous job of yours?"

"Someone has been doing their homework on me." He served the ball.

His serve was fast and the ball had some impressive spin on it, but she didn't have any problem returning it.

"It's a small town. People talk," she said, sailing the ball back over the net. Then she ran forward, ready to stop whatever he sent back her way. There was no way she was going to let him have two victories in a row.

"That's what they tell me." He hit the ball back. She had to jump to slam it back down on him, but she did. He stood and watched it fly by without any hope of returning it. "Nice shot."

It was her turn to grin. "Thanks."

"I'm going to have to step up my game."

"Don't hurt yourself." She winked. Giving him a hard time shouldn't be this fun. She was almost going to miss it when they were through.

The thought made her pause. Of course she wasn't going to miss it. The whole point of this dating exercise was to prove that she *didn't* need anyone. She shook off that train of thought and grabbed two more balls from the basket next to the net, one for her pocket and one to serve.

She took up her position at the serving line, and Jax got ready to receive.

"What fun facts about me did you pick up from the rumor mill?"

She served. "That you might be an art thief."

He laughed and sent the ball to the opposite side of the court from where she was. She had to dive to reach it, but her stroke sent the ball well out of bounds. Not one of her finer moves.

"And what do you think?" he asked.

"I think that was a lucky shot, and if I hadn't been flat-footed I wouldn't have missed it."

He gave a thoughtful nod. "Fair evaluation. But I meant about the art thief thing." He held the ball up to ask if she was ready for the serve.

She nodded. Once again, the ball came flying over the net with an impressive spin. If she weren't trying to get this guy to ditch her, he would make a great doubles partner.

She returned the ball to him. "Seems like an interesting . . ." She barely got the words out before she had to sprint across the court to make the play. "Profession," she finished.

"Most of the time," he answered as he returned the ball. They went back and forth three more times before he finally slammed a shot to the back corner out of her reach.

Even she had to admit when she had been outplayed. This guy was good. "Nice shot." She paused to wipe away the sweat beading on her forehead. "Clearly art thieves have plenty of time to play pickleball."

He shrugged. "There's a lot of downtime."

"Naturally."

He got ready to serve again. "One-four."

She was determined to stop it here. No way was she going to let him run up the score. She returned the ball with such perfect placement, there was no way he could get to it.

"Wow, that one was waspish," he said, clearly impressed.

She gave him a smirk. "Be careful of my sting."

"Apparently there's a lot of time for pickleball in the world of photography, too." He spun the paddle in his hand as he waited for her serve.

She grabbed another ball and took her spot. "Some, I suppose." She bounced the ball in front of her a few times to get ready for the serve while he wiped his face and resumed his position.

She served and got a quick point, then got ready to serve again. "What kind of photography? Wedding?"

"No. Too many emotions. Five-one." She served.

"Family portraits?" he asked as soon as he sent it back.

"No. Too much. Talking." The words seemed to come out punctuated between breaths as she scrambled to return the ball. Although she was too slow and Jax was ready for her at the net. As soon as her lob got to him, he slammed it back down, winning the ball back.

"I know. Don't you hate it when people talk too much?"

She wiped her forehead on the back of her arm. "Probably not a problem in the art thief world."

"Not when we're getting the job done, anyway. One-five."

He served and got the next two points before she won the ball back. She grabbed a ball and slowly made her way back to the serving line, giving herself plenty of time to catch her breath. If neither of them could score more than one or two points before losing the serve—if they scored at all—this had the potential to be a very long game.

"Back to your photography," he said as he lined up on his side of the court. "What kind?"

Break time over.

"Commercial." She served. "On the marketing side."

He focused on returning the ball before he spoke again. "Like those beauty shots of food that make things look too good to be true?"

"Beauty shots, yes." She sent the shot back over. "Food, no. Too fussy. It's always melting and drooping."

"You have a lot of opinions," he said as he sent the ball in her direction. As anticipated, she was able to hit it down at the net. It bounced twice on his side, then rolled to his feet.

She beamed, more than a little satisfied with the shot. "I just know what I like."

He picked up the ball and held it up with an impressed nod. "I respect that." He tossed it to her.

But would he really? She took the ball back to the serving line.

"And you own your own business?" he asked.

"Of course. I'm not really a 'work for the man' kind of person. Although you of all people should understand that." It was a bit of a taunt because if he weren't actually an art thief, what did he do? And seriously, there was no way she was playing pickleball with an international criminal . . .

Was there?

"Don't kid yourself, I very much work for the man. Although to be fair, I have just as many women bosses as men bosses, so I think it's more accurate to say I 'work for the human.'"

"Interesting. So you don't get to decide what you take?"

"Oh, I can decide if I take it or not. Just what's up for grabs is not always up to me."

"I hate when that happens."

"You have no idea."

Okay, now he was starting to make her nervous.

She served, trying to focus on the task at hand. Besides, who cared what he did? She was just here for the breakup.

"But I have big aspirations to be the man." He returned the ball with perfect precision. "And then I'll be the one calling the shots."

She sent the ball back over the net. "Is that what they call the kingpin?"

"Something like that." He grinned, which momentarily distracted her. He returned the ball to the far side of the court where she had zero chance of being able to get to it. And since it was hot and she was already out of breath, she didn't even budge in that direction.

Dang him and his annoyingly attractive grin.

"And what would be your first move as kingpin?" she asked, trying to push his handsome features out of her mind.

He shook his head. "Nope. Not going there until it happens. I don't want to jinx it."

"Fair enough. In that case, how about we play some pickleball." She wiped her forehead on her arm again and dropped into the ready position.

"Now you're speaking my language." He winked. "Four-six."

They finished out the game with less talking. It was close, but in the end, she won with a score of eleven to eight.

She walked to the net with her paddle extended. "Good game."

He joined her and tapped his paddle against hers. "You, Cora Prestly, are impressive."

"You sound surprised."

"Pleasantly." He stared at her for a second with a look she couldn't quite interpret. "Best two out of three?"

"Sure. But we're not going to need three."

He chuckled. "We'll see about that. But first, what would you say to a hydration break?"

"I'd say yes please, because I'm convinced the surface of the sun is not as hot as this court."

"I think you're right." He waved her over to the benches, where he pulled two ice-cold bottles of water from a cooler and handed one to her.

At the exact time she took her first sip, her phone buzzed in her pocket, right on cue. She pulled it out and checked to see who it was, as if she didn't already know. "Sorry, I have to take this. Sister drama. Our group text was blowing up while we were playing." She held up the phone and nodded to the other side of the court. "You don't mind, do you?"

"Not at all. It'll give me time to revisit my strategy." He swiped the icy bottle across his forehead. Once again, she momentarily found herself distracted by the muscles in his toned arms. The dark stubble on his chiseled jawline. The way his blue eyes seemed to dance every time he looked at her.

No.

No, no, no, no, no.

She was *not* attracted to this man.

She was here to destroy him on the pickleball court and to prove a point to her sisters. Just because he happened to have above-average looks and she found him intriguing didn't change her mission.

"In that case, I won't ask for the abridged version. That'll give you a little extra time to level the playing field." She winked to add a little sass and walked off, answering the planned call from her assistant on the way.

Beat him on the pickleball court, annoy him with all her personal drama, get him to break up with her. All she had to do was stick to the plan.

12

Jax

 ax sat in the middle of the court and waited while Cora paced back and forth at the far end. Her phone was pressed up to her ear, and her paddle waved dramatically as she dealt with yet another unavoidable work problem. Or was it another sister problem? He'd lost track since it was her third call during this specific game. And that wasn't counting all the other calls she'd taken since she'd been here. Either it was a really stressful day, or she was the most important person on the planet.

Or option three—which was far more likely—she *thought* she was the most important person on the planet.

But his job was to try to win her over, so he'd sit and wait. For as long as it took. No matter how many phone calls came in.

Although he wasn't above trying to figure out a way to disconnect her phone. Maybe losing signal for a while wouldn't be the worst thing.

Speaking of losing, revisiting his current game strategy might be a good idea. It had been a while since he was this far behind on the scoreboard. And he had to admit, seeing the game slanted in that direction didn't sit well with him.

Not that he minded losing. It wasn't like he was the kind of guy who had to win at all costs. Since it was fairly obvious that winning was important to her, he'd been willing to let her take home the *W*. After all, his ultimate goal wasn't to prove which one of them was better at pickleball. It was to prove to his uncle that he could be committed. If being committed meant letting Cora win, then that's what he'd do.

He wasn't going to throw the game, per se, because where was the fun in that? But he had decided to not play at one hundred percent. He'd just knock the ball around, have fun, and see what happened.

But what had happened was she was destroying him.

About halfway through the first game, he'd switched up his strategy. Letting her win was one thing. Being humiliated was something else entirely. Clearly he was going to have to up his game if he wanted to narrow the split.

When he came out at the start of the second game, he'd thrown out his strategy altogether. Best two out of three meant that he could at least win one.

But here he was, on the losing side of a six-ten score, and already dreaming about the rematch.

Of course, that would be dependent on her getting off her phone.

As if she'd heard his thoughts, she stopped pacing and stared at her phone. After typing for a few seconds, she slipped the phone back in her pocket and headed his direction.

"Sorry about that. Work."

He pushed himself up to standing. "Busy day, huh?"

She seemed confused by the question. "No. This is pretty standard."

Yep. He'd called it. Self-important. "A lot of emergencies in the commercial photography business?"

"A lot of *business* in the commercial photography business." She stepped into the zone to receive the serve. "But on the upside, I'm on vacation so it's a lot lighter than normal."

It took all his effort not to roll his eyes. Compliment. Charm. Woo. That was his plan, and he was sticking to it.

But he was starting to wonder if she was the right person for this project. Yes, she met all the important criteria. She was only in town for a limited time. She had no other ties to him or the town, which would yield a clean break when things ended eventually. She was looking for a serious relationship (or at least that's what she claimed). But no matter how hard he tried, he seemed to be having a difficult time winning her over, which was new territory for him. She was maybe the most independent woman he'd ever dated, which wasn't necessarily a bad thing. In fact, he found her independence quite attractive, but it was making the whole wooing thing harder than he'd expected.

"Shall we resume?" he asked, already backing up to the serving line.

She took up her spot to receive, bouncing on the balls of her feet as if she were ready to pounce. "We just need two more serves. One for me to get the ball back. And one to finish the game."

"I like your confidence. Misguided, but admirable."

"We'll see." She winked, which was all the motivation he needed to win the next point. He sent his serve flying over the net with enough speed to break the sound barrier and the kind of spin that guaranteed that even if she hit the ball, there was no way it would stay inbounds.

Which is exactly what happened. She managed to hit the ball, but it traveled in a wonky direction toward the other side of the court.

"Maybe three serves." He couldn't help the cocky smile. Yes, he was trying to compliment, charm and woo, but he had to be true to himself, too.

The comment didn't seem to faze her. "Just giving you a little extra court time."

"Aw, how thoughtful." He spun the paddle in his hand and backed up to the serving line. "But don't worry about me. I can take care of myself."

"We'll see." She flashed a sassy smirk and resumed her ready position.

He served again, although this time she was ready for it. Her return shot was perfect, and they volleyed back and forth. There was no banter this time, no casual conversation as they concentrated on playing the game, hitting hard shot after hard shot.

She was good. Impressively good, actually. He wondered if she'd played tennis on some sort of competitive level. Getting beat on the pickleball court by a semi-pro athlete made a lot more sense.

Because getting beat, he was. He had to scramble to return a well-placed shot, which ended up being more of a lob. It was the exact setup she needed to barely tap the ball over the net on the opposite side of the court from where he was.

The distance between him and the ball might as well have been a mile. He watched the ball bounce once, twice, and roll the rest of the way across the court.

He gave her an impressed nod, and he propped his hands on his hips to catch his breath. She returned the gesture with a slight not-so-humble bow.

Yes, he'd said she was intriguing after their first date, but he was starting to wonder if he'd gotten it wrong. Maybe the adjective he'd been looking for was *infuriating*.

She pulled a ball from her pocket and headed to the serving line. "Remind me of the score again," she said.

"Ten-seven."

"Oh, that's right," she said with a taunting grin. "Game point."

She was in the middle of her serve when he got distracted by a trio of people walking into the court area. Was that really . . . ?

He hadn't even finished the thought when he realized his fatal mistake. By the time he returned his attention to her serve, it was too late. The ball went flying right past him.

And he couldn't decide which was worse. That he'd lost both games back-to-back, that his date was going so poorly, or that Cora had to call in reinforcements . . . from her sister.

"Oh, hey! Look who it is."

The peppy voice of the trivia winner who'd set him up with Cora rang out across the court. Next to her was the guy who went to school with his cousin, with a little girl in tow.

Cora spun around. "What are you doing here?"

Bianca gave an innocent shrug. "We let Sylvie play while we were taking a break from setting up the private event. And then we saw you two." She clasped her hands together, looking delighted. "What a coincidence."

Cora, who seemed rather annoyed for someone who'd just won the game, waved her paddle in their general direction. "Jax, meet my sister Bianca and our friend Luke."

"I've already had the pleasure," he said. "At trivia night."

Bianca faked an epiphany. "That's right! So good to see you again. But you haven't met Sylvie yet. This is Luke's niece."

"Cool. Pickleball. Can I play?" the little girl asked.

Luke shifted uncomfortably. "I think they're in the middle of a game. We can't interrupt."

"Actually, we just finished. I won." There was nothing humble about Cora's brag. "I'll hit the ball with you, Sylvie. There's an extra paddle right over there." She pointed over to the bench where their stuff was.

"Thanks!" The girl ran over and grabbed the extra paddle and hustled onto the court. Luke took up a position next to the net, coaching her along.

Meanwhile, Jax took the chance to figure out how to get this date back on track. He'd never had a date go this poorly in his life. Maybe he was starting to lose his edge.

"So how bad is it? Is there any hope in saving it?" Jax asked quietly as he and Bianca pretended to watch the pickleball lesson from the sideline.

"What?" Bianca looked genuinely confused.

He gave a slight nod in Cora's direction. "She's been texting with you the entire time. It doesn't take a rocket scientist to figure out you're here to rescue her from the date. Is this some sort of sister code?"

Bianca studied him for a second, and then her expression melted into one of enlightenment. "Ah. I see what's going on here." She closed her eyes and shook her head as if she couldn't believe it. After a long breath, she fluttered her eyes open.

"First of all, Cora never needs to be rescued. And don't think you're being, like, chivalrous or something, because it will end badly. If she wanted out of this date, she would've walked away on her own." She paused and thought for a second. "Or she would've taken you down. She's been equally known to do both."

"Wait. If you're not here to rescue her from the date, why are you here?"

Bianca shrugged. "Like I said. Coincidence."

A new realization dawned on him. "There hasn't been an incredibly active sister group text going on?"

Bianca shook her head.

"Huh." She'd made it up. Interesting. He wondered how many of the other phone calls were just for show. She didn't think *she* was important. She wanted *him* to think she was important.

The only question was: Why?

"The thing about Cora is that she's not great at letting people in. The closer you get, the more her walls go up."

Walls? What Cora had going on made the Great Wall of China look like a picket fence. "And you didn't think to tell me this earlier?"

"I thought you said you didn't need any help in the wooing department."

Fair enough.

"But behind the walls, she's a deeply caring person. She just needs you to help her push past them."

"Do you have any tips? For pushing past them?"

"Now that's the million-dollar question."

Or at least that's what he thought she mumbled under her breath.

"What?" he asked.

Her bright cheerleader smile returned. "Relationship advice isn't really my thing, but I'm sure by now you've discovered Cora loves everything about nature. And she has a soft spot for someone who can make her laugh." She raised her eyebrows, looking expectant.

"So I should take her hiking and tell her jokes?" There was plenty of skepticism in his voice. Cora was faking phone calls, and that was the best inside tip her sister could give him?

Bianca shrugged. "I'm sure you'll think of something perfect."

Things weren't looking good in that department. Not yet, anyway.

He watched Cora high-five the little girl after her serve made it over the net. She was really sweet with the kid. Kind and attentive and encouraging. This different side of her intrigued him. The same way her wit intrigued him. And her pickleball skills.

"Did she play tennis in college?"

"Who? Cora?" Bianca asked. "I don't think so. Why?"

He shook his head. "No reason."

Luke looked over at them. "Bianca, are you ready?"

"Sure." She grinned innocently at Jax. "We don't want to keep you from your date." Then she grabbed the bag she'd set on the bench and joined the trio on the court. "Just wanted to pop in and say hi," she said to Cora.

"Hi." Cora didn't look like she was overly amused by her sister's impromptu visit.

Sylvie handed the paddle to Cora. "Thank you for playing with me."

Cora softened when she looked at the little girl. "My pleasure. Have fun at the park." The trio left, and Cora joined him at the benches.

Jax took a cold water out of the cooler and handed it to her. "Your prize for a well-earned victory."

She uncapped it and kept her gaze glued to his. "And if I had lost?" There was a hint of a grin there.

"You would've gotten the same thing with a different tagline."

He wouldn't have classified her response as a laugh. It was more of an exhale with the thought of a chuckle, but he still took it as a positive sign.

Okay, today might have been a hiccup, but he had this. He was Jax Verona. He'd never met a human he couldn't turn into a friend. People loved him. And while he didn't like to brag, he was pretty good with the ladies.

"I know it's been a busy day for you, but if you have time, I'd love for you to stick around a little longer."

"What? Looking to go double or nothing?" She had a challenging glint in her eyes.

He chuckled. "No." Not today, anyway. "I have something I thought you might like to see. Do you like baby animals?"

She studied him, looking unconvinced. "Is this part of your charming Jax Verona act everyone keeps warning me about?"

He looked amused. "No. In fact, I've never taken anyone to see this."

"So why me?"

"It's right here. And you look like someone who might appreciate it."

She seemed to consider that for a second, then shrugged. "Well, now I'm curious."

"Okay, but you have to turn off your cell phone. There's a thing about noise."

She pulled her phone out and toggled it to silent mode. "Where exactly are you taking me?"

"You'll see." He started walking.

She hesitated for a second. "What about all our stuff?"

"It'll be fine here. We won't be gone long." When he got to the gate, he kept going, not bothering to wait for her.

She caught up to him, and they walked to the far side of the park where the marina was located. Then they walked to the farthest side of the marina and headed where the last boat was docked next to the mangroves. He waited for her where they could easily step from the dock onto the deck of a sportfishing yacht.

He motioned to the boat. "Ladies first."

She gave him a quizzical look. "Is this your boat?"

"Nope."

"Do we have permission to be on this boat?"

"Depends on your definition of 'permission.'"

"How about the one that ends in us not getting arrested for breaking and entering?" She paused and stared at the boat. "Or whatever it is you get charged with when you go on someone else's boat."

"Now, where would the adventure be in that?" Without waiting for her, he stepped onto the boat.

This particular boat had a tower that went up three levels. On the second level was the main cockpit and could be accessed by a short set of steps.

But the third level, which was about twenty more feet up in the air, could only be accessed by a narrow ladder. It was more of an observation deck, used for spotting big fish, and had limited controls. Frankly, it wasn't used all that often, and there wasn't a whole lot of space up there, but there was enough room for the two of them. Especially for what they were going to see.

He started climbing hand over hand up the ladder without looking back to see if she would follow, because he knew she would. She didn't seem to be the type to turn down a challenge.

When he got to the top, he stepped on the platform and turned to check on her progress.

"Are we lifting the boat?" she asked as she climbed up the last few rungs.

"Are we doing what?" He offered his hand to help her onto the deck, but she ignored it. On her own, she climbed onto the small deck and took up her spot next to him.

"I don't know the correct term for this kind of thing. Nick? Pinch? Thieve? Or do y'all use something else nowadays?"

He eyed her. "Nowadays? What, are you sixty?"

She laughed. It was one of her authentic laughs that bubbled from her naturally, not from whatever facade she was trying to keep up. It was the kind of laugh that intrigued him.

"Let me try that again in layman's terms," she said. "Are we here to steal this boat?"

It was his turn to laugh. "No. We're here to see that." He pointed to her right, where the busy beach town faded into a swampy natural forest.

She squinted in the direction he was pointing. "And what exactly are we looking at?"

"There," he said again. He stepped close to her, leaving just a hint of space between them. With his body close to one side of her and his arm on the other, he pointed again.

Yes, it was a measured move. After all, this wasn't his first go at the dating game. But he wasn't ready for the way being close to her made him feel, almost like he was tipsy. He could feel her warmth and smell the flowery scent of her shampoo. There was something about her that drew him in, taking up all of his focus. When he was close to her, everything else seemed to fade away, and the air between them seemed to crackle.

He took half a step back. Maybe a little space was a good thing.

"Just at the top of the tree line, you'll see a nest on top of a platform," he said. "It's a sort of fake tree to give the ospreys a place to nest."

It took her a second, but then she brightened, "Oh, I see it!"

"Now look in the nest." He was quiet for a second, and as soon as the noise stopped, the sound he was waiting for filled the air. The sweet little chirps of the osprey chicks.

"There they are." Cora's hands flew over her mouth, seemingly captivated by the scene. "Aren't they precious."

Four little downy heads peeked up over the top of the nest. They were bigger now than when he'd last checked on them a week ago.

He dropped the arm that was around her and stepped next to her, draping his arms over the railing. "I like to call them Huey, Dewey, Louie and Frank."

She let out a little scoff that almost sounded like she was making fun of him, but her expression was soft. "Clever."

"I try."

"Are they ospreys?"

He nodded. "By my calculations, they're about six weeks old."

She shot him a suspicious side-eye. "I thought you were afraid of birds."

"Not baby birds. Who can be afraid of a baby?"

She seemed to consider that for a second, then gave a shrug of agreement.

"Plus, ospreys fascinate me. Did you know they mate for life?"

"I did not know that."

"Yeah, and you can tell how committed the couple is by the level of gifts the male brings to the female." He pointed again toward the nest. "This female seems to like the color blue, so notice how much blue material her hubby has brought to pad their nest."

"I had no idea. So fairy tales do come true." Cora studied the nest, captivated.

Jax, on the other hand, was captivated by her.

Cora was somewhat of a paradox. She was tough and determined but could be soft and caring. She seemed like the kind of person who didn't take anything from anybody, but he also got the impression she would walk to the ends of the earth for those she loved. The more he got to know her, the more he wanted to know about her.

That thought scared him a little. Because unlike osprey, he didn't do forever. He had only signed up for a summer romance, which meant he needed to solve the mystery of Cora Prestly by the end of the season.

She propped her chin on her hand, staring dreamily at the baby birds. "I wish I had my camera."

"We can come back," he said. "It's especially breathtaking at sunset."

She turned to him, eyebrows raised. "So we're not here to steal the boat?"

He chuckled. "No, we are not here to steal the boat."

She seemed to consider that for a second, then straightened and studied him with an intense gaze. "Jax Verona, do you steal things of great value? Like, say, art?"

"You don't beat around the bush, do you?"

She shrugged. "Like I said before, I know what I want, and I'm not afraid to go after it."

Yep, she was intriguing, all right.

"I do not steal things." He paused and thought about that for a second. "I mean, this one time when I was seven, I stole a can of Play-Doh from the grocery store, but my mom made me take it back and pay for it. Plus I had to write an apology note and hand-deliver it to the manager. Trust me, stealing is not worth it."

"Play-Doh?" She laughed, the legit kind again.

"It was neon orange. Do you know how many cool things you can make with neon-orange Play-Doh?"

"Mini traffic cones?"

"Um, yeah." He gave her a look like *obviously*. "The creativity options are endless. I might've been the next Michelangelo if I'd had neon-orange Play-Doh to work with. But as I previously stated, I didn't get to keep it." He sighed and let his shoulders droop under the weight of his disappointment. "Stealing is bad."

Cora laughed. "So that's a no to being an art thief?"

"I am not an international art thief."

"So then what do you do? And don't give me that nonsense about not being able to talk about it."

"I am a security logistics consultant."

Her eyes narrowed, and she looked skeptical. "I'm going to say this with the upmost respect. What the heck is that?"

He chuckled. "It's . . . complicated."

"Try me."

"The short answer is I work in the private security industry."

"And the long answer?"

"It's a long story."

She leaned back against the railing and crossed her arms as if she were getting comfortable. "I've got time."

Yeah, but did he want to tell her? It wasn't a story he usually shared with people. "A buddy from my Army days has been going through a tough time, and I've been helping him out." The words even surprised him. Apparently, he was doing this.

"You were in the Army?"

He nodded. "Four years after I graduated from high school. Army Ranger."

"You didn't mention the Army on your bio sheet."

He shrugged. "I wasn't hiding anything. It just didn't feel relevant at the time. Similar to the way I know you went to college, but you never said where."

"Rice University. For both undergrad and master's." She tilted her head as she studied him. "But this isn't about me. It's about being a security logistics consultant."

A grin tugged on the corner of his mouth. He liked her. She was tenacious. "It's a fancy name for 'bodyguard and transport team.' We specialize in moving people and objects that need increased protection during the trip."

"And what does that have to do with your Army buddy?"

He paused for a second, since he normally didn't get into this part of the story. In fact, he could count on two fingers how many people he'd told and both of them were related to him.

But for some reason he couldn't quite explain, he *wanted* to tell her. He wanted to share things with her. "He started the private security firm right after we got out of the Army. It became a pretty successful business. But he'd been struggling with some mental health problems that eventually took over. His marriage started falling apart, and his business was taking a hit. He needed help. That's where I came in."

"You went to work for him."

"Not at first. Not exactly." He tried to sort through all the complicated pieces that had made up his life for the past five years. "I started off just filling in on assignments he needed to bail on. Sometimes those calls would be last-minute. But it didn't matter how much warning I got. If he called, I'd go."

"Which is why you have the reputation for leaving town suddenly."

He nodded. "But as things got worse, the calls got more frequent, and it was more than just filling in on a job. He was having trouble running things. Recruiting. Setting up the jobs. Plus, I couldn't keep up with my responsibilities here when I was always flying off at the last minute." He shrugged. "I quit my position with my family's company and have been working full time with him for the last three years. Sometimes from here. Sometimes from his office in Chicago. Sometimes on jobs."

"Why didn't you just tell people that's what you were doing? Why all the secrecy?"

"Private security is a funny business. It runs on reputation. If it got out that he needed help because he couldn't handle it on his own, his company would've tanked. I couldn't exactly say *why* I was going. And the clients value their privacy, so I couldn't talk about *where* I was going. I wasn't trying to be secretive. There just wasn't a lot I could say."

"That explains the whole, 'I can't really talk about it.'" She nodded as if she got it. "And when you say nothing, people fill in the gaps on their own."

"Exactly. Which wasn't necessarily a bad thing. The longer I kept everyone looking the wrong direction, the longer my buddy had to figure everything out."

"Does your family know?"

"They know enough. But the less information I gave out, the easier it was to keep things contained." He waved at the air around them. "You've seen how information travels in a small town."

"I work in a small industry where rumors fly faster than our camera shutters." She paused for a second, mouth twisted to the side. "How's your friend doing?"

The fact that she asked touched him. "Really well. He's getting the help he needs. He and his wife are seeing a counselor and figuring it out. He's back to running the business mostly on his own."

"And that's why you're back in town."

"Yes." It was most of the reason, anyway. He considered stopping there, but as long as he was being honest, he might as well go all the way. "There's actually a pretty big promotion I'm hoping for. It's the job I've wanted for a long time, and it just came open." Okay, almost all the way.

Cora nodded as if it made sense. "Which is why you're back *now*."

She didn't miss much. "It did help speed up the timeline."

She stared at her shoes for a beat as she sorted through the information. "So you never pulled a single heist?"

"Not even one." He gave a shrug. "But I did have a job flying with a Monet."

"I'm guessing that client didn't talk too much."

"No. Art curators, on the other hand, never shut up. I have a whole arsenal of random art history facts, thanks to that ten-hour transatlantic flight." He gave her a wide-eyed look of being overwhelmed.

"I hope you charged extra for that."

"You better believe it."

She laughed again. She had a great laugh. It was deep and authentic, like it came from a place of pure joy. He found himself wanting to make her do it more often, which seemed to prompt the words that came next.

"I'd like to see you again."

The comment seemed to catch her off guard. The most authentic expression he'd seen all day flashed across her face. It was a mixture of shyness and nerves and excitement and hope and intrigue. It was a peek at what she was hiding behind those walls, and it made him more motivated to figure her out. After all, he loved a good mystery.

A second later her carefully composed, guarded exterior returned along with her signature sass. "You do, huh?"

He leaned in. "I do."

She seemed to consider the question, then gave a *What-the-heck?* shrug. "Fine, but this time I get to plan the date."

13

Cora

Three days later, Cora pulled up to a nondescript condo building on the other side of town, which didn't look anything like where she imagined Jax lived. In her mind, he lived in a fancy oceanfront penthouse, decorated in a style that could best be described as "bachelor pad–chic."

But this building was nothing like that. For starters, it wasn't on the beach but across the street from the water. And from what she could tell, there was no penthouse. There seemed to be modest-sized condos spread out on three floors.

She figured it was still pretty nice and probably had a great ocean view. It just wasn't what she expected, which seemed par for the course when it came to Jax. Every time she peeled back one of his layers, she got another surprise.

Still, her first instinct was to double-check the address to make sure she was in the right place. But before she got the chance, she saw Jax standing in front of the building with a coffee in each hand.

He was wearing exactly what she'd told him to wear for today's activities: jeans, a T-shirt, running shoes and a baseball cap.

Okay, she hadn't told him to wear the baseball cap, but she had to admit he looked good in it. It gave him a playful, boyish charm that made her feel all fluttery, which was irritating. She didn't need to feel all fluttery when she was trying to get this guy to dump her. She didn't want to feel fluttery at all. Nonsense emotions like that only clouded good judgment. Bianca was a living testament to that.

Still, he was handsome. And since she couldn't deny that fact, she stated it to herself and moved on.

He walked over to her car and leaned in the open passenger window. "Morning, sunshine." He reached through the window and held out one of the coffees. "Flat white with oat milk, brown sugar and a dash of cinnamon."

She kept her gaze locked with his as she took the drink. "How do you know my coffee order?"

He shot her a mysterious smirk that reengaged the flutters. "I have my ways."

She took a sip as he climbed in the car. It was perhaps the best flat white she'd ever tasted. "Did you have me followed, or is this part of your logistical consultant, tough-guy stuff?"

He looked amused. "You think I'm a tough guy?"

"No. I think you're a mediocre baker who needs to practice his dink shot. But you do have what some might consider a tough-guy job. I mean, if babysitting works of art qualifies as tough." She took a second sip of her divine drink and had to force herself not to moan.

"I think I made a pretty good claim for why that job required expertise." He took a sip of his own coffee. "Looks like you finally found your lost luggage." He gestured in the general direction of her outfit.

She looked down at the overalls she'd picked up for this particular event. "Found? Yes. In possession of? No. Its latest stop on its tour of the US is Dallas, where it is awaiting a new flight after its last one had to make a medical emergency landing." She gave a *this-is-ridiculous* shake of her head.

"It might be faster to drive there and pick it up yourself."

Cora chuckled. "You're not wrong. In the meantime, I'm getting to support local business." She gave her overalls strap a tug to illustrate.

"Silver linings." He fastened his seat belt. "So, where are we headed?"

"To do a little manual labor." She glanced sideways to gauge his reaction. "How are you with power tools?"

"A lot more proficient than I am at returning your serve." He sipped his own coffee, looking as confident as always.

"Not a high bar there," she said, then went on with the description of their date. "We're building beds. It's an organization I've worked with back at home that provides beds for kids who don't have one of their own. There's a chapter in the next town over that serves this area. Since I'm in Sunnyside for the month and have some extra time, I thought it would be a great way to give back."

"Sounds like a great organization. I can't believe I've never heard of them before."

"I think this chapter is fairly new, but they already have a lot of requests for beds, and today is the day to build them."

"Can't wait."

Neither could she. Because along with participating in one of her favorite charities, today was the day she was getting Jax to bolt.

She had to admit, she was surprised the pickleball win and over-focus on work didn't do the trick, but maybe she had underestimated his determination to find love. Plus, there was the whole baby bird thing that kind of redeemed the date. It was hard to walk away angry after looking at adorable animals in their natural habitat. So here she was for Round Three.

Also, she'd decided that admiring adorable animals was strictly forbidden on this date. Or maybe ever again. She needed to stay focused. She shifted the car into Drive and switched the playlist to her sister's horrible indie emo rap music. Technically, bad taste in music wasn't on the list of why men didn't hang around, but she figured it couldn't hurt.

"I know this is still over a week away, but mark off the last week of the month on your calendar. Chris and the girls will be in town, and we'll have a lot of activities planned. Basically, we'll be cramming an entire summer into one week. It'll be awesome."

Awesome seemed overkill, but she needed whatever it took to sell it.

"Who are 'Chris and the girls'?" Jax asked, confused.

"My sister's husband." She shot him a reprimanding look, as if he should've remembered every single family member she'd ever mentioned. And possibly even the ones she hadn't.

"Of course, Savannah's husband. And Genevieve and . . ." He paused as if searching for the right name. "Julia?"

Well, look at that. Someone *had* been paying attention. "Juliette."

"Sounds like a big family reunion." She couldn't tell if he was being sarcastic or conversational, because her focus was on the traffic. Or maybe it was because she was trying to not be sarcastic, which she assumed would be his go-to reaction, too.

"It'll be a packed week," she said, hoping to up his anxiety. "Tons to do."

"And you want me to be part of it?" His question was authentic, almost careful, as if he really wanted to know what his part was in all of this.

"Of course! We're dating, so it's kind of expected, right?" Normally it would take a lot more than two and a half dates for Cora to classify a relationship as "dating," and the kind of family commitment she was talking about would be way down the line. They could've been dating a year, and she still wouldn't be sure he needed to be involved in family events. But that was beside the point. The point was it would happen eventually. Probably.

"Okay." There was hesitation in his voice, which was good. That's what she was going for. "What kind of family fun is on the agenda?"

"I haven't seen the official schedule, but I hear Stingray Cove is a must-do. Beach days, of course." She looked at him. "Family pickleball tournament. But you'll be paired with me, so you don't have to be too concerned about that. Although you might want to work on your serve."

"Naturally." He nodded as if there wasn't a question about that.

To be fair, he had a nice serve. Under different circumstances, they might've had a lot of fun on the pickleball court together.

"And of course, we'll have to make dinner for everyone one night. It's our vacation tradition. Everyone cooks." She gave a dramatic pause to pretend she was thinking. "Fair warning, my sisters can be a little judgy about food. But that's okay, you *can* cook. Right?" She shot him an accusing glance to punctuate her point.

"I did make a great blueberry pie," he tossed back playfully.

"That was my mom's specialty, so don't go there. It wouldn't go over well." Was that a little harsh? Probably. But she was trying to up the family drama.

And also, blueberry pie at cooking class was one thing. But blueberry pie at the beach house? That was something entirely more tender. It's not like she wouldn't *ever* go there. But not right now. And certainly not with him.

So maybe she didn't need to fake all the family drama.

"I'm sorry. I didn't know." He paused, honestly looking remorseful. "Now I feel extra honored that I got to make blueberry pie with you. Although I would've enjoyed trying your mom's. She sounds like she was an amazing woman."

Before she could even help herself, the tenderness in his voice swelled a wave of nostalgia that swept through her, and tears stung her eyes. "She was."

For half a second she was lost in a memory of her mom laughing on the deck. Of all the happy moments that happened in that tiny two-bedroom cottage on the beach. Of a life that seemed to be perfect.

Wait a second.

Did he just make her lose her focus? Oh, he was good. He didn't get his reputation of town playboy for nothing.

Before she let herself get swept away, she shook off the nostalgia. He might be good, but she was better. And there was way more at stake here than simply winning a bet. Her baby sister's heart was on the line.

Okay, fine, a good portion was about winning, but that didn't make Bianca's heart thing any less important.

All that to say, it was time to focus on the plan. No more letting herself get distracted by Jax's hypnotic looks . . .

Antics. She meant *antics.*

She adjusted her grip on the steering wheel and refocused her conversation. "While we're on the subject of topics to avoid, do *not* bring up Bianca's upcoming wedding." She widened her eyes in a look of horror.

Jax nodded once. "Good to know. Anything else I should avoid?"

"Everything regarding last Christmas."

"What happened last Christmas?" His tone was genuinely curious.

She shot him some side-eye. "You do not want to know. And if the subject comes up, you should run."

He laughed, but she kept her serious expression. "I'm not kidding."

He shifted in his seat, looking uncomfortable. "Oh, okay."

Good. This seemed to be working. "But other than that, you should be fine. I mean, Savannah's a bit of a wild card. Just know that she's judgy and high-strung. Don't take it personally, that's just who she is."

Jax nodded. "Bring my A game in the kitchen. Avoid the taboo topics. Don't get offended by judgmental sister. I think I can handle this."

"But back to the more pressing topic," she said as they pulled into a gravel parking lot in front of a big warehouse-style building. The large warehouse doors were opened. Different workstations were set up just outside the warehouse with people already getting started cutting and drilling. "What was the verdict on you and power tools again?"

"Like I said before, baby. I got this." Every bit of his Gatsby-style swagger returned. "Let's go."

After they checked in and got a quick rundown of the process, they were issued safety gear and assigned a job.

"You two will be working in sanding today," the lead volunteer told them as he walked them over to one of the outdoor workstations where long tables held several handheld electric sanders all lined up and ready to go. "It's one of our most important steps in the process, but it's also one of the longest. We sure appreciate the help."

Sanding also happened to be the loudest station, which was perfect for Cora's plan. She stuck a foam earplug in one ear and smiled at the lead volunteer. "We're happy to do it."

"Then I'll leave you to it." He walked away and left Jax and Cora standing on either side of the table.

She tucked in the other earplug right as Jax's twinkling eyes looked over the table at her. "Are you ready to see just how smooth I can be?" He held up his sander, hitting the On button to give the machine an extra whirr.

It took all her effort not to laugh. Seriously? This was the guy who caused random flutters? For the record, her heart was ridiculous.

She pointed to her ears. "I can't hear you." Her voice was at least two decibels louder than necessary to exaggerate the action of the earplugs. Then she pointed to the pile of wooden boards that would eventually make up the headboards of the beds. "We'd better get to work."

She powered up her own sander as if to demonstrate. Then she grabbed the first board and got started on the dual project of sanding headboards and ignoring her date.

For the next thirty minutes she did her best to focus on sanding and to avoid any sort of eye contact with Jax, which was not as easy as she would've thought.

He kept throwing flirty glances in her direction and made comments that were just funny enough to make her want to laugh. She didn't, of course. The few times she knew he'd seen her paying attention, she wrinkled her face up and looked at him with a confused *What?* expression, then pointed to the earplugs in her ears.

But the truth was, he was funny. And the more time she spent with him, the more she started to realize he wasn't as arrogant as she'd thought. He was really kind and incredibly thoughtful.

He worked hard, carefully checking there wasn't a rough spot where a child might get a splinter. He was friendly to everyone around him, helping to do this and that. Answering questions. Making friends.

They were about forty-five minutes and three boards into their shift when the lead volunteer walked over to their sanding table. "We need one person to help work the drill press. Any takers?"

It was the perfect excuse to widen the space between them, which was all part of her master plan. Her hand shot up in the air instantly. "I can do it!"

"Great. Thanks. Come with me."

She looked at Jax. "You don't mind, do you? I'd love to get more experience on some of the other machines, and the drill press is the one thing I've never done when I've volunteered back home."

He smiled. "Not at all, go ahead."

"You'll be fine on your own, right?" She passed the board she'd been working on across the table. "And do you mind finishing this for me?"

"Absolutely. I've got Jamie here and the rest of the Honor Club to keep me company." He nodded at the teenage boy on his other side wearing a local high school service organization T-shirt.

"Great. You boys have fun. I'll check on you later." She gave him a nod, then followed the lead volunteer to the heavy machinery section on the far side of the outdoor work area.

All in all, things were going according to plan. She had Jax exactly where she wanted him.

Although she had to admit, she was enjoying her time with him a lot more than she'd thought she would. He was . . .

Well, it didn't matter. The next step on her plan was watching him walk away. After she learned how to use this massive drill press, of course.

14

Bianca

"Where are we going again?" Luke asked as soon as Bianca opened his truck door.

"A building day for some charity. I think they make beds for kids who don't have one." She climbed into the truck that was becoming familiar and shut the creaky door with the exact amount of effort required to make it latch on the first try, but not so much it would be considered slamming. It was a learned talent for a door that required a lot more *oomph* than the normal car door, and she'd finally mastered it.

Luke shifted into Drive and pulled onto the street. "Sounds like a worthy cause. But what inspired you to do it *today*?" He punctuated the last word with a questioning look.

"It's where Cora and Jax are."

"And you're stalking them. Again." There was a heavy note of accusation in his voice, and for a second she thought he might refuse to go. Which would be unfortunate because not only did she need a ride, but she also needed a cover story. And an ally.

She wrinkled her nose in distaste. "*Stalking* is such a negative word. I like to think of it as 'discreetly checking in on them to make sure everything is going well.'"

He gave her a look that said she was full of baloney, but didn't turn his truck around. "And why am I going on your wellness check?"

"Because you're my cover story."

Luke shook his head. "I have a feeling I'm not going to like this."

Maybe he wouldn't, but regardless of what he thought, this plan was actually perfect. "It would look suspicious if I showed up on my own.

But if I show up with you, someone who loves this charity and has done it before, it's not weird. You were already going to help out, and you brought me along with you."

"So we're going to lie?"

"Of course not." Again she wrinkled her nose at the negative word. "Think of it as a spy mission and this is our cover story. The well-being of several people is on the line here, and we have to do what it takes to protect them."

He shot her another glance that had a healthy dose of judgment. "You realize we're talking about your adult sister, who is on a date that she planned herself, right?"

"And?"

"And if anyone can take care of herself, it's Cora."

"Clearly you don't know my sister very well." Bianca crossed her arms in front of her chest defiantly. "Plus, like I said earlier, if you do this for me this morning, I'll do the whole dinner on the beach setup on my own tonight. Cleanup and everything."

"It would be nice to have a night off." He seemed to weigh the options. "Why do you care so much that this relationship works out? I mean, it's Jax Verona. I hate to be the bearer of bad news, but I don't think any relationship has ever lasted with Jax Verona. He's kind of known for it."

"Which makes him an even more perfect candidate." She caught herself just in time. "I mean, boyfriend."

Luke shot her an accusatory glance.

"It's complicated."

He shook his head but didn't argue. Instead, he headed in the direction the GPS told him to go.

Technically speaking, Bianca wasn't breaking any rule by following Cora on a date. Crashing her dates was nowhere on the official terms Savannah had drawn up. Was it a gray area? Maybe, but Bianca was willing to risk it because she had a lot on the line here.

It wasn't just about marrying Zander. Of course, she wanted her sisters' support—family was important—but she didn't need it. At the end of the day, she was an adult and could marry whoever she believed to be the best choice for her.

The main reason she wanted to win the bet, the far more important reason, was to prove that she wasn't a disappointment. And right now, that's what her sisters saw her as. A joke. Someone who couldn't get her act together in a world of people who were slaying it.

And maybe they were right. She didn't exactly have a stellar track record. Her career aspirations were still in the TBD category and, at twenty-five, her dad still paid most of her bills. She couldn't even seem to commit to a hobby long enough to finish it. But it wasn't because she wasn't motivated. She just couldn't find the right fit. Her future was there, she just couldn't quite see it yet.

And honestly, letting her dad pay some of her bills was just smart money management. The family plan cell phone was just a better deal for both of them. And why change car insurances when what she had was working?

Now that she'd met Zander, all of that was about to change, because she had a plan for her life. Sure, it might have been Zander's plan, but it was a perfect fit for her. Help Zander open his own legal practice; buy a house zoned for a good school. Have three kids three years apart. It was perfect. Her life was going to be perfect.

If her sisters couldn't see that, she'd have to prove it to them by winning this dumb bet and demonstrating just how capable SoulMatch was.

So, yeah, she was meddling in Cora's date. But it was the good kind of meddling. The justified kind.

"Okay, there's one thing you should know," she said to Luke.

"Please tell me I don't have to pretend to be someone else. I'm going to be honest, I'm not a good liar. I don't think I could pull it off."

"Of course not. We're not actual spies." She gave a slight *that's-the-most-ridiculous-thing-I've-ever-heard* shake of her head. "I was going to say we're getting there late. Everyone else has already been working for an hour out of their three-hour shift. I don't think our entrance will be all that noticeable, but just in case I thought you should know."

"And why are we that late?"

"Because I just found out where she was going this morning, and it took me a while to get us registered and out the door. But when I talked to the director this morning, he said being late was not a problem and they're happy to have us."

"I'm guessing there's a spy-games answer on why I'm late for my favorite charity?"

"Managing all those properties can be so unpredictable. Things come up."

Luke shook his head. "I don't know why I agreed to this."

"I do." She beamed at him. "Mostly because you're a great guy. And partly because you want the night off from setting up another romantic dinner on the beach."

"You can say that again. Which reminds me, I got three new requests today that I need to go over with you. Who knew private dinners on the beach would be such a big business?"

"People love a fairy tale," Bianca said in a singsong voice.

And she loved creating them. Dreaming up and then creating the perfect scene for each individual dinner was fun. Honestly, it didn't even feel like work. She almost felt bad that Luke paid her to do it. But since she quit her job before she came to Sunnyside, she sure wasn't going to refuse the money.

"Anyway, we can talk about the new jobs on our way home. After we make sure my sister doesn't tank her relationship."

And it was a good thing she'd come to check, because when they got there, Cora was about as far away from Jax as possible.

As soon as they got checked in, Bianca did her best to put herself in Cora's line of sight. It didn't take long before Cora saw her and did a double take.

Bianca feigned surprise. "Cora!" She waved across the busy stations full of people doing various woodworking jobs, pretending to be surprised by this turn of events. "Luke, look, it's Cora! What a coincidence!"

She left Luke, who was heading for the sanding table, and wound her way over to where her sister was.

"What are you doing here?" Cora glanced in both directions as if surveying who was listening to them, her expression leaving little guesswork for how she felt about her sister's unexpected appearance.

"Building beds." She gave her sister a look like *duh*. "What an incredible organization."

"I know. That's why I'm here. On my date."

"Really?" Bianca made a big show of scanning the area for Jax. As soon as she made eye contact with him, she gave him a little finger wave. "Look at that. Your date. On the other side of the workshop."

"It's a shared experience."

"It's something, all right."

Cora huffed. "You can't interfere with my date. It's against the rules."

"First of all, I'm not interfering. I'm volunteering." She held up her volunteer sticker as if she needed proof. "And secondly, I'm pretty sure tanking the date is against the rules, too. Jax walking away because you pushed him out the door isn't the same thing as leaving."

"You have no idea what you're talking about." There was a bite to Cora's words.

Bianca ignored it and smiled brightly. "Then my being here won't be a problem."

Cora huffed.

"Now, if you'll excuse me, I have some sanding to do."

Bianca sashayed away to join Luke at the sanding table. Clearly, he understood the assignment because he'd chosen a spot close to Jax. Bianca took up the spot right next to him.

"I hear you're stalking," Jax said with an amused grin.

Okay, maybe Luke hadn't understood the assignment as well as she'd thought.

Luke shrugged. "I told you I can't lie."

Bianca refocused on Jax with an innocent smile. "We're not stalking. We're just checking in to make sure everything's going well."

"Going great. Thanks."

She raised a questioning eyebrow. "Really? Do you often go on dates where you don't spend time with your, um . . . date?"

Jax didn't respond, but there was a slight hitch in his attitude that said maybe he wasn't handling this as well as he would've liked.

"What's your plan?" Bianca continued. "For after this, I mean."

Jax ran his hand along the board he was working on to check for rough edges. "I have no plans. This is her date."

Bianca gave him a disapproving look. "Does sitting back and seeing what happens usually work out for you?"

"Typically speaking, my dates tend to work out."

"Past the second date?" Again, with the raised eyebrow.

That one got him. "What are you suggesting? A double date?"

She pointed between herself and Luke. "We're not dating, so no. We're just here to sand." She held the sander up for emphasis.

"And stalk?"

"Support," Bianca corrected.

"Literally just here to sand," Luke added, focusing on running his sander along his board.

"Well, thanks for the support, but I think I got this." Jax tucked his earplug back into his ear.

"Ocean views," Bianca blurted out.

"What?" Jax paused the earplug task.

"She has a soft spot for ocean views. The more photographable, the better."

Jax stared down at the table, seeming to process that information. After a second he looked up, every bit of the confidence she'd seen that first night returning. "Good to know."

And just like that, she knew they were back in the game.

15

Cora

After three hours of standing on pavement and drilling holes into boards, Cora's feet were tired, and she was covered in sawdust and sweat. But she had a good feeling. A satisfied feeling.

When the shift ended the director of the program called the volunteers together. He thanked them for their help and pointed out the air hoses they could use to spray off the sawdust before they left.

Cora made her way over to where Jax was returning his safety glasses and gloves.

"Sorry to abandon you. I just really wanted to get some time on the drill press." It was not entirely untrue.

He shot her a dazzling smile. "I get it. Playing with new toys is always fun. If they had let me play with the forklift, I would've been all over it." He picked up the air hose and held it up almost like an offering. "May I?"

"Sure."

She stepped in front of him and held out her arms so he could blow off the layer of sawdust. He handled the task gently, making sure to angle the flow of air to avoid dust getting in her eyes or stinging her skin.

"You hungry?" he asked as she turned so he could get her back.

"Starving," Bianca answered, walking up.

Cora glared at her over her shoulder. "Are you always in other people's conversations?"

"Only when they involve something I'm interested in. Like lunch." She pointed at the air hose. "Are you done?" Without waiting for an answer, she stepped in front of it.

Cora surrendered her position and took the air hose from Jax. Abandoning his gentle method, she sprayed Bianca right in her face. "Oops. Sorry about that. Bad aim."

The only positive side to her sister crashing the date was that Cora didn't have to overdramatize the family drama. Bianca was kind enough to give an in-person demonstration.

"Should we all grab lunch?" Jax asked, seemingly good-natured about the whole situation. "Kind of like a double date?"

"Oh, I'd love to, but we can't. We have to get back for a setup," Bianca said.

"*She's* got to get back to set up. I have the night off." Luke gave Bianca a pointed look as they traded places in front of the air hose.

"Too bad," Jax said. Although Cora could've sworn his tone said the opposite.

"Another time. But we really should head out. We have a lot to do to get ready for tonight's setup." Bianca jerked her thumb toward the parking lot. "It was fun bumping into you, Jax. Y'all have fun on the rest of your date." She held her hand up in a wave, then she and Luke headed toward Luke's truck.

Cora watched them leave. "Sorry about that. That was weird."

"What? You don't think your sister showing up here was a coincidence?" He gave a look of fake shock.

Cora just shook her head. "There might be some boundary issues there."

"I think having a family who looks out for you is a gift."

"That's one way to look at it." There was more than a little sarcasm in her voice.

"But revisiting lunch, I happen to know that the best hot dog stand on the entire Emerald Coast is about five minutes from here."

Cora cocked her head to the side. "I thought everyone knew the best hot dogs are from The Original."

"The best hot dogs in Sunnyside? Yes." He raised his eyebrows, indicating that there was more to that statement.

Cora gasped in mock shock. "Are you, a Sunnyside resident, admitting there are better options outside of your beloved town?"

"It's not something we're proud of, but we're not too big to admit when someone does it better. Which happens. Occasionally."

"With a claim this bold from a hot dog aficionado, how can I say no?"

They finished de-sawdusting themselves before making their way to her car. He put the location in her GPS, and she headed in that direction.

The Hot Dog was a camping trailer that had been converted into a food truck. The side had a mural of a black lab sitting on the beach with a Frisbee in his mouth, and over the top was the truck's name in big bold letters.

It was parked in a large gravel area that looked like a pull-off for a scenic overlook. There was just enough room for the trailer, maybe a couple cars, and a picnic table. It was a pretty spot with an amazing view.

But the cute truck and the amazing view weren't even the biggest surprise. That honor went to the menu.

It was full of delicious-sounding gourmet dogs. There was the Blue Moon, which had a gourmet-style onion ring on top, and the Florida Footlong, topped with shrimp and mango salsa.

"This is not the hot dog stand for those who struggle making decisions." Her head was tipped back as she continued to read through all the ingredients in the different specialties. A BLT dog? Where had that been her whole life?

"Right? And just to make it more challenging, there's a 'make your own dog' option."

"I can feel my anxiety rising already." She gave up on the list and looked at him. "What do you like?"

He shrugged. "Depends on my mood. If I'm celebrating, there's nothing finer than a lobster dog. But if I'm commiserating it's gotta be a chili cheese dog."

"And today?"

"Today's one of those practically perfect days that calls for the practically perfect classic." He turned to the server. "I'll have the Wagyu Chicago Style. And a Coke."

That sounded delicious. "I'll have the same, thanks."

After paying, they stepped to the side to wait for the food.

"So now that you've gotten an up close and personal look at my family, tell me about yours." It was time to put him in the hot seat for a while, dredging up his own family drama.

Surely he had some, right? Someone with a background like his didn't grow up in a perfect sitcom family, did he?

"Well . . ." He took a sip of his soda before he got started. "My dad died when I was a kid, so we have that in common. The loss of a parent."

"I'm so sorry." The confession hit her in a different place than she was expecting, and suddenly she felt bad for trying to bring up tender topics just to throw him off his game. "It still stings, doesn't it?"

"It does." He shifted his gaze out to the water for a second as a vulnerable look she'd never seen crossed over his face.

She got it. It was the same one she felt when she thought about her mom.

"My mom remarried when I was in high school to a good man who we all like, so I can't complain. They live just north of Fort Lauderdale now, and she runs the hotel there." He paused. "I mentioned my family owns a chain of hotels, right?"

She nodded. "The Padua Resorts. I'm not sure you mentioned it, but it's pretty synonymous with you in any conversation I hear about the famous Jax Verona."

He raised an eyebrow. "Just how much did you ask around about me?"

"Enough to fill in the gaps of the subpar background check."

"Which gained you enough information to know . . ." He stared at her, waiting for her response.

"That nothing should surprise me."

He considered that. "Fair."

"But I'm guessing you have more than just a mom and a stepdad, since Padua Resorts is a family business."

"True. There are quite a few of us. Half are scattered around Florida and South Carolina running resorts while the rest are here in Sunnyside, working at the headquarters. Since everyone ends up in town for one reason or another, if you hang around long enough, you'll eventually bump into all of them."

She made a face. "And yet they haven't crashed one of our dates."

"Not overtly, anyway." He gave her a cryptic look.

"What? Do you have a brother who's been keeping tabs on us from some hidden lookout?"

He chuckled. "No brothers. But I do have a sister." He seemed to consider it for a second. "Although her husband is kind of a jerk. Maybe I should've spent more time stalking *their* dates."

"What is it about in-laws?" She shook her head.

"I know. They're the worst, right?"

"Although the way I hear it, *you're* the black sheep of the family." She shot him a side-eyed glance.

"Only because some of my life choices are . . ." He paused as if searching for the right word. "Misunderstood."

"They don't approve of your art-thief lifestyle?"

He twisted his mouth to the side in a perplexed look. "Oddly, no."

Being the black sheep because of making life choices the rest of the family didn't get? Yeah, she knew a thing or two about that.

But luckily, before they ventured down that rabbit hole, their order was ready.

They grabbed their hot dogs, then headed over to the picnic table next to the sandy shore. They sat side by side on top of the table, using the bench as a footrest, so they both could enjoy the unobstructed ocean view in front of them.

As soon as they were seated, he held up his hot dog in a *cheers* gesture. "Prepare for your world to be rocked."

"That's a lot of hype for a little hot dog."

"And it doesn't even do it justice." He kept his gaze locked with hers as they both took their first bite.

She'd had hot dogs before. She'd even had good hot dogs. But she'd never had a hot dog as good as this one.

Clearly her face showed her thoughts, because Jax's expressions flickered from amused to agreeing. His eyebrows went up in a *What-did-I-tell-you?* look, and a proud smile spread across his handsome face.

Wait, she didn't mean the handsome part. Just his plain ole face.

She covered her mouth while she finished chewing the too-big bite. "It's so good."

"Right?"

"How do you not come here every day?"

"It takes all my willpower." He took another bite.

"I have a new appreciation for your 'death by hot dogs' wish."

"If only Miss Mary's was in the same parking lot, we'd be in heaven."

"Now you're talking." She took another bite.

For several minutes, they sat on the table, enjoying their hot dogs and watching the crystal waves roll in with a rhythmic crash as the sun glittered off the surface. The breathtaking sight combined with the culinary treat and the company relaxed her, and slowly some of her defenses began to drop. Which is how she found herself answering questions she never meant to get into.

"Is it just you and your two sisters?"

"Technically speaking our dad is still in the picture. He's just not in *my* picture."

"Got it." But it wasn't just an offhanded response to a generic topic. The words, while generic themselves, were full of empathy and compassion. Jax's tone said, *I see you and your struggles.* She wasn't sure if she'd imagined it, but she could've sworn he scooted just a little closer, as if his entire being was offering her support.

Normally every response from Jax was a smart comeback or a sarcastic joke. She had no idea what to do with this soft, sympathetic side.

It threw her off-balance.

"You're not going to ask me about it?" Yes, her tone was probably a little more hostile than she'd meant, but she couldn't help it. When people got too close, she got defensive. That's who she was.

"I figure if you want to tell me about it, I'll be honored to know that part of your story. If not, it was never any of my business to begin with."

Again with the empathy and compassion.

When Jax was all measured charm and confident swagger, she knew how to handle their relationship. She had barriers in place to ensure she would never get caught up in the swoony side of a relationship again. She didn't swoon. Especially over guys like him.

It was this side of him, the side that was softer, compassionate, authentic, that left her feeling uneasy. The side that looked at her like he saw who she truly was and that he admired her.

This side of him was dangerous because she could connect with this version of him. This version of him threatened to break down the walls she'd so carefully constructed.

"My parents got divorced when I was in high school, and my dad moved out," she found herself saying. "It's the reason I don't see him anymore. He didn't need us, and I don't need him. Although my sisters don't see it the same way I do."

See? This was what happened when her guard went down. She shared things she didn't normally share on dates. Or ever. There were friends in Houston she'd known since college who still didn't know anything about the turning point in her life. In fact, most of them probably didn't know she had a dad, since she never talked about him.

Maybe she was spilling all of this because Jax had lost his dad, and she felt the need to justify why she'd cut ties with her own. Or maybe it was because she wanted him to know that it wasn't a decision she took lightly.

Or maybe it was the fact that for some unknown reason, the story felt safe with him. And at the end of the day she wanted someone to be on her side. She *needed* someone to be on her side.

"I'm so sorry. That must have been difficult."

Cora shrugged. "It just came out of the blue, you know? I thought we were the perfect family. We had just come home from a summer in Sunnyside and two days later, he was moving out."

Her thoughts drifted back to the day her parents sat the sisters down on the couch and told them the news.

"Anyway, Savannah refused to blame him. She said keeping the family together was more important than taking sides. And Bianca didn't really have a choice. She was still a kid and had to do the split-custody thing. But I didn't agree. If he had wanted us, he could've stuck around for us."

Jax didn't say anything, which she appreciated. What she realized she really wanted, what she really needed, was someone to listen to her side of the story.

"And then my mom got sick." She stared down at her hands, remembering how helpless she'd felt when her mom had called her with the news. "Of course I'm not blaming him for her getting sick, because I know he had nothing to do with it. But it didn't matter that it wasn't his fault. My mom deserved better, you know? She deserved the 'in sickness' part of their vows. It felt like he'd ducked out of the hard part."

Jax nodded.

She could've stopped there. In fact, she probably should've stopped there. But since clearly this was share-your-heart-with-a-stranger hour, she kept going. "Anyway, the last time I spoke to him was at my mom's funeral, which was not my finest moment." She paused to remember the single hardest day in her entire life and the conversation that sealed the deal on her relationship with her father. "And that was that."

Without any words, Jax slid his arm around her shoulder in a warm, supportive embrace. Which felt . . . nice. Really nice, actually.

And that's when it dawned on her: this was the first time she and Jax had touched.

It was hard to imagine that during the course of three dates, she'd never once touched this man. But as she raked her memory over their interactions, that's the verdict she kept coming up with.

She hadn't shaken his hand on their first encounter because they hadn't actually made any sort of introduction. He was a stranger in a drugstore, after all. Then she didn't do any sort of greeting on their first date because they'd already met. And in all the times she'd seen him since, she'd been actively avoiding touch of any kind because she didn't want anything complicating their already unique situation.

But it was complicated now because being in his arms felt a lot like coming home. It felt like she fit there, and she leaned into it, letting his strength and comfort seep into her.

"I'm sorry," he said.

"Thanks."

"Sometimes life stinks."

"You can say that again."

They sat there, watching the waves roll onto the sand, and she did something that surprised even her. She rested her head against his shoulder. Why? Because something about it felt right. Part of her felt like this was what she'd wanted all along. Leaning into him made it feel like the heaviness of the world wasn't quite as heavy.

That thought made her pop up, almost knocking his arm away, because of course she didn't belong there. And she absolutely didn't need him. She was Cora Prestly. Maker of her own destiny. She depended on no one. Especially not Jax Verona.

Yes, maybe it was a little colder over here on her own and the world felt just a little heavier, but at least she was standing. That was the important part.

That was the problem with leaning on someone else. If they stepped away, she fell flat on her face. She'd been there before and was not looking for a repeat performance. In fact, she'd made it her life's mission to never be in that position again.

Was there a chance she'd still fall on her face when she was on her own? Sure. But at least she was the one in control. She was the one to blame, and she could see any stumble coming. But nothing stung quite as bad as being dropped out of the blue.

"Anyway." She scooched to the side, hoping the additional space between them would help her regain more of her balance. "Maybe we should add my dad to the list of topics to avoid when we're with my family."

He nodded once to confirm. "Added."

"You know, just to be on the safe side, you should probably stick to a preapproved list of noncontroversial topics."

He cocked his head, looking amused. "Which are?"

She considered it for a second. "Lovely vacations spots."

He nodded thoughtfully. "And hobbies."

"Yeah. I could get behind that."

"How about favorite Taylor Swift albums?"

She cocked an eyebrow. "You don't want to start World War III, do you?"

"So I guess discussing who the best music artist is wouldn't go over well, either, huh?"

"You want them to like you, don't you?"

"Of course." He leaned in, and honest to goodness, the air between them actually crackled. "But I have to be honest, they aren't the ones I'm hoping fall for me."

The comment sizzled through her, sending excitement sparkling through her like a ticker tape parade. Her mind went all fuzzy, and the world blurred in the background, and all she could think about was how annoyingly perfect his face was and how the gentleness in his eyes made her want to melt. "No?"

"No." He reached up and gently tucked a flyaway piece of her hair behind her ear. In the process, his fingertips grazed her cheek, leaving tingles in its wake.

For a fraction of a second, she allowed herself to be pulled toward him by whatever magical, magnetic force that seemed to exist between them. And based on the way he was leaning into her and the gentle look in his eyes, she wasn't the only one under the spell. Her heart fluttered in her chest. He was going to kiss her, and honestly in this moment there was nothing she wanted more.

And that was the thought that broke the spell.

Wanting Jax? No.

What she wanted was to win her bet. She did not want Jax. That had already been clearly established.

Just as he was about to kiss her, she ducked out of it.

"Well, would you look at the time?" And since she didn't trust herself anywhere around him, she hopped off the table and walked around it, putting plenty of space and a large physical barrier between them. "I really should be heading back."

Jax looked a little dazed, but it only took him a second to recover. "Right. Of course." He blinked several times as if trying to reorient himself with the world, then he, too, stood up from their magical lunch spot.

Cora gathered her trash and tossed it in the can on her way back to the car. "Thanks for the lunch spot recommendation. You were right. They make a pretty good hot dog."

It was mindless chatter, but she needed her mind on anything other than what had almost happened. She also wouldn't mind if her heart stopped that annoying fluttering thing, too.

She hadn't even kissed him. It was nothing.

This whole thing with Jax was absolutely nothing.

16

Savannah

Savannah stood in front of the butcher paper bucket list stretched across the kitchen wall. They were two weeks into their stay, and over half the boxes hadn't been checked off yet.

She'd thought this would be easier. After all they'd been through, she'd thought her sisters would've loved the nostalgia of these activities. They used to do them every year. They had commiserated over missing them in the years after they'd stopped coming. Some of the stories that came from these beloved traditions were still the ones they told around the dinner table at family holidays. So why was this list—why was this trip—not helping them reconnect? What was she doing wrong?

Two weeks were gone, and she was no closer to reuniting her family than when they'd first shown up. In fact, they might've even drifted further away. Who knew trying to hold the family together would be so exhausting?

Or maybe it was the heart defect that was exhausting.

She slumped into one of the kitchen chairs and tried to catch her breath. Again.

Lately, everything had felt like an effort. She was far more tired than she had been just two weeks ago when they arrived. She was doing everything in her power to make herself feel better. She had followed her doctor's orders to a T, she was eating right, she was taking it easy, but nothing seemed to be helping.

It seemed to be a theme in her life. Nothing was going according to her plan, no matter what she did. She felt powerless.

But she wasn't giving up yet. Today was arguably the most beloved of all their Sunnyside family traditions: the Sunnyside Sandcastle Contest. Every year, the entire town from vacationers to local artists gathered on the powder-white beaches to create a sculpture out of sand.

It was also their mother's favorite Sunnyside tradition, and every year she would spend weeks drawing up a sketch for their family's creation and pass out jobs so each of the girls got to be in charge of a specific part of the design.

The festival seemed to be bigger than it was fifteen years ago. There were three categories now instead of the two she remembered. Savannah had signed them up for the middle level, the category for those who wanted to spend more time creating and paying attention to the details. It sounded like a better fit than the Family category that welcomed kids of all ages and skill levels. Besides, she liked the details. There was joy in the details.

The third category was for artists and sand-sculpting enthusiasts. Though she was excited to see what would be created on that section of the beach, she knew they had no place signing up for that category.

But winning their category wasn't really a concern for her. Her main goal was to spend time with her sisters, laughing and having fun. She needed them to connect, and they needed to do it now. They were starting to run out of time, and Savannah was not going to fail. Not at this.

"I know. I'm late. I'm sorry." Cora burst through the back door, dumping her camera equipment on the table. "I had to get a shot for a client, and I was hoping the morning light would give me the look I wanted. But it took longer than I thought."

"No problem. I haven't even seen Bianca yet." Savannah tried to keep her voice light and cheery, without any of the stress she was feeling.

"Bianca! Get your tush out of bed!" Cora shouted as she grabbed a Diet Dr Pepper out of the fridge.

"I could've done that."

"Yeah. But did you?" She raised a judgmental eyebrow and took a long drink.

Bianca stumbled into the kitchen, rubbing her eyes like she'd just rolled out of bed. "Why does everything start so early?"

"Early?" Cora questioned. "Restaurants have stopped serving breakfast by this point."

"The contest starts at *ten*." Savannah emphasized the number in case Bianca was confused.

"I know." Bianca grabbed a mug and filled it with what was left of the coffee. "I firmly believe nothing on vacation should start before noon."

"So the entire morning. You want to erase the whole morning from vacation?" It might have been a tad too much, but Savannah was starting to lose her patience.

"Not erase. Just shift." She pushed past Cora to get to the fridge and dumped at least half a mugful of flavored creamer on top of her coffee.

Cora shot Savannah a concerned look. "Luckily, we don't have far to go," she said in an uncharacteristically diplomatic moment. "If we bike fast we could probably leave at nine forty-five and still be there on time." She turned to Bianca. "That gives you at least fifteen minutes to get ready before you stress Savannah beyond her breaking point."

Oh, there she was. Normal Cora was back.

"I'm not stressed." Although even Savannah had to admit her tone wasn't convincing. Her arms started to cross in front of her chest, but she forced them to stay relaxed on the table.

Cora looked at her and held her thumb and forefinger up in a gesture that said, *Maybe a little bit.*

Bianca waved off the comment. "I'll be ready on time. Am I ever not?"

Savannah tried not to scoff. "All the time."

"Literally every day," Cora said.

Bianca huffed as if they were being ridiculous and turned for the bedroom. "I'll be ready," she called over her shoulder.

Cora sipped her Diet Dr Pepper and flopped into the chair across from Savannah. "Want to put a bet on the over-under on her being ready on time?"

"Minimum of five minutes over." And truth be told, that was being optimistic.

"I heard that!" Bianca yelled from the bedroom.

Cora's gaze met Savannah's in a knowing look, and they broke into giggles, which filled her with hope. Maybe all wasn't lost.

"I think I'll go ahead. That way I can get us all checked in," Savannah said. Plus there was no way she could bike fast. Slow and steady was the name of the game for her.

At least that's what she told herself.

"Good plan. Do you want me to come with you?" Cora asked.

Savannah shook her head. "You two can figure out how to bring the rest of the stuff with you. There's not a ton, but you know carrying things to the beach is always tricky."

Cora grinned. "Remember that time we tried to ride our bikes all the way to Castaway Beach with those beach chairs you could carry like backpacks?"

"But they were so big they kept hitting the back tire and making us fall over." She smiled at the memory of the adventure, one they'd taken one of their last years at the beach. "It was a wonder we didn't break something."

"I'm pretty sure we did. My favorite water bottle."

"And if I remember correctly, the cute boys we were going to meet were already there with other girls."

Cora shook her head. "Why we'd ever risk the perfect water bottle for some boys is beyond me. Clearly we were young and dumb."

"Clearly." Although even as she said it, Savannah remembered how devastated Cora had been when she saw the guy she had a crush on, the one who had invited her, was with someone else.

"He was a jerk," Savannah declared. "What was his name? Brandon?"

"Brennan." Cora's tone was casual as she got up to finish tidying the kitchen. "And they're all jerks. I'm pretty sure you got the only nice guy left in the world. Long live Chris."

"Yes." Of course Savannah knew that Cora's past with big heart-breaks, like her ex-fiancé Leo the Loser, had made her standoffish about relationships. But she'd never stopped to consider how much those little moments had really mattered. Or how many of them there were.

Cora always laughed everything off. Nothing bothered her. But maybe the truth was that plenty of things bothered her. She just hadn't let anyone see it. Even Savannah had somehow missed it.

It was a thought that required more of her attention, but now wasn't the time to focus on it. There were other, more time-sensitive things to conquer. Like getting her sisters to bond over building a sand sculpture. Or riding her bike less than a mile without her ticker giving out. Having a hole in her heart was a pain in the butt.

"Anyway, I'm going to head out. I'll see y'all there." Savannah grabbed her beach bag with all the things she thought she'd need and headed out the door to the shed.

Her bike, which was first in the lineup of bikes, stared back at her almost like they were in a face-off.

"Let's get one thing straight. We're in this together. You do your job, and . . ." She adjusted the bag on her shoulder and considered how to finish that statement. "I'll do my best."

It was a discouraging thought because her best at the moment wasn't anywhere close to what she wanted it to be. And it was nowhere near good enough.

By the time she got to the end of the block, she was huffing and puffing. By the time she was halfway through the neighborhood she had to get off and rest for a second.

Should she have driven? Maybe, but the parking situation would've probably prevented her from getting much closer than the bike ride from the house. Should she have invented a reason for one of her sisters to drop her off? Probably. Driving the supplies to the beach so they didn't have to lug them there didn't seem like an unreasonable request. In fact, it would've been a smart move. She could've made a valid argument for why it was the best plan.

But that would've required actually making the argument. Her sisters—Cora, especially—didn't do things without asking questions. And as far as the energy required to bike half a mile to the public access beach where the contest was being held, arguing with Cora and Bianca seemed like it would take more.

Side note: yes, she was going to tell them about what was going on, but now was not the time.

She was fine. She could do this. She'd just take it slow.

After stopping at every single park bench along the way, and walking a good chunk of it, she made it to the park and walked up to the check-in table.

"Hi." She had to take a breath before she kept going. "I'm checking in for the Prestly family."

"Are you just getting here?"

Cora's voice from behind her startled Savannah.

She spun around to see her two sisters approaching.

"Oh, I . . . um," Savannah started.

"Welcome, Prestly family!" the peppy volunteer said, saving Savannah from coming up with an excuse. "You'll be at spot fourteen in the blue section. Scan the QR code for all the rules. And if you have any questions, just wave down someone wearing a volunteer shirt." She handed Savannah the participant goody bag. "Happy sculpting!"

"Thanks," she said to the volunteer. Then she spun around to her sisters and held up their bag. "Just finishing checking us in. Spot fourteen."

She could feel her sister studying her, but luckily the volunteer stole Cora's attention.

"Wait, aren't you the girl dating Jax Verona?"

Cora nodded. "I am."

The volunteer gave her an almost sympathetic look that Savannah couldn't quite interpret. "Well . . . bless your heart." She turned to help the next person, and Savannah and her sisters headed for spot fourteen.

"What was that about?" Savannah asked.

Cora seemed unconcerned. "Apparently the community has thoughts about Jax's potential as boyfriend material."

Savannah shifted her stare to Bianca. "Who did your site set her up with?"

"Maybe he was just having trouble connecting with the right person before. He needed SoulMatch to help him find his full relationship potential." Bianca looked smug for someone whose main justification for her own relationship had just come into question. "And he is definitely not an art thief."

"Well, probably not an art thief," Cora admitted.

"You set her up with an art thief?" Savannah asked. Maybe they needed to set better ground rules.

They got to their square, which was roughly six feet by six feet, in the middle of the giant grid that made up the blue section.

"Huh." Bianca dropped her stuff in the space. "I guess that's what they call a blank canvas."

"Not for long." Savannah shifted her focus from Cora's new boyfriend to rummaging through her bag for the folder with the plans. "Ta-da!"

Cora eyed it skeptically. "And what is that?"

"Plans. You don't show up to a sandcastle contest and wing it."

"Some people wing it," Cora argued.

"Yes, well, not us. Mom used to plan for this for weeks."

Bianca smiled. "That I remember. She used to do the best drawings."

All right, this was working. Reminiscing was good. They were getting somewhere. "She would. Mine aren't as good, but at least they're something." Savannah grinned and handed Bianca the inspiration pictures, along with the scaled sketches on graph paper of their design. This year, she'd gone with a dolphin against a cresting wave.

Bianca studied it, her smile twisting into something more critical. "Huh."

The comment sparked Cora to look over Bianca's shoulder. "A dolphin again? They always end up looking like a wonky boomerang. Not good."

Bianca dropped the plans to her side, completely dismissing them, and turned to Cora. "Oh, you know what we should do? A mermaid."

"No." Savannah didn't even bother using her diplomatic voice. She grabbed the paper from Bianca. "This subject isn't up for discussion.

This is the only sketch we have. Therefore that's the plan we're going with."

"So we call an audible. That's a thing, you know. People change their plans all the time," Cora said. "Half of these other teams will be doing a dolphin. Let's do something original. Like an octopus. Or a blowfish."

"Or a mermaid," Bianca said again. "Think of all the cool ways we could decorate the tail."

Savannah stared at Cora. "You want to call an audible to do a *blowfish?*"

Cora shrugged. "Sure. It would be original. All round and spiky, with those big eyes and a cute little face." She sucked in her cheeks and puckered her lips like a fish to demonstrate.

"Cute. Yeah, let's do that," Bianca said.

"Absolutely not." Savannah stood up so she looked more in charge. "We're not tossing out our plan when we're in the middle of the competition because you two didn't want to be part of the prep. We always came with a sketch, and today we're doing it the same way we always did it." She could feel her face turning red.

"Wow, someone's in a mood today," Bianca said. "It's not a big deal. It's just a sandcastle."

And that's maybe what the problem was. This wasn't just about a sandcastle. It was about her family.

All the effort she'd put into this trip, all the fight she'd used to restore their relationships—suddenly Savannah felt like she was fighting an impossible battle. Everything was slipping away, and nothing she was doing was good enough to stop it.

She just needed one thing to work out. She needed one thing to go the way she'd planned.

What little energy she'd managed to hold on to seeped out, and her entire body felt heavy. "It's a big deal to me," she whispered.

The words hung in the air for a second, and then the person she least expected to jump in . . . did.

"No, she's right," Cora said. She gave Savannah a look of solidarity.

"We can do a mermaid or a blowfish next time. We really should stick with the plan. Like we always did."

Bianca shrugged. "Whatever."

Cora pulled two buckets from the bag Bianca had brought. "I'll get some buckets full of sand from the sandpile. We're going to need it for that wave."

"I guess I'll get a bucket of water," Bianca said. She reached down to grab an empty bucket, but she paused when she looked at Savannah, like something had just caught her attention. "Are you okay? You've got some really dark circles under your eyes today."

Savannah smoothed back the loose strands of hair that had gotten stuck to her sweaty forehead and tried to brighten her expression. "Yeah, I'm fine. I just didn't sleep well."

Bianca studied her, looking like she was going to challenge the claim, but she shrugged and grabbed the bucket. "I have a really good concealer. You should try it."

Cora nodded and pointed to the cooler. "There are cold waters in there. You know, if you want one. We'll be back in a sec."

"Thanks." She could use a water. And some rest. And probably a good concealer.

Savannah waited until they were a few steps away to sink down in the sand. She closed her eyes and pressed the cold water bottle against her face.

Maybe everything was slipping out of her grasp, but she wasn't going to let go of anything today. Today was going to be a success, no matter what it took to make it that way.

There was a lot more than just a decent sand sculpture riding on it.

17

Cora

*C*ora was on her fourth trip to the sandpile in thirty minutes. It wasn't necessarily because they needed more sand. The real reason she was scooping up two more bucketfuls was because she needed a break from her sisters.

For starters, something was up with Savannah. Everything about her from her attitude to her energy level seemed off, and if Cora was being honest, it was concerning. To make things worse, Savannah seemed to be compensating for whatever was going on by being extra bossy. She had zero acceptance of anything other than complete adherence to her plan, even if what wasn't adhering to the plan was the actual sand. They were one more landslide away from the entire beach getting a lecture.

And Bianca was being, well, Bianca. She was the queen of leaping without ever looking, and she seemed to be in overdrive today. The words *oops* and *well, that didn't work out* had been uttered so many times, Cora was starting to think they were the natural beginning to every one of Bianca's sentences.

Cora was running out of patience, and they still had ninety minutes of competition time left.

She figured if they sped up production, they could be finished with this "fun" family tradition early. She just hadn't figured out a way to do it yet. At least not one that interfered with Savannah's personal, undisclosed timeline.

It was times like these when Cora remembered why she lived eight hundred miles away from either of them.

She finished filling the second bucket and turned to trudge back to their sand sculpture when she saw something that instantly lifted her mood.

Or maybe she should say some*one*.

"Hey. I've been looking for you." Jax, dressed in a turquoise swim-suit and fitted T-shirt, strode her direction with his casual lopsided grin that had a hint of familiarity to it. This particular smile was different from his normal charming smolder or the hypnotic flirty grin he regularly used. It seemed more authentic, more personal. It was almost like it was just for her, maybe even caused by her.

It made her feel all melty inside.

"Hi, yourself. How's the spectating going?" During one of their many text-chats, Jax had told her he'd be there today. Since Padua Resorts was one of the main sponsors, he was there to shake hands and be the face of the company.

"Great. There are a lot of impressive sand sculptures." He pointed to her bucket. "What did you decide on?"

"A dolphin. Along with seventy-five percent of the other families here." She didn't bother hiding the annoyance in her voice.

"Naw, the dolphin market isn't that saturated. There are easily as many sea turtles out there. And I've seen a fair amount of manatees this year."

"I'm pretty sure most of those are dolphins that went awry."

"Huh." He twisted his mouth to consider that. "Well, in that case . . ."

His reaction made her laugh, which she seemed to do a lot around him. "Whatever happened to building a good ole sandcastle at a sand-castle contest?"

"They're sadly lacking," he agreed. And his gaze met hers in a look that seemed to sizzle.

What was wrong with her? Ever since their almost-kiss, she seemed to have caught a case of the feels, which was unfortunate. And she was having the hardest time shaking it. The way his T-shirt stretched across his toned chest and the sleeves wrapped around his chiseled biceps wasn't exactly helping, either. But it was just a phase. It would pass. There was no way she was falling for him for real.

Get him to dump her. That was the mission. She'd just have to get over the feels, which was kind of like getting over a cold. In due time it would run its course.

"Are you going to invite me over to see your dolphin? Or am I going to have to invite myself?"

Again with the familiar smile.

"I don't know. It's kind of a friends-and-family-only thing. I'm not sure you qualify."

"But I get to cook your family food while avoiding taboo topics as soon as your brother-in-law gets here?"

She shrugged. "Who we invite to eat with us and who we show our dolphin to are completely different levels."

"Naturally. But there's a third level, too. It's an all-access pass for the special people who made such a deep impact on our lives, we'll never be the same." He paused dramatically. "Like introducing you to the Wagyu Chicago Style."

She laughed. She didn't mean to, but she did.

Apparently this cold was going to be hard to kick.

"Come on, then. But I gotta warn you, temperatures are a little warm over there. And it has nothing to do with the heat from the sun." She passed him one of the buckets of sand and started toward their designated spot.

"Everyone knows it's not good family fun unless you question at least once if it's actually fun."

"You mean my family isn't the only one who does this?"

"Are you really bonding if someone doesn't cry at some point?"

"Hopefully it won't be you, but all bets are off today."

It was his turn to chuckle.

"Look who I found wandering around," Cora announced as she walked up to their space. She motioned to her sisters. "You already know Bianca, of course, and this is my other sister, Savannah."

He extended his hand. "Savannah, it's a pleasure."

Savannah stood and wiped away the stray hairs stuck to her sweaty forehead, leaving a trail of sand in their place. She looked at Jax and gave what Cora could only describe as an attempt at a smile. "Nice to meet you, Jax."

"Do you want to stay? We'd love some help." Bianca's eyes were wide as she looked at the mound of sand she was trying to sculpt into a wave. "Sand sculptures aren't as easy as one would assume."

He chuckled. "Yeah, I have some time."

"Are you sure? You don't have to." Cora wasn't sure *she* wanted to stay, and she was required to.

Although, if he was ever going to get his taste of family drama, now would be the moment. There was all kinds of tension going on here, and she didn't even have to exaggerate it.

"I'd love to. Give me a job."

"The wave," Bianca said without hesitation. "You can try to save that wave." She pointed at the sad pile of sand that looked nothing like a wave.

Savannah narrowed her eyes on Cora. "You're not planning on leaving, are you?"

Cora was caught off guard. "Of course not. Where would I go?" She threw a questioning glance at Bianca, who just shrugged.

"Good," Savannah said. "No one is leaving before this event is over."

Once again Cora noticed how Savannah looked worn out. Something was definitely up.

"Cool dolphin!" The voice of a little girl floated over from the walkway, and Cora turned to see Sylvie from the pickleball courts. Luke walked up behind her.

Bianca lit up. "Hey, you two! What are you up to?"

The little girl shrugged. "Checking out all the cool sand animals."

"You mentioned you'd be here, so we thought we'd stop by and say hi," Luke said.

For the first time, Cora noticed that Luke's smile seemed to go past friendly and bordered on smitten. Interesting.

Bianca didn't seem to notice. She dusted off her hands and stepped over the mounds of sand to greet them. "Welcome to our dolphin!" She gave Sylvie a high five, then turned to Luke. "I was going to text you. I have an idea for tonight's setup I wanted to run past you."

She pulled her phone from the back pocket of her cutoff shorts and showed him.

"You're not leaving, either." Savannah's uncharacteristically harsh voice seemed to catch all of them unawares.

Bianca stared at her, confused. "What?"

Savannah huffed and jammed her hands onto her hips. "I am *not* going to be left here all by myself again to finish this *family* project. The contest is supposed to last two hours. Everyone stays for the full two hours. We're doing this as a family!"

The other five of them froze, everyone staring at Savannah in an awkward silence. In fact, even the families in the spots next to them froze.

Yep, Cora couldn't have made up this family drama if she'd tried. Her sisters were certainly doing their parts to help her win the bet.

She would've glanced sideways at Jax to judge his reaction, but she was too focused on Savannah. Her sister was sweating, and even though she was certainly flushed from the Florida sun, she looked pale. Was that a thing? And while Savannah could be bossy, this type of reaction was completely uncharacteristic of her. What was going on?

"Hey, we're not going anywhere. We're all in it to win it." Cora's words and even her tone might have been casual and playful, but she met Savannah's gaze with a sincere, sympathetic expression.

It was the same combination she used to use when they were in high school and Savannah got so overwhelmed with schoolwork or life that she was headed toward a breakdown. Being a perfectionist, sometimes Savannah had had trouble with overcommitting and put too much pressure on herself. And she never wanted anyone else to see her struggles.

That's where Cora came in. At least, that's where she used to come in. When Savannah felt like her world was spiraling out of control, Cora would step in and help her hold it together. No one knew Savannah better than Cora did, and she knew exactly how to help Savannah keep things in perspective. Then Cora would stand next to her sister, shoulder to shoulder, and be her support until they got through whatever it was Savannah was going through. After all, that's what sisters do.

But they hadn't had this kind of conversation for a long time. At least since before the funeral, and maybe even before that.

Cora had assumed that was because Savannah hadn't needed her in that way anymore. Everything on her Instagram account looked so perfect, and when they got together everything seemed to be fine, so she'd assumed Savannah had figured that part of her life out.

But now she was starting to realize that maybe Savannah wasn't as put together as she'd thought. Maybe it wasn't that Savannah didn't need Cora's help anymore. Maybe it was that Cora hadn't been around to see that Savannah needed it.

"You think I'm about to walk away from this beauty? Not a chance." Bianca pointed at her phone. "This is for later. I can't exactly set up a romantic anniversary dinner before lunch."

Cora nodded. "Yeah, the Prestly girls pull through together, remember?" It was the line their mom had said after their dad had moved out, one they had echoed frequently through the years. Just maybe not in recent years. "I mean, technically you're a Prestly-Glasner girl now, but you know. Still applies."

"Always," Bianca reiterated.

"Okay." Savannah nodded, and Cora could see some of the tension that had been building up in her sister start to release. "Good."

"I'm not a Prestly girl, but can I help?" Sylvie asked. "I'm pretty good at sandcastles." She held up her plastic shovel.

Savannah turned to her, some of her kind and caring personality returning. "Of course." She even offered a smile, though it looked somewhat weak.

"From the looks of it, Bianca needs all the help she can get on that tail," Cora offered, trying to lighten the mood.

"Hey! I take offense to that very true statement." Bianca made an exaggerated expression of mock offense. She looked over at Luke. "Do you have some time to stay?"

"I've got all kinds of time. At the moment there isn't one problem at any of my properties, and I have the best event planner handling the other part of my job."

"First of all, I agreed to help. Not do it all," Bianca said. "And secondly, I wouldn't say that 'no problems' thing out loud. It's like you're asking for trouble."

Cora gritted her teeth together, looking remarkably like the nervous emoji, and shook her head.

He laughed and joined Bianca at the tail. "We'll see how long the good luck holds up. Okay, tell me how to do this."

The next hour was full of carefree, beachy fun. They told jokes. They teased one another. But they also worked together and supported one another. The only thing Cora regretted was that Chris and the girls weren't there to do it with them, because this was the closest thing they'd had to a Prestly summer tradition so far.

Did the sculpture still look like a broken boomerang resting on a smooshed sand dune? Yes. Yes, it did. But it was *their* broken boomerang. And *their* smooshed sand dune. And *their* memory.

For the first time since they'd gotten there, Cora started to think that maybe coming to the beach house wasn't an awful idea after all.

They were in the final efforts of finishing their sculpture in the allotted time when Jax suggested they get one more bucket of water for a last-ditch effort at making the wave look like, well, a wave.

"I'll come with you," Cora offered. "More hands, more water." She popped up next to him and grabbed one of the plastic sand buckets. "We'll be right back," she said to her sisters.

As they started off through the maze of other sandcastle construction sites, Jax gave her a suspicious look. "Your coming has nothing to do with me and everything to do with wanting to cool off in the water, doesn't it?"

She glanced around to see if anyone was listening, as if anyone even cared. When the coast was clear, she looked over at him and let go of her attempt to hold it all together. "Oh my gosh. It's so hot. It's like this beach is on the surface of the sun, and Savannah and Bianca keep hogging the umbrellas."

Jax chuckled. "Why do you think I'm going?"

She eyed him. "So it has nothing to do with wanting our wave to look more like a wave?"

He shrugged. "Of course it does. The sand sculpture thing is why we're here, isn't it?"

She raised an eyebrow to show she didn't believe him.

"Fine. I think I'm about to melt."

She chuckled. "Which leads to the real question. Are you just going in deep enough to fill your bucket, or are you going all the way in?"

"That's a trick question." He stopped just above the wave line and kicked off his flip-flops. "Because everyone knows the best water for sand sculpting comes from the bottom of at least a three-foot depth. In the nature of doing what's best for the team, I gotta go all the way in." He grinned at her before pulling his T-shirt over his head.

"I like the way you think."

Cora quickly slipped out of the shorts and shirt she'd recently bought to replace the neon palm tree monstrosity—on her last check, her luggage was currently in Houston waiting to be retagged—and followed him into the water.

After baking under the July sun, the cool, transparent waters of the Gulf felt so refreshing, and she let out an audible sigh when the water washed up around her waist. She closed her eyes and tipped her head up toward the brilliant blue sky.

"This is much better." She stood there for a second, feeling the gentle waves crash into her body as her feet stayed rooted in the sand and the sea breeze blew across her face. Her worries and cares seemed to melt away, and she felt herself relax. This was what paradise felt like.

When she opened her eyes, Jax was looking at her with an expression she couldn't quite decipher.

"What? Do I have seaweed on me or something?" She did a quick scan of her torso just to make sure.

"Nope. It's nothing."

But it wasn't nothing. The way he looked at her with a gentle sweetness, almost like she was adored, caused something to stir inside her.

The magnetic pull between them was getting stronger. These kinds of looks, the shared laughter, all the tiny, sweet moments that made up the time they spent together were starting to overpower all the barriers she'd tried to build between them.

But they weren't supposed to have moments. There was no future here, and the entire community backed her on that. Jax Verona was a playboy who didn't stick around. Everyone knew this. And frankly, it was a good thing because she actually wanted Jax to *not* stick around. She just had to figure out a way to not get sucked in to all these tiny, sweet moments.

She splashed him. "Then eyes on yourself, buddy. Aren't you supposed to be on the very important mission of fetching the best sand-sculpting water?"

"One I'm not taking lightly. But we might have to go a little farther out than anticipated. You know, to get the really good water."

"Agreed."

They bounced through the waves, pulling their buckets behind them.

Honestly, the problem with falling for Jax wasn't that it was Jax. And it didn't have anything to do with winning her bet or proving her point to Bianca. The real problem, the one she didn't even want to admit to herself, wasn't that she was worried all men would leave. Her bigger fear was that it was her, specifically. Everyone would leave *her*.

Yes, she was aware there were good men out there. Men who committed and who stayed and who were always faithful. No one was perfect, but she was willing to admit there were enough great guys that proved the whole Prince Charming thing existed. For some people, at least.

But that kind of thing didn't exist for her.

She was opinionated and determined and sassy, and truth be told, she could be a little outspoken about some things. Fine, a lot of things.

Yes, she still stuck to the belief that a lot of men, maybe even most men, took off when things got tough. But the real fear was that they *always* took off when *she* was involved.

Because maybe, at the end of the day, the real problem was her.

And for that reason, she was out. She didn't have a problem with who she was, and she wasn't willing to change just to be the kind of person some guy was looking for. But she also wasn't willing to risk heartbreak over something she knew had no chance at working out. She wasn't going to hang her hopes on a dream, only to realize there was never any chance of it being a reality.

Would falling in love be nice? Yeah, but she didn't need it. She was fine on her own. She thrived on her own.

Was Jax the kind of guy she'd be looking for if she were in the market for that kind of relationship? While she hadn't thought so in the beginning, she was starting to change her opinion.

But it didn't matter, because that was all in some fantasy world. She lived in the real world, and in the real world, it would never work. She was only in this relationship for the breakup. And the sooner, the better.

No more little moments or sweet looks. Playtime was over.

She jumped over a wave to keep her head above water. It felt nice to be fully immersed. She let her body relax in the cool water, enjoying the playfulness of being in the ocean.

Okay, so maybe playtime wasn't over just yet. She wanted to enjoy the water just a bit longer.

She turned back to the beach and searched through the crowds to check on her sisters.

"Do you think there's something going on between Luke and Bianca?" She hadn't meant to ask that question out loud, but watching them had caught her attention.

Jax squinted at the beach, too. "I don't know if anything's going on, but I can say with a hundred percent certainty that he's into her." He turned in the direction of where her family was on the beach. "She's engaged, right?"

Cora shrugged. "I mean, I guess. As engaged as you can be to someone you only know online."

"That bothers you." It was more of an observation than anything else, but she considered the truth behind it for a second, anyway.

"You have a sister. Would it bother you?"

"Fair point. Have you met him?"

"Kind of, I guess." She thought of the first time she'd met him, early in their stay. Bianca gave Zander a tour of the house, and Cora was part of that tour. "I was introduced while they were on a video call."

"And?"

"No one looks good on a video call. And he's always wearing these logoed trucker hats for his favorite fitness brands. It's like he's trying to get a sponsor."

"Maybe he just likes the brands."

"Maybe." She bounced over another wave. "But I think he's bald."

Jax laughed. "Is that a deal-breaker?"

"No. Just an observation. The deal-breaker is that I don't think *he* knows he's bald. And if challenged on it, he would tell you you're wrong before insisting the lack of hair is because he told it to stop growing, and he wears hats because they're cool. And then he'd fight you."

"I take it you're not heading up his fan club?"

"Absolutely not."

"Want me to run a background check on him? Mine are a little more thorough than SoulMatch."

"No way. That would be an invasion of privacy." But even as she said it, she vigorously nodded in an affirmative.

"Then I would never dream of doing it." He winked.

Was it an invasion of privacy? Maybe. But she didn't trust this guy. Who proposed over a video call? Knowing if there were any official red flags in his past made her feel the tiniest bit better.

And then another thought occurred to her. "Wait. Did you do one of your fancy background checks on me?"

He looked guilty. "No?"

She gasped and glared at him. But before she could let her righteous indignation soar out of control, his guilty expression faded into one of playfulness. "I'm just kidding. Of course I didn't. I reserve background checks for clients and creepers only." Then he cocked his head to the side and studied her. "Although I wouldn't mind finding out what part of your past makes you so good on the pickleball court."

"Still salty that I smoked you?"

"Salty? No. I'll redeem myself at the rematch."

"Keep dreaming big, little buddy." She patted his arm.

"Name the time and place, and I'll be there."

She raised an eyebrow. "This afternoon? After we finish up here, of course."

"Actually, I can't today."

She pressed her lips together and gave an *I-get-it* nod. "That's okay. I'd be afraid of the rematch if I were you, too."

"Not afraid of the rematch, I just have a commitment I can't back out of today."

"Another supersecret spy mission?"

"Something like that." He paused for a second. "Actually, would you like to come?"

"Learn how to steal priceless works of art from museums?"

"Technically speaking, I think most art is stolen from private homes or churches."

"Good to know."

"But today's mission is a lot more local and a lot less illegal." He shot her a taunting look. "Unless you have a problem with losing, in which case, you should probably sit this one out."

"Well, I can't back down from that challenge."

He grinned. "I didn't think so."

"In fact, should we go right now?" She started quietly singing the lyrics, "*All I do is win, win, win, no matter what.*"

He chuckled. "I have a few other things I have to take care of first. But two o'clock? I'll text you the address." His eyes twinkled with that good humor that she loved—

Liked. The good humor she *liked.*

"I'll be there."

"And on that note, I should probably get going."

She nodded, and they made their way back to shore.

When they got back to their designated station, he delivered the water and said his goodbyes.

"It was nice to hang out with you, but I have to take off." He pointed at Sylvie. "Best dorsal fin I've ever seen." Then he turned to Savannah. "I'm sorry I couldn't stay the whole time. I hope you won't hold it against me."

Bianca held up her hand. "Wait. Before you go, we should get a picture with everyone." She grabbed her phone and waved down a lady from the spot next to theirs to be their photographer, and everyone gathered behind the dolphin.

"Say 'world's favorite marine mammal,'" Bianca said, throwing her hands up in the air in a pose. Everyone repeated the phrase in voices that sounded like smiles.

Well, almost everyone. Cora said, "I prefer a sea lion," with the same photo-ready voice.

Savannah gave her a reprimanding look. "Really?"

Cora shrugged. "They're like the dogs of the ocean, and their facial expressions are ridiculously cute."

Savannah let out a tired exhale. Sylvie giggled. Bianca thanked the stranger and reclaimed the phone.

Cora ignored them all and focused her attention on Jax. "Anyway, thanks for, you know . . ." She motioned to the commotion behind her. "Putting up with this."

"I loved it. I'll see you at two." He tossed her one more lingering look before he turned and walked off.

She let the excitement tingle through her before she turned back to her family. Yes, she'd caught a case of the feels for Jax. She blamed it on the smoldering smile. Or maybe his ridiculously good looks.

Regardless, like any virus, this one had run its course. It was time to get back to business.

18

Jax

At two o'clock, Jax sat on the edge of the fountain in front of Sunnyside Memorial Hospital, waiting for Cora.

He hadn't originally intended to invite her here. Volunteering with the kids on the pediatric floor was his thing. Of course, it didn't feel like volunteering. It felt like playing. After all, play is exactly what he did. He pushed the game cart from room to room and played games with kids to cheer them up and take their minds off whatever landed them in the hospital.

He wasn't sure who got more out of it, them or him. It was his favorite part of the week and probably the biggest perk of being back in town on a regular basis, but it wasn't something he widely broadcasted. He rarely told the women he'd dated about it, and he'd never invited anyone to experience this part of his life with him.

But he'd invited Cora.

He didn't know what it was, but there was something about her that drew him in. He found her captivating, and the more time he spent with her, the more he wanted to be with her. The more he wanted to know her. But what he'd found surprising was his desire to have her know him. The real him.

So here he was, about to share with her something he'd never shared with anyone else.

He spotted her walking up to the fountain. Except, in place of her normal confidence, there was a hesitation in her step.

He walked over to greet her. "Glad you made it."

She glanced at the building behind them, looking nervous. "I didn't know your thing was at the hospital. I'm not really a medical kind of person."

"Understandable." He nodded sympathetically. "But what's your position on fun?"

She kept her gaze on the front of the building, looking skeptical. "I think it's safe to say I'm a fan."

"And games? You play games, right?"

She glanced over at him. "What kind of monster doesn't like games?"

He chuckled. "Then trust me, you're going to like it here." He nodded at the sliding glass doors. "Come on. We don't want to keep them waiting."

She stared at the front of the hospital again, as if she were trying to decide to follow him or ditch the whole idea. But if there was one thing he'd learned about Cora Prestly, it was that she didn't back down from a challenge.

And he was right. With a deep breath, she followed him.

Although her nerves didn't go away. In fact, the farther they got into the hospital, the quieter and more anxious she grew. She nibbled on her lip and repeatedly pushed the pressure points on her fingers. By the time they were in the elevator to the fourth floor, he was starting to wonder if this was a bad idea.

"You really don't like hospitals, do you?"

Her gaze was locked with the numbers at the top of the elevator. "The last time I was in the hospital was for my mom. It's not a great memory."

"I know that feeling. For a long time when I was a kid, I was terrified of this place because of all the hard memories. I started doing this about five or six years ago to help other kids not feel so terrified. Only I found that I was the one getting most of the benefits." He thought about his volunteer job and some of the amazing kids he'd met along the way. "I think you'll find that if you give it a chance, these kids might be able to show you just how much joy and hope this place can have."

He took her hand, hoping to calm some of her fears.

She continued to nibble on her lip as she thought. Eventually she gave a hesitant nod. "Where exactly are we going?"

"The pediatric floor." As if on cue, the elevator dinged, and the doors opened to reveal the big, bright murals of the space designed specifically for kids.

Tentatively, she stepped off the elevator. "And what are we here to do?"

"Play board games with some really great kids. Though I have to warn you, they won't let you win. Even if you're a first timer."

That made the corner of her mouth inch upward. "You think I'm going to try to beat sick kids at board games?"

"I'm telling you that these *resilient* kids are experts at their favorite games. You don't have to let them win, because they will beat you all on their own. Hope you brought your Uno A game. I mean you'll probably still lose, but hopefully you won't embarrass yourself." He nodded at the nurse's station and headed that direction.

"Hello, Jax." Lori, one of his favorite nurses, greeted him. "And this must be your friend. We're so glad you could be here today." She extended her hand, and Cora shook it.

"Thanks for letting me come."

"Any friend of Jax's is a friend of ours." She turned to Jax. "We've got some kiddos who've been waiting for you, so y'all better get to it."

Jax nodded, all business. "Okay, tell me who's here today."

"There's a six-year-old in Room 402 who's been pretty down. She's been here most of the week and could use a pick-me-up. The ten-year-old in Room 406 is up for a game and said to send you his way. But you should probably start with Haden in 415. He's already buzzed the nurse's station twice to see if you were here."

Haden was a funny kid who instantly won over everyone he met. He and Jax had played a ton of games together over the years, as he had been in and out of the hospital with a chronic illness. Jax hated they had become buddies under these circumstances, but he was honored to call him a friend. There wasn't anyone in the world who had a better outlook on life than Haden.

"Sounds good. Is the game cart in the toy closet?"

"As always," Lori said.

He thanked the nurses, and they made their way down the hall to the closet where they kept the toys, books, and other fun things to entertain the kids.

"Give me a quick rundown of the situation. What do I do?" Cora asked.

"It's pretty easy. First, we'll ask to be invited in. Once we get the nod, the rest is fun and games. Literally." He backed the cart out of the closet and positioned it in front of her. "Would you like to do the honors?"

She stared at it like he'd just asked if she wanted to brush a crocodile's teeth. "You mean push it?"

"The kids love the person who's pushing the cart. It gives you instant celebrity status."

She nibbled on her lip while she sized up the cart. Eventually her head started nodding like she was a boxer in front of her opponent. There was something about her determination amid her nervousness that made him like her even more.

Did he find it slightly disconcerting that he was using the word *like* a lot when it came to Cora? A little, but it wasn't like he was starting to think about forever or anything. He simply enjoyed being around her. It was a great quality for someone he was committed to spending his summer with.

"Okay, let's do this." She grabbed the cart, full of stubbornness, and started pushing. "He's in 415, right? Hope Haden's ready to bring it."

He chuckled. "Don't you worry about Haden. He holds his own."

He knocked on the door of 415 and stuck his head inside. "Hey, buddy, it's Jax. Is it okay if we come in?"

Haden sat up in bed, his smile lighting up his entire body. "Jax! I was hoping you'd come today."

"Of course I came." He walked in and did the secret handshake they'd developed years ago. "But I have a friend with me. Is it okay if she comes in, too?"

Haden shrugged. "Sure, I guess."

Jax waved Cora in. She pushed the door all the way open and pulled in the cart behind her.

"Haden, this is my friend, Cora."

"Hi, Cora," Haden said politely. Then he looked back at Jax and in a voice Jax could only assume was supposed to be a whisper he said, "Wait, is this the girl?"

"What girl?" Jax tried to play dumb, but it didn't work.

"You know. *The* girl?"

Okay, yeah. He'd told Haden about her last time he was here, but only because it was right after the pickleball date and only because he was still a little captivated.

Okay, a lot captivated. But he didn't think Haden would put it all together.

He let out a sigh and looked at Cora. "Yeah. This is the girl."

She had an amused look on her face. "People know about me?"

"*Of* you. They know *of* you. There's a difference."

She turned back to Haden.

"What do you know about me?" she asked, looking the most comfortable she had since she'd arrived.

"That you're really pretty and you make good pie."

She tossed a side-eyed glance at Jax before refocusing on Haden. "He thinks I'm pretty."

Haden nodded. "He said *really* pretty. And that you beat him at pickleball. By, like, a lot."

"Well, that last part is true." She had the sassy little smile he liked. "He's got to work on his dink shot. And returning the serve."

Haden nodded sagely. "That's what he tells me."

"All right, introductions made. Moving on," Jax interrupted before this little side conversation got out of hand. "Cora's a little nervous because she's never done a game day at a hospital before."

"Yeah, my first time was kind of scary, too," Haden said. "But it's pretty much just like playing games anywhere else. We're just playing them here. And my bed goes up and down, so that's cool." He pressed the buttons on the side of his bed to demonstrate.

"That *is* cool." She shot Jax a look and he could see her confidence building. "And maybe I'm not nervous about the location. Maybe I'm nervous about losing."

Haden gave her a serious look. "Yeah. You should probably be nervous about that. I'm gonna be honest, you're not gonna win."

Jax couldn't hold in the laugh. Even Cora looked like some of her walls were starting to fall.

"Well, since we've got that fear out of the way, I guess there's nothing to say except what should we play?"

"We should play Castles of Igon." Haden nodded confidently.

"You think it's fair to start her on the most complicated strategy game we have?" He leaned in and lowered his voice to a pretend whisper. "Maybe we should choose a game that at least gives her a chance. Like Candy Land."

Cora dropped her mouth open in a look of mock offense. "I'm offended. And also, I own Candy Land. Me and the Princess Lolly? Like this." She crossed her fingers. "I pull double colors every time."

Haden chuckled and looked at him. "You're right, she's funny. I can see why you like her."

"Okay," Jax jumped in. "I'd say it's time to start playing before anything else gets said that I'm going to have to make excuses for later."

He briefly glanced at Cora, and their gazes met and fused in an instant connection.

"Castles of Igon, right?" Haden said. Then he turned to Cora. "You'll lose this time, but don't worry. In a couple of months and with some extra practice, you might have a chance at beating one of us."

She looked at Jax and nodded at Haden. "Your protégé?"

Jax grinned. "I train them well."

Cora turned back to Haden. "That sounds like a challenge. Deal me in," she said. She pulled up a chair next to his bedside.

Yep, it was fair to say he liked her, but he didn't want to bother thinking about where that left him right now.

Right now, it was time to play.

19

Bianca

*L*ater that afternoon, Luke pulled up to the beach house in his old red truck at exactly four o'clock. He had barely shifted the car into Park before Bianca was out the door to meet him, her arms loaded with things she'd need for the setup.

"You're always on time. I love that about you," Luke said as she climbed into the passenger seat.

Bianca fastened her seat belt. "I think you're the first person who has ever claimed that about me. I'm actually chronically late." Just ask her sisters. Or any boss she'd ever had.

Luke shrugged and shifted the truck into Drive. "You're always on time when you're with me."

She considered the truth of his claim. Punctuality certainly wasn't her norm, but as far as she could remember, it rang true when it came to these private-event setups. Weird.

She pushed the topic aside and pulled out a folder full of things that needed to be addressed now. "Anyway, I have a few things I wanted to go over with you before we get there. You got my text about picking up the floral orders for today, right?"

He nodded. "I'll drop you off to get started, then go pick them up."

"Great. And I'll probably need help assembling those new lanterns I got. They arrived right before you got here." She checked that off her list. "Which reminds me, I have some ideas about bulk orders that'll save you money in the long run, if you're willing to part with a little up front. Especially on candles."

"Interesting you say that, because I was starting to think we might be single-handedly keeping the candle business afloat."

He wasn't wrong. They went through boxes of tea lights and pillar candles for every event. But there was something about the glow of an actual flame that made everything feel magical. Plus, there kind of had to be a lot of candles at a candlelight dinner.

"And while we're on the subject of bulk orders, I also have some ideas for a couple new standard setups. Something that'll appeal more to families and kids. It will be a way to expand your business."

"Expand?" Luke's eyes widened. "I can barely keep up with demand now. Ever since that proposal video went viral, requests have been out of control. This was supposed to be a side gig to help increase reservations."

"Your side gig that has become a decent revenue source."

"True. Did I tell you that Padua Resorts wants to meet with us to talk about possibly contracting with them to offer something similar?"

Bianca brightened. "Congrats, that's excellent news! Think of all the opportunities you'd have there!"

Luke let out an overwhelmed sigh. "Exactly my problem. I'll have to hire someone to handle all this."

Bianca gave his arm a reassuring pat. "Well, maybe I can help you find someone before I leave. I'll even teach them the ropes."

"Yeah, maybe." His tone didn't seem to agree.

"Anyway, we can look over all that when we're killing time before we have to tear down everything."

"You mean in the time we have to sit around and wait for them to finish eating their gourmet meals while we listen to our stomachs growl? I really need to start packing a sandwich."

Bianca beamed. "Then you're in luck, because when I was confirming everything earlier, I added two extra meals. They'll be waiting for us at the second location."

"You really do think of everything." They pulled up to the first location. "Okay. Time to work your magic."

They unloaded the truck at the site, and she got to work on setting up a thirtieth birthday dinner for six people. It was similar to a setup they'd done before, with a simple wooden rectangular table under a canopy of glowing white paper lanterns, with extra touches specific to the birthday girl. Bianca added clusters of candles in glass lanterns atop palm leaves on the ground for additional light and ambience, plus gauzy white bows with the birthday girl's favorite flowers on the back of each chair. Off to the side was a wooden Happy Birthday sign she'd had made just for this occasion to provide the perfect photo op.

She was just putting the finishing touches on the scene when Luke came back from picking up the rest of the supplies.

"Wow." He walked out to join her, holding two flower arrangements. "This looks amazing."

"Not yet." She retrieved the flowers from him and placed a few stems on the spots she'd reserved for the guests, rearranging a few of the other accessories to make sure the tablescape looked like it flowed seamlessly. Then she stepped back to admire it. "Now it's amazing."

A sense of pride swelled inside her as she took in the scene. It made her stand a little straighter and smile a little wider. She'd made this. She created that beautiful dream-worthy scene where there was nothing before, and it was impressive.

This was a new feeling for Bianca. Being born third in line after two amazing sisters meant she'd spent most of her life just trying to keep up. Yes, she was pretty. But she wasn't impressive. At least, not in the same ways that Savannah and Cora were.

Savannah could do no wrong. She was flawless in every situation. She was kind and gracious and creative and responsible and . . . well, the list could go on and on. She was a star student, graduating at the top of her class. She progressed through her career, earning promotion after promotion, until she decided to be a stay-at-home mom. And she then handled motherhood as if she were made for it. Her house, her kids, her life, it all looked like fairy-tale perfection. And if that weren't enough, she seemed to do it all effortlessly, like the world just fell in place for her. And maybe it did, because Bianca had never seen her struggle.

Cora didn't have quite the same practically perfect reputation, but she'd always been a force to be reckoned with. She was smart and powerful, and everything she did was a success. She moved away from home and thrived. She started her own business, and it soared. She became a leading name in an oversaturated industry because she didn't let anyone or anything get in her way.

Bianca, on the other hand, had always been the "someday" kid. *Someday you'll be as big as your sisters. Someday you'll get to where they are. Someday you'll have it all figured out.*

But the longer she hung in the game, the more she started to wonder if *someday* would ever come. She'd never quite gotten the hang of school. Her grades had been dismal at best, and she still hadn't finished college, not that it mattered because she didn't know what she wanted to do with a degree, anyway. While she'd had quite a few jobs over the past few years, she hadn't found one she was exceptionally good at. Or, as long as she was keeping track, a job she liked.

But this, creating these special events to make people feel celebrated and to create lasting memories, this felt different. This scene in front of her was fantastic. It was something she could point to and say, "I did that. And it's good."

And more than anything, she loved doing it.

"You ready to head to the next one?"

Bianca stood, staring at the beautiful scene with pride welling inside her, for just a little longer before she nodded. "Let's do it."

The rest of the evening was busy. They set up the second location, a romantic anniversary dinner for two at the same town houses where they did their first engagement setup. As soon as Bianca had that location looking inspirational, they went back to the first location to meet the caterer and set out the food. It was a flutter of activity until the birthday party was well underway.

Then, as soon as the birthday party was in progress, they headed back to the anniversary dinner.

They had just finished getting the food organized in the staging area, set up just out of sight of the romantic table, when she heard the couple walk out.

There was a gasp and then, with unmistakable excitement, a woman's voice said, "Oh, David. What have you done?"

Bianca snuck over to get a peek at them. They were probably in their late fifties, and Bianca thought they looked like coastal, sporty grandparents.

"Happy anniversary, my love." The look the husband gave his wife was adoring and loving and familiar, maybe even a little lustful. It was a beautiful representation of what happily ever after looked like, and it caused a yearning deep inside Bianca that made tears sting her eyes. She wanted that. She wanted someone to look at her like that after thirty-something years of marriage, with the promise of that love not fading anytime soon.

The woman stepped forward and admired the scene, her hands covering her mouth. "Is this why you canceled our dinner reservations at La Mer?"

Her husband watched her as if she were the most beautiful thing in the world. He was so captivated by his wife that Bianca was pretty sure he hadn't even noticed the picturesque table setup under the glow of a candle chandelier. Or the flowers in the middle of the table that were inspired by his wife's bridal bouquet. Or the watercolor sunset over the crystal waves. "Yes. Was I right? Is this better?"

The woman floated down the walkway outlined by rose petals and lanterns. "So much better." She turned back and held her hand out for him.

Bianca turned away just as they kissed. There was champagne chilling by the table and an appetizer already waiting for them. She'd give them some time to themselves before they took out the plated first course. After all, a private dinner was what they had wanted, right?

Luke walked up behind her. "Spying again?" he whispered.

"No." She gave him a *what-a-ridiculous-thing-to-say* look.

He tilted his head to the side, as if he wasn't going to accept her bogus answer.

"I was making sure the setup was acceptable. Which, I might add, is my job."

"And is it? Acceptable?"

She let out a dreamy sigh. "It was perfect. One of my favorite reveals yet." They walked back to their staging area. "I think that's my favorite part. Watching guests see it for the first time. It's worth more than any paycheck." She paused. "Don't get me wrong. I like the paycheck. I just really like this part, too."

"Naturally."

She busied herself with tidying up and rearranging things in the already-tidy and already-arranged space while she considered this notion. "I never really thought about this being a job before. But now that I've done it, I kind of wish I could do it all the time."

"Why don't you?"

"Why don't I what?"

"Do this all the time."

She looked at him like he'd lost his marbles. "Because I don't think they have a market for candlelight dinners on the beach in Idaho."

"So do something similar. You know, with Boise style."

She wrinkled her nose. "What do you think 'Boise style' is? Potato-themed dinners?"

Luke chuckled. "I'm sure there's more to Boise than that. Haven't you been there?"

His question jogged her out of her thoughts. "To Boise? No. Have you?"

"No. I just assumed you had. You know, since you're moving there." His tone was far from judgmental, but she felt defensive anyway.

"I don't have to visit a place to know it'll be great." But as soon as the words came out, she regretted her tone. She switched to one that was more optimistic and upbeat. And added a semi-forced smile along with it. "I mean, I already have a job lined up. And, you know, a fiancé and stuff. It's going to be great."

She didn't know why she said the "great" part again. It made her sound a little desperate. Which she absolutely wasn't.

"Great," Luke agreed. "What's this fun new job you'll be diving into?"

"I'll be working as a receptionist in my fiancé's law firm. Eventually he wants to open his own practice, and I'll need experience so I can run, you know, whatever it is that I'll be running." She waved her hands around, hoping the gesture made her seem more knowledgeable about the subject.

"Is that what you want to do?"

"What? Be a receptionist?"

"Open a law firm."

She considered the question. "I guess. I always thought I wanted to open my own business. Like maybe a floral shop or a cupcake bakery." Suddenly she felt embarrassed by confessing that out loud. To Luke, of all people. "I guess I watch too many Hallmark movies."

"If that's your dream, you should go after it. What's stopping you?"

"Mostly the fact that I don't know the first thing about floral arrangements, and I'm not a very good baker."

"That would make it a challenge."

"Anyway, a law firm is our own business, too. I mean, technically it would be his business, I guess, and I'd be running . . . stuff. But, you know, same thing."

Although it didn't sound quite as exciting when she put it that way.

But this plan was much more practical. Who really made a living running a cupcake shop or a flower shop, anyway?

"Maybe you could do something like this." He motioned toward the beach where their candlelight dinner was set up. "You could start your own event planning business. In addition to the law firm. Maybe you both need your own companies."

"Yeah, someday." After all, she was a "someday" kid.

"I meant what I said before." His face was full of gentle emotion, which surprised her. "I need to hire someone to run this, and you're amazing at it. If your plans change and you find yourself in Sunnyside instead of Idaho, you can take over this business. Maybe I'll help you out when my schedule allows it, instead of the other way around."

She laughed. "I'll keep that in mind."

It sounded like a dream. Would she love doing this full time? Of course. Who wouldn't love making magical moments for clients and spending afternoons and evenings on the beach? But that's all this was. A dream.

She didn't need a dream. She needed a reality, and she had that waiting for her in Boise. A job. A fiancé. A future. She had a five-year plan that made sense. For the first time in her life, Bianca had it all figured out.

So why was her sure deal starting to look less and less appealing as the summer wore on?

20

Cora

*I*t had been a while since Cora had gotten up before the sunrise to take pictures. This used to be what she lived for, what she most looked forward to on vacation. But somehow over the years, she'd just fallen out of the habit.

Of course she still got up early when she had to for work, but that was different. That was her job. She did that because she had to. She did this because she wanted to.

It wasn't that she hadn't wanted to in the past few years. She just *hadn't.*

But something about this trip reignited her passion. She wasn't taking pictures because she had to. She was doing it because she wanted to. Because she needed to. Photographing the world as it was just waking up was life-giving. It felt pure and optimistic and magical.

So when her alarm, which was set on the lowest volume so she wouldn't wake her sisters, went off in the wee hours of the morning, Cora crawled out of bed and dressed in the dark. She grabbed the camera equipment she'd left by the back door the night before and silently slipped out of the house.

Should she have at least brushed her teeth before she left? Maybe. But she wasn't going to see anybody, and even if a human happened to appear in her general field of vision, she certainly wasn't planning on talking to them. Mornings, while magical and optimistic for photography, remained her least favorite time to "people." No way was she conversing with anyone until she had consumed at least one Diet Dr

Pepper and the sun was a respectable distance from the horizon. At this time of day, she wasn't even willing to make direct eye contact.

Luckily for her, the beach was pretty much vacant at this hour. She lazily wandered down the shore, snapping shots here and there, enjoying the predawn light. After she'd walked a little ways, she found a spot that drew her attention. She sank down in the cool sand just behind a giant driftwood log that had washed up onto the shore next to a small section of the beach that was undeveloped.

The water was a perfect transparent sea glass color that rolled gently into the white sand, and the sky glowed a sort of rose gold. The colors were magnificent, and just thinking about the ways she could use them excited her. She took pictures of herons soaring in flight, sandpipers running from the waves and colorful crabs skittering across the sand.

This was her happy place. This was what gave her peace. She breathed it in, letting it fill her and cherishing the moment as her camera shutter clicked away.

She'd been to a lot of beautiful places in the world, but this one resonated differently.

The beach wasn't completely vacant. There were a few early morning joggers and some avid shellers who made their way out at this early hour, but none of them paid any attention to her. As the sun got higher, more people made their way out to the water's edge. It would only be a matter of time before people outnumbered the wildlife on this beautiful day.

She sat up on her knees to get a better angle of a pelican diving into the water, but a sheller walked right in the way. To be fair, she was completely unaware of Cora or what she was trying to capture. The sheller, whose attention was focused on the sand at her feet, paused to pick something up, something that, according to the look on her face, was a rare, precious find. Since Cora found her reaction fascinating, she took a picture of her, too.

When both the sheller and the pelican had moved on, she sat back and flipped through the images she'd captured to see how they'd turned out. It had been less than a minute of activity, but Cora had captured almost thirty shots, and several of them had real potential.

Her attention was so focused on the tiny screen that she didn't even notice someone approaching.

"Morning, sunshine. I wasn't expecting to see you out here."

Startled, she looked up. Jax, dressed in running clothes, trudged his way through the sand in her direction. He was sweaty and flushed from his workout, which somehow made him look even more attractive. His eyes had their usual twinkle, and his half-hitched grin was almost as radiant as the sunrise.

She couldn't help the smile. Okay, maybe there were some people she'd talk to before having a Diet Dr Pepper.

"Didn't expect to see me where I stay? I think the bigger question is, what are you doing running on my beach when you live on the other side of town?"

He looked amused. "You live almost a mile that way." He pointed down the beach.

"Really?" She looked around, trying to get her bearings. Had she really wandered that far?

He pointed to the ground where he was standing. "This is the turn-around point for the five-mile run from my condo. So technically, we're not on either one of our beaches."

"What you're saying is we're on neutral ground?"

He chuckled. "Something like that." He motioned to the spot next to her. "May I?"

She stared at the empty sand, then up at him with a skeptical look. "That depends. Are you planning on talking the whole time and disturbing my wildlife? Because it's kind of hard to take wildlife photos when all the talking drives the animals away."

He pretended to lock his lips with an imaginary key and sank down on the sand next to her. "What kind of wildlife are we taking pictures of?" he whispered.

"You're talking," she said, focusing her camera on a sandpiper in the glassy part of the sand where a wave had just been.

"Oops. Sorry. I hate when that happens." He pressed his lips tightly together as if he were trying to seal them shut, which made her laugh.

They sat there, side by side, for several silent minutes while she took more shots. After a while, she lowered her camera and reviewed the images she'd captured. When she got to one she especially liked, a heron perfectly framed in front of the round morning sun, she tilted the camera in his direction so he could see the image on the screen.

"That's beautiful." There was genuine awe and admiration in his voice, and he leaned in to study it closer, which was probably a good thing. It kept him from seeing the way his compliment sparkled through her or the involuntary smile it painted on her face.

Apparently he had a talent for triggering her involuntary smile reflex. Or maybe she just liked him.

Okay, who was she kidding? Of course she liked him. At this point it wasn't even worth denying. But so what? He was a likable guy. Was he a little cocky and at times infuriating? Sure. But everyone had their moments.

But once you got past his Casanova exterior—which she was starting to think was a defense mechanism—he was caring and thoughtful. He was the kind of guy who put his life on hold to keep his buddy's business afloat without taking any of the credit. The type of person who spent his afternoons playing games and encouraging kids in the hospital.

He was the kind of guy who helped her overcome her fear of the hospital. And maybe even her fear of trusting people.

Really, it would be weirder if she *didn't* like him.

But it wasn't like she liked him enough to call off the bet. It was just a fact. Something she was acknowledging. In a way it was kind of nice. He'd made the time she had to spend on winning her bet enjoyable.

And, as long as she was being honest here, she wouldn't hate it if they got to hang out a little longer. After all, the bet wasn't officially over until Chris and the girls got there. There was no need to rush things.

"May I?" He motioned to the camera, signaling that he wanted to look at some of the other pictures she'd taken.

Her art was one of the most vulnerable things she could share. It was an unfiltered look at who she was and what she loved and how she could capture it. Yes, she shared photos with people all the time. After all, she was a professional photographer. But pictures of products were different. They were business. She could look at them objectively for their specific purpose.

These pictures were personal. She didn't share these kinds of pictures with anyone until they were edited and perfect. And even then, sometimes they were just for her. While she liked him, she wasn't sure she was ready to completely open up to him.

"I, um . . ."

He looked deep into her eyes. "I would love to see them, but only if you're ready to share them. If not, I completely understand." His words were kind and gentle and safe. Much like, she realized, how she felt when she was with him.

She hadn't really wanted to spend time with someone before, but she wanted to spend time with him. And she hadn't wanted to open up before, but she was willing to open up to him.

What did that mean? She didn't know, and she didn't want to think about it right now. She might be willing to make an exception to talking to people before her Diet Dr Pepper, but she sure wasn't about to sort through deep thoughts without it.

She tentatively handed over the camera. "You should know that out of a hundred pictures, there are only a handful of keepers and maybe only one that is truly breathtaking. Which means there are a lot of really bad shots on there."

He flipped through the images, pausing every now and then to admire one for longer than the others. "Then I'd say you beat the odds, because most of these are amazing."

"Thanks." Once again, sparkles fluttered through her. She pulled her knees into her chest and looked out over the view she loved. "This beach was where I first fell in love with photography. I was fascinated by the beauty of nature here."

"It's easy to be captivated by it."

"You know, my dad gave me my first camera." She pulled up a mental image of her first Canon. It was fairly basic as far as cameras went. It did little more than point and shoot. But to her it was the fanciest camera in the whole world. "I was, like, eight or nine and totally enamored. My dad sat out here with me for hours that summer while I played with the light and angles. Lots of summers, actually."

"Sounds like a special memory."

She nodded. Funny how she hadn't thought about that memory in a long time.

"Has nature photography always been a passion?"

"Absolutely. Most of my photographer heroes are wildlife photographers."

"Why don't you go into that?"

She shrugged. "As much as I like the end result, I don't love spending all day laying on my belly in the dirt. It's a lot of waiting and hoping and spending hours in uncomfortable places."

He chuckled. "I could see that being a problem."

"Plus the money's better in commercial photography. Sooo . . ."

"Fair enough." He handed her camera back to her. "And you can still do this for fun."

"Exactly."

"Still, your pictures are exceptional. You should consider doing a show. The world deserves to see your work."

Heat pooled in her cheeks, and she quickly looked down at her lens, pretending to check it for any stray grains of sand in order to keep him from seeing her reaction.

The truth was he had just given her the biggest compliment she could receive. More than being pretty or funny or smart, Cora wanted her photography to be admired. And Jax did that. Everything, from the way he looked at the pictures to the tone in his voice, said not only did he get it, but he also genuinely liked it.

Maybe he even genuinely liked her.

It had been a while since she had felt seen and heard and validated the way she was when she was with Jax. That, combined with the way he looked at her, made what was left of her walls tumble down.

"Do you want to get breakfast?" she asked, jerking her thumb over her shoulder in the general direction of the town's restaurants.

At the very same time he asked his own question. "Are you busy Saturday night?"

He chuckled at the coincidence. "I wish I could get breakfast, but I have to be in the office this morning. There's a big meeting."

"Right. Of course." It was a completely legitimate reason, but she couldn't help the drag of disappointment that tugged at her. "I keep forgetting that not everyone here is on vacation."

"Speaking of work, my company is hosting their annual charity gala Saturday night. It's this black-tie thing to raise money for local charities."

"Sounds fancy."

"Apparently the town whose official dress code includes flip-flops likes to go all out on occasion. It's a thing." He gave a shrug, as if he didn't get it. "I'd love for you to come with me. As my date."

"As your date, huh?" She'd been on plenty of dates with him, but this invitation felt different. It seemed bigger.

"To be completely transparent, most of my family will be there along with everyone I work with, most of our vendors and half the town. And I'm sorry to say they all struggle with getting in the middle of your business. I can't wait for them to meet you, but if you're not ready to meet them, I totally get it."

"I think I can hold my own."

His eyes sparkled. "Of that I have no doubt."

She considered the invitation. "The challenge will be finding a dress for your fancy occasion in two days. It's not like I packed formalwear for the trip to the beach."

"The way I hear it, nothing you packed has made the trip to the beach."

"Good point."

"So, is that a yes?"

She pretended to consider it for a second, even though who was she kidding? Of course she was going.

"Sure, I suppose I could squeeze it in."

"Great." He leaned into her, and the ever-present sizzle that was always between them seemed to intensify. "I'll pick you up at seven."

"Just because you spend your free time cheering up kids in the hospital doesn't earn you the right to drive me places. I'll meet you there."

His authentic smile widened. "Of course. I would expect nothing less."

"Unless you want me to pick you up. I'll even open your door, if you want."

He chuckled. "I'll see you Saturday."

She wasn't expecting what happened next.

He kissed her.

Or maybe she kissed him. The specifics were a little fuzzy.

The bottom line was that they kissed.

It was almost like a reflex. Like, of course they would. Like the magnetic draw between them wouldn't allow for them not to kiss. It was hard to imagine it hadn't happened before now.

But there was also a part of the kiss that sent fireworks exploding in Cora's brain and down her body. His soft lips pressed against hers with a sort of gentle passion. Everything about it felt magical. His lips. His touch. The way he felt sitting next to her.

Excitement sparked through her in a way she'd never felt before. It was almost as if this was where she was meant to be, and this was what she was meant to be doing.

She really should have brushed her teeth before she left the house.

It was a quick kiss, but it was powerful, and it left her feeling off-balance.

"See ya Saturday," he whispered as he backed away. He lingered there for a second, his twinkling gaze locked on hers, before he pushed himself up. With one last long look, he turned and jogged off in the direction of his condo.

Well, it was official. He liked her, too.

21

Bianca

Friday afternoon, Bianca sat on the back deck snacking on taffy from the local candy shop and drawing up plans for their upcoming events. Ever since the proposal video had gone viral and she'd started sharing pictures of all the events on Luke's property management page, the bookings had risen steadily. Now with the Padua Resorts deal in the works, the business had the potential of really taking off. Keeping everything organized was starting to become a problem. It was a good problem to have, but a problem nonetheless. And since she'd be leaving in a little more than a week, she needed to leave Luke with a workable system for planning each event.

What made the private beach dinner experience so special was the amount of personalization that went into each one. A wedding bouquet–inspired centerpiece at an anniversary dinner, or an entire decorating scheme created around the birthday girl's favorite colors and patterns. Anyone could use the normal staples they used to create their scenes, and it would look fine. Maybe even great. But what made their settings and tablescapes resonate with their clients was the amount of themselves they saw in the displays. Bianca needed to figure out a system to help the next person have the same kind of attention to detail.

Although, she didn't really like thinking about not being part of this business. It was weird to consider handing over her binder full of ideas and sketches and letting someone else take it from here.

The back door slid open, and Savannah stepped out on the deck carrying a laundry basket full of supplies.

"Oh, hey. I didn't know you were out here." Savannah was out of breath, which was weird. How heavy was that basket?

"Do you need help with that?" Bianca asked.

"No, I got it." Her sister plopped the basket on the table and snagged a piece of taffy from the bag. "I was just about to set up for movie night on the deck. Want to help?"

Bianca motioned at the papers on the table in front of her. "Can't. Sorry. I have to finish these plans before Luke picks me up. I want to make sure to get these orders to the florist before they close tonight."

Savannah's forehead wrinkled with confusion. "Wait. When is Luke picking you up?"

"Four thirty. I hope that gives us enough time. Our two setups aren't close together this time. It's turning out to be a logistical challenge." Which was another thing she needed to help him figure out for after she left. She scribbled a note on the top of her papers to think about later.

"When will you be back?"

Bianca shrugged, still focused on her plans. "I don't know. Probably around ten."

"But what about movie night?"

"I guess I'll have to miss it. My schedule has gotten pretty packed."

"You can't miss it. It's been on our schedule since we got here." In true Savannah form, her mom-voice came out as if she were lecturing one of her kids instead of talking to her fully grown sister.

Which is what Bianca often felt like around her. A child. And frankly, she was a little sick of it.

"I'm sorry if *my* plans are getting in the way of *your* plans."

Cora chose that exact moment to come around the corner of the house carrying two beach umbrellas. "Got 'em, Van. But I don't know if they'll be tall enough to use as poles to hang a movie screen. Maybe taping the sheet to the house will be a better idea."

Savannah turned and glared at Cora. "Tell Bianca she has to stay."

Cora froze mid-step, and her gaze bounced between the two sisters. "Um . . . sorry?"

"Savannah is mad because I have a job and can't make her little movie night." Bianca pushed her chair back from the table and crossed her arms in front of her chest. "In fact, aren't you the one always telling me I need to get a job?"

Cora seemed to consider that. "She does have a point."

"But not now!" Savannah's voice started to rise. "Not when we're on vacation. Not when we're supposed to be bonding."

"Then maybe we need to pick a different time to do 'sister bonding.'" Bianca put air quotes around the last two words.

"This has been on the schedule all week. And I can't help that movie night on the beach is a nighttime activity we have to squeeze in between the sunset and the noise ordinance. But doing it is important. It's tradition."

Bianca had had enough. She threw her hands up in exasperation. "Why, Savannah? Why is this tradition so important? I barely even remember coming to the beach all those years ago, and I certainly don't remember all the stupid things we did. That was an entirely different life. It's not like watching some movie is going to make everything go back to the way it used to be. Times are different now. We are different."

"You know what, I'll come back with the umbrellas later." Cora slowly crept backward toward the corner of the house.

And maybe Bianca should've let her go, but anger boiled inside her to the point of overflowing. Things needed to be said, and now that she was on a roll, she was going to say all of them.

She spun around and jabbed a finger in Cora's direction. "No. You're part of this, too. You don't get to run away from whatever problem comes up because you're Cora and do your own thing."

Cora's eyebrows shot up. "That got personal fast."

Savannah's face was starting to turn lobster red. "You're no better than she is, Bee. You're about to move across the country to a place you've never seen, to do a job you know nothing about, with a man you haven't met just because you can't seem to figure out your life in Atlanta."

"Is that what this is about? Me moving?" Seriously, why did her sisters not get this? "In case you missed the memo, I'm getting *married*."

Savannah rolled her eyes. "Yeah, don't even get me started on that."

Bianca jammed her finger in Cora's direction. "If you're so mad about me moving, why aren't you mad at her? She left for college and never came back."

"Again, not sure why I'm part of this fight," Cora said.

"Of course she's part of the problem," Savannah shot back. "She's the one who can't figure out how to get along with Dad, so I have to do this choreographed dance over the holidays to keep everyone happy. She's like a sullen toddler, but at least she stays for movie night."

"I gotta admit, that's starting to look less and less likely," Cora muttered.

Bianca shook her head at Savannah's ridiculousness. "You are hopeless." She gathered up her papers and stomped over to the door. "Enjoy your stupid tradition."

She threw the sliding glass door open with more force than necessary, and it slammed into the stopper at the other end. She stomped into the house, not even bothering to close the door. She headed straight for the entryway, fuming the entire way.

Did she have any idea where she was going? Of course not. Luke wasn't supposed to pick her up for another thirty minutes, she had no car, and it was highly unlikely that Savannah was going to hand over the keys to her, given the current circumstances. And even if she would, Bianca was absolutely *not* turning around to ask for them.

But this felt like the kind of conversation that needed to be punctuated with a grand exit, so that was what she was doing. Even if that grand exit meant pedaling her bike down the street to . . . Well, she wasn't quite sure yet. She'd figure it out along the way, which absolutely did not prove Savannah's point of her never having a plan.

She yanked open the front door, prepared to storm out, when she almost stormed into someone.

A man. On the front porch. Holding a fancy leather duffel bag.

Startled, she jumped back and gasped. Instinctively, her hand flew over her mouth. Who was this stranger on their front porch?

"Surprise, babers!" the man said.

Babers? The only person she knew who used that word was . . .

"Zander?"

"Yeah, baby. It's me." His proud smile widened, and he held out his hands as if putting himself on display, the large Louis Vuitton duffel bag still dangling from one hand.

"Wow." She probably should've made some sort of move, but her brain was too stunned to focus.

This was Zander. Her Zander. And he was here. In Florida.

"I wasn't expecting you." Her feet stood glued to the ground as her brain tried to make sense of what was happening.

"I know. That's why it's a surprise." His voice had the kind of know-it-all tone that felt belittling, but it was possible she was interpreting it wrong. After all, she wasn't quite processing things at normal speed.

"Well . . . wow." She plastered something on her face she hoped resembled a smile while she tried to reconcile what she was looking at with what she knew. Or at least, what she thought she knew.

The man standing on her front porch sounded like Zander, but he didn't look like him. At least not the him Bianca was expecting.

For starters he was not almost six feet, like he'd claimed on his bio. She was five foot three, and he was shorter than she was. Probably by a couple of inches. Plus, he was pretty much bald. What little hair he did have on the front of his head looked like fairly recent implants. Which, one, he'd never mentioned and, two, she'd never noticed before.

Of course, it was then she realized she'd never seen him without a hat on. He always wore one of his trucker caps to the gym and his fedora to the office. It was part of his look. Except now she realized it might have actually been an attempt to hide his true look.

It was also worth noting that whoever had done his implants hadn't done a particularly great job. The tiny tufts of hair sticking up sort of resembled an old hairbrush that had lost half its bristles. She was having a hard time not staring.

None of those were necessarily bad things. They were just different from what he'd told her. And, yes, maybe she should have realized some of those things on a video call, but it wasn't like he was measuring his height during their conversations or showing her his scalp. She had no reason to believe anything other than what he'd told her.

Which made her wonder: What else was different from what he'd told her?

"It sounded like this place was getting so dull with all the small-town festivals and having to help out your friend with whatever those dinner things are, so I thought I'd come surprise you. Take you to do something fun. Liven up the scene a little." He glanced around with his nose hitched up in distaste. "This town is tiny. I don't know how you can stay here for a month. Is there even a decent place to eat? No wonder you've had to set up dinners for people." He gave the neighborhood one last glance. With a disapproving shake of his head, he refocused on Bianca. "Have you ever been to any West Coast beaches? 'Cause that's where it's at. La Jolla is legit. We should go there."

"Um . . ." There was so much to unpack about the entire scene that Bianca's brain had stopped working entirely.

Thankfully Cora chose that exact moment to appear out of nowhere. Or, Bianca thought, she probably chose that moment to announce herself. "Well, look who it is. Zander." She cruised toward them and took a spot right next to Bianca. "I didn't know we were expecting you today."

"You weren't. I came to surprise this beauty." He snaked his free arm around Bianca's waist and pulled her toward him.

It was probably meant to be a romantic gesture, but it had surprised her, and she sort of tumbled into him.

She was aware that she'd never hugged him before. She'd never even touched him, for that matter. But she thought when she finally did, it would at least feel familiar. She'd spent hours and hours talking to him, after all. Instead it felt . . . invasive.

But maybe that kind of thing took time. It had only been two minutes, after all. And it was a stunned two minutes.

He let go of Bianca and looked up at the house. "So this is it, huh? This is the old nostalgia house?" He walked between her and Cora and into the house without an invitation.

Maybe that shouldn't have annoyed her. He was her fiancé, after all, which practically made him family. But there was something about him just barging into her house that felt pushy.

And apparently she wasn't the only one feeling that way.

"Sure, come on in," Cora said to his back as she followed through the door. "Savannah! We have a guest," she called.

Savannah walked through the back door. "What?"

"Zander's here." Cora, who towered over him by several inches, pointed over the top of his head with both hands.

"In the flesh, baby." Zander posed, flexing the muscles in his biceps and chest.

Bianca just stared in horror.

This can't be Zander.

The man she'd spent hours and hours talking with over the last two months wouldn't walk into a room and flex. She'd seen him walk into a room, and he'd never flexed once. Loudly announced himself, maybe. But flexed? She would've noticed that.

And yet, here he was. Doing just that.

Although, now that she thought about it, he always flipped the camera around so she could see the room they were entering. She didn't actually get to see *him* as he entered.

On the other side of the room, Savanah's expressions filtered through emotions like someone flipping through a deck of cards. First she was shocked, then stunned, then confused, then horrified. But each expression lasted a fraction of a second before she eventually landed on her polite hostess smile. "What a fun surprise! We've all been dying to meet you in person. Please, come in."

That was the thing about Savannah. She always got it right, even when everything was falling apart around her. It was totally annoying.

Also, in this particular moment, Bianca couldn't have been more grateful for it.

Savannah waved him into the kitchen and pulled out one of the chairs at the small table. "Can I get you a drink? Or a snack, perhaps? I was just about to set out the popcorn bar for our movie night. You should try this white chocolate popcorn with a dark chocolate drizzle. It's made locally." She set a clear cylindrical container full of gourmet popcorn on the table in front of him.

Zander recoiled as if she'd just put a cobra in front of him. "I don't eat sugar. Only the best stuff for this temple." He flexed the muscles in his biceps one at a time, so the flex sort of bounced from one side of his body to the other like a ball. "Right, baby? We have that in common."

Cora seemed amused. "You don't eat sugar? How interesting."

Bianca felt like she was trapped in some sort of dream. None of this felt real.

"Anyway, Bianca and I were going to head out to dinner as soon as I get checked into a hotel and we can both get changed." He turned to her. "I'm going to take you to the best place this Podunk town has to offer and show you off, so wear something nice."

Bianca could tell Cora was about to step in again, and this time her response to Zander wouldn't be quite as pleasant. So in an effort to keep the house from exploding into the second fight of the day, Bianca pulled it together and finally found a voice to talk to her fiancé. "Actually, Zander, I can't do dinner tonight. I'm already booked. I have two dinner setups."

Zander shrugged as if they weren't a big deal. "Cancel them. Your plans have changed."

"I can't cancel them. They're both important celebrations. These people deserve them."

"So we'll send them to a restaurant instead. Or we can pay someone to set it up for you. Like that guy Lance you've been hanging around."

"Luke," she corrected. "And I don't want to pay someone to do it. I want to do it. I like it."

"You like working? As a waitress? On vacation?"

She could see Savannah flinch behind him and a look of regret in her eyes.

Today had gone wrong in so many ways, but Bianca didn't have the energy to figure it all out. One disaster at a time.

She shifted her focus to Zander and laid a hand on his forearm. See? Not all touch was so bad. They just needed time to connect. "I have to do this. But I can meet up with you afterward. There's a really nice French restaurant that might stay open late."

"Maybe I can go with you."

"No," she said almost before the words had even finished coming out of his mouth and definitely more emphatically than she'd intended. Or at least for what she'd intended him to hear. She regained control and tried again. "What I mean is, you shouldn't have to work on your vacation. You just got here. Go get settled in the hotel and I can call you when I'm done."

"I guess I could get in a quick workout. There's a nice hotel with a decent gym around here, right? Like a Four Seasons? Or a St. Regis, maybe?"

"There's a Padua's," Savannah offered with a cheerful grin.

Zander scrunched his nose up like he'd smelled something bad. "Never heard of it."

Cora looked like she found this whole situation hilarious. "Or Sunnyside Inn."

Bianca pulled Zander's attention back on her. "You'll like Padua Resorts. It's an independent boutique hotel on the water. Great views. And a great gym." She totally made up that last part because she'd never once seen their gym. But the rest of it was nice, so surely the gym was decent enough.

He nodded, looking a little more satisfied.

"I'll call you when I'm finished. We'll spend time together then." Because maybe that's all they needed. A little time to get acquainted in real life. Maybe his coming here was a good thing. She just needed to get over the shock.

"All right." He nodded again, as if thinking through the situation. "I'll call an Uber, and you can meet me at the hotel later."

"Or I can take you now," Cora jumped in. "We don't want to keep you waiting when there's a workout on the agenda."

"Yeah, that's even better." He stood up from the table and grabbed his duffel.

Thank you, Bianca mouthed over his head.

"I'll catch your act in a little bit." Zander leaned in and kissed Bianca right on the lips.

Their very first kiss.

Were there sparks or fireworks? Nope. In fact there wasn't even as much as a flutter. Instead, it felt kind of like kissing a fish.

But like she said before, maybe they just needed to get to know each other.

"I'll see you later." He winked.

"Can't wait."

He followed Cora out the door, quizzing her on what there was to do "in this tiny town."

They waited until the duo had left and the house was quiet again before either of them spoke. "So. That's Zander," Savannah said.

"That's him," Bianca said in her brightest voice. Although she had no interest in hashing out what had just happened. And even if she did, she certainly wouldn't do it with Savannah. Not after the fight they'd just had, anyway.

Nope, she needed some time to process everything that had happened on her own. And there was a lot to process.

But first things first. She had two very important dinners to set up. She headed to her room to get ready and tried to focus on the tasks she had ahead.

After all, everything else was going to work itself out. It would be fine. She was sure of it.

Maybe.

22

Cora

*I*t wasn't until the next afternoon, when they were both at the house getting ready for the gala, that Cora's path crossed with Bianca's again. To Cora, it seemed like there had been an eternity of silence since the events from the evening before, which made the air in the house seem fragile. There was a lot that needed to be said, and plenty of it by Cora, but she treaded slowly. She didn't want to star in *Prestly Sisters: The Civil War*. Not today, at least. So as she stepped into the tiny bathroom to share the mirror, she asked the most generic question she could think of.

"How was your day with Zander?"

"It was good. He's great." Bianca focused on applying her eyeliner instead of elaborating.

"He seems . . ." Cora had to pause to come up with something positive about him. She wanted to finish that sentence with *really proud of his muscle tone*, but since she thought that probably wouldn't go over well, she went with "very passionate."

Bianca nodded her agreement more zealously than probably necessary. "He is. Very passionate about all kinds of things. Like, just today he made a big donation to the Save Our Seas Foundation."

"How generous."

"And Luke was kind enough to give up his ticket to the gala tonight so Zander can go with me, which is good. It'll be great to spend some time with him in that kind of setting." She put on a second layer of mascara.

"Good. That's great," Cora agreed in a tone that sounded like she meant it. Almost.

"Besides, I think Trina mainly invited me and Luke to try to win us over for contract negotiations next week. But even if we do talk business tonight, who better to have negotiating for us than a lawyer? So really, it's perfect."

"So perfect." Although neither of them used the word with any sort of conviction.

"Plus, it makes sense for Zander to go, because he's staying at the hotel. It would just be awkward if he was there but couldn't be *there*, ya know?" She paused and looked at Cora in the mirror. "Thanks for calling in that favor with Jax to get him a room last night. I didn't even think about it being booked because of the gala."

Cora met her sister's gaze with complete sincerity. "I'm glad it worked out." Because at the end of the day, all she wanted was for her sister to be happy.

There was a pause while Cora rifled through her makeup bag and Bianca finished working on her eyes.

"Bee, you're happy, right?"

Bianca stopped her mascara application. One very long second ticked by in silence before she recovered her measured smile. "Of course. Why wouldn't I be?"

Cora went back to blending in her foundation. "No reason."

Of course there was a reason. Bianca was about to make a giant mistake with a man who apparently hadn't been honest about a single thing. At this point, Cora wasn't even convinced he was a lawyer. As far as she could tell from the thirty minutes she spent getting him checked into the hotel, he had nothing in common with her little sister. He certainly wasn't her soulmate. In fact, Cora wasn't sure he even *had* a soulmate, because the person he obviously loved more than anyone in the world was himself.

But she couldn't exactly say that to her sister. At least not while emotions were running so high.

"I just care about you and want you to be, you know, happy," she went with instead.

Bianca blinked several times in rapid succession, and it was obvious she had to work to keep her strained smile in place. "I am happy.

Getting to spend some quality time with Zander is good. Really, this surprise visit is going to be . . ." She paused as if she wasn't sure where she wanted to go with that thought. "Great," she finished, finally, and tossed her mascara into her bag.

"Good," Cora agreed. "That's great."

Bianca shrugged, some of her confidence returning. "It's almost like it was meant to be." She swiped lip gloss across her lips, then with a sassy waggle of her eyebrows, she disappeared from the bathroom.

"For your sake, I hope it is," Cora whispered to the empty space where her sister had just been.

23

Savannah

Savannah whistled when Cora walked out of the bedroom dressed for the gala. "Look at you! Somebody is looking to turn some heads tonight."

Cora ignored the comment and strolled over to the table where Savannah was sitting, her stiletto heels clicking across the tile floor. "You really think the crossbody bag is a no? It's way more practical." She held up the black bag she'd been carrying most of the summer.

"If you suggest it again, I will burn it." Savannah slid a new beaded clutch across the table.

"Thanks for driving me, by the way. I feel a little bit like I'm on my way to a junior high dance, but I figured it would be easier to let Bianca and Lord Farquaad have access to a car."

Savannah laughed. "That is the perfect name for him, but don't ever say it to his face."

"I'll try to restrain myself." Cora tossed a couple more things into the clutch, then looked over at Savannah with a more serious expression. "Did y'all get a chance to talk?"

A wave of guilt rolled through her. "No."

In fact, she was pretty sure Bianca had been avoiding her since their blowup the day before. It was the latest example of Savannah's failed attempt to fix what was broken. This summer was not going according to plan.

Savannah was just so tired, and nothing she did seemed to be good enough. It felt like she was always racing at full speed just to keep up, and things kept falling behind. There was always something else that she should be doing or something else that didn't get done. It was maddening and exhausting, and she felt guilty all the time.

"I just wanted the perfect night, you know. Where we could connect. Like we used to."

"I know."

"We used to love movie night." Savannah let her mind drift back to the summer nights of their childhood.

"We used to love a lot of things. Like getting a soda where you mixed all the flavors."

Just the thought of it pulled her mouth into an instant *yuck* face. "Fine. I wanted us to have an upgraded, grown-up version of the activity we used to love." She motioned to the glass jars half-full of what was left from the popcorn bar. "I did get the gourmet popcorn."

"Which was a nice start," Cora agreed. "That white chocolate popcorn is amazing."

"Right?"

"Give her some time," Cora said. "I think she's dealing with some of her own stuff at the moment."

"I can imagine." Besides the surprise of Zander showing up, he wasn't exactly the person they were expecting him to be. At least he wasn't who Savannah was expecting.

"Did you know there's not even one Michelin star chef in the Florida Panhandle?" Cora reported.

"I did not. However have we survived all these years?"

Cora chuckled. "Miss Mary's."

Savannah nodded as if that were, indeed, the only reason they had survived eating at subpar restaurants their entire lives. "Then it's unfortunate he doesn't eat sugar."

"I think there are a lot of unfortunate things there," Cora said.

"But in all seriousness, if he turns out to be her soulmate, I'll learn to love him." Which was what she should've said last night.

"Agreed." Cora nodded in solidarity. Then she closed her eyes and whispered, "Please don't be her soulmate. Please don't be her soulmate. Please don't be her soulmate."

Savannah chuckled because it was exactly what she was thinking. "You can spy on them at the gala. See how it's going and report back."

"Will do. But are you sure you don't want to go? You can spy on them yourself," Cora said. "I'm sure Jax could get you a ticket. I still have that second dress in the closet I was going to send back tomorrow. You could wear it." She hitched her thumb in the direction of her room.

"No, I'm fine. I'll actually enjoy having a quiet night with the house all to myself. Maybe I'll go for a sunset walk on the beach. Read my book. Go to bed early. A few of my favorite things."

Cora laughed. "If only Julie Andrews had sung about them in her song."

"It's the thirty-something, tired-mom version." She smiled at Cora. "But I might string up those café lights over the back deck. There was a ladder in the shed, wasn't there?"

Cora nodded. "I think so. But be careful. Bianca and I can always help you do that tomorrow."

"If she's talking to me tomorrow."

"She'll come around. After all, who can stay mad after dancing all night in the arms of their fiancé?"

"Well, there is that." She dangled the keys in front of Cora. "We should go before you turn back into a pumpkin. Your carriage awaits."

24

Jax

 ax stood in front of the mirror to tie his bow tie. This event was the whole reason he'd come back to town. Or at least, it was the reason he'd come back when he did. This was the night his uncle and the board of directors would announce the new Senior Vice President of Operations. The night they would announce *his* name.

And yet, now that he was here, the anticipation felt different than he'd imagined.

There was still plenty of excitement. He was giddy, like a kid getting ready to go to his birthday party. He couldn't help the goofy grin plastered to his face. He felt like yelling out random phrases like *let's go*, and he had an odd feeling there was a decent chance he'd high-five the next person he saw.

But very little of that excitement had to do with him getting the job he wanted.

He pulled his tie into the perfect knot and stared at his reflection, his goofy grin spreading wider across his face. "Let's go!"

He grabbed his jacket off the bed and slipped it on as he headed out of the room.

The entire hotel was gleaming. This event was the pinnacle of the year at their flagship hotel, and it was always a chance to show off. There were cocktails in the lobby. The formal dinner was set up in the grand ballroom, and a silent auction to raise money for local nonprofits was set up in the smaller conference rooms. There was dancing and a live band out by the pool and bonfires with relaxing seating areas set up on the beach. And every single space was dressed accordingly.

But this year's event had an added layer of anticipation with the announcement of the new SVP.

It had been ten years since there was any sort of change at the top, and in that ten years, their business had boomed. Since his uncle had already announced his plan to retire in five years, this position came with even more weight.

What they were really naming was the next CEO in training.

Jax cruised into the lobby, taking in all the ways the space had been dressed up for the occasion. There were flower arrangements on every surface. Several new drink stations had been erected throughout the room, and tuxedo-clad servers were manning them. There was a wall completely covered in fresh white roses with the hotel's glittering gold logo hung in the center.

He didn't care who you were, it was impossible not to be impressed.

His brother-in-law was standing in the middle of it all. And since he couldn't be avoided, Jax walked over to say hello.

"Big night," Travis said. Technically speaking, his wife—Jax's sister—was in the running for the job, too. But they all knew she didn't want it. Even if his uncle was trying to prove a point to Jax, he wouldn't have appointed her just so power-hungry Travis didn't try to take it over.

Jax wasn't the only one in the family who wasn't keen on his sister's husband.

But it didn't matter how Travis tried to bait him. Tonight, nothing could shake his mood.

"It is." Jax swiped a stuffed mushroom off the tray of a passing waiter and popped it in his mouth.

"You think you really pulled off the coup by rolling into town with your *I-charm-everyone* attitude and taking your uncle's ridiculous bet?"

"What bet?" Jax played innocent.

"Really? You forget I know everything that goes on in this place."

"Which is what makes you such a great assistant GM *of this hotel.*" He put an extra emphasis on the last three words because as far as Jax was concerned, that was the highest role he would ever get. The only reason he had the role to begin with was because he was married to Trina.

Travis seethed. "You think you've got this all figured out, don't you?"

Confidence surged through him. He tucked his hands in his pockets, standing firm in his position. "I guess we'll see. Now, if you'll excuse me, I'm expecting someone."

Without waiting for a response, he strolled out the giant automatic glass doors to the covered arrival area.

The valet station was a flurry of activity. Cars pulled up. Well-dressed guests stepped out as the valet team rushed to move their cars so the long line of vehicles could cycle through.

He greeted a few guests as they walked past him and paused to talk with a couple he knew. When he turned around he saw another familiar face. Bianca, with a man he didn't recognize.

He walked over to greet her. "I heard you were an addition to the guest list. My sister tells me they've been impressed by your work and are looking forward to your possible partnership."

The compliment made her glow. "That's the hope. We're excited to work with Padua. Well, Luke will be, at least." She held her hand out toward the man who was with her. "Let me introduce my fiancé, Zander. Zander, this is Jax Verona, the man Cora is seeing."

"Zander." Jax extended his hand. "I've heard so much about you. It's nice to meet you."

Zander took it with a grip that Jax would have classified as *beyond confident* and bordering on *aggressive*. "A fellow fitness enthusiast, I see. What do you bench-press? Like, two-fifty? Two-eighty?" He said the numbers as if they were meant to be belittling, but the insult rolled right off Jax.

"Something like that." He took his hand back and discreetly wiped the sweatiness on his pant leg.

"Zander showed up in Sunnyside to surprise me," Bianca threw in. "How fun."

Zander snaked his arm around Bianca's waist. "I thought I'd come down here and treat her well on her vacation. Why have money if you can't spend it spoiling your lady, am I right?"

"Right." He had a whole new appreciation for Cora's aversion to her sister's fiancé. Maybe he would run that background check after all.

Bianca motioned to the bar. "We're going to grab a drink."

"Absolutely. Enjoy your evening." He could've asked if Bianca knew any details of her sister's arrival, but since he didn't want to prolong his time with her fiancé, he opted to end the conversation there.

Although, he couldn't wait to hear Cora's thoughts about the surprise visitor. He wasn't sure how it was possible for anyone to be more ridiculous than Cora's description, but somehow Zander managed to do it.

He scanned the lineup of cars waiting for the valet, looking for hers, when his uncle Anders walked up.

"It's a fine night for a gala," Anders said, taking a position next to Jax.

"It's a fine night for the Senior Vice President announcement." He gave Anders a confident side glance.

"Yes. It's that, too."

"You know you want it to be me." Jax didn't even try to hide his cheekiness.

His uncle looked at him with a serious expression. "Wanting it to be you was never part of the problem." He let the words hang in the air for a second before he continued. "On that note, I hear I will be meeting someone tonight. A date? Perhaps something more?"

Excitement sparkled through Jax as he thought of her. "Cora."

"And what do I need to know about this Cora?"

"You're going to like her." There wasn't even a hint of hesitation in his response. "She's smart and funny. And she doesn't put up with anything from anyone, but she also has this compassionate side. She's an artist and a businesswoman and loves her family but is also fiercely independent. She can be so incredibly difficult, but so incredibly . . ." He let the words trail off as the corner of his mouth tugged upward.

In a word, she was perfect, but he kept that description for himself.

His uncle looked at him, amused. "Has the untamable Jax Verona really been tamed?"

"Tamed? No." There might have been a scoff attached to his emphatic answer because he wasn't some wild stallion who needed someone to make him settle down. In fact, no one said anything about the future. While he liked Cora, maybe even a lot, no one was talking about settling down.

He looked anywhere but at his uncle, trying to separate this notion from whatever this thing was he had going on with Cora. "It's only been three weeks. It's not like we're—" He turned back to look at his uncle to deliver the last line, but his words fell away when he saw her.

It was almost as if a spotlight was on her. Everything else seemed to fade away, and the only thing in his awareness was her.

She was breathtaking.

She was wearing a long silky dress with thin straps and a sort of draping neckline but was fitted everywhere else. Technically the color could've been classified as blue, but it wasn't like any shade of blue he knew. It was the color of the ocean on a perfect day and every bit as magical.

Her long dark hair hung in soft curls perfectly framing her beautiful face. And silvery, strappy high-heeled sandals peeked out as she strode down the sidewalk with the confidence and determination he loved.

He had no idea where her car was. She cruised past the long line of vehicles waiting for the valet from the direction of the main road. The only parking lot in that direction was over a block away. From what he could see of her shoes, they didn't exactly look like they were made for walking, but things like that never seemed to stand in Cora's way. She took life by the horns, which was maybe one of the things he loved most about her.

There was that word again.

"It's not like we're putting a title on it," he finished. It wasn't exactly how he thought that statement was going to go, but then again, nothing with Cora had gone how he thought it was going to go. In the very best way possible.

"I have to admit, I didn't think you had it in you." His uncle regarded him with a bemused look. "She must be something."

At least that's what he thought his uncle had said. It was kind of hard to listen when his focus was somewhere else.

"Excuse me a moment." Jax stepped around his uncle and took a few steps toward Cora so there wasn't anyone in between them. Her gaze met his and his heart, which had been rapidly beating in his chest, seemed to soar.

Or to be technical about it, his entire being seemed to soar. He felt lighter. Freer. Happier in a way he couldn't quite explain, because he would've said he was happy before he met her. It wasn't like anything was missing from his life. It was just that with her everything seemed . . . better.

She was the most beautiful, interesting, amazing person at the party. Possibly in the entire world. And she was here with him. He had to be the luckiest guy alive.

He held up his hand in a wave and she paused, a sassy smile pulling at her lips. From her position about twenty yards away, she motioned to her dress, then did a little model–style turn to show off the plunging back, keeping her gaze locked with his over her shoulder.

His heart skipped a beat, and he put his hand over his chest to show that he loved her dress. And the truth was, he might've loved more than that, although he wasn't quite ready to go there.

Not yet, anyway. Not out loud.

He took a couple slow steps toward her as she finished walking the rest of the way up the sidewalk.

"You are stunning," he said as she got close. He put his hand on her waist and greeted her with a kiss on her cheek.

"Thank you." She looked him up and down, and he did his own little model spin, which made her grin widen. "You look very dapper yourself. You've got a kind of James Bond thing going on."

"I get that a lot," he said.

"Occupational hazard, I suppose."

"Something like that." The way her silky hair cascaded over her bare shoulders was making it hard for him to think. Before he could get completely lost in her, he offered her his arm. "But now that you're here, there's someone I'd like you to meet."

She draped her hand through his arm. "Ah, the family. I promise to be on my best behavior."

He chuckled as they made their way to his uncle. "Cora Prestly, let me introduce you to my uncle, Anders Padua."

She let go of Jax's arm and extended her hand. "Mr. Padua, it's so nice to meet you."

Uncle Anders shot Jax a knowing look before he took her hand into both of his. "Trust me, my dear, the pleasure of this meeting is all mine. Have you enjoyed your time in Sunnyside?"

"I have, thank you."

"Then perhaps you'll make your visits more permanent?"

"I guess we'll have to see how the rest of the summer plays out, but it's not completely out of the question."

"You don't know how glad I am to hear it." He stepped back and looked confidently at Jax. "I'll be making the announcement later tonight." He gave a slight nod, then returned his attention to Cora. "It was lovely to meet you. Enjoy the party."

Cora smiled brightly until Uncle Anders had disappeared into the hotel. She looked over at Jax. "What announcement?"

"Remember the SVP position I told you about?"

She brightened as the dots connected. "You got it?"

The excitement in her voice sounded like she was on the verge of giving him the high five he was looking for earlier. He had to admit he felt a level of excitement, but not altogether for the same reason.

To think that he would care more about the woman standing in front of him than the job he'd wanted since he was a kid. Talk about a plot twist.

"It's not official but starting to look like more of a possibility."

"Then I'd say this calls for a celebration. Surely we can find a glass of champagne in this place."

"I think that can be arranged." And he knew exactly the best place for that celebration. "But first I have to do a little business. Are you okay with doing my obligatory meet-and-greet with me?"

"Of course." She smoothed out her dress. "Although, I have to warn you, I don't always keep my opinions to myself, and I've been known to offend people."

"Isn't that your finest quality?"

"I think so. But apparently some people see it differently." She gave an *I-don't-get-it* shrug that made him chuckle.

"I don't think you need to change who you are." He offered her his arm. "And if you happen to see my brother-in-law, feel free to offend away."

For the next thirty minutes, they worked their way around the lobby, welcoming people and greeting special guests. Cora was the perfect partner for the activity.

Yes, she spoke her mind, but most people responded to that. They enjoyed the authentic conversation because she didn't just talk, she also listened well. Better than most. There wasn't a single one-sided or generic conversation the entire time. Even Charles Hooper, the hard-to-please city councilman, walked away looking appreciated and heard and, dare he say it, charmed.

After they stopped to say hi to the mayor and her husband, Jax leaned in and whispered, "Have you met enough new people?"

"Like twenty people ago."

He nodded at the side door. "Want to escape?"

"It's like you know me."

He swiped two champagne glasses off a passing tray, and they headed in the opposite direction of the crowd. With a quick look over his shoulder, he pushed through a somewhat hidden door on the far side of the hotel that led to a small hallway.

Turning down the hallway to the left took them to the pool and the gardens by the gym. Both were beautiful spots, but since he had something a little more private in mind, he turned to the right.

They wound their way around the hall and then up two flights in a narrow staircase. Cora gave him a questioning look as they walked down another hall to a small elevator at the end. "Maybe I should've had you clarify where this mysterious people-free place was located."

Jax handed her one of the glasses of champagne. "Trust me."

She eyed him skeptically. "You keep saying that."

"And haven't I been right every time?"

She narrowed her eyes, not looking sure she believed him.

"Well, was I at least right about the hot dogs?"

"I'll give you the hot dogs."

He chuckled and stopped in front of the doorway at the end of the hall. "Prepare to be impressed again." He pushed open the door that led to the outside and allowed her to go out first.

They stepped out onto a wide rooftop deck that was six floors above the ground.

Most of the hotel focused its design so that guests would look out the back to maximize the views of the pool and beach, but this deck faced off to the side. It still had sweeping views of the water and the beach, but it was a different view. It focused more on how far the beach stretched down the shoreline.

"Welcome to the Moon Deck." He strolled out to the middle of the deck between a row of rattan loungers and sun umbrellas in their down position.

"It's pretty." Cora sauntered past him to the wide concrete railing that wrapped around the deck. "But don't you mean 'sundeck'?"

"No. I mean Moon Deck. Because it's the best place to look at the moon." He pointed where the perfect half-moon hung in the velvety sky, its silver reflection splashed out over the inky waves. "You should see it when it's a supermoon."

"I'm sure it's amazing. But if it's the Moon Deck, why is it covered in suns?" She pointed to the emblem stamped into different parts of the deck.

He waved away the idea. "That's a moon."

She cocked an eyebrow. "With squiggly rays coming off it?"

"Those are moonbeams."

She studied him for a second. "You're pretty committed to this moon theme, huh?"

"It is the best place to do stargazing."

She laughed. "Then 'Moon Deck' it is." She held up her glass. "And if I remember correctly, we're out here on the *Moon Deck* to celebrate."

He raised his glass, too. "That we are." But his focus was on her. He'd never noticed the golden flecks in her mahogany eyes before. Or the way tiny freckles perfectly dusted her nose.

"Is it bad luck to toast something that hasn't happened yet?"

"Possibly." He took a step closer to her, and sparks seemed to fill the air between them. "Maybe we should toast to something else to stay on the safe side."

"What do you suggest?" Her eyes locked with his in a sizzling gaze, and she took a small step toward him.

"How about to AI?"

"I think you mean 'a revolutionary scientific method.'" Her signature sass and the look in her eyes pulled him toward her.

He took the last tiny step, closing what was left of the gap between them. "To science," he whispered. He let his fingertips trail down her arm from her shoulder to her elbow as her intoxicating scent of flowers and confidence washed over him.

"I think this is the part where we clink glasses." Her voice came out in a husky whisper.

"Is that how it works?" His lips hovered right over hers.

"Generally speaking. Unless you kiss me. Are you going to kiss me?"

He grinned, placing his hand on her waist and pulling her ever so slightly closer. "That is the plan, yes."

"That could get in the way of the toast."

"I'll take my chances." He paused for a second. "As long as that's okay with you."

She tilted her face up to him, and without answering she kissed him first.

25

Cora

C ora had to admit she had been wrong about a lot of things.

Jax wasn't the villain she'd thought him to be.

Apparently dating apps weren't as bogus as she'd once claimed.

And it was possible to fall in love in less than three weeks.

Turns out, Jane Austen was onto something, after all.

She let herself get lost in the kiss. The way his arm felt wrapped around her, holding her close. The way her fingers felt laced through his hair. The way she was trying not to spill her champagne but had zero focus left to worry about keeping the glass upright. She wanted to stay just like this, in his arms, lost in this moment forever.

And she might've, if it weren't for the incessant buzzing happening between them.

Not the emotional kind. The physical kind. From some sort of electronics.

Without adding any more space between them than necessary, she looked into his eyes. "I hate to ruin the moment, but what is that?"

He gave her a sheepish grin. "My phone." He let go of her waist and pulled the buzzing device out of his jacket pocket. He held it up as if proving his point, then flipped it over so he could read the screen.

She stepped back to give him room and took a sip of her champagne, trying to recenter herself with the physical world around her.

"They need me in the ballroom." He typed something on his phone, then looked over at her. "Sorry. I have to, um . . ." He nodded at the door but there was hesitation there, like he didn't want to go.

She didn't blame him. She didn't want to go, either. Being here with him, in the moonlight, felt magical. Almost like a dream. She didn't want it to end.

She was so practical and controlled ninety-nine percent of the time that she'd forgotten what this felt like. She'd forgotten what it was like to let go and let herself fall in love. To let herself be loved. And now that she remembered, she wanted to stay here, in his arms. Something about being here with him in the soft light of the moon made her feel safe. It was like they were separated from reality. The dangers of the real world couldn't affect them, and she could allow herself to let go.

Although maybe it wasn't the Moon Deck that gave her a feeling of security. Maybe it was Jax.

The thought both excited her and scared her.

"Is this *the* announcement? Are we finally going to have a legit reason to celebrate?"

He slid his hand around her waist again and pulled her into his strong chest. "As I recall, we were celebrating a perfectly legit reason. Us."

"Us," she repeated, letting the word echo through her. In the past it would have made her want to sprint away from here. The farther and faster, the better.

But not tonight. Tonight the possibility—the reality—of "us" made her want to stay. It made her excited not just to be in this moment but to see what the future held.

He pressed his lips against hers for a quick kiss. "I hate to say this, but, shall we?"

"If we must." Reluctantly, she untangled herself from his embrace, and they made their way from the magic of the Moon Deck back to the real world.

Cora had to blink against the harsh lights as they reentered the hotel. As they cruised down the hall toward civilization, she ran her hand through her hair in an attempt to look less disheveled. Next to her, Jax did the same thing, although she had to admit he looked as confident and in control as ever. He laced his fingers through hers.

When they got to the ballroom, most of the guests were already seated at the round banquet tables. A woman with a two-way radio headset and an iPad met them at the door.

She gave a quick glance at Cora, then ushered Jax around the perimeter of the room to the stage set up on the other side. A well-dressed, distinguished woman was already on the stage giving a greeting.

Cora wondered for a moment if she should follow them, but decided against it. Headset Lady looked like the kind of person who would've told Cora if she wanted her to follow, and she probably had zero patience for people who were where they didn't need to be. Besides, Cora had a better view of the stage from here, anyway.

She leaned against the back wall and halfway listened to the opening remarks, cherishing the warm glow of being in love.

The room was full of people sitting at tables draped in crisp white tablecloths and decorated with towering centerpieces. Guests dressed in tuxedos and sparkling dresses shimmered in the light. The clink of crystal and the happy hum of conversation provided the background to the formal remarks from the stage. Cora couldn't help but be swept up in the magic of the moment.

The woman onstage introduced CEO Anders Padua, and the room broke into applause as Jax's uncle took the stage.

"You must be the one." A young woman about her age in a low-cut, sparkling dress sidled up to Cora in the midst of the applause.

"I'm sorry?"

"Jax's new love interest." There was a hint of scandal in her whispered voice, and perhaps a little jealousy. Cora figured she was probably someone on the very long list of women Jax had dated. She was most likely here to give Cora yet another warning about what a heartbreaker he was.

"That would be me." A memory of the kiss swept through her, making her feel all warm and floaty. She didn't need another warning against Jax. At the moment, she felt pretty good about her decision.

"Are you new to town?"

"No, I'm from Houston. I'm only in town for the summer."

"Ah, that makes a lot more sense." Gossip Girl settled against the wall, seeming satisfied with the answer.

Although the comment struck Cora as strange. She probably should've let it go, but since letting things go wasn't her strong suit, she didn't. "Sorry, what makes sense?"

"We were all wondering how it would work. An out-of-towner makes sense."

Cora pulled her attention off the stage and focused on Gossip Girl. "How what would work?"

"The deal. You know, the *rumor*." She winked at the last word, as if it were an inside secret.

Cora was starting to get annoyed. "And which rumor might that be?"

"The one that Anders Padua would only give his nephew the SVP position if the untamable Jax Verona could figure out a way to settle down and find a committed relationship. But we figured there would be some kind of *arrangement*. Jax always finds a way to work the system."

It took a second for the words to register, but as soon as they did, understanding hit her with the force of a bomb. The rest of the room faded away, and Cora was standing there fully exposed with Gossip Girl and all her tea.

It was all a bet.

Of course it was. Jax wasn't in love. He was only with her—had only stayed with her—because he needed her to win some sort of bet with his uncle.

And Cora had been the fool who'd gone along with it.

"Right." Cora wasn't sure if she was agreeing with Gossip Girl's assessment, her own realization, or the fact that she was telling her body it had to continue standing despite her mind spinning out of control.

How could she have not seen this?

Gossip Girl leaned in like she was sharing a secret with her new bestie. "And since you and I both know committing isn't Jax's style, we were all wondering how he'd pull it off." She shot a side-glance in Cora's direction, sizing her up. "But you're brilliant. We should've known Jax would come up with something like this. Someone from out of town who can silently slip away after the announcement. No one knows you, so there won't be a mess when it's over."

"When it's over." Cora repeated the phrase.

Gossip Girl must have misinterpreted her tone, because she widened her eyes in an *oops* expression and covered her mouth with her dainty hand, all while maintaining her sly, knowing smirk. "Oh, we're still pretending it's real, aren't we? I mean, technically speaking the announcement hasn't been made yet." She leaned in again. "But between us, you're good. All anyone can talk about is how smitten Jax's new date is with him. Very convincing."

"It is my job, after all." Cora's voice was flat.

How had she missed the signs? How had she managed to let her walls, her well-constructed, well-justified walls, come down for the town playboy who needed a fake date?

Gossip Girl brightened. "Oh! Are you an actress? I read this book once where the main character needed a fake boyfriend, and she hired an out-of-work actor to do the job. It's kind of smart, actually."

It was at that exact moment that Anders announced Jax's name and the whole room broke into applause.

Everyone except for Cora.

After all what was the old saying? *Fool me once, shame on you. But fool me twice . . .*

Yeah, Cora wasn't going to let it happen.

Ever. Again.

She turned to Gossip Girl amid the thundering applause. "I'm a commercial photographer from Houston in town for the summer. Now, if you'll excuse me."

"Right." She winked again as if it were their little secret. But when Cora walked away, Gossip Girl's expression fell. "Wait, but you were in on it, right? You knew it was fake?"

Cora didn't bother to answer. She just kept going.

On her way out the door, she caught sight of Bianca seated at one of the tables in the back. Her expression must have said it all, because Bianca instantly went from a carefree wave to a look of concern.

Her sister whispered something to Lord Farquaad, and Cora didn't bother to watch to see what would happen next. She pushed through the door into the lobby.

She stomped out into the now-vacant area, her footsteps echoing off the marble floor. Red-hot anger bubbled up inside her.

She wasn't sure who was making her more furious: Jax for deceiving her, or herself for falling for him.

Geez! She should know better. This was the exact thing she warned everyone else about. Relationships didn't work. Men were selfish and always left. It happened with her dad. It happened with her ex-fiancé. Of course it would happen with Jax.

"Cora!" Bianca called behind her. Cora spun around to see her sister rushing toward her. "What happened?"

Tears stung Cora's eyes, which only made her angrier. She was *not* going to cry over this. Jax didn't deserve her tears.

With a frustrated huff, she blinked them back. She refused to even dignify them by swiping them away.

"It was all a ploy. Just some sort of deal he made to get the job he wanted." Cora motioned to the door that muffled Jax's voice.

Bianca stopped next to her, looking confused. "What?"

"Jax. SoulMatch. Whatever this was." She waved her arm around as if trying to encircle the entire summer so far. "Turns out he was only doing it so he could get the job he wanted."

"I mean, maybe at first," Bianca said.

Cora froze. Her eyes narrowed on her sister. "What?"

"That might have been how it started, but it's not the case anymore. He—"

"Wait, did you *know* about this?"

Bianca looked like a deer caught in the headlights. "Um . . ."

And a new truth dawned on her.

Jax wasn't the only one with a bet. Bianca was, too.

Suddenly, everything was becoming clear. All of Bianca's questions. The way she kept showing up at every date. Her seemingly friendly relationship with Jax.

Cora had never felt so stupid in her entire life.

Bianca launched into a flurry of excuses. "It was all really innocent at first. I happened to overhear him make the deal with his uncle. And it seemed like a good idea at the time, because I was so mad at Savannah. You were both looking to connect with someone and . . ." She let her words trail off, which Cora kind of expected. After all, where does one go with that kind of statement? *And we thought it would be a good idea to deceive my sister?*

"And you knew he would stick around, making you the winner of the bet," Cora finished.

Bianca stared at her feet and shrugged. "I was trying to beat Savannah at her own game. I just wanted to even the playing field because you—"

"Drive people away?"

Bianca looked into her eyes. "I had no idea you'd actually fall for him. No one thought he'd fall for anyone. I thought it would be harmless, and everyone would get what they wanted."

"And you'd get to marry Lord Farquaad while sticking it to me and Savannah."

Bianca looked confused. "Who?" Then enlightenment slowly dawned on her. "Ohhhh. Yeah." She looked at the closed doors, a different expression taking over. "Except you did fall for Jax. I mean, why wouldn't you? You're perfect together. I should've seen it then."

"I can't believe you." Cora seethed.

"Me?" Bianca took a step back. "Yeah, I was wrong. But in case you've forgotten, your reasons for dating him weren't exactly innocent."

"But I never tried to get him to fall in love with me. In fact, I was trying to do the opposite. I made my intentions known from the beginning. If he wanted out, I gave him an open invitation to get out." She held out her hand. "Give me the keys."

Bianca seemed confused by the sudden conversation switch. "What?"

"My car keys. You drove my car here, and I had Savannah drop me off. But I'm not staying. You can find your own ride home."

Bianca glanced around like she was searching for the right answer. "I, um, valeted."

Cora's hand was still outstretched when the doors to the ballroom opened and Jax rushed out, a concerned look on his face.

"Is everything okay?" There was genuine compassion in his voice.

Cora dropped her hand and focused on Jax, the anger burning inside her. "Congratulations on your promotion. I hope it was worth it." There was venom in her words, and she turned for the exit.

She had to manually tell herself not to run because she didn't want to look like some wounded animal. She was dignified and confident. She was bruised but not broken, and stronger than any of this nonsense.

At least that's what she told herself. It's what she wanted them to believe.

She would not let them see how much they hurt her. She held her head high, kept her posture perfectly straight, and strode out the door.

She didn't stop at the valet station. She had no idea how she would find her car in the parking garage, or get the keys, for that matter, but she didn't care. She certainly wasn't going to wait on the sidewalk like a sitting duck while someone pulled her car around.

She'd rather walk all the way home than be a captive audience while her sister and her so-called boyfriend tried to justify their actions. She didn't want one more reminder of how she'd been so stupid. Frankly, she'd rather walk all the way back to Texas than to ever have to see Jax again.

Except not in these shoes.

She paused as she entered the garage just long enough to rip the four-inch sparkling stiletto sandals off her feet and swipe at the tears streaming down her face. It didn't matter how nasty the floor of the parking garage was. She didn't care about a lot of things at the moment. She dangled the sandals from her fingers, gathered her skirt in one hand, and kept on marching up the steep incline of the parking garage ramp.

And that's when she saw it. Her car. Four spots ahead of her.

She also saw a horrified teenage boy wearing a valet uniform on the opposite side of the aisle from her.

She probably was a sight to see, with her bare feet, skirt gathered up, and mascara streaks running down her face. Later she would send him some sort of gift basket full of things teenage boys like as retribution, but right now she needed his help.

"That's my car. I don't have the tag so you'll have to trust me. But I need you to get it and bring it to me. I'm headed that way." She pointed in the direction away from the property. "Just keep driving until you see me."

The wide-eyed teenage boy just stared at her, not quite sure what to make of the task.

"If anyone asks, tell them it's for Jax Verona."

"Right." The name caused the kid to spring into action, and Cora changed her trajectory.

She had just reached the corner of the property and was about to turn on the main road when her car pulled up beside her. The passenger side window rolled down. "Mr. Verona asked me to tell you he's sorry and please call him."

Cora walked around the car to the driver side. "Tell Mr. Verona that's not happening." She switched places with the valet, and before he could even make it all the way back to the sidewalk, she was fastening her seat belt and driving away.

She wasn't sure where she was going. She might've headed straight for Houston, except her camera equipment was at the beach house, which was the one thing she wasn't willing to leave behind.

Although she didn't want to go back to the house right now. Even if Bianca wasn't there, she didn't want to talk to Savannah about this. The last thing she needed was a lecture from Savannah.

Which left . . .

Well, she wasn't sure, so she just drove.

Her phone rang over the car speaker. Her first instinct was to send it to voicemail, because as she told the valet, she had no intention of talking to Jax. Ever.

But as her thumb hovered over the End button, the name on caller ID made her pause.

Chris Glasner.

Savannah's husband?

She pressed Accept and mustered up the most normal-ish voice she could. "Hey, Chris."

"Cora, I'm so glad you answered," he breathed out as soon as she picked up. There was undeniable panic in his voice. "There's been an accident. They've taken Savannah to the hospital. Can you—"

He didn't even get the words out before Cora pulled a U-turn in the middle of the street, tires screeching, dust flying up from where she went off the shoulder. When the car was facing the correct direction, she pressed on the accelerator until the engine revved, and her car shot forward like she was on the Daytona International Speedway.

"I'm on my way. Tell me what happened."

26

Bianca

Fear. That's what gripped Bianca first.

It seemed to grab her with its icy clasp. She couldn't breathe. She couldn't think. She couldn't move.

She stood frozen in the middle of the lobby, still holding her phone in midair, like she couldn't even move enough to let it drop limply by her side. She wasn't sure if she blinked. It was like every function in her body had been stunned into a stupor.

Since all the speeches were over and dinner was in the process of being served, there were more people walking in and out of the ballroom between courses. The lobby wasn't busy, but it wasn't as vacant as it had been during her fight with Cora. If that could have been considered a fight. It was really just Cora yelling and stomping off.

Was it deserved? Probably.

Okay, fine. Yes, it was deserved. Once again she, Bianca the baby, had messed up. But she would've liked the chance to talk it over instead of watching Cora walk away without any sort of explanation.

And now there was this.

Several people passed Bianca as she stood like some sort of living statue. No one said anything to her. If anyone even cast a questioning glance in her direction, she didn't notice. Although to be fair, her brain wasn't functioning, either. The only thing she could think about was the fear.

She wasn't sure how long she'd been standing like that when Jax walked past and did a double take. "You okay?"

"I'm . . . It's . . ." She licked her lips, trying to get her brain to start again, but the fear seemed to have stolen her voice. "My sister," she whispered.

A concerned look wrinkled Jax's forehead. He took a step closer and lowered his voice. "You're still upset about the thing with Cora? Because I'm working on it." He ran a hand through his hair and stared off in the distance. "I think if I can just get her to talk to me, we can figure it out. But the valet said she took her car. Any idea where she'd go?"

"The hospital." Her whispered voice sounded choked, which was probably about right because it felt like the fear was squeezing every part of her.

Jax looked confused. "What?"

"There's been an accident. I have to go to the hospital." Tears began to slide down her cheeks.

Jax went pale. She could almost watch the color drain out of him from his head down to his feet, like someone had pulled a plug. "Who's been in an accident? Cora? Is Cora hurt?"

Bianca squeezed her eyes shut. She gave her head the slightest of shakes. "Savannah."

"Savannah," he repeated in a voice that sounded like half an exhale. A beat passed before he spoke again. "So Savannah had an accident and is in the hospital?"

With her eyes still shut, she nodded.

"Is she okay?"

Bianca shrugged. She wasn't sure why her eyes were still shut, except everything seemed less real when she was surrounded by blackness. Like maybe it was all a dream.

She felt Jax rub the outside of her arms. "Okay. No problem. I'll drive you there. Come with me." His voice was more confident now, more in control, and she felt some of her own shock start to wear off.

With one hand on her back, he led her toward the front door. "How about Cora? Does Cora know?"

Bianca nodded, the tears flowing in a steady stream now. "She called because Chris couldn't get ahold of me. I didn't answer. I didn't think it was important."

"It's okay," Jax said again in a calm, confident voice. "Let's get you to the hospital, and we can figure it out when we get there."

He left her standing just outside the door while he talked to someone. In what seemed like an instant, a black sedan pulled up and someone was opening the passenger side door for her.

"This is us," Jax said. He gave her arm another encouraging rub, then walked around and got in the driver's seat.

They drove in silence. Now that she was moving forward, some of her fear started to melt away. That was always how it worked. Maybe doing something gave her more of a sense of control. There was a plan.

Or at least when she was with a person who had a plan. Jax seemed to know what he was doing, and she was hitched to his plan, which seemed to be her go-to strategy in life. When things went sideways, find someone else to straighten them out. Was it a winning strategy? No. But it seemed, at least at the time, like an easier strategy.

And her life was going sideways in so many different ways, most of which were thanks to her stupid attempts to try to fix her own broken situation. And, if she were being honest, her own situation was only broken because she'd messed that up, too.

She stared out the window and watched the world speed by. There were a lot of things she needed to make right, but she needed to start with Cora and Savannah because family was the most important. And Bianca was most upset that she'd put that at risk.

They pulled into the emergency bay at Sunnyside Memorial Hospital, and Bianca was out of the car before Jax even had it in Park.

She went through the automatic doors, her head swiveling in every direction to figure out where she needed to go. Her heart thundered in her chest as she stopped at the counter with a giant Information sign. It seemed like a good place to start.

"Hi. I'm here for my sister, Savannah."

The lady behind the desk smiled brightly. "Who?"

"Savannah. Savannah Glasner. She's here. Maybe . . . I mean . . . Can you tell me where to find her?"

"We can try. Is she a patient here in the ER or at the hospital? Because that will change how I look for her."

"ER, I guess. I don't know."

"And was she a self-admit or brought by ambulance?"

"Ambulance, maybe?"

The woman tapped on the computer in front of her. "How do you spell that last name?"

Bianca was about to lose her patience when she spotted Cora on the other side of the large waiting area, in front of a set of swinging double doors, talking to some official-looking woman wearing scrubs. "Never mind."

She rushed across the room to where Cora was standing. "I'm here. What happened? What's wrong? Where's Savannah?"

Cora thanked the scrub-clad lady and waited until she walked away before she turned to Bianca. "All I know is they found Savannah unconscious and think maybe she blacked out and fell. She's stable and awake, but they're running tests. CT scan, X-rays, echo-something or other." Cora seemed shakier than Bianca had ever seen her, which did nothing to help her own fear. If strong, confident Cora was shaken, then . . .

"Is she going to be okay?" Bianca didn't really want to go there either, but she needed to.

Cora shrugged again. "All they'll tell me is that she's stable, which I guess is good." She let out a frustrated huff. "But it's hard to get anyone to talk to me in this place."

"So, what? We just . . . wait?"

Cora huffed again, then walked over to a row of empty chairs. She slouched down in one of them, her dress pooling on the floor around her feet.

"Look, Cora, about earlier—"

Cora held up a hand. "Don't."

"But—"

"Not right now. Not here." She crossed her arms in front of her chest and stared straight ahead.

"I'm sorry," Bianca whispered. Then she joined Cora in the row of uncomfortable hospital chairs to wait.

27

Cora

*I*f Cora could've wished for one thing in this moment—besides this moment not existing at all—it would've been a scrunchie.

It was probably an odd wish, given the current situation. She was sitting in an uncomfortable hospital chair in a dress that made it hard to breathe and shoes that were four inches tall.

But her hair was in her face, feeling sticky and heavy from the product she'd used to style it, and she just wanted to pull it up. She'd be able to think better if she could just get it off her neck.

It didn't have to be a scrunchie, per se. Any sort of hair tie would do. She'd even had some success in the past with twisting her hair up with a pencil when nothing else was available. At this point, she'd take anything that would get her hair out of her eyes.

She gathered it up and twisted it into a bun, hoping it might magically stay.

It didn't.

She sighed and shifted positions, hoping her sticky, heavy hair would at least stay off her shoulders.

It had been almost ten minutes since they'd sat down to wait. Ten minutes of listening to every second tick by and wondering what was happening behind those ominous swinging doors.

Unconscious? Like she'd fainted? Cora knew Savannah had been looking tired. She kept telling Bianca something was off. She should have pressed Savannah harder for answers.

Or she should have stayed home from the dumb gala. That would've solved a lot of problems.

In frustration, she gathered up her hair again and twisted it into a tight bun, only for it to instantly cascade down around her shoulders like a shampoo commercial.

Dang fancy hair masks and expensive blowouts.

"Do you have a hair tie?" It was the first thing she'd said to Bianca since they sat down, and it came out as more of a demand than a question.

Bianca looked hopeful. "Are you talking to me now?"

"No." She had no intention of talking about what Bianca had done. She didn't want to hear whatever pathetic excuse she had for why her actions were justified, or what she did or didn't think actually happened. And even if at some point they had that conversation, Cora sure wasn't having it here. "But I could use a hair tie."

Bianca held up her phone. "This is the only thing I have with me. This dumb dress doesn't even have pockets. Everything is in my clutch that I left on the table with . . ." She gasped. "Zander."

She stared down at her phone and rapidly sent off a text. Cora was watching her when a voice interrupted them.

"Hi. Are you Cora?"

Cora looked up to see a woman with a hospital ID badge and a friendly smile standing in front of her.

"Yes. Yes, that's me." She leaped out of her chair, forgetting she was wearing a tight dress and four-inch spiky heels. She wobbled unsteadily, trying to find her center of balance, almost knocking into the woman. "Sorry about that."

"No problem. I always have a hard time in heels, too." The kind woman held out her hands to steady Cora and let out a light, tinkly laugh. "I'm Diana."

"Do you have news? About Savannah?" Cora pushed her hair out of her face as she fired off the frantic question.

"I'm not involved with her care plan, so I don't have specific information. But if you're ready, I'm here to take you back to see her." She waved her hand in a *follow me* gesture and turned for the swinging doors.

Cora and Bianca followed Diana, who pushed through the doors to the hallway behind. The setup looked similar to the halls she'd already walked with Jax, except the rooms seemed to be smaller, and there were no cheerful murals of cartoon characters at the beach.

Adults really did miss out on all the good stuff.

"You can't stay long," Diana explained. "Savannah's only in this room while they're waiting to take her to imaging and admit her to the cardiac unit. In the meantime, they're trying to keep everything calm and quiet around her because her heart is still pretty weak."

"Her heart?" Cora asked, her fear spiking.

Diana gave her a reassuring smile. "But a quick hug never hurt anyone, right? Besides I tend to think family makes things better. We're all stronger when surrounded by our loved ones."

They stopped at a door midway down the hall, and Diana pushed it open. "Just keep it light and encouraging."

Cora nodded and ventured in first. The room was dimly lit, and Savannah was laying in the hospital bed with her eyes closed. All kinds of wires were attached to her and running in different directions. Monitors on both sides flickered in reds and greens and bright whites as various bits of information flashed across the screens. Savannah's right arm was propped up next to her and wrapped in some sort of splint.

The scene took Cora's breath away and once again, tears stung her eyes. She blinked them back, because while seeing her sister this way seemed like a valid reason to shed tears, that wasn't what Savannah needed at the moment.

"Hey, Van," Cora said in a soft voice. "We're here." She laid a gentle hand on Savannah's blanketed leg.

"Hey, sis." Bianca used the same soft, soothing tone.

Savannah's eyes fluttered open, and a weak hint at a smile somewhat brightened her pale face. "What are y'all doing here?"

Her voice was soft, but it sounded stronger than Cora was expecting. The smile looked less like someone who was sick and more like someone who was going to be okay.

"I think the better question is what are *you* doing here?" Cora raised an eyebrow.

Savannah pushed herself up to a seated position, wincing a little in the process. "Well, that's a funny story," she said.

"Funny like 'ha-ha' or funny like 'y'all will never believe this'?"

Savannah gave them a sheepish look. "Probably the second one."

Then she told them about her heart defect and how she'd likely had it since she was born, but having kids made it worse. How it had been getting a lot worse recently, which was why she was tired all the time. And probably the reason she fainted and fell off the ladder she was standing on to hang the café lights on the deck. Luckily, a couple who was walking on the beach saw her fall and called 911.

She held up her splinted arm at the end of the story. "And I probably broke my wrist. Not really the souvenir I wanted from this summer."

"Why didn't you tell us?" Bianca asked, sitting on the corner of Savannah's bed.

Savannah shrugged. "I don't know. I wanted to, but I couldn't find the right time. What was I supposed to say? 'What do y'all want to do for lunch? By the way, I have a hole in my heart that seems to be getting bigger.'"

"Is there anything they can do for it?" Cora asked. She couldn't exactly give her sister her own heart, although she would've if she could have. But if Savannah needed a new heart, or even an entire new circulatory system, Cora would storm to the ends of the earth to get it.

"Actually, it's pretty treatable. As far as heart defects go, they tell me this is not an awful one to have. We've been trying to manage it with meds, but it's looking more and more like I'm going to need surgery."

"And the surgery will fix it? Like, completely?" Bianca asked.

Savannah nodded. "That's what they tell me."

"Holy smokes." Cora flopped into the chair next to her, letting the panic she'd been feeling since she had gotten the call start to dissipate. "Then why on earth haven't you done that?"

Savannah shifted uncomfortably. "Oh, you know. Trying to schedule it has been a trick. There are holidays and my kids' birthday parties. Plus, you know, a stay-at-home mom doesn't exactly get medical leave. Who's going to do all the stuff?"

"That's what we're here for. We'll help. We are your medical leave policy," Cora argued.

"But you live in Houston, and you . . ." She turned to Bianca. "Are about to move."

"Yeah, but you still have a guest room, right?" Cora stood up and took Savannah's hand. "Tell us what you need, and we'll do it."

"How about making it so I don't have to have surgery at all?" She jabbed her finger at her chest. "Because I don't even like to get shots in my arm. This is surgery. On my heart."

"So we find you the best heart surgeon in the country," Cora said.

"You won't have to do it alone. We'll all be with you every step of the way." Bianca joined them on the other side, resting her hand on Savannah's leg. "We'll even let you make us a chore wheel for while you're recovering."

Cora gave Savannah's hand a squeeze. "We'll get through this. Because the Prestly girls always pull through together."

The nurse popped her head back in the room. "Okay, Savannah, we're ready to take you down to imaging."

"I guess that's our cue to leave." Cora reluctantly backed away from the bed as the scrub-clad staff came in to get Savannah ready.

"Smile pretty for your pictures," Bianca said. "We'll be waiting for you when you're finished."

"Thanks." Savannah adjusted herself in her bed, getting ready to be wheeled away. "I'm sorry I ruined your night."

Cora shot a knowing look at Bianca. "Trust me. You didn't ruin it."

They backed out of the way, and the hospital staff rolled their sister out of the room.

Diana was waiting for them in the hall. "I'm going to take you out this way. Her room is almost ready on the cardiac floor. After they're done in imaging, they'll work on transferring her up there. The main lobby is a much more comfortable place to wait than the ER." She motioned in the opposite direction from where they came.

"Thanks," Cora said. She felt so much lighter than when she'd walked in through the other set of doors.

Obviously, she didn't want her sister to have any health problems, but this health problem was fixable. It was one they could conquer. There was hope.

"Thanks for letting us talk to her. I needed that," Cora said.

"I'm glad I could do it."

"And I guess I should thank the other nurse, too."

"The other nurse?"

"You know, the first one I talked to. I can't remember her name. I assume she's the one who set this up."

Diana shook her head. "I'm not sure which nurse you talked to, but Jax was the one who made this happen." She pushed through swinging doors on the other end. "Typically we would've waited until she had been transferred, especially since you're not the spouse. But he insisted we let you see her now." She shot Cora a knowing look. "And Jax can be pretty convincing if he wants to be."

"Jax did this?" Cora was completely shocked. How did Jax get involved in this?

"You can wait here or out in the courtyard, and I'll come find you when she's in her room," Diana said. She gently rubbed Cora's shoulder, then disappeared behind a different set of doors.

Cora stood in stunned silence, trying to make her sluggish brain decide where to sit, when Bianca blurted out, "I'm sorry."

She let out a tired sigh. "I thought we weren't doing this right now."

"I know that's what you said, but for what it's worth, I never meant to hurt you."

Cora glared at her sister. "And this is the place you want to have that conversation?"

Bianca didn't back down. "I'm willing to do this wherever you'll listen."

"Fine. Talk."

"I know it sounds stupid, but I honestly thought it would be harmless. I never, ever thought you'd fall for him."

"Why? Because I have a heart of stone?"

"No." Bianca dropped her gaze to her feet, her shoulders slumping with guilt. "I just thought you didn't do love. Like maybe it wasn't your thing."

"I've been in love before." Cora didn't bother to hide the offense in her voice.

"I know," Bianca said. "At least, I know the story. But I wasn't there. You were in Texas, and I was in high school dealing with moving from Mom's house to Dad's apartment and trying to manage graduation parties with Mom's chemo schedule. Your life, and you in general, were . . ." Bianca paused for a second as if deciding on a word, then shrugged. "Distant."

The confession hit Cora like a slap to the face, surprising and stinging.

For so long she'd been so busy pointing a finger at everyone else that she'd missed all the fingers pointed back at her.

She'd never thought about what that season of life must have been like for Bianca. She had been completely occupied with trying to manage her own life of building a business, being engaged and flying in and out of Atlanta when she was needed. It was such a painful season for Cora, and she realized now that she used the distance as an excuse to not have to think about how hard it must've been for her sisters, especially Bianca.

"I'm so sorry," Cora said. "You're right. I should've been there for you more."

Bianca shrugged. "It was fine. I had Savannah and Dad."

"But you didn't have me. And you should have." She let that truth settle for a moment. "But you didn't miss anything by not getting to know Leo. He was a jerk."

Bianca cracked a smile. "That's what I hear. How did you end up engaged to him, anyway?"

Cora shook her head, thinking of all the things that had led up to that moment. All the warning flags she'd missed. "A lot of bad decisions and being blinded by love. I promised myself I would never let it happen again."

It was how she had lived her life ever since. She'd blocked out every relationship that had the potential to blindside her, and not just the romantic ones. That meant she'd blocked out pretty much everyone, even keeping her sisters at arm's length.

But not Jax. Somehow Jax managed to break through the barrier, which was baffling. How, when she was so determined to keep everyone else out, had he managed to get in?

"For the record, the relationship might have started out fake for him, but that's not how it ended up. His feelings for you are real."

Cora crossed her arms in front of her chest. Maybe she'd forgive her sister, but she wasn't about to forgive Jax. He'd used her. He'd tricked her. And even worse, she'd let him.

Nope. When it came to Jax, she was out.

"He used me."

"Maybe." Bianca twisted her mouth to the side, as if considering the whole situation. "But you know what they say. Those in glass houses . . ."

That hit a little close to home. But she hadn't been playing with his heart. She hadn't been trying to make him fall in love with her. In fact, she was trying to prove that he *couldn't* fall in love with her.

Bianca lifted her gaze to her sister's. "Are we good?"

Cora nodded. "Yeah. We're good."

"Is this where we hug it out?" Bianca held her arms out.

Cora looked at her sister's outstretched arms skeptically. "I—"

But before she could get an argument out, Bianca wrapped Cora up in a tight embrace. Cora gave in and let the healing power of a hug seep into her body.

They stood like that for several seconds before Bianca mumbled, "Oh, good grief."

Cora stepped away from the hug and turned in the direction Bianca was staring.

Zander was at the hospital information desk, and even from all the way across the lobby, she could see him flexing his pecs through his too-tight dress shirt.

Bianca had a disgusted look on her face. "To think I almost lost my sisters over *him*."

"He is a sad, strange little man," Cora said, quoting Buzz Lightyear in *Toy Story*, one of their favorite childhood movies.

Bianca laughed. "You can say that again."

She felt for her sister, because she'd been there. She knew about wanting something so badly that you started to dismiss all the reasons you needed to let it go. "Being blinded by love is a real thing, you know."

"I was blinded by something, all right." She shook her head at her own ridiculousness. "Excuse me while I fix another mistake."

Cora was watching Bianca meet up with Zander so they could "talk" when she spotted her own mistake on the far side of the room. Since it seemed to be fix-it hour, she headed over to do a little repair work of her own.

"I guess I should say thank you for driving Bianca here. And for getting us in to see Savannah. She's doing fine, by the way." Her voice was flat, almost annoyed as she delivered the obligated appreciation.

"I'm glad to hear she's doing well. They wouldn't actually give me any information."

Cora crossed her arms in front of her chest. "You've done your good deed. Why are you still here?"

"Because no one should have to go through a moment like this by themselves." His tone was gentle and caring, and yes, there was probably compassion in his eyes. But it wasn't enough. What he had done was inexcusable.

"And you assume you're the person I'd want here with me?"

"Probably not. But I'm still not willing to let you go through it alone. I'll sit over there, out of your way. Just know that you have someone on your side. You're not alone."

She shrugged. "Fine. Whatever."

He held up a bag. "And I thought you might want this."

She stared at the bag like it was one of his sad playboy tricks to try to win her back. "What is that?"

"Clothes." He held it out to her. "I thought if you were sticking around here for a while, you might want to change into something more comfortable."

"You brought me clothes?"

"Yes." He looked at the bag. "Although to be completely honest, they're my sister's clothes. She picked them out. I'm not entirely sure what she put in there, but I think you're close enough to the same size. Since I had no idea about your shoe size, I just put some of the slippers we have at the hotel in there. Not an ideal solution, but I figured they would be more comfortable than what you had on."

Cora took the bag from him and looked inside. There, on top of the folded clothes, was a note that said *Our prayers are with you* in loopy, feminine handwriting. Along with two hair ties.

"This does not mean you are forgiven."

Jax shook his head. "Of course not. I get it."

"But thank you for this, too." She took out one of the hair ties and immediately pulled her hair into a ponytail.

"I'll be over here." Jax nodded toward the chairs on the far side of the room. "If you need anything else, just text me. Or, if you already blocked my number, just tell the hospital staff, and they can pass it on. Or write it down and send it by paper airplane. You know, whatever."

Despite being so mad, she couldn't help the hint of a chuckle.

Her dumb, traitorous heart.

"And for the record," he said, looking into her eyes, "it may have started out as a bet, but somewhere along the way I fell for you. Everything I said, everything from tonight—that was all real."

If only that were enough.

28

Jax

Jax slouched on one of the plastic upholstered armchairs in the hospital lobby, thinking about how his life had gotten so off track. In an attempt to secure the life he thought he'd always wanted, he lost the only thing he needed. Or maybe he should say the only *one*.

That's where fate was cruel. Without the bet, there would be no Cora. He never would've met her in the first place. He never would've been on SoulMatch. He never would've abandoned his two-date rule. He never would've met the woman he fell in love with.

But with the bet, there was never a possibility of a future with her. Their relationship was doomed before it even started.

Of course, when he made this ridiculous deal with his uncle, that hadn't mattered to him. His only goal was to get the job. The job he thought he always wanted. The job he thought he deserved. Falling in love was never part of the plan.

He wasn't sure when their relationship had stopped being about the bet for him. Was it when they were sitting in the sand, looking at her photographs? Or when he watched her connect with the kids while they played games? Or over hot dogs while they gazed at the waves?

Or maybe it had happened even before that.

Somewhere along the way, his time with Cora had stopped being about getting a job and started being about Cora.

He'd never met anyone who tempted him to want to look at forever. The idea of a commitment like that had sounded so restrictive, he had trouble taking full breaths. But here he was, not being able to imagine a future without her.

Except he'd ruined it.

"Hey, Jax! Is that you?"

A familiar voice pulled him out of his slump. He sat up to see Haden being wheeled across the lobby, his parents behind him, carrying a crate with all the comfort items he kept in his room.

Jax jumped out of his chair to meet them. "What? Are they springing you out of this joint?"

Haden pressed his lips together in a proud smile and nodded. "No more Jell-O for me."

"That's the best news I've heard all day. Congrats, my man." He held out his hand, and they did their secret fist-bump.

"It's nice to see you, Jax," Haden's mom said. "We're going to pull the car around while you chat." They left their son with Jax and the hospital aide, who was manning the wheelchair.

"Why are you here?" Haden asked. "It's a little late for games, isn't it? They almost didn't let me go home tonight since it was so late."

"I'm here for a different reason. Remember my friend you met? Her sister was just admitted."

The ten-year-old nodded sagely. "That's a bummer."

"Big time," Jax agreed. "But it looks like she's going to be okay."

"That's good. So why are you down here instead of up there with them? I bet they'd let you use the game cart."

"The truth is, I did something dumb, and my friend is mad at me."

"So that's why you look like that." He waved a hand in front of Jax as if to sum up his entire appearance.

Leave it to kids to tell the whole truth.

"Did you say sorry?" Haden continued.

"I did, but sometimes saying sorry isn't enough."

Haden thought about that for a second. "Maybe. But a wise game player once told me that everyone makes dumb moves once in a while. It's what you do to fix the dumb move that counts."

Jax smiled. "I did say that, didn't I?"

Haden shrugged. "You have good game advice every once in a while."

"Glad I can help. But in this case, I don't know if my dumb moves can be undone."

"But do you like her?"

Jax nodded. "I do."

"Then don't give up. Sometimes it takes a couple of tries to get it right." He leaned in and lowered his voice to conspiratorial tones. "You told me that once, too."

Jax chuckled. "I did. Maybe it's time for me to start taking some of my own advice. Thanks."

Just then they spotted Haden's parents pull their car under the carport. Haden's mom got out to open the door for him.

"Looks like my ride's here. Gotta go." He held out his hand for another fist bump. "I'll see ya next time."

Jax nodded as the hospital aide wheeled Haden away. "I hope not," he whispered once Haden was out of earshot. Because nothing would make Jax happier than Haden not ever having to spend another night in the hospital.

Okay, not nothing. Fixing things with Cora would make him pretty happy. Ecstatic, even.

Don't give up.

He might've taught Haden a few life lessons, but Haden had taught him plenty, too. The biggest one was to keep fighting, even when the odds seemed stacked against you. And if Haden could keep fighting, so could he.

29

Savannah

*A*fter being in the hospital for less than twenty-four hours, Savannah was released to go home under the strict conditions that she take it easy for the next week and keep the pre-op appointment with her own cardiologist a week from Monday.

"I promise," Savannah said as she signed her discharge paperwork.

"And I promise to make her," Bianca added, giving her sister a serious look. "She's been bossing me around my entire life. It's my turn now."

The nurse gave an approving nod. "Sounds like you're in good hands."

They wheeled Savannah through the hospital doors to where Cora was waiting next to the car. "There's a surprise for you at home," she said.

"What is it?" Savannah cradled her casted arm, which was broken in two different places, against her body to try to avoid any more pain.

"Nope," Cora said, climbing into the driver's seat. "If I told you, it wouldn't be a surprise, would it?"

"But you're going to like it," Bianca said from the back seat.

They were right. When they pulled up to the beach house, there was a banner hanging across the front that said "Welcome Home, Mommy." Two giggling girls and a very handsome man were standing in front of it.

She really was the luckiest woman alive.

"What is this?" Savannah said as soon as she stepped out of the car.

"We're here! Two loops early!" Genevieve announced.

"At the ocean!" Juliette threw her hands up in the air and spun in a circle.

"I'm so glad because I have missed you." She held out her good arm, and both girls ran to her for the best single-arm hug she could manage.

Chris joined them, giving her a kiss. "You gave us quite a scare."

"You gave us all quite a scare," Cora added.

"I know, and I'm sorry. But starting right now, I'm putting my health first."

"Good, because we've implemented some new house rules. Starting with a mandatory chore chart," Cora said.

"A chore chart, huh?" Savannah raised a skeptical eyebrow since she'd seen how well the first chore chart had worked.

"Yep. Except unlike last time, this time everyone is required to do their jobs. No exceptions. No excuses. Even from you." Cora gave her a stern look.

"I'll do my best," Savannah said.

"Ta-da!" called Bianca, who had snagged the chore chart from inside and held it triumphantly over her head before handing it to Savannah.

It was the same wheel that she'd made weeks ago, but it had been revised. The pies in front of Cora's and Bianca's names now had extra jobs written in with a black marker. And the pie next to her name had a whole new paper taped in place.

She only had three jobs: rest on the couch, rest in a lounger, and rest on the bed. Savannah pointed to the second choice. "I choose the lounger on the deck."

"Perfect choice," Cora agreed. "Because we're grilling hamburgers tonight. Right after Chris and I take the girls for a quick swim."

"Hooray for waves!" Juliette danced around, and for the first time, Savannah realized they were already dressed in swimsuits with the matching cover-ups she'd bought them for the trip.

It wasn't exactly how she'd imagined the scene would look. The girls' hair wasn't styled in the perfect, photo-ready braids she'd imagined.

The umbrella wasn't up, and the beach loungers weren't set for the first trip down to the water. Every single beach picture from here on out would have her arm in a cast, and she'd be spending far more time in a chair than she'd intended.

In fact, the whole summer didn't look the way she'd imagined. The Summer Bucket List had more empty boxes than checked-off ones. Even the activities they *had* done hadn't turned out like she'd thought they would. And of course, there was the impromptu sleepover at Sunnyside Memorial Hospital, which hadn't been comfortable for anyone.

Even now, the flurry of activity around her was chaos. People bumped into one another as they gathered floats and towels and snacks. Genevieve cried because sunscreen stung her eyes and Chris had white streaks on his face from where he hadn't rubbed his sunscreen all the way in. Juliette was walking around with a Twizzlers rope hanging from her mouth, and the entire house fussed over Savannah getting settled in a lounger, as if a tiny hole in her heart somehow made it hard to sit down without missing the chair. As if she hadn't been practicing that move every day for the last thirty-three years.

But as she watched the scene unfold, she realized that while it might not have been what she'd envisioned, what was in front of her was even better. There was laughing and talking and togetherness. These moments, as messy and unexpected as they were, were memories in the making.

"Auntie Cora, I'll race you," Genevieve was saying. "Last one in is a rotten egg!"

"You're on!" Cora started running before she'd even finished speaking.

"Wait for me, wait for me!" Juliette cried, always half a step behind her big sister.

"I got you, Jules. We'll catch 'em." Chris scooped her up and set her on his shoulders. He turned back to Bianca. "Will you light the charcoal?"

"On it."

"I want a hot dog!" Juliette called from her perch on Chris's shoulders.

"On that, too."

It wasn't a perfect day, but maybe that was the problem. She'd been trying so hard for so long to make everything match the ideal vision she had in her mind that she missed the everyday perfection that was happening all around her.

Bianca reappeared from the side of the house with all the required supplies for the charcoal grill. "I hope a quiet environment wasn't part of your relaxation requirements. Because I'm pretty sure that's going to be impossible."

"Naw. This kind of noise is good for the heart." Or at least it was good for the soul.

Bianca busied herself with the grill. "How are you feeling? Do you need anything?"

Savannah shifted in her seat. "Are you my designated babysitter? Making sure I don't overexert myself?"

Bianca chuckled. "No, although it's not a bad idea to put someone in charge of making sure you take it easy. Apparently you haven't been the best at self-regulating." She gave Savannah a mock stern look.

That was fair. "I promise from here on out I'm going to be better about that."

"Good." Bianca finished lighting the charcoal, and she dropped onto the lounger next to Savannah. "I have to leave in a few minutes to go do a setup. But I wanted to help out by getting things rolling for dinner. I'm sure the girls will be starving when they get back from their swim."

"Thanks. Swimming always makes them ravenous."

They both watched their crew splashing in the waves in the distance and a silence fell between them. After a few silent minutes of staring off at the water, Savannah shifted to face her little sister.

"I'm sorry I made you feel like you're not good enough. That was never my intention."

Bianca looked at Savannah. "What?"

"I've had a lot of time to reflect over the last couple of days, and I realized that my actions may have not lined up with my intentions." She paused, trying to choose the right words. "I think you are one of the most amazing humans I know. You're smart and funny and creative. And I want the very best for you. But sometimes I get so determined to make that happen, I forget to stop and think what would be the best thing for *you*."

"My life doesn't look like yours. I'm not you."

"No," Savannah agreed. "And that's a good thing. You're more daring than I could ever dream to be, and I admire that about you."

"Thanks."

"I realize I haven't been as supportive of your decisions or as trusting of your intuition the way I should have. And I apologize for that."

"Well, you're not always wrong," Bianca said. "There have been a lot of bad choices in there."

"Yeah, but there have been a lot of wins, too. And if you want to marry Zander and start a new amazing life with him, then of course you have my support. You will always have my support."

Bianca scoffed. "Yeah, that's definitely one for the Fail column." She stared down at her hands, lost in thought. "I actually broke up with him. He's probably back in Idaho by now, or whatever place he thinks is posh enough for his glamorous lifestyle."

"What? When?" Although Savannah was surprised, she wasn't necessarily disappointed. She was trying to embrace life looking different than she'd imagined, but Zander was going to take a little warming up to.

"Yesterday. At the hospital, actually." She stared out at the water and drew in a deep breath. "You know, I think you were right about the gym-rat thing."

Savannah nodded. "He definitely gave off those vibes."

Bianca looked at her with a mystified expression. "I mean, what was with the flexing?"

"Maybe he's just really proud of his muscle control?"

"He's really proud of something."

They looked at each other and both dissolved into a fit of giggles.

After they stopped laughing, Bianca shook her head. "I have no idea how I let myself fall for that."

Savannah did. "You see the best in people and the most optimistic side of every situation. It's one of your best qualities."

"I'd say it makes me blind."

Savannah shrugged. "Sometimes, maybe. But you get it right when it counts."

Bianca seemed to let that resonate for a second. "Thanks."

"And if I start to overstep again, don't be afraid to call me out. Because I don't always get it right, either."

Bianca leaned over and engulfed her in a hug. "Maybe. But I wouldn't be where I am without you."

"Me, either," Savannah said, wrapping her good arm around Bianca.

"Although you should know," Bianca mumbled into her hair, "now that I'm not marrying Zander, I actually have nothing. No apartment. No job. No plans."

Savannah sat back and looked into her sister's eyes. "Sounds like what you really have is no restrictions. You're free to follow your heart any direction it takes you."

"I know. Which is scary."

"Yes. But you've never let that stand in your way. You're going to figure this out." She gave her sister's hand a squeeze. "And if you need to stay with us for a bit until you do, you're always welcome."

"Who's always welcome where?" Cora asked as she walked up the sandy path carrying a towel-wrapped Juliette.

"Involved in other people's business much?" Bianca said.

Cora climbed the few steps to the deck and set Juliette on Savannah's lounger. "I know, right? A wise person told me I needed to be more present, so I'm trying it out. What do you think?"

Bianca just shook her head. Then something near the back door caught her attention, and she shot up. "Oh, shoot. Is that the time? I gotta go." She sprang out of her chair and grabbed her things.

"Have fun at your setup," Savannah said.

"You're not mad I'm missing hamburger night or whatever this tradition is?"

Savannah shrugged, cuddling with her damp daughter. "I think it's time we start making some new traditions. And maybe one of them can be coming to see your beautiful dinner settings in real life."

Bianca grinned. "I'd like that." She gave everyone a quick hug, then dashed into the house.

When Chris and Genevieve got back, Chris took the girls into the house to give them a bath while Cora carried out a platter of hamburger patties for the grill.

As soon as she flipped the first one onto the grill, she looked over at Savannah. "I take it you and Bianca made up?"

Savannah sighed. Being back on good terms with her sister felt like a huge weight had been lifted off her chest. "Yes. But while we're on the topic of making up, there are some things I need to tell you, too."

"Okay, shoot," Cora said as she put the rest of the hamburgers on the grill.

"I might have let you believe some things that weren't exactly true about Mom and Dad's divorce."

Cora paused mid-flip. "What?"

Savannah swallowed. "The night of the big fight, I said you were acting like a sullen toddler when it came to Dad, which wasn't a nice thing for me to say—"

"You're forgiven," Cora said before Savannah could even get the whole phrase out and went back to her grill responsibilities.

Savannah continued. "But I realized that might be because I kept some things from you."

"Like what?"

"Well . . ." Savannah paused, trying to think through the best way to word the truth she'd conveniently concealed for the past sixteen years. But the time for thinking of the best way to say things had passed. Since she'd already started the conversation, it was time to lay it all out on the table. "You put all the blame on Dad for leaving us, but the truth is Mom wanted the divorce as much as he did."

Cora shook her head, her focus still on the grill. "No, she was devastated. He left us."

"Yes, it was hard on her. Her marriage had fallen apart. But that didn't mean she didn't want the divorce. And Dad didn't just leave. She asked him to move out." Savannah paused. "I can't begin to try to understand all the details of their relationship that led them to that decision. And maybe it isn't really for us to understand, anyway. But I do know it was very mutual. If you want to blame someone, you have to blame them both. Equally."

Cora narrowed her eyes skeptically. "Who told you that?"

"Mom." She considered that for a second. "And Dad. In multiple conversations."

Cora flipped a burger on the grill. The only sound was the sizzle of the meat while Cora considered what she was hearing. It took actual physical effort for Savannah not to fill the silence with words.

Finally, Cora looked up. "Why wouldn't they tell me that?"

"They tried," Savannah said gently. "But I think you weren't in a place where you wanted to hear it. To you, the divorce was a feeling of abandonment."

"Yeah. Because Dad left. And Mom had to fight her own battles. Even cancer."

"Well," Savannah said slowly, "not exactly."

"What?"

"Actually, Dad was pretty involved in her treatment. He drove her to her chemo appointments. Remember that book we kept all the notes in about what the doctors said so we could keep everything straight? He was the one who started that system. In fact, half of the handwriting in there was his. He talked with doctors and helped manage the never-ending mountain of medical bills. Especially at the end."

Cora blinked, looking off-balance. "I don't remember any of that."

Savannah shrugged. "You were in Texas at college. The day-to-day stuff wasn't your responsibility."

"But I came back. I was there on every break. I looked through the book and went with her to appointments and slept in the hospital. Why did I never see his involvement?"

"Sometimes we only see what we want to see."

Cora sank into a chair and stared off in the distance. Several silent minutes ticked by before she spoke again. "Why didn't you tell me this before?"

And this was where Savannah was at fault. In her attempt to keep the peace, she might have made things worse. "I should have. But I was trying to protect Mom. You were so mad. And you funneled all your anger at Dad. I was afraid that if you knew Mom was equally at fault, you'd stop talking to her, too." Savannah dropped her head, feeling ashamed. "And I was afraid if you stopped talking to Mom, you'd stop talking to all of us. I couldn't stand losing you, too. So I helped you build the belief that it was his fault so you wouldn't hate us."

"Oh, Savannah," Cora breathed out, tears glistening in her eyes. "I was just angry. I never hated you."

Savannah nodded. "I know. And I should have told you the whole story, but I thought if you were only mad at Dad, eventually you would come around. I didn't realize it would make things worse. I'm sorry."

They sat there for a second, savoring the truth laid bare before them.

Cora got up to flip the burgers. "So, what else haven't you told me about Dad?"

"He came to your college graduation."

She paused and stared at Savannah, looking shocked. "Really?"

Savannah nodded. "He has your photographs hanging on his walls of his house. And he takes your ads to show his golf buddies so often that they're about to ban him from bringing more pictures."

Cora was quiet while she pulled the hot dogs off the grill and stacked them on a plate. "Why are you telling me this now?"

"Because he might have stopped being married to Mom, but he never stopped loving us. It just dawned on me that you might not have realized that. And part of that was because I let you believe he was the one who left."

Once again she could see tears glisten in Cora's eyes, but her sister stayed focused on the grill. "So, what? I'm just supposed to forgive him and act like nothing happened?"

"Keeping the information from you was on me. And I apologize for that. I should've trusted you with it a long time ago. But what you do with the information, now that you know? Well, that's on you." She reached over and gave her sister's hand a squeeze. "But take it from me: life is too short to hold on to grudges."

30

Bianca

For the first time since she'd started doing these dinners on the beach, Bianca stayed for the whole thing.

Part of that was because this was her only setup for the night, so she didn't have to bounce around from location to location. Part of it was because she didn't have a ride. Luke had left about five minutes after unloading to go take care of two different property emergencies.

But most of the reason she'd stayed was because this dinner, a romantic candlelight dinner for a young married couple with two little kids, was nothing but one disaster after another.

Bianca had messed up the florist order and ended up with the wrong flowers on the wrong day. The caterer delivered the meal without checking her note about food allergies and had to remake the whole thing, causing a delay. The wind knocked one of the tiki torches onto some of the decorations, which started a small fire on the beach. Bianca had to run and help the couple stomp it out before anything important was damaged. And just to ensure that wouldn't happen again, she had to make sure the remaining tiki torches were anchored deep enough into the sand.

And for reference, nothing kills a romantic vibe like someone running around, manhandling burning sticks in the background.

Then, as if that weren't enough, the wife leaned too hard on the edge of the table when they were taking a picture and accidentally tipped the table over. Everything went sliding off, including her plate, which landed upside down in the sand. Only by the grace of her lightning-fast reflexes was she able to save her husband's plate.

So to summarize, the entire night was a disaster.

Except the couple didn't seem to think of it as a disaster.

"Life doesn't always go according to plan. But that's what makes it fun! You just have to go with it," the wife said. "Sometimes the best memories come from those unexpected turns." Then they scooted their chairs together and shared spaghetti off the same plate, like the scene from *Lady and the Tramp*.

And now, after they had finished dessert and the candles were getting low, they were dancing together in the moonlight.

"Spying again?" Luke whispered as he walked up.

Bianca shook her head. "Thinking."

He pulled up one of the plastic bins they used to carry their supplies and sat next to her. "About what?"

"About unexpected turns."

She twisted around so they were sitting knee to knee and looked into his eyes with a serious expression. "Were you serious when you said I could stay and take over this?"

Almost instantly, his demeanor turned more serious. "Yes."

"But I'd be taking over the business you started. You're really willing to give it up? To me?"

He leaned in, matching her seriousness. "Bianca, there would be no business if it weren't for you. I had an idea to put a table in the sand. You were the one who built this." He motioned to the scene on the beach far away. "People weren't excited about a table. But they can't seem to get enough of this."

Bianca gazed out at the dreamy setting where the couple was still dancing. "I've never felt as alive as I have doing this. I love it. Even when it doesn't go according to plan."

"That's good. Because rarely does anything in the hospitality industry go according to plan."

"Maybe that's why I like it."

"Or maybe it's because of moments like these." He nodded at the couple in the sand.

"Oh, it's definitely about moments like these." And the passion-filled engagements, and the special birthday dinners. And who knew? Maybe she'd even venture into weddings at some point. Really, the sky was the limit.

"Does that mean you're staying in town?"

Bianca sucked in a deep breath. It was a big step. A scary step. But it felt like the right one, at least for right now.

"Yes, I think it does. Of course, I'll have to find a place to live and iron out some of the logistics, but it looks like I'm moving to Sunnyside!" She threw her hands up in the air and let out a squeal—a quiet one, of course, as to not interrupt Fred and Ginger.

A smile spread across Luke's face. "That's great news. We'll be glad to have you. But how did you convince Zander to move his law practice to Florida?"

She waved a hand in the air. "We broke up. Turns out, he wasn't the man he said he was. I sent him back to Idaho, and I've never been so thankful for how far away it is."

Luke chuckled. "I'm sorry it didn't work out."

Bianca breathed in a deep, confident breath. "I'm not. I fell in love with the idea of a ready-made life, but honestly, I don't think I was ever in love with the man."

"Does that mean you're unattached?"

"Single and ready to mingle." Bianca grinned. "And ready to start my whole new life."

Luke licked his lips and paused, looking down for a second. Then he looked up at her. "In that case, since you're staying in town and all, maybe I could take you out to dinner sometime?"

Bianca almost said *of course* without even pausing to think about it. Because of course she'd go to dinner with Luke. She loved spending time with Luke.

And that's when it hit her. "Like, on a date?"

Luke looked bashful. "Yeah. I mean if that's what you want, too. But it's okay if you . . ."

"I'd love to," she said. And as soon as she said it, a sort of giddy anticipation filled her chest.

Wait a second, did she like Luke?

When had that happened?

He held her gaze, a broad smile spreading across his face. "Great."

"Great," she echoed.

All this time, Luke had been right there, and she'd almost missed it. For some reason she imagined that falling in love was all-consuming and all-encompassing, like a powerful wave that rolled over everything in its path. Every relationship she'd ever been in, she'd been looking for huge feelings that knocked her off her feet.

But maybe love didn't have to be like that. Maybe it was more like a sunrise. It started off soft and slow. So soft, in fact, that she'd almost missed it. But now that she was looking at it, she couldn't look away. It warmed everything inside her.

And she had a feeling it would turn into something breathtaking.

31

Cora

Two days after life had gone topsy-turvy (aka the gala fiasco), Cora sat on the sandy beach and stared at her phone. She knew what she needed to do. On some level she even wanted to do it. It was the right thing. She'd talked about it with her sisters. She'd done some deep introspection, thinking about some of the issues she hadn't wanted to deal with over the years. And all those conversations pointed to the same conclusion.

She needed to send a text.

It was a simple task, really. She sent thousands of texts every day. All it took were a few taps, a few words, and they didn't have to be spelled correctly. Punctuation wasn't even required.

But this wasn't just any text. It was a text to her dad.

She needed to be the one to send it. She had rejected every attempt he'd made to reach out over the years, and she realized now that some of her reasons for doing so were based on faulty information, combined with her blinding anger. She wasn't taking all the responsibility in what had happened, but it was time she took responsibility for her part. So here she was, offering the modern version of an olive branch.

Now all she had to do was do it. With the steady rhythm of the waves lulling her nerves, she started.

Hey, Dad. It's Cora.

Well, it was the text opening of a seventy-eight-year-old trying to figure out how "this newfangled technology" worked, but at least it was something. She briefly considered deleting her name because she was well aware of how texts worked. But on the other hand, it had been years since she'd sent one to her dad. Or called him. Or had any communication with him of any sort. If she got up the courage to send this message, she sure didn't want the response to be *new phone, who dis?*

So she was sticking with the generic Boomer opening. And now that she'd gotten the greeting out of the way, it was time for the meat of the message. She drew in a deep breath and before she could rethink it, she kept going.

> I'm going to be in town in a couple weeks. Maybe we can grab dinner?

Okay, so she was going with complete sentences and full punctuation. But as long as she was going Boomer style, she might as well own it.

As far as owning the question . . .

Her hand hovered over the Send button. It was such a simple question, but it felt like a giant step. Dinner? There were still a lot of hurt feelings and anger there, still a mountain of healing that needed to happen. But Savannah was right. Life was too short to spend it being mad at him.

Because without even realizing it, Cora had let her anger affect every single relationship she had, including her relationship with her sisters. It was time to start looking at forgiveness.

And yes, she knew that one dinner wasn't going to fix everything with her dad, but it could be a start. She needed to start down that road. She owed it to herself.

She read the question one more time. Then before she could talk herself out of it, she pressed Send.

Almost instantly her phone buzzed.

> Hi, Cora.
> It's really good to hear from you.

I'd love to go to dinner. Tell me when and where, and I'm there.

She stared at the last message.

He'd love to.

Okay, they were doing this.

Her stomach did a nervous flip. She had no idea how dinner would go or where it would lead, but just putting the wheels in motion made her feel lighter.

Great, I'll be in touch.

"I thought I might find you out here."

Bianca walked up and sank down into the sand next to her.

"I'm going to have dinner with Dad." Cora held up her phone as if she needed to prove it.

Bianca nodded. "Savannah told me you were thinking about that."

"And?"

"And I think it's a good idea. You two have a lot to talk about."

Yes, they did. And at some point she would think about the conversations they needed to have. But not right now. She'd taken enough big steps for one day.

So instead, she gave her sister a playful nudge with her shoulder to lighten the mood. "Maybe our first topic will be why he's still paying for your cell phone."

"Maybe you need to mind your business," Bianca joked.

Cora laughed. She'd missed this kind of relationship with her sisters.

"Anyway, it will be nice to have everyone talking again," Bianca continued.

Cora nodded. "Yeah. It will."

"Speaking of talking, have you talked to Jax yet?"

Well, that was a sneaky conversation change.

Almost instantly, her mood changed with it.

"No." Maybe she was short with Bianca, but that was because she was done talking about it. She'd said everything she'd needed to say to Jax at the hospital. And she'd even returned the clothes he'd kindly lent her to the hotel check-in desk. As far as she was concerned, things between them were over. She was moving on.

"Not at all?" Bianca asked.

"Nope." Of course, part of that could've been because she'd blocked his number, but whatever.

"You're not even curious about what he has to say?"

"Not really. He got what he set out to get. Now we go our separate ways. That's how it was always supposed to be, right?" Why were they still talking about this?

"Except everything changed when you fell in love," Bianca said.

The statement made Cora pause. It was weird to hear it out loud. It made her feelings for Jax somehow seem more real. Yes, she had fallen in love with him. She wasn't even sure how it happened. She wasn't someone who fell in love, not anymore. And yet, she had fallen in love with him.

"What did or didn't happen doesn't matter," Cora said. "It's over. Time to move on." She stood up and dusted the sand off her legs. "In fact, I'm not sure if Savannah told you, but I'm heading to Houston tomorrow. I need to get a few things in order before I fly out to Atlanta to help her out after her surgery. They scheduled it for the week after next. My flight has officially been changed."

"So that's it, then?"

How many different ways did she have to say it? "Yes, Bianca, that's it. The relationship had an expiration date from day one, which I knew. And I fell for him anyway. Which I was warned would happen by nearly every woman in town. But did I listen? No." She shrugged. "So I'm not sure if that makes him a jerk or me a fool. But either way, the end game is the same."

"So, what? You just fall out of love with him?"

Cora was starting to lose her patience. "Me loving him never mattered!"

"It matters to me."

The deep voice came from behind her. It was so unexpected she actually had to take a tiny step forward to keep from losing her balance.

Her first instinct was to stomp off and pretend Jax didn't exist. It was over. The damage was done. She didn't feel like she needed to hash it out over and over again while, as Bianca had so eloquently put it, she was trying to figure out how to fall out of love with him.

Although if she didn't at least acknowledge him, he'd probably follow her, and she had no desire to have whatever exchange was bound to happen at the beach house. He'd never actually been there before, so at least she had one Sunnyside memory that wasn't tainted by him, and she wanted to keep it that way.

With an annoyed sigh she spun around to face him.

Then her heart did the most ridiculous thing. Even though she was furious with him, even though she never wanted to see him again, her heart still fluttered at the sight of him.

Love was such a strange thing.

He was holding a white poster that said I'm Sorry in big black letters. Under it, in smaller letters, it said I Was a Fool.

"What do you want?" She didn't bother masking her hostility.

He tapped his poster. "I think I made it pretty clear." Then he leaned in as if sharing a secret. "It was all me. I was the fool. And the jerk. Guilty on both accounts."

She turned back to Bianca, motioning to Jax. "Were you in on this?"

Bianca shook her head. "No. I've interfered in this enough. But this is a pretty perfect coincidence, if you ask me. You might almost call it *serendipity*." Bianca gave her a nudge in Jax's direction. "I'll be at the house if you need me."

Cora let out a long, tired breath. As soon as Bianca was out of earshot, she turned back to Jax. "Okay, fine, you got your conversation. What do you want to say?"

"Did you mean what you said before? About the love thing?" He took a step toward her, and the magnetic draw that had always been between them tugged at her.

She could've lied. She could've said no, of course she wasn't in love with him, and walked away. This whole relationship had already been humiliating enough.

But she was tired of the lies and tired of the games. If she was going out, she at least wanted to go out with the truth.

"Yes."

He took another tiny step toward her. "You fell in love with me?"

She threw her hands up in frustration. "What is it with people not understanding answers today? Yes. I fell in love with you. Happy?"

"Yes, actually. Very." He grinned. It was the authentic one that made it hard for her to think clearly. "Now it's your turn to ask me a question."

She huffed. "Like what? How's the new job?"

"Good one." He nodded at her question choice. "Yeah, I turned it down."

That news caught her off guard. He what? She felt some of her defenses, along with her anger, start to drop. "What? Why?"

"Turns out it wasn't a good fit." He shrugged like *What do you do?* "The job kept me here. And I realized I don't want to be here."

For a moment she didn't say anything.

So this had all been for nothing? Seriously? Why would he even come here to tell her that?

"You're not going to ask me why not?" Jax prompted.

"Do you have a script you want me to read from, or are you just going to keep feeding me lines?"

He chuckled, but her sass didn't slow him down. "Because I'm at a place where I'm looking for a forever kind of relationship. Someone to share my life with. And I know enough to know I'm not going to find that here."

That's when the realization started to dawn on her, and optimism began to kick in.

Was he saying what she thought he was saying?

This time, she was the one who took a tiny step in his direction. "No? So where are you going?"

"Houston."

She couldn't help but grin. "Well, as you pointed out before, we have two million people in Houston. That'll give you a nice little candidate pool to choose from."

He closed the rest of the gap between them, dropping his poster to the side and sliding his free arm around her waist. "There's only one out of that two million I'm interested in. In fact, there's only one in the entire world. If she'll have me."

"But—"

She didn't know where she was going with that argument, except it was her natural instinct to put her walls back up. She'd already been hurt by Jax once. And as much as she was trying to open up and let love in, she wasn't sure she could handle having her heart broken by him twice.

But he didn't let her finish her argument. Instead, he launched into one of his own.

"I'm so sorry I hurt you. The truth was I never planned on falling in love. Forever was never in my picture. Then I met you. You're strong and independent and passionate and funny. The more I hung out with you, the more I couldn't imagine not being with you. I'm not even sure where it happened, but somewhere between the blueberry pie and that amazing dress, I realized that what I wanted more than anything in this world wasn't a job. It was you."

Tears that, once again, had no business being there stung her eyes.

He slid his other hand behind her head and caressed her cheek with his thumb. "I love you, Cora. Now and forever. In the easy times and hard times and whatever else is thrown our way. I promise, I am not leaving you. Where you go, I go. Whatever you go through, I go through."

She let the words resonate inside her, calming the fears she'd held on to so tightly for so many years.

Was letting herself fall in love still a risk? Absolutely. But she trusted Jax.

"I've got a better idea," she said, sliding her arms around his waist and staring up into his eyes. "How about we do it all together?"

He smiled down at her. "Sounds about perfect to me."

And then she kissed him. It was long and slow and perfect. And the only thing she could think was that she couldn't wait to do this for the rest of her life.

"So you really gave up the SVP job?" she asked when they finished the kiss.

"I did. I realized that my uncle was right about one thing. I'm not ready to settle down quite yet. But I'll still be involved with the company, just in a different capacity. And who knows? When he retires, we might reopen the conversation."

"So what are you going to do in Houston? Besides live out your blissful days with your one in two million, of course."

"I've been talking with my buddy about expanding the security transport business. Seems like a second office might make a lot of sense."

"You're going back into the spy business?"

"Something like that." He grinned. "Plus, I realized I liked it more than I thought I did, which was probably one of the reasons I kept letting myself get pulled into new jobs."

"But we can start telling people what you do, right? No more secrets?"

He nodded. "No more secrets."

"Well, in the spirit of full disclosure, you should know I'm going to start spending more time in Atlanta. I'm making an effort to spend more time with family."

"I fully support that decision. Family is important. And in full disclosure I'm going to have to travel for my job."

"Maybe we can coordinate schedules for when we have to be out of town," she said.

He grinned. "I think we can figure something out."

She narrowed her eyes, as if they were negotiating. "And what would you say to spending summers at the beach?"

He seemed to consider the question. "Since that's where my family is, too, I'd say it sounds like the perfect plan."

"Are you sure you can handle my big, loud, meddling family?"

He pulled her in close to him. "I love your big, loud, meddling family. Without them, I never would've met you."

"What happened to serendipity?" she teased.

"Like they say, sometimes it needs a nudge." He pressed his lips against hers in another quick kiss.

"I mean, I know I said take your time," Bianca called from the distance. "But, like, we can't wait all night to start the movie. It's a bucket list item, you know."

Cora shook her head. "Family," she said in mock annoyance. "Can't live with them . . ."

"But life isn't worth living without them," Jax finished. He offered his hand. "Shall we?"

They walked hand in hand through the sand to join her family. Together.

For the first time since they'd arrived, Cora thought something on Savannah's Summer Bucket List lived up to its name. Movie night on the deck was perfect.

Okay, it wasn't perfect in the sense that everything went according to plan, because pretty much nothing went to plan.

Besides having to wait on her and Jax to join them, Bianca had burned the popcorn. Cora had no idea how their dad used to get the sheet to stay between the two umbrellas, because it didn't matter how much tape they used, it refused to stay put. They ended up going with Cora's original idea to hang the sheet on the house. Where it also didn't stay.

But none of it mattered anyway, because by the time they got the sheet figured out, the Wi-Fi went out.

Even in the midst of the mess-ups, they were having fun. There was laughter and talking and sparklers and games. By the time Chris whisked the girls off to bed and Luke and Jax headed home, Cora thought it had been the best night of the summer. And most of that was because they were all together.

She was sitting out on the deck, chatting with her sisters in the moonlight, when they heard the doorbell ring through the screen door.

Instantly the conversation froze, and they all looked at one another. "Are we expecting someone?" Bianca asked.

Savannah checked her watch. "At nine fifty-five at night?"

Cora laughed. "Haven't we had this conversation before?"

"Well, I can confidently say it's not an ax murderer," Bianca added.

"How about a future business partner and potential boyfriend?" Cora asked, eyebrow raised.

Bianca shrugged. "Then he's out of luck, because the position is already taken."

Savannah laughed and pushed herself out of her seat. "I'll get it. Luke or Jax probably forgot something."

They all made their way through the house, except when they opened the door, it wasn't either one of the men they were expecting. It was a woman dressed in a polo shirt with an airline logo stitched onto it.

"Hi!" she said in a chipper voice. "Sorry to disturb you so late, but I thought whoever this belonged to would want it tonight. I have a missing bag for . . ." She checked her clipboard. "Cora Prestly." She motioned at the suitcase by her side.

"That's me." Cora pushed through her sisters to sign for the suitcase that had made it around the better part of the country. After thanking the woman, she pulled it inside.

"Well, look at that," Savannah said. "Everything worked out in the end. Even the suitcase."

"I think this is what they call the 'better late than never' rule."

"Agreed." Bianca nodded. "Speaking of late, should we clean up tonight, or can we leave it until tomorrow?" Bianca eyed the movie night mess in the kitchen and everything left out on the deck.

"Tomorrow," Cora said confidently. "Tonight is for enjoying."

"I second that," Savannah said. When her sisters looked over with shocked expressions, she shrugged innocently. "What? Y'all aren't the only ones trying out something new."

"Well, if we're trying something new, how about a midnight"— Bianca checked her watch—"I mean, 10:00 p.m. swim?"

"Absolutely not," Savannah said instantly. "I might be trying new things, but I'm not going crazy."

"How about a midnight wade? I'll put my feet in the water," Cora said.

Bianca shrugged. "I can go with that."

The three of them headed out the back door with their phones lit up like flashlights, heading for the water's edge.

"Next year we go skinny-dipping on the first full moon," Bianca said.

"Swimming at sunset," Savannah compromised.

"I love the ocean, but if I can't see below the surface, I'm pretty sure nothing except my feet are going in," Cora said.

"She does have a point," Savannah added.

Bianca just shrugged. "You laugh now, but it'll be a thing. Just wait and see."

When they got to the shore, they kicked off their shoes just above the waterline. Then, with their arms linked together, just like they used to do when they were kids, they waded out into the dark water.

"You know, Mom was right when she said we needed to come here," Bianca said as the waves washed over their ankles. "We needed this."

Savannah nodded. "They say the beach has healing properties."

"This beach does, for sure," Cora agreed.

Although it occurred to Cora that maybe it wasn't the beach. And maybe life wasn't perfect like they thought it was all those years ago. Maybe what was perfect, maybe the thing that had brought them healing, was just being together.

"We're doing this again next summer, right?" Savannah asked.

"Absolutely," Cora replied.

"Wait." Bianca tilted her head to the side like she was thinking. "This will be my home then. That's weird. I guess you can count me in, because I'll already be here."

Cora looked over at Savannah. "But next time Chris and the girls should stay the whole time, too. I mean, the family's not just us anymore."

"Agreed." Savannah nodded. Then she paused for a second, as if thinking it all the way through. "Although maybe we can have a little time when it's just the sisters."

"Of course. Sister week. It will be a new tradition," Cora said.

"I like it," Bianca agreed.

"Because the Prestly girls always pull through together," Cora said.

"Always," Savannah agreed.

"Always," Bianca echoed.

Cora, who was in the middle, rested her head on Savannah's shoulder and pulled Bianca in a little tighter.

Always, she thought. Because no matter what else came their way, they always had one another.

Epilogue

Cora

Four years later

Summer is still my favorite season. Every year I look forward to June 1. Of course, it looks a little different now, but that's okay. Life should look different. It's always growing and changing and evolving.

We don't all stay in the same house anymore because there are too many of us now, especially for the blue clapboard house. Savannah and Chris took that house for their family. It just made sense for them to take it because she's the one who values traditions. And I have to say, seeing Genevieve and Juliette live out their childhood summers there does warm my heart.

Besides, Bianca and Luke have their own place, naturally, since they're full-time Sunnyside residents. For the first year and a half, Bianca lived in Luke's sister's garage apartment, where Sylvie loved having a surrogate big sister. But after Bee married Luke last fall, she moved into his house. So far they seem really happy. And her event planning business? It's been voted a Sunnyside Favorite for three years in a row.

Which just leaves me and Jax.

We decided to buy a vacation place of our own on the beach. In fact, it was our wedding gift to each other. Part of it was to signify our commitment to spending time with our family, but part of it was for ourselves. After all, Sunnyside was where we fell in love.

We pull up to our house for the first day of the season.

"Should we go inside first?" Jax asks.

The question barely has time to settle before we both look at each other. "Naw," we say in unison. As always, the first thing we want to see is the water, especially this time. Because this is a particularly special summer.

"Do you think he needs a hat? It's pretty sunny." Jax grabs one from the backpack he's holding and hands it to me. I look down at the two-month-old snuggling against my chest and try to arrange the hat on his bald little head without waking him.

"We made it, Will," I whisper.

"There's zero chance you'll remember this visit, little buddy," Jax says to him. "But hopefully this place will become so familiar, you won't ever remember not coming here." My husband puts a hand on the small of my back to offer support while I carry our son across the sand to get his first look at the ocean.

To our surprise, everyone is on the beach waiting for us. Or, maybe it's more accurate to say waiting for Will. Savannah, Chris and the girls. Bianca and Luke. Even my dad is there. And they all take turns getting peeks at the sleeping baby while we talk and catch up. Because there's something about coming to the beach that just feels like coming home.

Sometimes I think back to the summer when everything changed. I wonder what would've happened if our mom hadn't made that last request before she died. Or if Savannah hadn't had to have heart surgery, prompting her to plan the trip. Or if Bianca hadn't gotten engaged to not-a-gym-rat gym rat, forcing the famous bet.

I never would have wished for any of those things, but sometimes what we think are life's biggest disappointments turn into the biggest gifts. It's how I got my family back. It's how I learned to forgive.

It's how I met the love of my life.

Although we did meet on the toothbrush aisle first. So maybe there's something to serendipity after all.

Acknowledgments

Seeing a book that was once just an idea in my head turned into something beautiful that I can hold in my hands is always humbling. There are so many people along the way who helped make my dream a reality and words can't describe how grateful I am for each of you. But since we all know I love words, I'm going to give it a try anyway.

A very big thank you to my amazing editor Lizzie Poteet. You always take my vision and make it even better than I could've imagined. I appreciate your enthusiasm and encouragement. You are an amazing human, and I'm so lucky to get to work with you.

Thanks to the whole team at Thomas Nelson including (but certainly not limited to) Amanda Bostic, Savannah Breedlove, Kerri Potts, Taylor Ward, and Colleen Lacey. I so appreciate everything you do to make this book so beautiful (I mean that cover!) and get it out there into the world. I am immensely thankful for you and your encouragement.

I owe a world of gratitude to my amazing kids who put up with me being locked away in my office for days at a time when I'm on deadline or walking around in a daze while I'm in the middle of working out a scene in my head or eating frozen pizza way more often than any of us would like to admit. You two are my inspiration, and I'm so very proud of you.

And maybe the biggest thanks of all to my real life MMC, Mike. Thanks for always believing in me and encouraging me to do whatever it takes to chase after my dreams. I love you more than you'll ever know.

Finally, thank you, dear reader. I wouldn't be here without you. Thanks for getting lost in my stories. I hope you loved Savannah, Cora, and Bianca as much as I did and you walked away with a smile after reading this book.

xoxo,
Rachel

Discussion Questions

1. The Prestley sisters are heading to Sunnyside to relive their childhood summers. What special memories from your childhood do you always remember fondly?

2. Despite growing up in the same family, Savannah, Cora, and Bianca have very different personalities. Which sister do you most relate with? Why?

3. After a long and frustrating travel day, Cora makes some impulse purchases that she later questions (the neon palm tree coverup). Tell us about a late night and/or impulse purchase you later realized was hilarious, embarrassing, or just What-on-earth-was-I-thinking? (Come on, you know we all have them.)

4. Bianca and Zander met online, and because of their long distance relationship, most of their interactions were virtual (which Bianca claims during that famous fight was as good or even better than being in person). In this technology driven world we live in, virtual meetings are becoming more and more common. Do you think virtual conversations are as powerful as in-person conversations? Why are why not?

5. On their first night in town, Luke tells Bianca, "The beach has a way of healing things. They say it's the saltwater." Do you agree? What place has healing qualities for you—it just makes you feel better when you're there?

6. There's a lot of talk about serendipity throughout the story. Bianca thinks these happy accidents mean it's destined to be. Cora's more on the side that they are just coincidences, nothing more. What's your take on serendipity?

7. After her conversation with Savannah, Cora realizes that she's been holding on to anger and chooses forgiveness. It was a big, hard step, but a good one! How does holding on to anger affect a person emotionally, and what does Cora (or anyone) have to gain by choosing to forgive? Have you seen this in your own life?

8. In the end, most of our characters end up going in a completely different direction from where they were intending to go when they started out. Do you think they all ended up doing the right thing? Why or why not?

I'd love to know your answers!
Email me at Rachel@RachelMageeBooks.com. I'll even tell you some of my most hilarious impulse purchases.

About the Author

Photo by Christi Mule

Rachel Magee writes rom-coms and women's fiction with relatable characters, witty dialogue, and plenty of happily-ever-afters. Her stories are usually set in fun, sunny locations where she doesn't mind spending lots of time "researching." When she's not out scouting the setting of her next book, you can find her at home in The Woodlands, Texas, with her amazing husband and their two adventurous kids.

Connect with her online at rachelmageebooks.com
Facebook: @rachelmageeauthor
Instagram: @rachelmageeauthor
X: @rachell_magee